EPHEMERA

*Also by Andrew Bell
and published by Authorhouse:*

Unguarded Instinct
Every Heartbeat Counts

EPHEMERA

BOOK ONE:
THE GHOST OF AARON BROOKES

ANDREW BELL

authorHOUSE®

AuthorHouse™
1663 Liberty Drive
Bloomington, IN 47403
www.authorhouse.com
Phone: 1-800-839-8640

Published by AuthorHouse   12/17/2012

ISBN: 978-1-4772-5161-4 (sc)
ISBN: 978-1-4772-5162-1 (e)

This work of fiction is dedicated to some *very* special people. I can not begin to express the indelible imprint that they have made upon my life. To Claire, for her undying love, and for their support and friendship, this book goes to Margaret Cowley, Rita Kuhlmann, Sarah Williams, Susan Riedel, Amanda Cockburn (the best friend I ever had), Denise Sparrowhawk and last but by no means least, Martin Old.

We all remember that one special teacher that made you believe in yourself, raised you up and made pretty damned sure that you stayed there. Martin helped me to *see* rather than *look*. Thank you for being there for me, Martin.

But to three little ones who will never know just how special they really are, again this one is for you. To Reece, Megan and Connor, love always from your Daddy xxx

It has been a year since the secret war at Hamsterly forest, the fight that gambled the lives of the entire human race . . . and lost.

Now 19 years of human existence remain.

And time, like the beating of a heart, is limited.

But who is the more deserving of time, the living or the dead?

PART A

I was no stranger tow pain.

I enjoyed it as much as the next person.

Didn't the song say it was so close to pleasure?

I liked the pain that lasted a second or two though. After that the body went numb and the mind took over; at least that's the way it worked for me. It was a learning curve that had to be felt to be believed; something I knew deep down would always elude me.

I played along with their games because they made me believe that I was the only one, that I was special, made from molten gold and poured into the mould of a small, clumsy boy. I was made of no such thing. I wasn't special because I hadn't been the first, and would certainly not be the last.

I'd often help them along, tease them with the promise of something a little more; press their fingers against, around and into the most sensitive areas of my very body and soul. But when the torture came cold and calculating, when plans were drawn and ideas passed around like Chinese whispers to be cogitated and approved, their initial concept was not a patch, not a damned shadow, of what was to come alive. It was then that I wished I had never been born.

When the mind awoke like a dying dog, begging to be put to sleep once more, the second would grow to three then nine then eighteen, then . . .

That initial split second of pain seemed to repeat itself over and over again, tearing my nerve endings apart like nothing I had experienced before . . .

The scraped knees, the twisted ankles, and the broken arm from the time I fell in Rossmere Park pond after wrestling my scooter from the clutches of a bunch of school bullies was nothing . . . nothing compared to the pain I felt that instant, that very moment.

I remember the sudden yelp issuing from my throat, the tear of flesh when the blade squeezed between two of my ribs . . . the look in their eyes as I bled over their hands. The ones who were supposed to love me, nurture me and protect me from the monsters of the world, I guess were the real monsters after all; they just knew better hiding places than me is all . . .

I knew that hunters sometimes stalked in packs, but I never knew my family would take their turns and violate what they once loved.

Me.

I was just a child who had gazed into the eyes of cruel children . . . after they had blackened mine with their fists.

I was just a boy who had tried taking back what belonged to him. Sometimes I failed, dabbing my wounds with toilet tissue, holding my head up high . . .

It was the pain of dying . . . or rather that moment of being murdered, which will be forever etched onto my mind.

That . . . split . . . second that plays its self over and over and over and . . .

But now there is little time to waste.

It's wasted me for ten long years.

I curse the day I died.

They used my body, like they did so many after me and indeed before me . . .

That's why the other children in the street hated me; that's why they wished I were dead. They knew my suffering.

They buried me where the authorities would never imagine, never dare look.

But I know where I am, where I rot . . .

I hate the ones who killed me.
Mum, Dad, my English teacher . . .

What started as a game had turned bloody.

My name is Richard Pearce. I was 11 when my life was taken from me.

Now I'm taking it back . . .
But first there is someone in need of help. The only adult I can trust. She was there for me when I had nowhere else to go.
I trust the boy as much as I do her.
I just hope I'm not too late.

1

The fingertips tapped against the rain-lashed window pane; gently at first, trying to keep up with the heavy droplets. But as they failed to rouse the sleeper tucked away cozily in his bed, they struck harder, almost to the point of breaking the glass.

David Reed dreamed, his chest rising and falling as the heat of the house bathed him with sweat. For this time of year the days should be growing shorter and cooler, but this night his underwear clung to his body almost like another thin layer of skin. The crying wind and rain drowned out the thudding noise that would have threatened to wake the rest of his family, but even if his Mum and Dad strolled into his room, they wouldn't have seen nor heard a thing. And as Reed shifted and turned his pillow over to feel the cold softness against his fevered cheek, the boy at the window looked on, his body shivering as the rain fused his muddied clothing to his rotten, charred skin.

His face was torn, burnt and bloody. And as he pressed the hot bones, exposed through the gaping slash running from his left eye down to his jaw line, he shivered against the icy glass. Fragments of the ragged flesh had dried to a husk over the months and now it hung over the crumbling bones as though defiant. An eye, which once seemed to change colour to match his moods now glowed a dirty bottle-green, the colour Reed associates with hunger and desire. When they're dark and somewhat sparkly that was when it was time to worry; its lid torn to shreds, rolled in its socket, searching in the

6

darkness of the room for signs of life as he had done many times before-

Maybe he would do this until the end of time?

Maybe tonight Reed would accept him and learn to see the funny side to their relationship?

Just who the hell was alive here, anyway?

'David . . . Wake up, sunshine,' he whispered, his breath frosting the glass before him. A smile twisted his broken lips as he watched the sleeper sit up, rise from his bed and slowly cross the room. Now the boy giggled as the figure, his white tee-shirt and pale blue boxer shorts, glowing dully in the dark, approached the window-

Now the fingers tapped harder against the glass, threatening to shatter the old single glaze if he failed to control his excitement. Lightning cut across the sky, exposing the horridly torn face in all its hideous glory. And he pounded harder and harder against the glass. Piercingly blue arc-sodium light from the street lamp behind him bleached the skulls exposed cartilage, the flesh there hanging like ribbons from his broken jaw . . .

When their knives had cut him from ear to ear he had bitten the tip of his tongue . . .

And now he could taste the familiar coppery tang mixed with the petrol they had used to sear the flesh from his-

He shook the images from his mind . . .

He would learn to live with his scars for a while, like a soldier returning from a bloody war to an unforgiving world; a world of self-appointed judges . . .

But they can't see him.

He's a ghost.

And the rain trickled through the cuts in his death-like mask as he glanced up at the pearls dropping from the black sky, cleaning the bones underneath to an almost phosphorescent whiteness.

'It is time,' whispered the face at the window, his hot breath misting the cold glass.

Reed nodded then turned about, gently opening the bedroom door so as not to wake the rest of his family. Then, as his body shook with the coolness of the hallway, the sound of the house unwinding, floorboards creaking beneath his bare feet, he slowly made his way along the landing and down the stairs, being careful to avoid the fourth step. It had a habit of screaming like a living thing.

His eyes were wide open but he slept like the dead. He was aware but helpless to fight it. It was the way it had always been.

2

The punishing winds had weakened over the course of the evening but it still managed to push at the branches of the trees that lined the avenue, clawing at cars as they passed by sluggishly in the dark. And the rain continued to bludgeon the streets, permeating the air with the scent of burnished steel. Suddenly a warm breeze shook the litter along the guttering outside of Reed's house, rattling cans and bottles across his path as he left the garden and stepped out onto the road. The air was already growing hotter, and he glanced up at the heavens, hearing a delicate rumble of thunder. He counted the seconds before lightning cut the sky in two. Almost nine seconds, he thought, a cold sweat breaking beneath his armpits and lower back. The fabric of his clothing thinned with the rain drops, gooseflesh spreading about his entire body as though he had grown some kind of reptilian carapace. Nine seconds was pretty good, or so he was told by his dad. The longer the time between the thunder and the lightning meant it was going away.

Piles of brown and golden leaves choked the guttering. And despite the occasional sharp pain, whether it was from a tiny stone or shard of glass, he strode through them with his bare feet slipping occasionally in the thick muddy puddles beside the curb.

Anybody who had faced this nightmare as many times as David Reed would have given up by now; maybe even tried to do something . . . stupid.

But it was just a dream, he thought. Like no other, or more to the point, a dream that no other *person* would have. It had taken its toll, depriving him of much needed sleep of late, but, just like someone having to take a pill to get through the day, he knew just what he had to do, as if he could control it? All he had to do was gently usher the child away from his street, even if he *did* get soaking wet in the process. A few muddy footprints on the hallway carpet were a small price to pay and could be easily cleaned up.

Reed just wanted to know why it was happening all over again.

Why *now* after so many weeks? Why did the boy at his window stay there longer each night, begging him to stir from his sleep? Why wouldn't he take the hint and just go away?

He marched the boy to the edge of the street, as usual without a single exchange of words, delivering him safely to the puddle beneath the lamp post at the corner of Silverfield Avenue, where the asphalt broke away to the soft carpet of mud and leaves, beyond which the shadows in the woodland paced to and fro in the blackness like a bloodthirsty pack of wolves.

Just another tedious dream, thought Reed. Another night in wet clothes. And when morning came there'd be another bloody smear to wipe away from the window.

Reed then turned away from the small boy, looking over his shoulder once before making his way back home, watching the figure watch him back as he stood in the harsh glow of the lamp post.

Reed waved.

The boy waved back, his fingers clenching into a fist as though he had caught a freshly blown kiss from the air.

Then he spoke, whispering words that traveled on the warm breeze like a twig on the shoulders of a mighty stream.

'They can't see me, David,' he said, glancing over his shoulder at the trees behind him. 'But you can . . . You know the rules . . . You know what you have to do-'

'I'm not listening to you, Aaron,' Reed said, walking up the garden path. 'And I don't need you.'

'Say my name,' the boy whispered. 'Easy as ABC . . .'

3

December 2013

'Bastard!' he shouted. 'Not again, Davey-boy!'

The steering wheel slipped through his clammy palms, but he only realized just what was happening when he felt its thick rubber surface meet his forehead; jolting him up straight in his chair. He blinked his eyes a dozen times it seemed, trying to focus on the rushing cats' eyes and stripes as they hurtled towards him between the headlights twin beams. The road was dark and misty, its surface slick with rain.

'That was a close one,' he muttered, not quite grasping the gravity of the situation. He shook his head, wondering just how many lives he had left.

The dashboard clock read half past one in the morning, and he grinned, knowing that by law he had already traveled too long and too far. He shrugged. What the hell, it wasn't the first law he'd broken. He couldn't sleep even though his body cried out for his bed. In fact sleep had kept its distance for three days now-

'Thank God!'

Heaven was just a couple of metres away.

David slowly pulled the Long Goods Vehicle into the motorway lay-by, the heavy eighteen wheels cutting through the deep puddles along the curb. He looked over at the small window of orange light of 'Sheila's Greasy Spoon' café and almost cried. Suddenly he felt just how a weary sailor might noticing the tiny spoke of light from a lighthouse, cutting through the mist to guide him home. All he wanted—no, *craved* was a good starchy plate of cholesterol, a pint of something resembling coffee and three or four cigarettes to get his heart pumping.

He tried to remember the figure he had seen in the rain of his dream. But like all dreams it had vanished-

'David,' he muttered under his breath. 'It was just a dream.'

Besides, he thought. That was a long time ago.

A very long time ago.

Dreaming and driving should also be a criminal offense, he thought, quickly climbing down from the cab.

He stopped for a moment to scrutinize the other three vehicles parked along the verge but failed to recognize them. For that he was grateful. At least he would get a little peace and quiet. He wasn't unsociable by any stretch of the imagination. Hell, he'd have a beer and chew the fat with anyone who had the time, but right now he needed the solitude.

4

The little trailer certainly lived up to its name. It was no spoon but Sheila had certainly mastered the art of keeping it greasy! Cigarette smoke hung like a pale blue cloud in the low lit room, and he could just make out a couple of old photographs hanging on the walls. One depicted a waterfall from God knew where and the other was of the Statue of Liberty cutting through the New York skyline. He saw the Twin Towers in the back ground, pointing to the sky like two fingers. Sometimes he wondered if Sheila knew what had happened to the Trade Center. Or if she did, did she refuse to believe 9/11 had ever occurred? Hell, maybe she refused to believe the Holocaust ever happened! Maybe it was a reminder of just where she sees herself in the future . . .

Who knows?

Who cares?

David knew what lay in *his* future-

'Stop it,' he mumbled. 'Don't think about it. Just don't think about it.'

He glanced at the peg board to distract him from his thoughts. The large cork square which now clung to the wall as if for dear life such was the weight of the business cards tacked to it was at an awkward angle. But apart from that, the place had never changed. Judging by the smell of oil and eggs neither had the frying pans. He was glad to see that three of the four tables were occupied. He wished they could be spaced out a little more but it would have to do.

'Now then, gorgeous,' said David, tipping an imaginary hat at the lady beside the gas cooker. Sheila, a cigarette clamped at the corner of her mouth, shook her head and smiled crookedly. God, she was aging like a dog, he thought, reaching for his own dwindling pack. He jammed one in his mouth and lit up, blowing a stream of blue smoke into the air. Smoking in any work place was illegal, but out here in the sticks, at this Godforsaken hour of the night, rules were not just broken. Hell, they were bent, shattered and snapped.

He always made a point of sweeping his hand across the chair before seating himself down, just habit he'd once chuckled at the unkempt proprietor some time ago. But he wasn't the only one who had suddenly developed this uncanny habit. It was always prudent to remember the last time you had your tetanus jab.

He sat down and reached inside his pocket for his mobile phone. After jamming the number on the key pad he sat back, listening to the slow beeps.

And he waited.

Of course it was early, he thought.

'I'm not putting the phone down,' David mumbled the words, a yawn almost paralyzing his jaw. 'Come on, for fuck's sake. Pick up!'

And he waited-

'Why the hell are you phoning me at this hour?' said the sleepy voice.

'Tabby? Thank God,' David replied, clearing his throat. 'Good morning!'

She's alive! Thank fucking God! They haven't gotten to her . . . yet.

'Look, I know it's the middle of the bloody night,' he said, 'but I wanted you to . . . to know that I am okay . . . And that I love you.'

For a moment there was silence on the line. Then Tabby cleared her throat. 'Aww, baby, I love you too. Why can't you be this lovey-dovey on your days off?'

Her voice was warm but he recognized the hint of concern, could sense it.

'Are you sure you're alright?'

He shrugged, trying to relax and somehow convey that through the bloody line.

'Of course, sweets . . . Why wouldn't I be?'

'Well now I know you're fine,' Tabby yawned loudly, 'then maybe you'll let me get some bloody sleep!'

Just glad to know you're alive is all! God, if you only knew—and I hope you don't find out-

'I've nearly delivered all the beer now and have only a couple of breweries left on my list,' David replied, squeezing his mobile phone, trying to sprinkle a little optimism in to his voice. But he felt as though it wasn't working at all. 'Then I'm on my way back up north . . . hey, put Paul on the line. I want to speak to my little future England footballer-'

'David, it's one o'clock in the fucking morning and the baby's asleep,' Tabby replied, trying to whisper. 'All he'll do is gabble anyway-'

'The words of a King, I tell you, flower. The giggling gibberish of a future monarch,' he replied, a tear running down his cheek. Were they of happiness or sadness? He didn't know any more.

'Look, darling, I'm really tired. Can you ring me a bit later? I've a lecture at the University in ten hours and I'm bloody wrecked,' said Tabby, yawning loudly.

'Of course, babe. Sorry . . . I just wanted to make sure-'

'Well, we're just fine. So stop worrying. Just like an hour ago when you rang. And the two hours before that-'

'Okay, okay, I get the picture,' David laughed. 'I just love you both to bits is all.'

'We know that, love,' said Tabby. 'See you when you get back home, okay? And please be on time. You don't want to anger Jay-'

'I know, I know. See you later.'

'Goodnight, sleeptight,' said Tabby.

'You too, sweet heart,' replied David. 'You, too.'

The line went dead.

He lit another cigarette, his smile quickly disappearing.

Beyond the window to his right, where a cold wind swept the rain-slicked road, he thought of his vehicle. How it waited for him to complete his journey. He thought about the darkness inside the cab and icy fingers raked across his back, sending goose bumps dancing along his arms and legs.

God, the journey was just beginning, he thought, feeling his heart sink.

If he didn't have to lug about a load of beer the trip would've been over hours ago. He'd calculated approximately nine hours for a round trip from Hartlepool to Cambridge; providing he kept within the speed limits of course. But now at least he could ease on the pedal and take his time. The job, as he had informed Tabby, was indeed coming to a close, but he knew that he would be facing the dole queue in a few days . . .

That's assuming you live to see another sunrise, David!

Reed felt the tear at the corner of his eye and quickly wiped the stinging thing away with the back of his hand. Homesickness was not a word he'd normally use to describe how he felt at times like these, but after hearing Tabby's smoky voice, his heart seemed to deflate as though a knife edge had slit its under belly and let the blood drain out.

He shook his head, and thought about the revolver in the glove compartment, and he wondered if he would ever change.

But he already knew the answer to that bloody question.

5

Three days and no sleep, thought David.

God, you're really going for the record.

Is sleep deprivation really going to save your skin?

It was the voice of his conscience interrupting his thoughts. He supposed its heart was in the right place. Advice and help, an extra hand and a different point of view: it would all help. He knew that he needed all the strength he could ever hope for; needed to keep alert, alive-

Let's just concentrate on staying awake for now. Staying alive?

David thought of Tabby and Paul . . .

Let's just think about keeping awake . . .

'Come on, David,' he mumbled. 'Keep the old blinkers on the road. Keep the mind on the job . . . home's for later.' He knew that chatting to one's self was one of the many signs of madness, but out here on the black road, who cared?

He glanced at the photograph tacked to the dash board, its instruments casting a soft warm glow across its surface. It was Tabby's favourite picture, that's why the one he possessed was just a facsimile. The original took pride of place on the family room's mantel piece, its silver frame always shining; the glass as clean as a mirror. It was his favourite too, and his copy wasn't a patch on the real thing but it would help to keep the wolves at bay. Not only was it the first picture of Paul it captured the magic of their most cherished moment. Tabby had just given birth to Paul and she lay there half asleep, clutching the little bundle closely to her chest; sweat glistening on her fevered brow. Closely guarded was not quite the right choice of words he would describe the love Tabby had for their child. 'Touch-my-baby-and-you'll-be-wearing-your-balls-for-earrings' was a touch closer to the mark. After four miscarriages-

Shut up, David. Just shut the hell up!

He couldn't help glancing at the picture, smiling at the contrast between mother and child. Tabby had her golden hair tied back tightly in a pony tail, her face as pale as chalk. And round, Jesus! "Well, babies did that to you" she had once said. "What the fuck's your excuse?" Her eyes looked so dazzlingly brown, but now they were closed, the tiniest of white shining between her right eye-lid as though she silently kept vigil over her most prized possession.

And wasn't he just? Where the hell did Paul's shock of black hair come from? Many people, his family included, said a child never looks like its father for the first sixth months. Some even said he might not be the father, especially after their poor luck of falling pregnant . . . then Tabby announces the good news-

It was fair to say that Reed didn't break bread with those fuckers any longer.

He couldn't quite remember who took that photograph, probably some passing nurse, he thought. But that guy holding his wife and child, how the fuck dare he! But then . . . it had been him. Any one would have been forgiven for thinking that it was some body else holding his family, after all, Reed failed to recognize himself; the muscular arm around the sleeping woman, his short brown hair gelled firmly to his tanned forehead; blue eyes full of joy and hope for the future-

Now he looked in the rear view mirror again; but somebody different stared back.

Those same glistening eyes were now dull, lifeless, witness only to fear and anger; dark rings were etched below them and crows' feet scarred their corners. Joy was now a stranger; a luxury he couldn't quite afford. The tan had faded, hair peppered with grey at the temples. His chin was sporting another. And his muscles once toned and tight, were now reduced to rolls of fat that hung over his belt and pushed at his clothes. God, how he had let himself go!

But Tabby would get her man back, he thought, nodding to his pale reflection in the glass of the windscreen before him. Times were changing and so would he when this nightmare was over.

Tabby would have her husband back, the man she had fallen in love with . . .

He just needed to survive the next couple of days. That was all.

David grabbed a cigarette from the packet on the dash board and lit up, wondering what time it really was out there in the real world. As a roadster the sun, stars and moon guided him through time and darkness like a sailor upon the ocean-

Suddenly David noticed the blossoming sun illuminating the horizon like a slit in the belly of a fish. So it must be about five in the morning, he thought, yawning. Dawn was breaking wide open and he was relieved. He had survived another night on the road.

He thought about the conversation earlier. Tabby wouldn't have dozed off immediately following their conversation a couple hours ago. Hell no, he knew her like the back of his hand. Well, who could blame her after what had occurred almost a year ago, thought David, shaking his head at the memory of the night he had cheated death. A grin spread across his face but it slowly faded when I remembered how distraught Tabby had been.

It had been one of the worst nights of his life as a lorry driver. Rain came down in sheets and he could barely discern a thing in the bobbing arcs of his headlights. The icy wind had bludgeoned the sides of the vehicle so brutally he hoped to keep all eighteen wheels on solid ground. Yes, although Scotland was renowned for its harsh weather David rode the wind and sleet like a rodeo star. And all things were going to plan. That was until he did something he had promised Tabby he would never do-

For Christ's sake, the lightning lashed at the black sky, dousing the land! He just didn't have the heart to see the poor fucker drown by the side of the road. So he had picked up the hiker.

'I know it was a fucking stupid thing to do, Tabby!' he had hollered down the hospital phone. 'Don't lecture me . . . Of course I won't do it again . . . I promise . . . You—Tabby, you know . . . I do love you, don't say that!'

The line went dead, but he had listened to the tone; it resembled the laboured cry of a dying wasp.

It had happened so fast. The steel blade came from out of nowhere, cutting through the air towards his face. Luckily, after a minor struggle, he was able to kick the bastard out of the cab;

after slowing down first of course. Fuck him! Looking back, David wished he had been belting a hundred when the hiker's arse had met the roadside! At least that way the creep wouldn't have returned. After such a bad fall, for the doors were pretty high up from the road, and hitting the rain slick tarmac wouldn't have been as soft as cotton, David hadn't expected the fucker to be waiting for him in the hospital car park.

But he was.

'If it hadn't have been me, Tabby,' he said as calmly down the phone, that night at the hospital, 'then some other poor bugger would be lying in the morgue right now . . . That's what the police said . . . Yes, they did! As I was about to discharge myself I quickly nipped out for a fag—I don't know what time it was . . . about three-ish, does it matter—anyway, he was standing beside the truck . . . No, sweets, just like I said . . . yes, yes . . . I went back inside—yes, phoned the bizzies . . . well, it must've done the trick, flower, 'cos he wasn't there when I went back outside . . . '

David looked down at the scar on his forearm, a reminder of that night; how the blade had cut so deeply it had scraped across the bone. He never told Tabby of just how lucky he had been to survive that night; two pints of blood and a lot of stitches. She didn't need to worry. Hell, he'd brought her enough misery, she didn't need this too.

So now the cab was a mobile fortress fitted with extra locking systems should he run into that same kind of trouble in the future. Despite Tabby's protests, no matter how much she hated it, David had to work. Driving was all he had *ever* been good at.

Right now, hikers were the least of their problems.

Mom and dad loved me, at least I thought they did because we had played football in the park and had our favourite meal that beautiful summer afternoon. Well it was my favourite anyway: Pizza with extra pepperoni. Mom didn't like pizza . . . Come to think of it she couldn't look at pizza let alone eat it. But this day she did.

That should've been my first warning.

But I thought nothing of it.

And we played football, taking turns shooting between two trees that served as goal posts. I thought I had died and gone to heaven. Mom and Dad hated football . . . Come to think of it they never sat down with me to watch a game on television.

That should've been my second warning.

But I thought nothing of it.

They were just some of the many lies they kept from me; just an example of what they'd tolerate at the weekends when they both had time off from work. Saturdays and Sundays had become forty eight hours of awkward silence and discomfort. It was like they had no choice but to while away the hours, watching the clocks hands slowly move around and around, yearning for Monday morning so their shifts can allow them to pass each other in the house like ships that pass in the night . . .

I'm just a child and they think I'm stupid; that I don't see these things.

So when the game was over, they settled down to play the one pass-time they had mastered a long long time ago: Mommy and Daddy. Dad told a joke and Mom laughed even though the warmth of her smile failed to reach her hazel eyes. They had lost their sheen years ago it seemed. Mom told Dad some of the hot gossip currently flying round the office: who was being naughty with whom, what he said and she said, and Dad rolled his eyes. He had mastered another art: laughing, nodding and agreeing in the right places, at the right moment. His laugh seemed just as false as hers.

Why could silence be so uncomfortable?

They nibbled at the home made meat loaf and sipped long glasses of iced orange juice, watching other children kicking around on the field with their parents. They were probably wishing and yearning for some kind of spore to come flying from their proximity—anything to burrow its teeth beneath their skin—to infuse the hot blood that would shake off the numbness they felt for each other . . .

No such luck . . .

They held the falling pieces of their marriage together . . . for me.

Such a sacrifice doesn't come without its share of guilt; after all, they awoke in the mornings (in separate beds I hasten to add) exchanging fake pleasantries as they passed one another down the hall from the bathroom. There were small words at the table and I always felt the tension between them as they watched me open my presents at Christmas . . . I think they thought I couldn't feel the hatred they shared for one another, that I couldn't count the years the magic had been dead between them.

I guess they never knew me at all.

Such a sacrifice.

As we left the park I knew that something very bad was going to happen to me that summer day twenty seven years ago . . .

Something very bad indeed.

I was right.

They started to talk—no shout at each other, finally breaking the wall down that had built its self between them over the years.

Dad was seeing another woman behind mom's back. But Mom didn't care, she'd known about it for weeks. She's seen the credit card receipts in his pants pockets before placing them in the washing machine. It was simply a habit that one day ended everything. Maybe . . . and I've come to think of it after so many years, that maybe dad left the receipt there on purpose. His secret had to come out sooner or later!

That day at the park was pretty tense because mom had ideas of her own: she was going to tell him on our way home that she was going to leave him and take me with her.

So she did.

Silence wrapped around me like a flea infested blanket; my skin wouldn't stop itching; itching to jump from the moving vehicle—into the path of an oncoming car I didn't care! We would stay with her sister, Veronica. It was all arranged; even our clothes were packed and ready-

What about me? I wanted to scream out.

What about my friends I would be leaving behind just because they didn't like each other any more?

What about my toys? Would I be able to take them with me?

Didn't they love me any more? Was it my fault, I wanted to scream until my throat bled. But now, looking back, it was life.

Simple.

That's when dad turned the car around back to the park, found a quiet spot where the other families couldn't see; then took the knife from the picnic hamper and slit our throats.

I guess if he couldn't have us then no one would.

Dad's still on the run.

I think the police have given up trying to find him.

But I know where he is.

I sit and scream in his face every day.

When he looks in the mirror I'm there at his shoulder.

I see the state of my throat and I have to turn away.

He didn't need to be so nasty. The knife hurt like nothing I've felt before.

He could've just let us go . . .

But he had to have things his way.

My name is Kyle Henry.
I was seven when I had my life taken from me.

Now I'm taking it back . . .
Because the coffee lady with the kind eyes said I could.
The boy says she's in trouble. And I'm scared . . .

I just hope I won't lose my nerve when the time comes.

6

As darkness lifted Reed was able to read the list of breweries on the clipboard beside him. There were so many that he had yet to visit; together with their individual inventory, it would help him take his mind from his worries.

He looked at the glove compartment
Don't, David! Don't think about it.

Night was safely tucked away behind him once more. He yawned loudly, shuffling in his seat. Every bone and muscle in his body seemed to crackle and snap as he stretched. He looked at the clipboard once more, shaking his head at the number of breweries he had yet to deliver to. Was that ten or twelve? He switched on the cabin light for a second. Then he turned it off with a sigh. Yes, his eyes were not deceiving him: twelve fucking stops.

Jay was expecting him back at the depot in three days. Jay, as in, head honcho of Jay Duckingham's Distilleries Limited; knee-cap breaker and home wrecker extraordinaire-

Just stop it, David. This is another chance to hold on to your job!

He shook the thoughts away like cobwebs from his shoulder. Tabby knew that he was treading on thin ice with Jay, but she had no idea of just how close he had been to losing his life to the bastard.

'Please be on time. You don't want to anger Jay.'

Tabby's words echoed in his mind, but like that cobweb, he brushed them off too.

'Everything's going to be alright,' David said softly, his fingers squeezing the steering wheel until his knuckles turned white. 'Everything's under control.'

'Didn't you say that the last time, David? When Jay hit you so hard for fucking up an order and almost destroying his business, didn't you plead with him for one more chance?'

He shook his head, grabbing a cigarette from the packet just poking out from his breast pocket, and jammed it in his mouth. With his eyes still on the road he struck a match along the dashboard, the pungent smell of sulphur permeated the air as he inhaled deeply. The nicotine rush sent shivers through his body. Then he thought that maybe it wasn't the drug that made his hair stand on end or his skin crawl as though maggots writhed beneath its surface.

Public houses had inundated the phone lines, land lords spitting their rage at Jay and his late deliveries. Each time the line went dead another driver received his cards. These were hard times. And the customers paid dearly for Duckingham's spirits and beers. They were at the forefront in quality alcohol and prided themselves at offering the best in competitive prices. They were unbeatable; a reputation nobody was going to ruin. Christmas was rapidly approaching and cellars needed stocking.

So, If David didn't make his rounds on time—this time being his fucking *last* time—then he could surely kiss his arse goodbye! But, as much as it pained him, and despite the promise he had made to Tabby, the deliveries would have to wait. If he was fired, then fuck it! It wouldn't be the first time. Hell, it probably wouldn't be the last either.

'If it comes to that,' he mumbled, reaching a hand under his seat for the road Atlas. 'Then I'll have to deal with it then.' Tabby knew just how competitive the industry was and that every day he skated on thin ice. He could tell her that the business went bust and there was no alternative but to let him go. Easy.

David smiled. And it felt real, warm and . . . natural.

'You can do this, matey,' he whispered. 'You can do this.'

His hand lit upon the hard backed book, and his smile widened. A driver had to thank more than God as personal possessions had a habit of growing legs and walking; even from the shabby lockers. Everyone wanted a piece of somebody else's life, not content with their lot. He just kept himself to himself and liked it that way. He took a last drag from his cigarette, wound his window down and flicked the butt into the rushing winds. Traffic passed sluggishly, and as a break appeared he pulled into the lay-by and switched off the engine.

By the force of bad habit David looked about the cab, bending down to peer under his seat for castaways. But, as always, he was alone. It was a silly thing to do but he had his reasons, and the fucking scars to prove it.

The motorway was practically deserted, he was pleased to know. Driving long distance could be a pain in the arse at the best of times; the unending hours, sleep deprivation and time apart from his family. Having to watch out for incompetent coasters along the way really raised his hackles. But all was calm. He switched on the windscreen wipers to rid the glass from condensation, noticing how the streets and houses had given way to large sprawling fields of corn, rolling towards the blood red horizon like a golden wave.

It was cold out and he smiled as the heaters beneath the dashboard panel whirred into life. It was like a home from home, thought David, switching on the radio. He flicked through the stations, static filling the speakers about the cabin as he eavesdropped on a dozen broken songs and conversations-

'Fuck it!' he mumbled, turning the dial until finally stumbling upon an old pop song. He lit another cigarette and opened the Atlas. It fell open, almost eerily, on the page he should not . . . or shouldn't he?

'God, I just don't know what to do!'

But deep down he knew exactly what he had to do; knew what direction to take. It was the only way.

David peered over at the digital clock glowing on the dashboard:

6:30 AM 8TH DECEMBER 2013

He sighed.

'Three days and you'll be dead!'

'Shut the hell up!' David scolded, shrugging off the voice inside his head. 'Everything's under control . . . I promise . . .'

He stole a glance at the photo of Tabby and Paul once more before studying the map before him, at the fork in the road he had thought of so much it was almost etched onto his mind; wanting the look in their eyes to decide for him-

'Grow a set, David!' he snapped, shaking his head. 'Decide, and do it now!'

Should he turn right towards Sheffield and deliver the beer like a good boy . . . and keep his job, but lose Tabby and the baby in the process? Or turn left towards Lincoln, crawl to Cambridge . . . to the end of the line, screw the job and finally have a chance to drag his wife and kid out of the shit they're in?

David closed his eyes for a few seconds as he turned the key in the ignition, listening to the engine burst into life. He bit his bottom lip, his stomach turning somersaults as he realized what he was about to do. He opened his eyes.

'You've got to be fucking crazy,' he said, as he slowly pulled away from the lay by; his heart hammering in his chest as he turned the steering wheel to the left.

7

The map was etched on his mind. He didn't need to look at it. Leeds, Doncaster . . . Lincoln. All the way to the red dot; the fucking 'X'. Like red veins leading to a clot . . .

And too much time to get there. Now there was no excuse to be late. Not like his usual beer runs-

I couldn't give a fuck about that! This was not your usual outing!

This was the real deal, he thought, trying to calm his self down, his heart skipping.

With the route firmly etched upon his mind he tried to follow the road the best he could; one mile at a time. A mixture of revulsion and excitement suddenly flushed through his face, goose flesh gently tip-toeing up his back and shoulder blades at the sheer thought.

He knew a way out!

It would hurt, but it was worth the try. He clicked open the glove compartment and stared at the pistol.

Just one in the head should do the trick!

His heart was beating hard, faster by the moment. And each beat accompanied images in his mind; Tabby and Paul, their faces flashing across-

How about in the mouth? Surely I couldn't fuck that one up!

At least it was a way out . . .

What about Tabby and Paul?

Tabby . . .

Paul . . .

Your little England footballer-

'Fuck it,' he mumbled, once again pushing the weapon out of sight. He had looked at it countless times since setting off, hoping he would have the guts to use the bloody thing if it came to that; hoping that he may never need to.

David pushed aside the thought and sighed heavily, thinking about all the money he didn't have, all that did not belong to him, and all that he could not ever hope to pay back. He shook his head and wanted to curse the day he was ever born.

God, the promises he had made to Tabby, about his gambling addiction-

"Don't worry," he'd said one night whilst holding a buzzing telephone receiver. "I make enough to pay it back, Tabs. Everything's okay." Then he placed the phone unsteadily in its cradle, hands shaking. But Tabby was in hysterics, her face flushed. His smile faded the moment she turned her back, making her way slowly out of the kitchen, her stomach turning somersaults, repulsed in her husband's presence. "They're just empty threats, flower!" he'd called after her. But they were just words; empty words that she'd heard a hundred times or more.

"I'll stop this," he'd shouted, hearing the Lounge door click quietly shut behind her.

"I promise," he'd whispered finally.

Except this time he couldn't promise a fucking thing, and there was no way of repaying what he had borrowed. Not this time, he thought, pulling up to traffic lights, breathing deeply and firmly. He had no money-

'I guess you can like it or fucking lump it,' he said, his voice trembling. It was a stone cold fact, one he had to get pretty darn used to and quick. 'God, you make it all sound so . . . so bloody simple, Davey-boy-'

He noticed the family snap, and it caught the words in his throat like a rat in a trap. It made him wish that he was apart from something so good, that he didn't deserve to be a part of the miracle; a family . . . a loving partnership. He wished he had nothing to lose. That way everything would be so fucking easy-

'I'm going to do us all a favour, Tabs,' he said, taking his eyes from the road a moment to pull the glove compartment down.

The gun fell into full view.

He grabbed it and pushed the muzzle to his temple, his right hand keeping the wheel steady. The cat's eyes hurtled towards him and he knew that there was no way out. He had to be strong, had to keep his shit together and see this through! His hand trembled, finger pushing the trigger-

'FUCK!' he shouted, throwing the pistol back into the glove compartment, punching his fist into the door over and over with anger and frustration-

Then he breathed deeply, trying to compose himself. He knew he had to keep his mind in one piece and this time he would have to stand his ground and be a man; a father; a husband. For once in his sorry life he would have to cultivate a spine!

Then he did something he'd promised his wife he would never do again.

He spotted the figure standing in the distance, its arm raised, thumb pointing upwards. A bright, cold winter sun blurred David's vision, making the hitcher look as though he was swimming on the spot. He slowed the vehicle, a voice yelling in his ear, telling him not to, but he ignored it.

Tabby, if you knew just how lonely I am right now . . . If you knew what was spinning through my mind, you'd do the same! I can't be alone, baby. Not tonight.

He grabbed a cigarette from a crushed box on the dashboard, jammed it in the corner of his mouth and left it there unlit. He just wanted it there. And he wondered what the hell he was doing.

8

'A bit early in the day for hitch-hiking, isn't it, mate?' said David, watching the heavily clad figure climb up to the cab. 'I suppose it's a bit safer though—anyway, name's Dave,' he said, proffering his hand.

'Charlie,' replied the passenger, now facing David.

Their hands clasped for a moment as David's smile faltered, shocked that the newcomer was indeed female. He knew it was wrong but he knew that his journey could get a lot more interesting—Jesus Christ, he was a human, a man . . .

She removed her black woolen hat and unbuttoned the top three buttons of her coat. Long blonde flaxen hair hid her face for a moment before she gently flicked it over her shoulder. She revealed a pale, but gentle face, untouched by make-up. In fact, David thought rather guiltily, she was pretty enough without it. With her full lips, large brown eyes, hell—early twenties, he thought.

David looked at the dashboard, his family grinning back at him—no, Tabby was *glaring* back at him.

Get a fucking grip!

'So . . . where're we headed?' he said, quickly pulling away from the side of the road.

'You know the dark—I know this sounds crazy, but have you ever heard of the dark wood of Grandalask?'

David shook his head. 'Ermm . . . sorry, never heard of it. Sounds like a place from a horror movie.'

'Well, that's what they call it-'

'Who are they?' said David, slowly making his way along the road now.

Charlie unbuttoned the rest of her jacket and pulled it off, proudly presenting the tee shirt beneath.

David was more drawn to her rather large chest than the symbols and colourful slogans emblazoned across the fabric.

'"Save the tree"?' he said, lighting the cigarette that hung from his lip. He offered her one. She took it. Not the most original of slogans, he thought. But said instead: 'Hey, haven't I read that somewhere before?'

'Well, mock if you must,' she replied. 'But some day it'll happen.'

'Like I said,' replied David. 'Who are they?'

'Just a bunch of . . . people I have been meaning to catch up with. It's been quite some time, I tell you.'

'Just a bunch of people, eh?'

'Well . . . old friends; like-minded students who care about the world in which we live in, that's all.'

A student . . . More like a fucking eco-warrior!

He wished he had kept his promise.

'Save the trees? Woods? Hold on,' said David, clicking his fingers, realizing where he'd heard this all before. 'You lot were on the news a couple of weeks ago, right? Protesting about that new road the council is going to build through the forest-'

'They won't,' she replied matter-of-factly.

'Have I touched a raw nerve?' he replied, knowing full well that he had. 'Hey, did they untie that bloke from the top of the tree?' he said on a lighter note, breaking the ice that had so suddenly formed between them.

'Who? You mean, Skunk?' replied Charlie, finishing her cigarette. She wound down the window and threw the spent butt out into the air. 'No, he's still there,' she said seriously.

'That was three weeks ago.'

'I know.'

'Three fucking weeks ago I was sat at home on the couch watching you lot fight off landowners. Punk-'

'Skunk.'

'Sorry, Skunk, was hanging from a branch by his waist *then*!'

They glanced at each other, a split second of silence that suddenly turned to laughter.

'Please don't-'

'He's *still* there? What a crazy fucker!' David sniggered, unable to remember the last time he had felt this good. 'You people are really serious, aren't you?' he said, finally catching his breath.

'There are a lot more to trees than fire wood, apples, garden furniture and attractive laminated flooring, you know?' she told him, still smiling.

David waited for the fully prepared speech, a spiel she'd saved and probably repeated a hundredfold. But it never came. 'Okay, Charlie,' he said wearily. 'Enlighten me. What do you see in those woods apart from poison ivy and bear shit?'

'It's not just about the environment, you know?' she replied, the warmth quickly disappearing from her eyes. Now she stared forward, a lock of blonde hair crossing her pale cheek. 'Although that's what everybody seems to think. You see . . . the woods are full of spirits.'

'What?' David chuckled. 'I think you bloody students have too much time on your hands. Either that or you read too much Tolkien!' He shook his head, smirking. 'Spirits? I think the only spirits in these woods are the forty percent proof stuff swilling about in your veins, m' lady.'

'You know,' she said, shaking her head, 'you sound so old, I mean, don't you believe in an afterlife?'

I wish I never fucking started this now!

He was tempted to stop the lorry and kick this little shit out onto the road, but instead he said, 'I guess everybody has their own beliefs. You don't have to push them down another person's throat. You believe in spirits and fairies and what you can't see, feel or touch. But others, like the council, believe in currency. Without it we all become spirits, don't we? Am I right?'

Charlie was silent.

David looked away from her, surveying the passing traffic on his right, so she couldn't see the beaming smile on his face.

I've always wanted to knock one of you work-shy bastards down a peg or two!

'You're simply narrow-minded like the rest of them,' she said finally, her eyes still on the road.

'You want to know what I believe?' David snapped, hitting the dashboard with his knuckles. 'This.' Then he tapped on the windscreen. 'And that. Things that are real.'

'I love the trees,' replied Charlie as though he hadn't uttered a word. 'I love the forest, for it's where we go when we die.'

David shook his head, sighing heavily.

This is too much. What have I started?

'Trees give us life, you see? I hope I'm lucky enough to be swept away by the wind and thrown to the branches and leaves when it's my time. They take the tainted air and keep us alive, yet we cut them down. What happens when we cut them *all* down? Won't we all die-'

'Hey, calm down, I get your point!' he snapped. 'But I think we'll survive.'

Suddenly he remembered his dream from the night before, the boy at the window; his torn fingers tapping against the glass. The lamppost, the trees behind the boy-

'Deep down, you believe me, don't you?' Charlie said, facing him now, a bright smile cutting the gloom in two. It matched the sparkle of her eyes. 'There's a part of you that believes me . . . maybe something happened in your childhood perhaps-'

'Hey, look, we're there,' said David, relieved to finally have rid of the nutter beside him. She was beautiful, he thought, but she had gone fishing a long long time ago.

'Well,' she said, pulling on her coat and woolen hat, 'people sometimes hate to hear the truth.'

'Just be careful, Charlie. I heard someone got killed up here last year.'

'I know,' she said softly. 'I'll be careful.'

He slowly pulled up to the side of the road. Up ahead he could barely make out a small camp fire, a cluster of what appeared to be bodies huddled together around the flame, jabbing at it with sticks; sparks spun through the air like fireflies.

'Hey, won't you anger those spirits by burning branches and stuff?' said David, stifling the laughter bubbling up inside.

Without another word, Charlie opened the door and quickly climbed down from the cab, slamming the door behind her. David heard the splash as her feet landed in a thick muddy puddle, a very *deep* muddy puddle by the sound of her language, and as he watched her join her friends in the gloom, he chuckled.

'Well,' he said, lighting another cigarette. 'I hope you lot haven't seen the Blair Witch Project.'

9

David remembered the telephone calls.

The ones that got you out of the bath, trilling as though the caller was burning in a fucking house fire—then cease the moment your dripping-wet finger tips touched the receiver.

Those fucking calls!

But then they got worse . . .

The caller would hold on, only for a couple of seconds then cut him off.

Then the silence became heavy breathing.

But never a word was spoken.

Tabby wasn't stupid. She didn't have to ask her husband questions to know what was going on in his mind. She could see it written all over his face as he'd slowly replace the receiver. The way his face had drained of blood, such paleness. Then he'd light a cigarette and smoke one after the other. Sometimes she'd sleep alone, reaching out a hand but brushing empty space where David should be sleeping; his side of the bed as cold as stone. After a while she'd get out of bed and look for him.

"Can't bloody sleep again, petal," he'd say, switching on the Playstation in the living room, the bright screen silhouetting his face, wiping away his eyes. 'I just thought I'd see if I can beat my score, y' know?' His chuckling faded as she would leave the room to go back to bed.

Indeed, she wasn't stupid.

David would stare at the screen, wanting to punch his fist through it! He could hear the words go through his mind, over and over again—the promises! Of what they'd do to Tabby and Paul if he failed to comply-

Tabby . . .

Paul . . .

He looked over at the glove compartment once more and wondered how easy it would be-

'Shut the hell up!' he snapped, bringing the lorry to the side of the road once more. Cars sped by, their horns screaming, lights flashing, but he didn't care. His heart was racing in his chest now. He thought about what Charlie had said. And he hated her more than words could say. Memories were flooding back to him now, his head swirling, eyes watering. He rubbed away the tears but his head was starting to ache, as though someone had struck a match right in front of his face.

You know it makes sense, David-

'Get the fuck out of my head!' David screamed, sitting down heavily in the dirt, the iciness of the wet mud sending shivers up his spine. But the sensation revived him, shaking off the tiredness that had afflicted him over the past few days. But he needed to keep his composure-

You know I'm always here should you ever need me-

'Who's there?' David hollered, hearing birds scatter through the branches of the trees that overhung the road.

You know.

David got to his feet and steadily made his way to the lorry. And as he tried to climb up to the cab, he fell back down into the icy puddle beside the wheel, his hands shaking.

'You'll be fine,' he whispered, breathing heavily now. 'It's just a memory. Nothing more.'

As he started to climb back up to the cab, the sound of the heating whirring, wrapping the warmth about his face like a hot towel, he glanced over his shoulder and surveyed the darkness of the trees.

10

It was some time before he started the engine.

Reed couldn't shake off the chills that rushed through him. He tried to turn the key in the ignition but his hands shook.

'Just fucking hold on for one minute!' he hissed to no one in particular, his hands gripping the steering wheel now as traffic passed lazily, the cab rocked gently.

Why are you doing this to yourself? Why rake through the old ashes—Not now, not now!

Then he started the engine, felt the soft rumbling of the lorry, vibrations that never failed to shake him awake.

'Don't do this, Davey,' he mumbled, taking a deep breath, turning the lorry around. 'Don't do this. Not now. You're not twelve years old-'

But what about the dream-

The torn finger tips tapping at the glass-

The rain beating against the window-

'Fuck off!' he shouted, glancing momentarily in the rear view mirror, catching a glimpse of his face, the redness about his forehead, beads of sweat formed there. 'You've picked the wrong time to start falling apart, David. Not when they need you the most . . .'

Tabby.

Paul.

But . . . what about you, David?

'What about me?' he replied with a snort.

How do you feel right now?

He shrugged, trying to concentrate on the road, traffic hissed passed.

'As much to be expected, I guess . . . Don't have long to live, put my wife and child in danger—feel pretty fucking good actually!'

No need to be like that, David—just remember who threw you in the shit you're in-

'I know,' he replied, grabbing his box of cigarettes from the seat beside him. He lit one and inhaled, holding the smoke for as long as possible before his head swirled. 'It's all my fault.'

He watched the dark clouds drift across the sky, spreading like fresh bruises on a beaten face. The tired sun blinked occasionally, dust motes upon the icy wind caught in its eye.

I'm in the trees, Davey-boy-

'What?' he replied, knowing that he should've kept his thoughts to him self. 'You mean like Charlie and the other wastes of space-'

Keep joking, pal . . . It's what your whole life is about! I'm here if you need me . . .

'Always have, always will be,' Reed whispered.

Later . . .

'Bye,' said Reed. Then he sighed heavily, wondering what was happening to his mind.

He glanced in his rearview mirror, watching the tiny flame of the fire lick at the darkness like a friendly hound. Small silhouettes were crowded about, and he envied them, as much to his dismay. The gatherers had vision, and they saw something that he didn't . . . or maybe they saw what he used to see-

Reed shook the thoughts from his mind. All he knew was that he believed-

There, are you happy now? You believe what Charlie was going on about! The spirits in the trees!-

He pressed on the brakes.

'I'm going to settle this right now!' he said, pulling up to the curb once more. As he climbed down from the cab, jumping in to a muddy puddle, he turned his collar up to the cold breeze, tiny needles of rain dashing across his cheek. He wished for a heavier downpour, then maybe he would have an excuse to return to the lorry.

The shadows seemed to converge upon him, bathing him in goose flesh as he approached the roadside. Behind him he could barely hear a thing. Not even traffic passed by. He expected to see a little smoke from the student's bonfire but even that was sucked in to the forest like the air of some vast lung. Only dark clouds filled the sky.

Reed took a deep breath and blinked hard. The pain and flashing sparks behind those lids reminded him of his sobriety. It was what made everything real, he thought, watching his feet move forward. The trees closed upon him; their leaves crunching beneath his feet, limbs embracing him, hooking onto his collar and sleeves. They felt like fingers, prodding and scratching him. Their shadows waved and chased each other like children; simply giddy silhouettes cast by a cruel sun.

Reed struck a match, a cigarette dangling at the corner of his mouth. The sound of the match was like a harsh breath, a curse squeezed from between gnarled, gritted teeth. The scent of sulphur and pine permeated the air.

You can turn around and go, if you'd like . . .

'I know . . .'

Reed spun round, the cigarette falling from his lips.

'What?' He was sure that he had heard something, a voice just a little louder than a whisper, a real voice. But he had heard it nonetheless. So he held his breath to try to concentrate, straining his hearing to pick up the slightest reprise should it occur.

And he waited . . .

'Screw this!' he snapped, bending one knee to retrieve his burning cigarette. He brushed the dirt from the filter and placed it in his mouth. It was a little damp but he didn't care; the fuckers weren't cheep-

Suddenly he heard the voice once more.

'If it's one of you fucking hippies taking the piss, you can kiss my arse!' shouted Reed, flicking away the cigarette after all. His voice was thunderous amongst the surrounding trees.

You're not alone-

'I know-'

I've always been right by your side-

'I FUCKING KNOW!' Reed screamed, falling to his knees. He raked his fingers through his hair and pulled at the roots. 'Shut up! Just shut the hell up!'

Say my name.

'No . . . this can't be happening,' Reed whispered. He shook his head. 'This isn't happening . . . Not again. NOT AGAIN!'

Just say those two magic words-

'No! I won't do it-'

Not even for your wife-

'Please,' Reed cried, tears falling freely down his face. 'I don't need you . . . I CAN DO THIS ON MY OWN!'

Not even for your son-

'Aaron Brookes! AARON BROOKES! Are you fucking satisfied now?' Reed shouted, his vision blurred by tears, but he surveyed the surrounding trees for the twinkling of an eye or a shadow that didn't quite belong . . . or was it the stench of charred flesh he searched for?

Silence replied.

Reed turned about and ran towards the lorry, his feet slipping through puddles of mud and dead leaves. Thin roots seemed to grab at his ankles and toe caps like hungry hands wanting a piece of him.

'God, I'm so stupid,' he muttered breathlessly, over and over again. 'Say something . . . Why aren't you saying something? What the hell have I done—SPEAK TO ME!'

Once again silence replied, this time louder than ever.

Reed climbed up into the cab of the lorry, looking over his shoulder at the darkness of the trees for a moment before slamming the door behind him. His hands shook wildly and he had to stop a few seconds and simply breathe, the keychain jangling between his fingers, before inserting the right one in the ignition once more.

He felt as though a million eyes were looking at him-

The branches creaked, hissed, moved-

'Come on, for God's sake!'

The keys slipped from his fingers, landing in the darkness by his feet.

The cab shook, buffeted by a strong gust of wind-

His hands swept the dusty patch of carpet around the pedals-

Something as strong as a fist hit his door-

'FUCK! COME ON! Yes, you bastard!' he hollered triumphantly, the keys held aloft between forefinger and thumb like a piece of solid gold. He jammed the key in the ignition, a bead of sweat trickled down his back, as hot as a lover's fingertip. And as the engine purred into life, Reed wondered just what the hell he had done.

With that thought he turned back to the road, the smile now gone from his face.

11

The day grew old and the shadows stretched to breaking point. Vehicles passed by in a blur of colours, and they could have been insects for all he cared. Concrete tower blocks, harsh sunlight sparkling in their window panes pointing drill bits at his temple with their brightness soon gave way to the gloomy atmosphere of an industrial estate; the dark cloud suspended above a cluster of factories, reluctant to move no matter how strong the winds were becoming. He could feel the darkness tug at the lorry, trying to hold on as he cruised through the estate. But as he stepped up the speed, only for a few seconds, he felt the oppressive gloom float away as though the dark hands had been torn away from the wrists.

Reed glanced at the dash board clock:

3:53PM 8th DECEMBER 2013

Then he glanced at it again.

'Where the fuck's the day gone to?' he mumbled, noticing how his fellow roadsters had switched on their headlights—'Christ!' he snapped, following suit. The last thing he needed was a couple of points on his license.

As the sun started to fall, Reed thought of home. It's what got him through the dark hours. Warmth, late night television to rot the brain and cold beer was what he missed. That and of course Tabby and the baby.

The baby . . .

Reed smiled, thinking of how much he missed the little devil. Shitty arses and snotty noses he didn't mind. He would trade his life to walk bare footed through the living room, relishing in the pain of breaking his toe on one of Paul's razor sharp toys—anything to be home again!

'Anything?'

Reed heard the voice but he chose to ignore it.

'You just couldn't be content with what you had, could you?' he mumbled, shaking his head.

'You can have it all back, you know-'

Reed noticed the twinkling lights of the roadside café and felt his stomach rumble and twist. He slowly pulled into the lay-by and turned of the engine.

'Did you hear what I just-'

'I heard you the fucking first time!' Reed snapped, jumping down from the cab. He cut his way through the deepening gloom, heading for the café like a moth to a flame.

Everyone knew the story circulating number 32 Whitman Drive, and despite the house's run down façade, the trash scattered about the yard like broadcast seeds, broken roof and cracked windows, it would be its charm that so many found alluring, feeding the imagination of neighbours to bursting point . . .

An obsession which proved to be their undoing . . .

And mine.

It was a hard choice to make. Alas, a choice that was almost as important to me as Mr. Giggles, my pet tarantula . . .

The mummy, a zombie, Dracula and the wolf man.

'Live a little,' said Tommy, the store keeper, rolling his eyes, exuding a barrage of excitement . . . or maybe not! After all, it was approaching closing time and a football game was about to start.

Four measly costumes, as predictable and over priced as ever!

Those were the only costumes left to rent from the store. Not the best choice, but . . . the mummy was simply a bag of bandages, so I crossed that off; Dracula looked about as scary as a soft, cuddly kitten, the zombie outfit resembled my dad on a boozy night with the boys, but the wolf . . . now that looked pretty fucking good. So I parted with eighteen dollars and fifty cents and made my way to my best friend's house to get ready for what was to be our last ever Halloween. The holiday was as important as our first times . . . well, maybe not! Well, as much as it hurt, we were in our senior year in High school . . . we knew it was time to grow the hell up!

I left the store—the door slammed behind me, the crunch of locks and chains followed like my shadow. Even the sign in the door switched from OPEN to HEY! CAN'T YOU SEE WE GOT A LIFE?

I never made it home that night.

I often wonder how things would've transpired had I just crossed the street and minded my own business. Would I have become the doctor I set out to be? Would I have had the three children I envisioned myself rearing? The two boys and the girl . . . Would they have my eyes? Their father's nose (the mister right who didn't even know it yet!) grand father's feet-

Broken windows, ugliness and a reputation as being the town's most haunted house, was one thing, but also being the focal point of countless camp fire ghost stories and speculation was another. If monsters were real, if ghosts and all those other gems that made their way through the small hours were real, then they fucking occupied number 32.

When I close my eyes to allow my other senses to take a hold of me, all I can hear are the cries coming from that house . . . that damned fucking pile of shit that caught me in its web and wouldn't let go. Like a fat spider, bulging with blood, yet hungry for more, It seemed to beckon me toward it-

I heard the crying child or whatever the hell made that noise!

I looked around but I was alone. I called out for assistance but silence shouted back at me as though I had touched its most private and intimate of parts. The street was deserted, a sun as red as freshly drawn blood edged the horizon, and I imagined a million people holding hands, every one of them ablaze with fire along the very bottom of the sky line, separating the earth from heaven.

That's when the cries grew louder.

Ignoring my instincts to keep on moving forwards, homewards, I slowly crossed the road and walked up the garden path.

I shouldn't have peeked through the gap in the front door.

But it was ajar . . .

Who the hell leaves their front door wide open and not expect interlopers?

Who?

I shouldn't have called out to whoever may be in trouble somewhere in the darkness . . .

WHY?

WHY?

WHY?

Three identical questions . . .

As simple as W.H.Y.

It was Halloween and the night was warm. The grass beneath my feet was freshly cut—not of number 32 I hasten to add, I'm talking about the abodes that seemed to give this fucker a wide berth. Monster 32 was a bloody wreck! If it was an island not even pirates would step ashore! Not without good reason, you understand? But it was alluring, the fear as juicy and tasty as the burgers grilled not two blocks from this very pile of bricks and glass. God, the place was . . .

How can I describe it?

Yeah . . . sexy. That's the word!

Resurrected from the cutting floor of some seriously fucked-up movie director, 32 was everything I needed this Halloween; the proverbial icing on the cake. I almost chuckled aloud but called out instead.

Yet no body replied.

Perfect . . .

The floor boards screamed beneath my feet, my voice echoing back to me.

Pure nirvana . . .

Hey, I was getting older! How many adventures have you had?

Then I heard footsteps. They surrounded me-

Silence.

I called out, trying to strain my hearing in the darkness, the costume in its paper bag under my arm, the child's voice crying again.

The façade.

It was all fake . . .

He was there, waiting.

My friend was at home, waiting.

I shook my head, laughing. Thinking all the while that this was just a dream-

The noise caught in my throat like a chicken bone as I turned to leave, the hand covered my mouth and pulled me into the shadows and dust motes.

I could smell his tobacco scented breath and body odour, taste his saliva as he clamped his mouth over mine. I wanted to scream, to run from the house but the gun poking my stomach turned my legs to concrete and my blood to iced water. I did everything he asked of me. I begged, screamed, smiled and caressed. I did everything he wanted. But he still dragged me to another place, somewhere cold and damp.

My body is in the dry wall cavity behind the bathroom. I've lost count of the years. They don't matter any more.

I didn't even have the strength to attend my own funeral. I know I should've been stronger, to look my loved ones in the eye; even stand beside my empty grave. But I couldn't. It was all fake. All of it! That wasn't me in that hole.

I should feel something, anything . . . but it's simply numb.

The new residents of the house don't even know I'm there. I see them, feel them walk by. I even call out but they don't hear a thing.

All that is going to change.

My name is Penny Stadler. I was 17 years old when Kev "the butcher" Turner took my life from me.

Now I'm taking it back.

Christine is like the older sister I never had. I love her.

And nobody hurts my family . . .

12

Reed stared down into his hot coffee cup and saw his pitiful reflection glare back at him as if hoping, waiting for some answers. If it was tea he would have tipped it down the sink just to get to the bloody leaves at the bottom of the mug.

'What the hell's wrong with me, Tabby?' he whispered.

Behind him fellow travelers tucked into all-day breakfasts, greasy fry-ups washed down with gallons of coffee. If it kept sleep at bay, thought Reed, his stomach growling with hunger now surrounded by the irresistible aroma, it was worth the heart attack. A long goods vehicle hissed passed, the cabin rocking gently. The radio crackled then fell silent a moment, only to spark into life once more after the truck sped away.

'Aren't you going to fucking say something?' he mumbled, glancing at the small list of home made food on offer, glancing sharply out the corner of his eyes, but nobody had heard him over the din of the radio. But there came no reply. 'Just checking.'

He ordered a piece of home made steak and kidney pie, only devouring half of it before pushing his plate away. Loss of appetite? Now he knew that there was something seriously wrong. He reached for his mobile phone and hoped he could find a signal. He noticed the tiny bar in the screen and smiled. He closed his eyes, a migraine building there, punched the keys on the phone and waited.

'Come on, come on! Pick up for God's sake!' he mumbled, noticing a couple of diners glance over their shoulders at him. 'Have I got a TV on my head?' he said, watching them turn back around in their seats. He wanted to laugh but thought he had already used up his nine lives with that outburst. 'Come on-'

'Hello?'

Yes!

'Tabby, why the hell haven't you been picking-up? I've tried ringing four times in half an hour!'

'Hey, chill-out, David,' she replied breathlessly. 'Picked up as quick as I could-'

'Where have you been?'

'Stuck in the house with little man all day, what do *you* think?'

'I've been ringing-'

'Look, we had a visitor and I couldn't get rid of him.'

Oh, God, no! They've come for my family. The bastards said I had four days to pay them back or else—the fuckers went back on their word!

'Jesus, honey!' he snapped. 'I'm coming home right now!'

'No, you're bloody-well not,' Tabby replied. 'We need the money. Remember what your boss said to you the last time you fucked up a job? Let's face it, David, you're working on borrowed time here. The firm won't be lenient all the time-'

Working on borrowed time? I'm living on borrowed time!

'I don't care,' he shouted, hands shaking. 'Who was at the door? Who?'

'Don't worry,' Tabby chuckled. 'It was only a double glazing salesman. I couldn't get rid of the cunt. That's why I didn't answer the phone.'

Reed felt the proverbial stone roll away from his shoulders, his heart hammering crazily in his chest.

'Are you alright?' she asked, her voice now as soft as silk. 'You're beginning to scare me.'

'Yeah,' he replied, feeling a tiny bead of sweat run down his back. 'I guess I'm okay.'

'Hey, I know you want to be home-'

You've got no fucking idea, Tabs! No bloody clue!

Tabby's voice was so soft, thought Reed, that he could just wrap it's sound about him and happily fall asleep.

'I miss you,' he whispered.

'I know you do, sweetheart,' she cooed. 'We miss you. But you know how important your job is to us. We need the money, baby. If I could work, I would. You know that. But after having Paul-'

'Look, darling, you don't have to explain-'

'And pretty soon,' said Tabby, interrupting him. 'When I get a little better, I can get my old job back. The boss said so.'

'Tabby, don't worry about that. You hated that job.'

'Yeah, I know,' she said, giggling. 'I hope the place burns to the fucking ground. But it'll do until I finish my degree.'

'What the hell are you doing with a loser like me?'

'Well . . . you got me up the stick for one!' she replied, bursting with laughter.

Reed could've sat listening to his wife's voice forever. He didn't realize up until now just how good her laughter sounded. But most of all he couldn't believe how he had taken her for granted all these years. Then he shook his head-

Admit it, David. You only feel this way when you're afraid!

'Stick it out, eh?' Tabby said softly. 'And I'll tell you what . . . When you come home we'll go to the job centre together and find you something else, eh? Something that doesn't take you away from home . . . How does that sound?'

Reed wiped the tears from his eyes. 'That sounds lovely, baby—I'm sorry-'

'Why are you sorry, sweetheart?'

'I love you.'

'Aw, it hurts so much when you're not here beside me,' she replied gently. 'I want to kiss you and hold you all night. The bed's so big without you.'

'I know, baby,' Reed replied, wiping away the fresh tears from his eyes. 'And I promise I'll find it—a new job—then I can be home *every* night. For you and the baby . . .'

Home.

God, I wish it were that simple-

Beep, beep, beep-

'Shit!'

'What's wrong?' Tabby sounded crackily, shocked and distant.

'Nothing, really. Just my bloody mobile phone. Running out of credit!'

'Running out of credit?' she replied jovially. 'That's our life story.'

'Look, I'll ring you soon, honey. I love you,' said Reed, quickly.

'I love you too. And remember what I said: stick it out, please—you'll be home soon. We love you.'

'I love you, too. See y-'

The line went dead.

13

Reed reviewed the road map for the hundredth time it seemed, following the thin lines down the page with the small torch, as though they represented the depth of despair to which his life had become. He looked at the tiny, red cross in Sheffield, where Tabby thinks he's heading, and sighed, slowly shaking his head. 'I'm so sorry, sweetheart,' he mumbled, wiping the tear from his eye with the back of his hand as the memory of the morning he had planned the route returned to haunt him. It had been two in the morning when his boss, Jay, had given him the job:

"I don't give a fuck if I *have* woken the baby up, Dave," snapped Jay down the phone. "This is your last chance. Take it or leave it!"

He had glanced over his shoulder at Tabby, Paul wriggling in her arms. She smiled even though she barely had the strength to stand.

"Okay, I'll be at the depot in-"

"Don't fuck up this time!" replied Jay before cutting him off.

"It's money, baby," yawned Tabby. "Can't knock it back."

But Reed was going nowhere near Sheffield-

"You know that you're on borrowed time," Tabby's words cut through him the first time she had spoken them and now, as he slowly traced his right index finger down the route on the map, they seemed to hurt him all the more. "Your boss won't be so lenient all the time."

He shook his head once more, firstly to clear his head and secondly with something akin to shame.

'Baby,' he mumbled. 'I lost my job the moment I turned left . . . Lincoln then sunny Cambridge, here I come.'

Fuck it! What's done is done!

Reed flipped on the radio and pushed the atlas back under his seat. He thought about putting it in the glove compartment as reaching down all the time was starting to irritate his back, but then he decided against it. He just didn't want to put his hand in there; simply too tempting-

He winced as a heavy metal song broke the silence. He detested the bloody stuff, but if it kept him awake and blew the cobwebs away then it would suffice, he thought, shaking his head with the onslaught of screaming guitars and thunderous drums. Night was falling quickly and he almost welcomed the cacophony.

'Alice fucking Cooper?' laughed Reed, wincing once more, this time at the blindingly bright fog lamps of passing vehicles. 'Alice?'

Reed switched on the screen wipers as tiny drops of rain pattered the glass. He could see the mist crawl from the side of the road like the smoke from a forest fire, and already he felt the temperature in the cab plummet.

It was then that he noticed the figure standing beneath a lamppost by the side of the road. It slowly raised its hand to the oncoming traffic, but the vehicles passed by sluggishly.

'Oh, not again! Not another fucking eco warrior,' said Reed. The rain had become heavy now and with it came string gusts of wind. 'I don't envy *you*, mate.'

I know, Tabby! I know you hate hitchers . . . But you have no idea how lonely it gets out here on the road—and this weather!

He pulled over to the side of the road.

The dark sharp didn't run, didn't even walk briskly. It strode calmly despite the lashing rain, towards the lorry. Then the door handle turned slowly, clicking loudly. And Reed watched the hitcher climb aboard.

14

'Cigarette?'

'Those thing's will kill you,' the hitcher replied, staring down at his hands, watching the fingers move.

'Suit yourself, mate,' Reed replied, already beginning to feel the tension dissipate. He wished the rain would, he thought, noticing the stranger's shaking hands. 'Sorry about the cold. Here,' he said, the cigarette dangling unlit at the corner of his mouth as he flipped a couple of switches on the dash board. 'Central heating,' he chuckled. 'Warmer than my fucking house, this bugger!' The sound of fans spinning within the cab's panels burst into life and Reed could already feel the goose bumps across his neck relax as a warm breath of air escaped the filters behind him. 'It'll warm up soon, you'll see.'

'Where do you want to be dropped off then?' said Reed, quickly lighting the tip of his cigarette. As he blew out a stream of smoke he could just see through the darkness beyond the arc sodium glare of his headlights. 'I'm going as far as Cambridge—'

'Wherever you finish . . . I'm fine with that,' the figure replied, looking up for the first time since getting in the cab.

'You're not in any trouble with the law or anything, are you?' said Reed, permeating the air with a gust of blue smoke. 'Because if you are I'm finishing right now,' he added, quickly easing gently on the brakes.

'Keep driving,' the stranger replied. 'I swear I'm in no trouble. Please, keep going.'

'Just kidding, mate,' said Reed, nervously. 'Just kidding!'

Reed laughed, but icy fingers clawed at his back. He looked over at his passenger sitting in the glow of the dash board light, as alone as a lost soul.

'What?' he said, looking back at him, the whites of his watery eyes glistening in the darkness of the cab.

'I just hope you don't turn out like my last hiker.'

'Turn out? You mean in a small shallow grave amid a boggy cluster of trees?'

'Ha ha, I like you,' said Reed, sucking on his cigarette. 'No, I mean, she turned out to be a wacko eco-warrior. Save the trees and all of that fucking shit!'

Well, you believed her, didn't you, mister tough guy-

Reed's smile suddenly faded.

'Save the trees, eh?' replied the stranger. 'Well, cut the fuckers down, I say. They take up too much room.'

'Too right, mate. Spirits in the trees and bollocks hanging from the branches—load of bullshit—bloody students!'

'Yeah,' replied the stranger. 'Cut the bastards down. That's after the spirits have found a home, that is.'

The laughter soon turned to silence. Confined, strangled silence.

'Yeah, whatever . . . that's all shit talk,' said Reed, reaching out his hand. 'The name's Reed. David Reed.'

The stranger looked down at the hand proffered, then met the driver's eyes. They twinkled in the darkness like exploding stars. He slowly reached out and held his hand, his grip, thought Reed, was a little weak as though the act was some kind of alien custom.

Reed shuddered as their flesh met. He blinked hard, his vision blurring a little as though he had suddenly awakened from a reverie.

'Bob,' said the stranger, looking out at the road before him. 'Just call me Bob.'

David tried to resume concentration on the task at hand, the headlight's bright beams swaying from side to side, but the sudden smell of . . .

Just what the hell is that fucking smell? Petrol . . . Is that what this creep smells of-

'Hey, steady, mate. Don't want to have an accident,' said Bob, his eyes didn't sparkle now. They were darker than the shadows now, thought Reed. But they sparkled at their edges.

15

Reed's hands shook as he tried to grip the wheel but its surface was slick with sweat. Outside, rain tapped against the windscreen, smearing his vision. He switched on the wipers, watching them sway hypnotically left and right. He blinked hard again to shake off the malaise.

'Bob?' he said. 'That's it? What kind of a name is that?'

'It's short for Robert,' Bob replied flatly, staring out at the dark endless road; cats eyes narrowing to razor sharp slits in the scouring beam of the headlights.

'I know that!' snapped Reed, shaking his head. 'No surname?'

'Smith.'

I give up!

'So what's waiting at the end of the road for you then, Bob Smith?' said Reed, swallowing hard. 'I think I know what might be waiting for *me*.'

'So what *is* waiting for you?'

Reed shook his head.

'Do you have a cigarette?' said Bob. He wasn't shaking but Reed sensed movement, could feel it through his seat and the panels about him. The cab vibrated, momentarily dousing the dash board instruments.

'Holy shit!' snapped Reed, bashing a fist against the warm plastic, hard enough to break its ticking innards. He suddenly understood how a pilot would have felt in the same situation. He turned the ignition key then started her up once more. Then he whistled, feeling his heart hammering as the lights on the dash board burst into life once more.

'What the hell just happened?' gasped Reed. He felt tiny pearls of sweat roll down his back. 'We lost everything for a few seconds-'

'Can I have a fucking cigarette or what?' Bob replied, his voice as dry as Reed's throat. He stared ahead at the aura from the headlights as it cut through the darkness as though it didn't even exist.

Reed jammed two cigarettes in his mouth and lit them. Suddenly the cab illuminated, carving ghosts and shadows on his retinas. And it was in that second that he saw his passenger in full living colour, and his blood ran cold. He took a cigarette from his mouth and handed it to his new friend-

I've got to get some fucking sleep-

Their fingers touched-

His small fingers wrapped the cord tighter about the wooden handles. Swollen, dry throats whimpered behind the closed doors.

He felt the hot breath stroke his cheek and goose bumps crept across his shoulder. But he couldn't move a muscle, feeling the clammy hands forcing his face forward. And as the breath turned to twisted, razor sharp laughter, he finally lost control of his bodily functions-

"Listen," it said. "Listen to the bastards!"

He wanted to spit and scratch at the face perched on his shoulder, now wheezing like a dying man's lung.

"Please let them go . . ."

The laughter grew louder, courser as fingers once furious, like the desperate hands of a drowning mass slowed against the wooden panels; air tightening, entrapped souls choking on the fetid air. And slowly the voices died . . . one . . . by . . . one-

His fingers untied the cords, scrabbling at the knots, pulling one of his nails right back. But he ignored the pain.

"Fine," it said. "You'll never learn. And neither will they!"

That's when-

Reed started in his seat, pressing his foot down on the brakes, his body lurching forward, hitting the windscreen like a lifeless crash test dummy. Light swirled, piercing the darkness that had become his world. Pin pricks of diamond-sharp light spread across the black canvas of his mind. There was blood in his mouth; he could taste its coppery foulness. And a pain that pulled at his neck also gripped his temples and squeezed, as though his head was in a vice.

'I don't fucking believe it,' Reed grumbled, numbness spreading across his cheek as he pulled his face away from the glass. There wasn't a crack, the pane was far too tough for that, but he *did* feel as though he had been thrown at a brick wall. 'What the hell . . .' he said, tracing a shaking finger tip across the bloody smear on the glass.

'Maybe you should take more care,' said Bob flatly, looking at the glass. Traffic swept by like fireflies, gently rocking the lorry.

He chose to ignore the remark, hearing the distant siren wailing like a banshee, white noise now scratching in the radio speakers to his left—or was it the right? He couldn't decide where it came from-

Then he looked at the dash board clock, which read:

11:23AM 9th DECEMBER 2013

'. . . And it is time to wake up,' said Bob finally, shielding his face from the shard of broken light which forced its way through the passenger window like a knife attack.

Reed spun in his seat, facing the stranger. The sudden movement blurred his vision and turned his stomach. 'How long have I been . . .'

'You've been asleep for a few hours-'

'How the fuck's that possible!' Reed snapped, wincing with the noise, instantly regretting his outburst. Traffic rushed by, and he remembered plunging his feet down the brakes. 'This can't be happening,' he whispered. 'This can't be happening.'

'My name's not Bob.'

There came a silence so long that time itself seemed to stop and watch.

Reed kept his eyes on the road.

16

Reed tasted fresh blood as his tongue pushed against the two loose teeth in his bottom right hand jaw.

'My name is-'

'I know your name,' said Reed, his whole body shaking.

You're in shock—That's all it is: shock—This is insane and you fucking know it! That scruffy bitch you picked up has planted the seed-

'I just don't want to hear you say it, okay?'

This isn't happening, you dickhead! Sleep, that's what you need! Just listen to yourself, David! How do you know? HOW DO YOU KNOW-

Reed detected movement from the corner of his eye. The figure was looking at him as though for the very first time.

How can you be sure? How?

I . . . just . . . know

'I can help you,' said Bob. 'I can help you right the wrong-'

'Just get the fuck out of this cab, Aaron! Go back to wherever it is that you came from!' shouted Reed, wiping his bloody mouth upon his sleeve, forcing himself to face the—whatever the hell it was!

Aaron Brookes had green eyes. Instead of a pupil a tiny pearl drop of blood sat at their centres, occasionally spreading in ever decreasing circles across the whole of his iris; like the ripples on a pond, the surface broken by a thrown pebble. For a moment Reed had mistaken the two bright orbs as all-seeing nothingness, the windows of a soulless entity—but he had been wrong. They were only eyes; bright and full of life.

Life?

The boy had grown, if that was possible-

No, it can't be . . . What ever happened to the burns, the exposed bones? How can . . . How can he age-

His features seemed more angular, chiseled rather than rounded and smooth. The skin was taut about his throat, augmenting his jaw. He was completely bald; etchings of some kind, like interwoven vines of ivy, covered the right side of his head. Fine lines covered his entire face, joining tears and cuts that seemed to meet below his slightly pointed chin. His smile creased his thin lips. He lit one of Reed's cigarettes, holding it between two heavily burnt fingers-

He's grown but hasn't changed!

Reed craved the smoke. But it wasn't solely to feed his habit; there came a stench he couldn't quite place, and the blessed smoke eradicated such a foul odour.

'What're you doing here, Aaron?'

'I knew you were going to ask me that,' said Aaron, exhaling a long cloud of blue smoke. He spoke quietly, his words seemed long and protracted as though each one required care and thought. 'I could predict everything. What you're thinking, what you were about to say . . . always could.' He allowed the words to trail off, gazing out of the window at the midday traffic as it passed by. He slowly shook his head. 'After all these years, David . . . You're in deep shit. Shit so deep you can't even move-'

'You don't have a clue about what's going on in my life,' Reed replied. 'So why don't you just get out and fuck off!'

Aaron shook his head, grinning. He didn't even glance at the door to his left. He wasn't going any where.

'I don't know who convinced you or shook that tiny mind of yours,' said Aaron, his smile now fading. 'But I sure as hell would love to shake his or her hand.' He took a final drag from the cigarette and crushed it in the palm of his left hand. 'You see that, David? Smell that?'

Reed watched the tiny wisps of smoke rise from Aaron's hand, and he could almost hear the hiss of melting flesh; almost smell the stench of cooking pork.

'I'm still asleep, aren't I?' said Reed, his voice now barely a whisper. 'I'm still asleep-' Pain fired through his jaw as the two loose teeth finally broke free, filling his mouth with the sweet coppery taste of blood. 'God!'

'You're not asleep . . . And before you think it again, you're certainly not away with the fairies,' said Aaron wearily, his eyes still on the road.

'But I sent you away all those years ago!' snapped Reed, his heart beating fast now, flashes of light appearing before his eyes. 'You don't exist—in fact you never really did in the first place!'

The lorry rocked like a rowing boat in a high wind as three cars sped by.

'I'm very much real,' the passenger replied, turning round in his seat to face him.

Reed was unnerved by the intensity burning like tiny emerald fires in Aaron's eyes, so much so that he stared straight ahead, afraid to disappear in those miniscule flames.

'I'm so real, David . . . that you believed in me-'

'I do *NOT* believe in you!'

'You called my name.'

Silence.

'Didn't you?'

Reed felt small and stupid, shrinking almost in his seat like a disobedient school boy. He held his aching jaw, felt the cold clamminess of his palms and shivered. Then after a couple of seconds which seemed to last hours, he finally spoke through the cold digits, still unable to face the-

Say it! You can say GHOST . . . it wouldn't kill you-

'I . . . can't go through all of this shit again, Aaron,' said Reed, his throat now as dry as parchment. 'I really can't. I have a real life now, I've moved on-'

'Don't you think I know all of that, David? Your wife is called Tabby, you have a pup called Paul, whom you want to be a footballer when he grows up—*blah-de-blah-blah-blah . . . but now you're in the shit with sharks—the end!'*

Reed couldn't move or speak. His jaw chattered and he had to clench his jaw to keep it still.

'I've never been away,' said Aaron softly.

'But I sent you away, all those years ago,' Reed replied, desperately trying to convince himself of the fact-

It's concussion! I've had a bit of a knock and now I need a doctor!

'David-'

'I walked you to Silverfield Avenue myself, in the pouring rain . . . the place where we met—I sent you away—and you turned around in the rain and disappeared—under the lights-'

'Didn't I tell you that I've always been here?' he tapped his forehead with a burnt finger, a grin spreading across his face. 'Your baby has four blankets; two Jurassic Park ones, Bob the builder, and—well, some baby goo-goo lambs and shit on it—I forget!' he said, waving the triviality away as though it were a pesky insect. 'You read the Incredible Hulk comics to him even though he can't understand a bloody word, and always when Tabby's not around because she hates those rags . . . Oh, and I also know that you keep ecstasy tablets under your bed in the red Nike shoe box—boy, you two really know how to throw a party—let me tell you!'

Reed felt his stomach somersault, his guts churning. A bead of sweat trickled down his collar, raising the hairs along the nape of his neck. He lowered the window a fraction to let in some cool air and remembered the heating still filtered hot air through the cab's walls. He flipped the toggle beneath the steering wheel and listened to the fans slow, finally stopping with a squeaky click. It didn't take long for the cab to cool down.

'You,' Reed stammered, reaching for the dwindling pack of cigarettes beside him. Even though his hands shook he managed to light one. 'You've never been away? For over twenty years . . . you've watched me-'

'You and your, shall we say, *lovely* wife,' Aaron winked, but without the trace of a smile on his dark lips.

'Would you have . . . you know, been with us 'til I died—unseen, I mean?'

'I *have* to stay. I knew you'd need me eventually,' Aaron replied, nodding slowly. There was an edge of despair to his words that chilled Reed. He took a drag of the cigarette and he felt his stomach turn. 'Adulthood . . . has a habit of clouding your mind. You forget your real friends, you see? Funny how you ever get back in touch with them when you need something? Human nature, I guess-'

'For fuck's sake, stop rambling on!' Reed shouted, his voice deafening in the close confines of the cab. 'You know why I sent you away! You know why!'

'You didn't need me any more,' said Aaron, softly, wiping the condensation from the windscreen with his right hand. His fingers barely left a trace on its cold surface. 'I know that for sure . . . You learned to stick up for yourself and therefore I guess you kind of *outgrew* me-'

'That's right, I *did* learn, you bastard!' Reed snapped, despite the pain in his jaw and the taste of blood on his tongue. 'I learned to do things for myself—you just cocked everything up . . . then expected me to pick up the pieces. Not chatty now, are you? Then you'd have me return your . . . favours.' Reed winced, shaking the thoughts away, unable to believe that they were still as fresh in his mind as the day they had happened. 'The things you made me do, Aaron . . . to those innocent people . . .'

'I was trouble,' Aaron chuckled, shaking his head. 'I admit that. But at least you've grown not to care about that part of me-'

'Is that meant to be some kind of fucking joke?'

'Well, when you called my name back there, last night,' Aaron pointed over his shoulder. 'In the trees, I mean. You said my name . . .' his words trailed away, for he knew that he didn't need to explain any further.

'Don't . . .'

'That's all it ever took. You know that. You were so desperate that-'

'Shut up.'

'So desperate that you followed your instincts and just let it all out-'

'I SAID SHUT UP!'

To Reed, the next few seconds were a complete blur.

He stopped the vehicle.

One moment he was nursing a swollen, bloody jaw, the next he had bridged the tiny distance between himself and . . . whatever the hell it was sitting beside him. The door opened and they fell in a twisted heap of arms and legs. Reed felt his bones jar as they hit the edge of the road, barely missing the asphalt. Mud splashed his clothes and now he could taste that too. Horns from passing vehicles sounded, screeching by like angry insects. They could have been surrounded by a squad of Police cars-hell, the SAS could have turned out to try and break them up! But Reed didn't give a fuck. His world was falling apart at the seams and he was damned if he'd let some joker completely push him over the edge! He got up as quickly as he could.

'You're in trouble,' Aaron spluttered, Reed's hands about his throat. 'It's . . . big time! Don't pretend that it's not-'

Reed's fist struck Aaron's jaw, creating a dull flat slapping sound. He couldn't remember the last time he had actually punched someone. But it certainly didn't sound as dynamic as it usually did on the silver screen, thought Reed, grabbing his fist in his left hand. God, it felt as though an armoured tank had backed up over it.

'You have no idea what I'm going through!' shouted Reed, kicking the fallen man as he clutched his face, squirming in the quagmire. 'No fucking clue!'

'Hit me as much as you want to, David,' said Aaron, spitting blood. 'You're a loser . . . the only thing going for you is your wife and kid-'

'Just go away,' said Reed, making his way, somewhat unsteadily, back to the lorry. The grit from the muddy puddle crunched between his teeth. 'You're nothing to me.'

'Nothing, eh?' Aaron shouted, kneeling in the mud. 'You narrowly escape knee-cappings, and almost had to re-mortgage your home because of your stupid, fucking gambling habit!'

Reed stood with his back to the ghost, unable to speak or move.

'I'm right, aren't I? I've been there,' Aaron continued, now getting to his feet. 'I've been there through it all . . . And don't think for one second that I don't know what you keep in that fucking glove compartment up there.'

Reed spun round, fists clenched.

Aaron laughed.

'This isn't over . . . David. *We* aren't over.'

'I don't need you any more.'

'Yes, you do,' Aaron replied, grinning like the burned skeleton child he had been all those years ago, scratching at his bedroom window. 'You need me now more than ever . . . Am I right?'

Reed tried to maintain eye contact but it was futile.

Aaron laughed, but it was silent.

'I said . . . Am I right?'

I hated seeing mummy cry. She was such a beautiful lady and I always told her so; watching her big blue eyes light up when I gave her bunches of flowers I picked for her on my way home from school everyday brought me joy too. On summer days the bright warm sun could catch her no matter how hard and fast she ran from it. Her golden hair cascaded over her tender shoulders, where I saw my daddy kiss one day beside the Christmas tree. But that had been a little time ago and such nice things were of the past.

I was six years old but to 'good mummy' I was already a princess. And when she held me and squeezed me tight I knew that maybe the 'bad mummy' would stay away, even for a short while . . .

I remember when daddy tried to take bad mummy away; pouring the bottles of water she kept hidden from him down the sink. I hated those bottles of water, it made mummy talk funny and cuddle me too tightly. Why didn't she drink from the tap like me and daddy did, I wondered, often watching her wrap big glass bottles in old newspaper and stuff them deep down at the bottom of the bin. I think daddy found them one day. In fact I think he kept finding such bottles day in and day out, but kept his mouth shut. Mummy could get very angry sometimes when daddy opened his mouth . . .

Then one night, mummy and daddy were shouting and they had the bedroom door open a little. They thought I was fast asleep but I was looking through the gap in the door, watching their red faces bulge with anger, daddy's fists closing and opening by his sides as though he was holding hot coals . . . and mummy was laughing . . .

Daddy said nasty words, so did mummy; words I was told never ever to say-

Then he saw me standing outside the door.

He wiped the tears from his eyes and smiled at me, and told mummy that we can sort everything out in the morning. But as he opened the door and knelt down to pick me up, he screamed. It took a bit of time to release just what happened, but then I saw the blood pour down his forehead, into his eyes and open mouth. If I didn't jump out of the way he would've fallen on me . . .

Mummy looked dizzy, her blue eyes as grey and still as a dolly's . . . She held the broken bottle in her hand, blood dots on her nightie. I knelt down and cried at daddy's side, shaking him so he'd wake up but deep down I knew he was in heaven . . .

That's when the bad mummy grabbed fistfuls of my hair and dragged me to the bathroom, turned on the cold tap and held my head under the icy water until I knew no more.

My name is Lisa Wayne. I went to heaven with daddy last year.

He's coming back with me because he said he has a plan and I'm too little to be on my own.

He won't tell me what his plan is because he said it was a secret.

I wonder if the lovely lady with the sweeties and beautiful smile has anything to do with it? She gave me some coloured crayons, a book of pictures and a glass of fizzy orange pop that tickled my tongue because my throat was really really dry. I heard them chatting over coffee and doughnuts in the small, brightly lit café two nights ago while I was busy trying to keep my crayons within the thick black lines. I tried but I'm just a little girl.

I think daddy likes her. I can't remember the last time he smiled this way. It was so warm and bright. And I smiled too when they both looked toward me. It was almost like seeing mummy and daddy back together in happier, warmer times.

I can dream, can't I?

We know where bad mummy is and we're going to get her.
But the kind lady is in trouble . . .
Bad mummy will just have to wait.

I asked the boy his name but he had already walked back into the shadows . . .

17

'You know the way it has always worked, David,' said Aaron flatly, watching the trees and buildings pass them by on their way up the motor way. Dark clouds, the colour of fading bruises slowly drifted by on a breeze that failed to shake the vehicle. The heating had dried their muddy clothes some hours ago and now, as the sun started to fall, their weary bones called out for a soft and safe place to sleep. But they would find no such thing this night.

Reed shook his head, trying to wake up. But sleep deprivation had him by the throat and it wouldn't let go. He squeezed his eyes closed for a split second, almost letting the steering wheel slip through his fingers.

No, I won't do it! I know what you want from me and I won't do it!

'If you think I'm going to harm another person for you, then you're fucking mistaken!' Reed snapped, steadying his grip on the wheel, the road's cats' eyes swerving a little to the left. 'Do you understand, Aaron? I have a life now-'

'I can drag you out from the shit you're in, David,' said Aaron as casually as commenting upon the weather. Then he smiled, seeing the lights flicker in Reed's eyes as they made eye contact. It was only for a moment but it was enough. 'I promise no harm will come to you or your little family. But-'

'But?' Reed chuckled dryly. 'There's always a but—Jesus, Aaron—you haven't changed at all. So what's the catch now, eh?'

Aaron grabbed the last cigarette from the crumpled pack beside the seat, struck a match and inhaled slowly.

'Come on, you bastard,' snapped Reed. 'You can't honestly believe I'm falling for this! You don't need to think. You know what you want, so stop fucking with me! It's all part of your plan, right?'

'You are a strange one, David,' replied the ghost, smiling. 'So unwilling to harm the hair upon any being's head. Funny, judging by that little pop-gun you have there I would've thought that you'd finally grown a pair of balls-'

'Cut to the chase-'

'I will help you,' said Aaron, his smile fading. 'But you will help me too.'

'Okay,' Reed hissed, bringing his fist down hard upon the steering wheel. 'I will not kill any body. You understand? No murder, no hurting any one—none of that—do you fucking understand?'

Aaron stared straight ahead, watching the road beyond the cracked glass, his emerald eyes surveying the glimmering lights of the passing traffic-

'Understand?'

'That, I can not promise.'

18

'How long before we reach the rendezvous?' Aaron wanted to know, tapping his hands on his knees along to the beat of the rock music on the radio. The crackly interference made Reed wince as though he had been skewered from ear to eye. He switched it off.

'Thank fuck for that,' said Reed, wishing they had more cigarettes. They'd have to stop for some in a short while. Nicotine cold turkey was the last thing he needed right now.

The sun had closed like a swollen, blood shot eye, darkening the cab.

Another day gone

'Not long,' replied Reed, yawning loudly. 'Besides, why are you asking me? You're the ever-present, all knowing, invisible guest in my home—you tell me.'

'Calm down, David,' said Aaron.

'I'm fine. There's nothing the matter with me.'

'I know where you're heading and who'll be there-'

'There's a thing. If you do know my business; the shit I'm in, where I fucking live for crying out loud—even the colour of Tabby's underwear-then why now? Why didn't you help me earlier when we were drowning in debt?' He glanced briefly at Aaron, waiting for an answer. 'Why now?'

'Because I needed to know that you needed me; that I existed to you,' replied Aaron, his emerald eyes shining cat-like in the darkness. 'Especially after everything that had happened between us-'

'If you're trying to send me on some fucking guilt trip, then you can go to hell!' Reed shouted, hands squeezing the steering wheel; wishing it was his passenger's throat. 'You know fine well why I sent you away. Don't you think I needed you? You know how desperate we were-'

'I know,' Aaron said, nodding at the glove compartment.

'I know?' Reed grunted, shaking his head. 'You know bugger all—you'll watch me torture myself with worry; you'll stand over me when I'm shagging my wife, but you won't help-'

'I can not help you unless you ask me too,' replied Aaron quietly, opening his mouth to yawn. 'That's how it goes, you know that.'

'Oh, you mean you're like one of those vampires that can't enter a house unless he's invited?'

'Not quite,' said Aaron, flexing his weary fingers as though trying on a pair of tight, leather gloves. 'You know I'm dead . . . I can't be of any use to you unless you believe in me,' he added, his voice now barely a whisper.

'So . . . all I had to do-'

'All you had to do was believe—look, I'm here now, in the flesh!' Aaron snapped. 'That's all that matters.'

'A whisper in my ear at the bookies,' Reed sighed, shaking his head in disbelief. 'Being tipped off would've been a good idea at the time-'

'I can't see the future, David. Christ, you watch too much TV,' Aaron chuckled. 'Neither can I change the future. You got yourself into all that shit, not me.'

Reed nodded, glancing at Aaron for a moment, before a smile creased his lip.

'If I'm talking to a ghost, then how come you've aged?'

Aaron looked up now, surveying the road ahead, as though the right answer to that question lay beyond the cracked glass. So near yet so far away.

'Boy, when people get irate they really go for the poison,' he said finally, eyes gleaming with tears. 'We move on, grow older. I'm not alone this side of the wall, you know? I know of a dead girl who waits tables in a café . . . counting down the days until her family are wiped out so they can all be together again—but that's not important, David. What I'm saying is that in death, like in life, your fingernails and hair continue to grow—only for a short while. You see, we age too-'

'I don't understand a bloody word you're saying. And I don't care!' Reed snapped. 'I just want out of this hell. Do *you* understand *me*?'

The ghost nodded.

'I understand,' he said flatly. 'Let's calm down, grab some cigarettes from somewhere and think about our next move.'

Reed exhaled loudly, tapping the steering wheel in tandem with his beating heart. It was some time before the beat slowed.

19

'What's this bloke like then?' Aaron wanted to know. The service station grew smaller in the rearview mirror until its lights disappeared entirely, swallowed whole by the converging darkness. It wasn't long before his face lit up, the match burning the tips of the two cigarettes he held at the corner of his mouth. He passed one to Reed, who accepted it as though they were going out of fashion.

'Which bloke?' he said, feeling his head swirl with the nicotine rush.

'What do you mean: which bloke?'

'Like I said, for fuck's sake! I'm not too popular at the dog stadium either, you know?' Reed tried to laugh but his jaw still ached from his collision with the windscreen earlier.

'I know. Okay . . . Why don't we start with the one who wants you dead?'

Reed glanced over at the ghost, only for a moment. But that was all the time he needed for an accident to occur. Two cars swerved around the lorry as it hurtled towards the opposite lane, cutting the peace with their horns.

'Maybe you won't live long enough to find out,' Aaron laughed.

'Johnny Gladstone doesn't want me dead,' replied Reed, getting them back in line. 'He just wants the money I owe him. Besides, he's not such a bad 'un when he's on his own-'

'How *dare* he want his money back? *That* wasn't part of the deal-'

'Okay, be a sarcastic bastard-'

'You owe him seventeen grand, David. Not exactly a fucking king's ransom, is it?' the ghost replied as casually as describing the weather. 'And he will *not* be alone . . . Christ, was this all worth it?'

'Well, that's not important any more. Pretty soon this'll all be over and I won't have to worry about him any more, right? You'll help me, right?'

Aaron looked out of the passenger window, beads of condensation racing down the glass, traffic light passed by like bare, unguarded electricity.

'Right?'

'Right,' the ghost replied softly.

20

Johnny Gladstone was like any other loan shark, thought Reed, shaking his head. Mr. Friendly, how's-the-wife-and-kids? Here's-a-lolly-for the bairns, how's-your-sick-mum? Kind of guy. They all were when the repayments flooded in regularly, without a scratch or nudge, straight into their wallets. A hard day's work without breaking a nail; or knee cap, for that matter. Missing a repayment to Gladstone was like forgetting to breathe: it wasn't possible.

In Reed's world, *anything* was possible.

As Reed described the shark, Aaron occasionally nodded and grunted in all the right places, not paying much attention at all. He didn't need to know. He knew Gladstone by sight, but guessed that inside they were all made of the same stuff. Aaron had been the cold presence that chilled Reed to the marrow that day. As he sat huddled between Reed and one of Johnny's minders in the back seat of a brand new black Mondeo, breathing in the scent of fear hidden beneath layers of cheap aftershave, he felt Reed's flesh harden with goose bumps.

Even the minder shivered despite Reed's proximity, a chill seeping through his thick woolen coat and suit that unnerved him somewhat. After all, he was no stranger to violence—hell, he got off on it. And being given full rein of the punishment due, he found the notion of putting a gun to Reed's head and having done with the bastard pretty irresistible. But he did resist. And for this, the ghost was grateful . . .

He needed Reed alive.

Closing his eyes, even covering his ears failed to drown out the screams, so Aaron had left the back of the Mondeo. And as he slowly walked away he could hear the sound of flesh hitting flesh and the cracking of bones. He stood for a minute or two, breathing in the cool, wintry air, before making his way back to the car. As he passed through the metal, he saw the blood. And there was somebody else there sitting beside Reed.

'Do you want 'im finishin,' Mr. Gladstone?' the minder grunted breathlessly, beads of sweat trickling down his round face.

'No need, Jeff,' Gladstone sneered. 'I think any more exercise will be the end of you, mate.'

The shark's brown eyes narrowed, like sharp slits, diamonds glistening at their centres. His pale face, almost phosphorescent in the car's dark interior, was only an inch from Reed's pulped nose . . .

Those eyes . . .

Aaron closed his eyes, and sighed.

God, Reed, you don't stand a chance . . .

Then he glanced at the glove compartment once more and he understood what lengths the poor bastard was willing to go to. He looked over at Reed, a pale figure steering the wheel like a ship's captain in a torrential storm; turning his head from left to right as though searching for the blessed beacon of a lighthouse; looking for some way out of this sea of madness.

'What're you thinking about?'

'What?' Reed replied, starting almost as though pushed from some reverie.

'You were miles away. What's going on up there?' said Aaron, tapping a finger against his forehead.

'Tabby and Paul,' he said, finally, breathing deeply. 'I hate being away from them for days on end . . . not knowing if they're alright or . . .'

'You should be ashamed of yourself,' said the ghost. 'But don't torture yourself-'

'Well thank you so much for the words of encouragement, my friend,' Reed snapped. 'Why do you ask questions in the first place? I thought you knew everything. Besides, you know fine well how I feel . . . But at least it's all getting sorted out. Tabby need never know. We can go on with our lives and grow old; watch Paul grow . . .'

Silence fell between them as Reed's words trailed away.

'As though nothing's happened, eh?' said Aaron.

Reed nodded, glancing for a moment at the ghost's emerald eyes, before turning to the road once more. He felt his heart start to thud against his ribs and wondered if things would ever be the same-

You have to try, David! That's all you can do!

'Yeah,' Reed exhaled loudly, straightening up in his seat, steadfast and resolute. 'Yes, everything will be okay.'

'I thought you were married,' said Aaron, smiling broadly.

'What the hell are you babbling on about now?' Married? What does that have to do with anything?'

'Well, you're not wearing a band of gold,' said Aaron, pointing at Reed's left hand.

'For crying out loud, man! You know I'm married. Besides, you were probably there, but my ring's been missing for weeks now. All I can remember is taking it off, placing it on the edge of the sink before taking a shower. Later on it wasn't there; haven't seen it since,' he said, smirking. 'Hey, you're the creepy crawly, why don't *you* tell me where it is, eh?'

'I know exactly where it is.'

Reed sniffed, his smile fading somewhat.

'The pawn shop.'

'You . . . what?' Reed chuckled. 'The-'

'Yes, the pawn shop on York Road. You know the one? It's opposite the library-'

'Yes, I know the fucking place!' Reed snapped. 'And don't try to be clever with me, okay? Stop playing games.'

'Well, that's where it is, and I'm not even going to dignify your next question with an answer. Okay?' replied Aaron, calmly tapping another cigarette from the box on the dash board. He lit it and inhaled deeply.

And he waited.

Seconds turned to minutes.

'Come to think of it, David,' said Aaron. 'When was the last time you actually saw Tabby wearing jewelry?'

I know what you're going to say, you bastard . . . I'm not falling for it!

'Believe me. Tabby isn't stupid. If you gave her the same amount of credit as you run up on your cards-'

Reed slammed on the steering wheel, but kept his mouth shut.

Do I need to spell out how you're making me feel right now?

'She knows what you're up to on this little trip, David-'

'You're talking rubbish,' Reed said, shaking his head. 'Talking crap just like always.'

'Remember, I spend more time at home than you do,' said Aaron softly, dragging deeply on the cigarette. 'While you're at the bookies, I'm at your house watching your wife reach down the side cushions of the couch for stray coins. When she nips out for a pint of milk she returns with less jewelry. Haven't you ever noticed? Man, you are so naïve, it's laughable. Tabby knows about everything . . . Jesus! You should hear the 'phone-'

The ghost stilled his tongue before he could twist the knife too deeply.

'Phone calls? What phone calls? That's what you were going to say, wasn't it? I should hear the phone calls—Well, I'm here now, Aaron, and you'd better believe that I'm listening!'

'Gladstone has a very colourful vocabulary, hasn't he?'

'I don't know,' said Reed. '*You* tell *me*.'

'Remember that night you came home from the pub and Tabby was crying? And you asked her why?'

'Yeah, she said she'd been watching a sloppy video—Titanic, I think she said, so?'

'Come on, man. Did you really believe that? She'd received a phone call from the big guy himself. Yep, Johnny Gladstone told her everything: how much you borrowed, the interest to be returned—oh, and before I forget: what he'd do to her and the baby if he didn't get back what he's due. He said he knew a few blokes who liked children a little too much and-'

'Don't, Aaron!' Reed snapped, his fingers gripping the steering wheel until his fingers went white and the blood stopped at his wrists.

'The bastard was willing to drop a payment if Tabby gave him a blowjob,' continued the ghost as casually as discussing the weather.

Reed looked away, a passing lamppost illuminating his face for a split second. Aaron smiled, watching the knot of veins twist in his jaw like steel ropes.

'But instead, the portable TV from the spare room made a mysterious trip to the repair shop on York Road, remember? Come to think of it . . . haven't seen that TV for a while now.'

How could I have been so fucking blind!

Reed slammed a fist down on the steering wheel once more.

'So she knows everything?'

Aaron whistled. But then his smile faded. This reality check was killing Reed. It wasn't fair, and besides, he needed him strong, focused. Not some fucking nervous, emotional mess of a man that he appeared to be at this moment.

Try something new! Can't lose him now!

'Yes,' replied Aaron, softening his voice. 'Tabby knows. And she loves you so much. She's a strong lady. But she just thinks you're off to pay Gladstone back. That's why she doesn't want you to lose your occupation. Poor girl has no idea what you really have in mind.'

Reed sniffed back the tears, trying to smile. But it wouldn't come. 'It's safe to say that I've well and truly lost my job now!'

'But we can put an end to the whole thing,' replied Aaron, seriously. 'I promise that the next time you both place your heads on your pillows, you'll sleep as soundly and peacefully as newborn babes. Gladstone will be no more. And it will be because of what we are about to do-'

'God, why did I turn out to be such a jerk? I have everything!' Reed shouted, shattering the still. 'You know I love Tabby, don't you,' he said, tears falling down his cheek at the thought of the fear his wife must have endured at the hands of that bastard. 'Please help me sort this mess out . . . please.'

'This time tomorrow night, your problems will be . . . a thing of the past,' said the ghost quietly, watching the grown man cry. The tears were real, thought Aaron. Each one burned . . . but not for Tabby or the baby. He had seen this same person cry many times, especially as a young boy. And Aaron knew why he was breaking down. He smiled crookedly and turned to face the passing trees and vehicles, moving like spilt oil across a madman's canvas.

I know what you're thinking, David . . . You know how we play this game. I may have changed but the rules have not!

Reed knew that even with Johnny out of the way and his family safe from harm, his problems were far from over.

21

Reed noticed a razor sharp ribbon of red light appear on the horizon, cleaving a bank of gray smoky clouds. He refused to look at the dash board clock; he didn't care for time any more. He'd get to wherever he needed to be when he was ready and not a minute earlier—fuck Gladstone, he could wait. As the sun's warm rays gently stroked the windscreen, making him wince, he felt its warmth caress his cheek. He smiled, wondering if this was some kind of sign. Not from God, no, from Tabby.

Beside him, the ghost slept.

Your chest's rising and falling . . . so you must be real . . . Not the little boy from all those years ago! Can't be . . .

Now was the time, thought Reed.

Not wishing to wake him, Reed reached out his left hand; had to touch the figure sitting beside him; had to find out if he was real and not a figment of his imagination-

Just one touch, my friend . . . That's all it takes to make everything real . . .

Reed knew that this whole situation could be the product of the cocaine he sometimes took to take the nightmares away, but he supposed the added addiction of old horror movies and tatty paperback novels were partly to blame. Hell, when sleep kept its distance what else could he turn to but TV-

What the hell are you doing, David? Don't do it.

Reed prepared himself, for what he didn't exactly know. His fingers moved closer to the dark fabric of Aaron's coat. Any second

84

it's going to happen, and the lorry would leave the motorway—for that, Reed was certain. The fucker is going to wake suddenly, his eyes flickering open like those of a giant demonic doll—lifeless, glass and full of hunger; his hands would reach out and tear the larynx from Reed's throat-

But the ghost slept peacefully, chest continuing to gently rise and fall, shivering slightly at Reed's touch as though their flesh had been joined momentarily by a live wire.

Reed's heart sank somewhat. Maybe it was a mixture of fear and the thought that this whole promise of freedom was not real after all.

Where's the magic, Aaron? You're superhuman for crying out loud!

His fingers rubbed the fabric of the wraith's coat and he sighed heavily, drawing his hand back to the steering wheel. The cloth was damp and cold, but nothing more. Aaron was real, undoubtedly as factual as the sun light on his face and the troubles on his mind.

The previous night, Aaron had wanted to know when they would reach their rendezvous, and how Reed planned to face Gladstone.

Silence fell between them.

How the fuck do you think I'm going to settle the matter?

Reed looked at the glove compartment.

This wasn't how it was meant to happen, for God's sake!

He looked up through the windscreen, at the warm sun and brightening sky, green fields rolling by like waves on a sun-dappled ocean. He pulled up to the nearest lay by and turned off the engine. His hands shook as though they had been encased in ice. He looked for his cigarettes and cursed at the small amount that was left in the sleeve he had purchased the night before. Aaron had hit them quite heavily during the night, but he didn't care. He lit one and immediately started to relax, his body juddering with the nicotine rush.

His stomach churned and he wanted to vomit, all the while telling himself that this was not the way life was supposed to be—not his life! His stomach growled now with hunger-

'Fuck this,' he mumbled, unable to contain himself any longer. He opened his door, reached forward and emptied the contents of his tummy into a dark muddy puddle by the wheel; eyes watering and throat burning. With the fresh air on his face and the rush of noise from passing traffic cutting through his tired, aching head, Reed threw-up once more.

'Nerves,' the voice echoed in the cabin.

Reed started slightly, hoping that when he turned around, the thing—what ever it claimed to be—would be gone. He sighed heavily and slowly closed the door on the cold breeze.

'Disappointed, David?'

The ghost's eyes were wide and bright as though he had slept like a God, and what Reed had mistaken for carvings in the side of his face were in fact deep scars. His entire forehead looked as though it had been crafted from warm wax and left to dry and harden; its sculptor's finger nails still apparent in its surface.

Aaron turned away, somewhat self consciously; looking ahead at the sun.

'To be honest,' said Reed after a time, 'I thought this was all a nightmare.' He grabbed a bottle of Coke from under his seat, unscrewed the cap and took a long slug of the liquid, wincing at its flatness. But at least it was wet and helped rid his mouth of the taste of vomit. He offered it to the ghost, who declined with the wave of a hand.

'As you can see,' said Aaron, 'I've aged. Scars never heal no matter how many years pass-'

'You never *did* tell me how you got so badly messed up, did you?'

'That is irrelevant,' the ghost snapped. 'It happened such a long time ago.'

Reed detected the urgency in the ghost's voice, and despite the part of him that wished to press on with the subject, he realized he was simply wasting his time.

'I guess you'll tell me eventually,' Reed said quietly, taking a final drag from his cigarette before flicking it from the small gap at the top of the window. The cool breeze stole it and carried it off to God knows where. Then he closed the window and rubbed his hands together to generate some warmth.

'How many times have we traveled about the moon?' said Aaron suddenly. 'I mean, Christ Almighty! We must have fallen off the edge of the planet—we've driven so far. Are you sure you're not just riding around in circles in the hope of avoiding-'

'Fate? I know what's coming, Aaron,' replied Reed, a little harshly. 'Don't worry about me.'

'Do you really know what's about to happen?'

I know I could be dead within the next couple of hours!

'I'm avoiding bugger all, mate,' said Reed smiling. 'I'm not the secretive one. Take a look outside, Scarface.'

The ghost leaned forward in his seat and surveyed the land beyond.

'What is it I'm supposed to be looking at? All I see are factories, a bunch of trees, the motorway . . . and a river on our right. So what?'

'And you said you know where we're going and who'll be there,' said Reed, grinning. 'So you should be telling me, shouldn't you? Don't you remember the map?'

Aaron smiled, his eyes narrowing to bright slits as realization dawned on him.

'Cambridge?'

'See that tall building? The one between those ones you thought were factories?'

The ghost nodded slowly, his right hand now shielding his eyes from the brightening sun.

'Well, that's actually an old store house. Nobody works there-'

'For what?'

'What do you mean?'

'I mean,' Aaron turned to face him, his eyes now as wide as saucers, 'what's stored there?'

Reed shrugged his shoulders. 'I'm not sure . . . As far as I'm aware, it's old carnival stuff—hey, I don't know,' he replied, closing his eyes a moment as if the answer was there on the canvas of his mind. 'Like old roller coasters that aren't fit to ride any more . . . worn out merry-go-rounds and things.'

'You mean like carousel horses and the like?' The ghost sat back in his chair, smiling broadly.

'What are you so damned happy about? That's where this whole mess is going to end,' said Reed, igniting the engine. Slowly they pulled away from the side of the road, unable to take their eyes from the store house. It grew closer, tearing itself from the horizon; moving towards them like a chess piece on the chequered fields beyond the road. The sun skipped across the silver disc of the river, keeping up with them. The lorry couldn't outrun it, there was nowhere to hide.

They all look at me but they don't see me. Not the adults anyway. I sometimes detect the glimmer of something in a child's eye, I can't quite describe it but they see, those little ones. I know they see. I often wonder how I would look to me should I be the one gazing through the tiny square frame of old glass.

Amongst the old toys of this dusty attic, a museum I used to love, I wander. Sometimes I press my bloody hands against the glass but it leaves no trace. And I taste the gore mixed with dust and it doesn't affect me any more. I knew that deep down I should never feel hunger again. It's just a useless craving, like cigarettes. I didn't need it and I knew it. Yet I tasted the blood, just to fill my stomach. Sometimes when the rains beat fists against the windows beyond my prison, I smell the dampness creep through the walls of the old room like daddy long leg spiders, reaching the ceiling, coming towards me as I huddle scared in the corner . . . Even though I can feel its chill surface, often wanting to cover the pane with blood so nobody can peer in at the display . . . and not see the young boy pushing the rickety old wooden train set along the same old track, I try to keep the window clean so I can survey the pale walls beyond.

They think this room is haunted, and they're right. After all, ghosts are what they pay to come and see . . .

But I don't want to push toys around any more . . .

I feel like a circus freak: watched, pointed at, laughed at . . . even though I'm invisible to anyone taller than four feet! I know it's all in my head but that's just how my mind is starting to operate. I'm gone but I feel human again.

89

Every moment I try to move a doll or knock over a block of wooden building bricks, my strength takes another small bite of my soul . . .

I am a ghost and sometimes even I wish to die.

I can't endure seeing the children's faces, looking straight at me and through me, noticing my face amongst the rows of cuddly bears and porcelain dollies. I see the shock in their eyes. They pull on their parent's hands and point through the glass. I read their lips. But they move on and forget me . . .

THEY SEE ME! THEY SEE ME, I TELL YOU!

I am not alone here in this dimly lit room. Other like minded individuals stand at their prisons opposite mine, writing obscenities in blood across their glass walls, toys of different eras skulking in the shadows behind them.

We're all tired of the nightmares, the memories of the night we were brought here.

The incantations, the circle of salt, the . . . the pentagram-

The seven of us—the magic number, lying naked, shivering, crying, waiting for the pain to end, hoping the hooded ones would be satiated soon . . .

I awake every night to the cry of other ghosts that share my dreams. Of how they had seen the merciful light rush along that blade's razor sharp edge, smiled when it came down and ended the suffering . . .

But it didn't end.

We call ourselves the Preston Hall Seven; we were eleven years of age when they used us.

They took our lives, our innocence . . .

Now we're taking it back.

Monsters exist, I know that now. But seven kids against the countless?

Maybe we don't stand a chance . . . But maybe . . .

I believe his hand print still stains the glass window of my cell, invisible to the living. He came with news and was gone . . . I didn't catch his name.

22

Reed felt his innards turn to iced water. He moved in his seat, peering out of the window; trying to survey his surroundings through wide, tear-blurred eyes, his nerves destroying themselves one by one. He wiped the tears away with the back of his hand-

Keep calm . . . Just have to keep calm, that's all!

The vehicle's wheels dipped occasionally in the potholes in the road, splashing through muddy grooves as the asphalt turned to a gravelly track. Now that they had broken from the motorway, tiny pebbles skittered across the windscreen as the road grew narrow and increasingly water-logged.

Why the fuck should I care about a few scratches to the bloody paint work? I could be dead in the next few—STOP IT!

Reed shook his head, eager to be free of Gladstone once and for all; wondering what life would be like without the bastard . . .

'Where the hell is he?' said Aaron.

'I don't know,' Reed whispered, stopping the lorry. He watched the road in the rear view mirror, its branch-like track broken from the black clean macadam of the motorway. He couldn't help feel as though they *had* driven off the edge of the Earth; expecting an iron gate to swing closed behind them.

"He won't be alone," Aaron said, remember-

In all the time he'd spent on the road, Reed enjoyed driving at night least of all, especially since the attack. And now he felt betrayed by night *and* day, for none could offer him refuge now. No quarter, no sanctuary and no mercy—the clichés kept coming to him-

STOP IT! Just ride it out, David! The nightmare will soon be over!

A cold breeze scattered litter across the gravel, empty crushed Coke cans tumbled noisily along as though caught by a magnet beneath the earth. Reed watched the crisp packets and torn newspapers scatter towards the warehouse entrance, which was little more than a jagged gash in where a roller door used to be.

Reed couldn't shake of the sinking feeling, unable to pinpoint exactly what he felt inside. He just knew that there was no turning back. A dark galleon of a cloud sailed across the sun, dousing the earth with darkness. He felt its chill as he opened the door and climbed down from the cab, his feet splashing in a small puddle. He jumped at the sound of the passenger door slowly opening. And the ghost joined his side.

'Where the hell is he?' Reed whispered, looking left and right. For some idiotic reason he even looked up! 'This is crazy-'

'Everything will be fine,' replied Aaron calmly.

'Don't pretend everything's alright,' Reed snapped. 'You have no idea what it's like to have the living shit kicked out of you-'

'Is that so?'

'Well done!' said Reed, patting his pockets. 'Now you've made me forget the-'

'Here,' said Aaron, placing the object in Reed's hand, his eyes shining in the early morning gloom.

For a moment time and everything in it seemed to stop-

This is the time, David! Now! Today it will end—no more pain, no more tears-

Tabby . . .

Paul . . .

No more pain-

Reed looked down at the pistol, realizing just how heavy the machine felt in the palm of his hand, and wondered just how much can be changed with one bullet.

23

Johnny Gladstone lit a cigarette, watching from the enveloping shadows of the dead machinery as Reed slowly approached the warehouse. He grinned. There were eyes and ears everywhere. Funny how loyalty can be bought for a few pounds, he thought, wondering just how far his minion's loyalty would stretch should he pile the notes into their hands, one on top of the other. Would they kill their own mothers, their own children—themselves? But for now they would strike, they just waited for his signal. He felt the cell phone in his pocket and thought of how easy it would be to end this problem-

Just press the button and it's all over, Johnny! But where's the fucking fun in that?

Gladstone smiled broadly, the sleeper ring glimmering in his right ear lobe, seeing the fear on Reed's face as he stepped over the threshold. He could almost smell it. But he sure had balls coming alone, thought Gladstone, dropping his cigarette in the dirt.

Boy, you have reason to be scared stiff right now, David . . . this is too easy!

The shark weaved through the graveyard of twisted engine parts and hills of dead Dodge 'ems, casually stepping over obstacles large and small; metal cables gleamed like oily snakes in the gloom, but they posed no threat as he stepped over them.

He knew the damned place like the back of his hands because he owned it. Old abandoned factory units such as this were hard to come by. It had proved useful over the twenty years in the money-lending game. But he knew from the start that he needed something else to

94

fall back on. Well, not all of his clients paid on time and he had a mouth to feed: his own. To the untrained eye the room resembled nothing more than junk. Metal hulks weren't left there to crumble to dust like cattle out to graze, much of the machinery was stored here until the so-called health and safety authorities lost their scent. Such as dangerous fair ground attractions that were fit only for the scrap yard. And farming machinery that had taken its fair share of careless limbs in its time; waiting for the proverbial dust to settle before seeing the light of day once more. It was a storage facility, but with a twist. It cost twice the price of any where else to use but it hid the kind of secrets that could either destroy a life, take away its owners freedom for a very long time or take the life of whoever wished to gamble using it. It was all the same to Gladstone, and none of it mattered. It didn't have a lock on the door, it didn't need one, after all, who would dare disturb one speck of dust around these machines let alone set a foot in the building without Johnny's permission?

He'd find his way through the darkness eventually . . . he had all the time in the world.

24

Reed felt like a suspect in an identity parade. Shafts of sunlight speared through slits in the vast roof, almost blinding him as he stood at the threshold of darkness. He couldn't see a thing in the black before him but that didn't make him invisible to whatever waited-

Come on . . . there's no time to be afraid now, David. You should've left that behind a long time ago!

'Ready?' said the ghost, his voice was barely a whisper, yet easily heard above the brisk wind and the beating of Reed's heart.

He nodded, then stepped over the terminating line; from blessed light to cursed darkness, the temperature plummeting somewhat as though he had stepped beneath a rushing waterfall.

'This is it, David-'

'Shhh!' Reed hissed tight-lipped. 'Don't say a word.'

'No one can hear me, except you,' Aaron replied, shaking his head. 'Christ, you really have forgotten . . .' He allowed his words to trail off, for he knew they fell on deaf ears.

Reed held his breath for a few seconds, his eyes watering at the heavy scent of oil and scorched paint. When he exhaled memories flooded back. Of his first job, a steelworks labourer, the deafening crunch and grind of overhead machinery, the potentially lethal pounding of approaching cranes, rumbling and shaking the foundations, brakes squealing across the rusty tracks.

Breathe it in, David. It's alive, the memory, you . . . even though everything around you is dead.

Reed hadn't felt this insignificant and small since his childhood; surrounded by so much metal, its limbs intertwined to the point that he failed to determine where one contraption ended and the other began; that such hulks of scrap could crush him in the blink of an eye, should the mountains of rotten steel tumble down, chilled him to the bone. He was in awe of the vastness of the room, could feel his head spin a little. He imagined this was how the toy chest of some spoilt deity would resemble; broken, dismantled playthings, forgotten and bereft of attention.

To think that I used to like the carnival as a kid!

He looked over at Aaron, and smiled.

'What the hell have *you* got to be smile about?' the ghost whispered, looking about curiously, his emerald eyes now shining cat-like in the darkness. 'Have you forgotten why we're here?'

'Why are you whispering?' replied Reed, mocking him. 'No body can hear you-'

'Go fuck yourself-'

Reed chuckled, scratching his right temple with the muzzle of the pistol. Maybe it was through fear or madness, he didn't know which.

'Did you ever watch that film: Willy Wonka and the chocolate factory?'

'I'm dead, remember,' snapped Aaron, looking about like an ant in God's palm. 'Besides I've been too busy to watch cartoons-'

'Well it wasn't a cartoon,' replied Reed, smiling a little. 'That would've completely fucked the effects up—anyway. This was a story about a weirdo who owned a factory full of orange dwarves with green hair, wearing white bib overalls. It was so bright and colourful that me and a couple of old friends once popped a few acid tabs whilst watching it.'

Aaron shook his head.

'That would explain it,' he said dryly. 'Your point is?'

'Just look at all the colours in this place,' replied Reed, smiling at the recollection as he looked about. The place spun with dust-covered colours of all kinds. Mechanisms from miniature trains and spitfire airplanes to torched 'Haunted House' facades; ghostly faces peered from between burnt black fingers as though they had hidden their faces from the flames of some bye-gone conflagration. He noticed the crushed body work of a vehicle that looked like it had worked an eternity in the fields, carving up the earth and sowing seeds. But now the engines of labour seemed incongruous amongst the arms and legs of funfair rides-

He almost screamed when he noticed the pile of mannequins a few feet to his left, the roving sunlight now caressing the broken limbs. Some were clothed, others as naked as the day they fell from the assembly line.

'When will it begin-'

'You know what?' said Reed, unable to contain the joy in his voice.'I think we missed them. I mean, maybe we're late? There aren't any cars outside so Gladstone's been here but grew tired of waiting-'

'Maybe you should think again, pal.'

25

Reed almost screamed at the sound of the voice, his heartbeat accelerating at an alarming rate now as Gladstone emerged from the shadows, stepping over what looked to be the broken jar of some cabaret freak; its plastic appendages had broken free from its formaldehyde-filled prison a long time ago and now lay prostrate in the dust.

'You made it,' said Gladstone, ignoring the sickening crackle of ruptured ligaments as he stood on one of the creature's three heads; a sound made all the more real in the silence now permeating the air like mustard gas.

Reed wanted to turn on his heel and get the hell out of there. And it would be so easy, too.

The bloke's on his own, David! Don't you see? You can turn around and-

No . . . it's not going to be that easy.

His finger twitched against the trigger. He just had to pull it and bury the bastard in broken machinery and rusting metal and run away as far away from this god forsaken place, no one would know, no one would know where to come looking-

Shut the hell up, David! For once just listen to reason: me! Listen to me-

On his left, Reed heard the unmistakable dry click of a weapon being cocked, the creaking of a car door being opened on his right.

What did you expect?

Reed turned-

Aaron had disappeared but his two footprints remained.

What did you expect? The spineless fucker!

'Nice wagon you've got out there,' said Gladstone, wading through the gloom to join Reed in the pool of sunlight. 'I assume that it's very secure, 'cause you're not actually carrying a briefcase full of dosh . . . So it must be in that lorry somewhere-'

'Johnny, I-' Reed's words caught in his throat like a fish bone.

The other man rubbed his forehead wearily with two heavily ringed hands as though the mother of all migraines was slipping between the folds of his skin like lovers between silk sheets.

'Well, you've certainly got balls, mate. Ever heard of the telephone?' continued the shark, cruising exquisitely slowly in the light, getting closer to his prey; fists clenched, hanging by his side like massive clock weights. 'Especially coming all this way to tell me you want me to kill you quickly 'cause you don't have *MY FUCKING MONEY-*'

Reed raised the pistol.

His hand shook as though he could barely lift the damned thing, but it had the desired effect. The muzzle focused just a couple of inches from the shark's studded nose and wide sparkling eyes. A bead of sweat formed on Gladstone's forehead, it broke the skin and gently trickled into the corner of his left eye. It twitched, but he never blinked, the hatred and anger burning there would not allow his enemy from his sight.

You feel that, David? You feel the eyes upon you-

Reed didn't need to listen to his conscience to know that he was heavily outnumbered. If they were there, he didn't care any more.

'Screw it,' he said, pulling back the trigger. 'They hit me, I hit you and we both hit the ground.'

'I like that, Dave,' chuckled Gladstone. 'Would you mind if I used that-'

'You're not going to get the chance to use it.'

The shark's smile faded.

Reed heard the sound of rifles clicking and crunching, hammers locking and rounds sliding—to his right he heard the crackle of gravel, as though glass shards were being ground beneath heavy feet—and to his left the snap of a magazine in the grip of a pistol.

But his eyes never left his target.

Now you're talking, David! You're really doing it!

'Did you really expect me to believe that if I returned your cash you would just let me turn around, get back in my fucking cab and go home? *Well, did you?*' Reed shouted, his voice resounding, ricocheting from one fallen metal titan to another, as though his words were white hot coals. He was defying the fear inside, denying its insistence, crippling its fingers and throwing its grip from his throat before it could truly take hold.

'A simple phone call would have done the business-'

'So you said, *Johnny*,' said Reed, turning the other man's name on his tongue like a sour sweet. 'But I needed you here . . . This is after all where we agreed-'

'You don't have a bloody clue what you're-'

'*Shut the hell up! For once in your sorry life—SHUT YOUR FUCKING MOUTH!*'

God is my pistol, the sheath separating flesh from flesh, the fabric against outer-space, the cage between man and beast-

'At least you can't touch Tabby and Paul down here-'

'And you believe there's nobody touching them both right this minute?' Gladstone sneered, the sleeper shining in his earlobe. 'She's already paid off two of your repayments in the sack!'

'Liar!' Reed hissed, gripping the pistol tightly, knuckles white, flesh to the point of bursting, his teeth grinding; lip quivering.

'And Jesus Christ, she doesn't stop sucking 'til she draws blood-'

'Fucking liar!'

The finger twitched on the trigger now . . .

The shark grinned as he watched the tear trickle down Reed's cheek.

'I don't lie when it involves my money,' said Gladstone, laughing.

'Die,' said Reed, squeezing the trigger.

The hammer fell.

26

Click!
Click!
Click!

'"Did you really expect me to believe that if I returned your cash you would just let me turn around . . ."' said Johnny, mocking Reed in a high-pitched voice. 'Blah de blah. Of course I did. What did you think? I mean, look at this! You can't even get this one right!' he shouted, grabbing the pistol from Reed's hand. 'It's not even bloody loaded.'

All colour seemed to drain from Reed's face, his blood chilling in his veins with the realization that his time was really up-

This is really it, David . . . You're whole buggered up life has been worming its pathetic way through the flesh and now it had rushed headlong into the stone! But what would you have done if the gun had been loaded?

He stepped away from the shark, holding up his shaking hands to protect his face from the barrage of blows that were destined to come. He knew there was nowhere to hide but that would not stop him from at least going down without a fight.

Reed took another step back, trying to clench his fists, to maintain some excuse of a guard, a tired boxer's stance.

And Gladstone followed, laughing now as he reached a hand into his jacket pocket.

'Where the hell are you, you bastard?' Reed shouted, looking about frantically in the dark around him, scouring the heaps of metal

for the ghost's face, his shining eyes. 'Where are you, Aaron?' But his voice echoed a thousand times, joining forces with the shark's derisive laughter.

Reed fell to the floor, curling up into a ball. For there was no better, warmer and cozier way to die, he thought, settling in the dust like a dying fetus.

So now you're just going to leave the world like the day you entered it? I see, that's clever, David. Now you can be the real you . . . some blubbering, terrified insignificant nothing, blinded by fear-

Reed felt the cold steel press against his forehead, fiery patterns danced in the darkness behind his tightly closed eyes-

He held his breath, the sound of the hammer pulling back-

And he waited . . .

And waited.

Reed, still afraid to open his eyes, to look upon his executioner, felt a rumbling vibration course through the earth beneath him. Something was burrowing it seemed through the ground. He slowly opened his eyes.

Gladstone stood still, the gun still pointing at Reed's head, but his eyes were wide with-

Is that terror, David? And . . . Christ, the man's wet himself!

Reed wanted to laugh, but he didn't have the strength, and as the pistol was still at his head he didn't wish to make any sudden movements either.

Gladstone searched the gloomy interior of the torn ceiling, for what, he didn't know. Countless bars of bright sun light pierced the layer of tin as though riddled with shells from a WWII spitfire, something neither of them had noticed until the sun had reached its zenith. Now the air hummed as though a supercharger was operating somewhere, shaking the metal armour of this warehouse and all that was rotting within it. It ran through the twisted machinery like blood squeezing through a collapsed vein, pumping straight to their rusty hearts.

'Kev! Stewy!' Gladstone hollered, but his voice lacked the edge it cut with earlier.

The air seemed to shake, dust falling from the ceiling like snow flakes.

'Chris? Tony? Where the hell are you lot!'

The shark spun round on his heel, almost losing balance, as the blindingly bright head lights of a dead machine burst into life. And only when it slowly growled and twisted, pulling itself from the ground like a rotten tooth from a swollen gum, stumbling towards him in the shadows and shards of broken sunbeams, did he realize what it was.

27

Reed wasted no time.

Galvanized into action as the rollercoaster came thundering towards them, he soon discovered muscles he never knew he possessed. The hulk followed no track, neither did it move on wheels—in fact the bugger *had* no wheels! Its dark undercarriage was being . . . *dragged* along by some force-

Don't think this isn't happening, David! Move your arse. NOW!

Sparks erupted beneath its crumpled body work. Smoke permeated the air with the stench of melting plastic and rusted steel, flames licking the underbelly of the dented coaster as it pushed onwards; scraping through the earth and stones.

Reed dived out of its path as it hurtled towards Gladstone, crashing into a couple of rickety chairs. They shattered beneath him as though they were made from balsa wood.

'What's going on?' Gladstone shouted. 'Tony, Stewy—where the hell are you, you sackless bastards!'

Reed quickly untangled himself from the chair legs, wincing at the pain screaming down his right leg. There was a little bit of blood on his jeans and a tear in the fabric exposed a superficial cut-

What's wrong with you! MOVE!

He felt the hot sun on the back of his neck. There was a way out right behind him! Reed scrambled for the blessed light while he still had legs to get him there; his heart beat a tattoo on his ribcage. He found the gaping hole in the corrugated steel wall and jumped through, falling into a puddle of mud-

Who cares, David? You made it . . . You made it.

Out here he was safe. He lay on his back in the cold water, his skin crawling with goose bumps as he stared skyward, smiling broadly. He wanted to laugh but his lungs felt like they were on fire-

Just calm down.

The sky was blue . . .

The grass was green . . .

The brightest sun he'd ever seen . . .

Reed chuckled, running his hands through his hair, feeling tiny pieces of grit and glass as the filthy water washed over them.

That was close . . .

He crawled from the mud and broken glass, feeling pain hit him from every angle he could imagine. He could feel the dirt beneath his finger nails as he clawed in the dirt, trying to steady himself. His stomach churned, the bile in his throat spinning his mind. But eventually he turned, infinitely slowly, towards the gash in the side of the ware house.

He would survive.

Out here he was safe.

But beyond the tear in the wall the carnival had just begun.

I didn't mean to set the Christmas tree alight last year. I was angry, and when that happens I try to get as far away from the house as possible, so that hopefully the feel of the fresh air rushing through me will take away the edge of this madness. Sometimes rushing headlong with my eyes closed helps me relax. Unfortunately, this time I couldn't hold it. It was late, I was scared, and the shakes pulled me from the shadows behind Sarah Jane's headboard . . .

I had to get out of there . . .

So many obstacles blocking my way: the toys beside the door, the wardrobe in the hall. I think I accidentally pushed it aside on my way, but it's not important; it hadn't been the first piece of furniture to be replaced.

The tree . . . just . . . burst into flames!

I reached the front door, passed my hand through the small pane of glass . . . so near . . . se close . . . But then I looked over my shoulder, watching the smoke drift slowly up the staircase like a thief . . .

I managed to fight my fear and rush back to the sleeping, overturned their beds; heard the confusion in their weary voices . . .

They survived.

They were not to blame for my anger; they were not the ones responsible for my demise. I couldn't take the innocent. That is not who I am.

Besides, I hadn't finished with Sarah yet. There was still so much fun left to be had. We had developed such a bond, Sarah and I. I even had my own place at the dining table, complete with crockery and cutlery. The little one found it necessary to spoon feed me, and in front of her mum and dad to boot. It used to make me smile but I'm not five years old any more; now I want out of this endless maze . . .

I'm a boy, or at least I was before I drowned in the small pond in the back yard. That was eleven years ago. I should be leaving school now–

I close my eyes and clench my fists, trying to hold on, to keep control. I can't count very far at all before the numbers get all jumbled up. So when they start to sound strange and repetitive I return to one and keep going over and over and over until my heartbeat slows . . .

On the night of the fire, I had awoken from a nightmare. But how can I call it a bad dream when in fact it was a recollection, a black memory? I was dead so why did I carry this emotional baggage? I'd often wonder. But those questions meant nothing when all I could see were moving objects along the ceiling. A bright orb shifted, developed a thousand fractures, disappeared then reformed brighter than ever. The endless draughts of ice cold water entering my lungs weighed me down, made my thrashing limbs slow. Stones scratched my bare knees, my toe nails coming away as they tried to gain purchase with the floor, but . . .

Every time I see the bright, flickering orb it sends shivers running through me. I know it was the sun dancing on the surface of the dark pond water. And I know there were other shapes there too . . .

It was the other shapes that angered me: poisonous smiles swirling across the faces that looked down through the opaque water.

They weren't watching me when they should've. Mum and dad trusted them. But they were cruel and sometimes hurt me. They kept me quiet with sweets and toys, made me feel special. And they made me promise not to tell . . .

But I couldn't take it any more.

They chased me down from my room, pulling on their clothing, almost tripping down the staircase. I was screaming and wiping the tears from my eyes as I headed for the back garden. Luckily the kitchen door was unlocked.

Outside the rain had just begun, it trickled down the window panes and pocked the surface of the pond. I could hear their voices behind me, gaining on me. I cried but it was useless-

I tripped!

Into the water I fell, the tiny goldfish brushing their frightened fins across my face, scratching my eyes as I looked up . . . A sharp pain lanced through my back. It seemed to push right through my spine, forcing me to the bottom of the pond. Scrabbling for the object, my vision fading, pulse thundering in my ears, I realized it was a broom shank . . .

They were keeping me beneath the water . . .

I knew that pain was real. When mum told me not to touch the clothes iron . . . I touched; and it burned. When they kept the bottles beneath the sink tightly capped and told me to keep away from them I opened one and held the top to my lips, but the smell made my eyes water and I couldn't drink.

I knew pain.

My aunt and uncle held mum and dad as they took me away. I didn't like the blanket over my face but I think ambulance men always do that. I wanted to throw off the wet cover and tell mum and dad about the ones standing beside them, their poisonous arms about them, holding and comforting them. But I couldn't move . . . It was too soon.

Aunt Beverly and Uncle Peter are still together. I don't think they're in love; just afraid the other one will break and confess to what they had done to me. It's the fear that keeps them together. I want to keep them feeling this way for a little while longer. I want them to suffer just like I did.

Now mum and dad have moved on, leaving me behind. I heard mum say she couldn't bear to be within a hundred miles of the house and its pond. It had been almost a year after all since I died . . . Dad couldn't have agreed more. He wanted out too. I wanted to go with them, but when Sarah Jane and her mum and dad took a tour of the house, the little girl saw me . . . I knew it.

That's what makes us hold on. She believed I was real . . . and so I was trapped.

I grew to love my new family . . .

There are rumours. I know I shouldn't listen . . . But I think they're true. I can feel the tiny remains of my soul deep inside, yearning to be free, to come back . . .

I do love my new family, truly I do, but I either break free now or forever regret not doing so . . .

I know where Beverly and Peter live. They sometimes drive by the house, sometimes slowly, craning their necks through the windows to see if any police cars were parked out front. It was on one such occasion that I tagged along. Got right to their house too . . .

It was easy . . .

They should keep their garden tools locked away, the sharp ones at least.

I watch the figures shift behind the bedroom curtain as I peer up through the darkness of their back yard. There was a lot of grass, almost enough room for a small football goal post and a swing; a garden I would have loved. Such a thought made me all the angrier, my hands now squeezing the handles of the shears.

I made my way to the back door and put my fist through the small pane of glass.

My name is Robert Dickinson and I was five years old when they took my life.

Now I'm taking it back.
Christine says I'm a very brave boy . . .

Let's see just how brave I am.

28

'You call yourselves minders—fuck!' Gladstone hollered, stumbling back a couple of feet as the freak he had crushed only moments earlier, stirred once more. A claw-like hand reached for his ankle, nipping the fabric of his trouser leg. 'Get the hell away from me!' he shouted, stamping on the appendage.

But it kept moving, getting closer, its nails clawing through the earth, pulling the rest of its carcass along through the dust.

Gladstone stamped on it once more but soon gave up as the creature-

It's just a bloody toy, man! It's not real!

Then he froze.

The roller coaster had ground to a halt at the opposite side of the warehouse, colliding with the thick corrugated wall, becoming one with the steel. Above the machine smoke plumed like an ungodly halo, and the air was heavy with the scent of burnished metal and rusted iron.

As Gladstone looked down at the cabaret freak he almost screamed, for the creature was looking at him, its arms crushed and broken, three heads, six eyes, staring straight at him! He drew his pistol from the holster beneath his arm.

CRACK!
CRACK!
CRACK!

Gladstone fired at the creature's faces, wishing the bastard was real. And as the dust settled and the alien finally stilled, he noticed the wires and pieces of metal peeping through the bullets gaping entry wounds.

What did I tell you, man? It's just a toy . . . it can't hurt you!

SCREEEEEEETCH!

Gladstone shook, the gun falling from his hands.

SCREEEEEEETCH!

'Jesus Christ . . .' he whispered; his eyes wide with terror.

The roller coaster.

It was moving again . . . backing up away from the wall, its engine screaming in agony with the effort it seemed. The sparks and flames had died but whatever galvanized the machine into action was far from ready to give up.

Gladstone wasted no time in disappearing into the darkness of the warehouse. He knew the place like the back of his hand. He had lost count of the bodies he had buried here in the dust. Unfortunates who couldn't pay back their dues were everywhere. One just needed to know where to look. Some were encased in concrete, others under car bonnets. But most of them were just bones, rotting in the earth. Just how much damage three pitbulls, starved for over a week, were capable of, was beyond him-

Gladstone fell down, snagging his shoulder on a piece of blunt steel. Although it didn't pierce the skin it still sent shockwaves of pain through his arm like a heart attack-

No, Johnny-

He felt the warmth spread about his crotch, the dark stain appearing like spilled ink.

Don't piss yourself-

But he couldn't help it.

Stewy's torn body sat opposite him in the gloom.

The minder's bloody face and upturned eyes sat motionless, head twisted at an angle way beyond extreme to be natural.

Gladstone stifled the scream that welled up inside. But his whole body shook as though the temperature had plummeted a hundred degrees or more as he surveyed his friend's bludgeoned face. There were tiny bone fragments jutting from his torn throat-

No—get out—you can't do this any longer—get up!

Gladstone got up unsteadily, pain screaming through his arm, and made his way through the junk. But despite the pain he quickened his pace, feeling his heart batter against his ribs. He trampled over the bonnets of old cars and dodge 'ems-

Their headlights suddenly bursting into life at his very touch-

'WHAT THE FUCK IS GOING ON?'

Old doors, rusted shut, squealed open as he ran by-

Then another-

And another-

But Gladstone moved out of their way, being careful not to catch his clothing on a door handle or wing mirror-

That's right, Johnny! Keep moving . . . you stop, and it's got you!

He could just see the Volvo parked up ahead-

Chris's lolling head on the steering wheel, dark fluid pouring from a gaping wound!

'NO!' Gladstone screamed, but there was nothing he could do but keep moving and save his self.

Fuck 'em all!

And as for David Reed . . . Well, he would have to wait-

Johnny's mind went blank as his body flew eight feet high and twenty feet through the air, his face grinding into the hard dirt and grit as he skidded across the ground. Then he lay still, feeling as though every single bone in his body had been pulverized. Time passed slowly as he lay in a heap of dust and stones.

What the hell . . . just happened?

He opened his eyes, but his right eyelid flickered as though something sharp had pierced the damned thing. He rubbed at it with frustration-

'God, NO!' he hollered, pulling his finger tips away from where his right eye should have been. He tasted blood on his lips but fought the urge to investigate-

Suddenly something wrapped about his wrists, pulling him forwards. They were thick cables of some sort, creeping out from beneath the earth like tree roots. Before Gladstone could draw another breath he felt the crushing grip about his ankles; the slipknots squeezing the blood in his veins into submission. He tried to muster the strength to move, but it was futile-

'What?' he gasped. 'What . . . the fuck . . . are you?'

A sparkling circle of light floated before him, no more than a foot from his bleeding face. And as the seconds passed like an eternity, he noticed-

It can't be!

But his one remaining eye was not lying to him, nor was madness playing tricks on him either.

It's a face, Johnny! See how the mouth is cracking a smile—laughing at you! Yes, those are eyes you can see . . . But who-

Gladstone felt the stranger's hot and fetid breath on his face, turning his stomach. But he didn't have the strength to throw up.

My God, Johnny, look at its eyes! Have you ever seen eyes so green?

The face drew closer . . .

Closer . . .

Smiling.

'Goodbye, my lucky ticket,' whispered Aaron. 'You have no idea how valuable your death is to me.'

Gladstone wanted to break free of the ropes.

Come on, Johnny, you can do this! Come on, break out!

Something moved.

Gladstone froze, staring at the shadows. For a moment he completely forgot about the cables holding him to the ground; even the numbness in his feet and hands from the lack of blood circulation escaped him as he tried to push away the shadows. But his one remaining eye was quickly blurring-

Johnny, if you stay here you-

'SHUT UP!' Gladstone hissed, tasting blood on his lips. 'Just shut the fuck up!'

He could see the sparkling white paint of their eyes shining in the darkness about a hundred feet away. They blinked—THEY FUCKING BLINKED! He shook his head; wanting to laugh aloud at the insanity of it all but Gladstone was transfixed by . . .

The carousel horses!

They twisted and stirred from their slumber like reluctant slaves facing a new but repetitive day. Out of the silence they came, steam pluming from their nostrils; shaking their tussled manes. Wooden eyes rolled in dead orbits, hooves cracked and twisted, feeling the earth beneath their weathered-

They froze, eyes fixed upon him, baring their teeth.

Gladstone's flesh crept, his bladder giving way. He felt the hot liquid spread down his legs as the horses turned their heads from side to side as though studying him, analyzing him.

There are four of them, Johnny!

'You again?'

Four horses, Johnny! But look closely-

He did, shaking his head.

'So what? I don't get it' He whispered, twisting his neck, hearing the ligaments crackle loudly, like broken twigs.

Think about it . . . they're turning away from us-

The voice was right: the beasts were turning about, like some weird ceremony, something they had practiced many times before.

Don't you get it yet?

Within seconds the four horses charged towards the four corners of the warehouse, weaving between broken machinery, anything that got in their way.

You know why they're not heading for us, don't you!

'SHUT THE HELL UP!' Gladstone hollered, feeling the cables tighten.

The horses disappeared in the shadows, their once beautiful, bright colours blurring in a wave of motion and dust. They cried but it permeated the air like a crackling cry. It was the last sound to Gladstone's ears as they quartered him.

29

Reed witnessed the horror then backed away from the vision. Into the blindingly bright sunlight he turned on his heel and searched the horizon; looking at the green fields and factories for what, he didn't know. He just didn't want to see. He'd seen enough. He squeezed his eyes closed and tried to force the image from the canvas of his mind but it was etched there, indelibly so.

'God, no . . . I don't want to see.'

The blood was spreading from the four stumps-

'Please, no-'

But it was no use. It was there. And he knew it would be quite sometime before he'd forget, that's assuming that he ever would.

He fell to his knees; hands covering his ears, drowning out the recorded scream which repeated itself over and over-

'NO!'

'Wake up, David.'

Reed backed away from the voice, blinking myopically. He shook from the revulsion of the madness he'd just witnessed, and looked up at a sun that played between the two factories opposite; darting behind a cluster of trees to his right. And he watched; his back saturated with dirt, sweat and muddy water.

'Wake up!'

Before he could draw another breath, two cold, bony hands enveloped his, pulling him away from the crack in the side of the building. Somewhere Reed heard the clinking of thin metal, his nostrils flaring to capture the unmistakable aroma of cigarettes. He raised a dirty hand to shield his eyes from the blinding sun; watching the smoke circle Aaron's face, like an aura, yet more deadly.

116

'What do you mean, wake up?' said Reed, groggily.

'Why? From your nightmare,' replied the ghost, grinning. 'It's over. You can wake up now.'

'So that's it?' said Reed, slowly walking a few steps away from the ghost, a little unsteadily on his feet. His heart hammered in his chest, spots thumping before his eyes. 'I can't-'

'It's over! Don't you understand a word I'm telling you?' snapped Aaron. 'You don't have to worry any more. That pile of shit is dead and so are his cronies!'

Reed shook his head. His eyes were wide with fear and adrenaline-

Calm the hell down! Listen to him. It's over!

'We can't just walk away and leave a corpse—no, more than just one, for crying out loud! Not out here in the open-'

'You call this out in the open?' said Aaron, with arms wide open, motioning towards the derelict buildings about them. 'Who the hell is going to find his bloody parts-'

'Don't-'

'The one bane of your life is gone and now you're worried about this? Jesus Christ! Are you *ever* going to be free?' Aaron said, shaking his head. He spat at a puddle at his feet, and as he looked Reed in the eye once more, he noticed the spots of blood on his forehead.

Good . . . I don't know where the blood came from, I don't particularly care; I'm glad you've shed some of it! Now you know pain!

Reed looked at the tear in the side of the building.

'Nobody will miss your friend,' said Aaron, softly. 'Nobody will come looking . . . You don't believe he's gone, do you?' The ghost smiled crookedly, suddenly grabbing Reed's elbow.

'Get your bloody hands off of me!' Reed shouted, but the ghost was too strong for him to resist. In three strides they had crossed the threshold of what had become a charnel house.

'It's the only way you'll forget it all and move on!'

Reed shivered at the ghost's icy touch, feeling goose bumps spread across the skin where Aaron clawed him-

'Get off me!' Finally he pulled free, but he held eye contact with the ghost for an eternity it seemed before turning to face the carnage.

30

Reed shook so badly that Aaron had to light the cigarette for him.

They sat listening to the engine purr, waiting for the heaters to cook up the cab. Reed thumped the generator with his fist to speed the damned thing up. He reached down the side of his chair and produced a cloth to wipe the condensation from the windscreen, letting the hot sun light brighten the interior. It felt good against his dirty skin-

'Convinced?'

Reed nodded, drawing deeply on his cigarette, catching Aaron's eye for a second before putting the lorry in gear. 'As long as that stuff can't be moved-'

'Bloody hell!' snapped Aaron. 'You've just watched me bury those bastards in thousands of tons of carnival rides—without your help, I hasten to add! They're well hidden. Besides, if you're worried about the police then don't be. You saw me crush Gladstone's vehicles and scatter them to the four fucking winds in that warehouse . . . and I made sure that him and the others were in them when I did-'

'What if the police can trace me-'

'There's not a damned thing in there bearing your fingerprints, okay?'

Reed breathed slowly, trying to compose himself. Finally he nodded

'Okay, Aaron . . .'

The ghost placed a hand upon Reed's shoulder, only for a second.

'I know you're not convinced but it's true,' he said quietly. 'It's over. It'll take a while to wean off the negative when that's all you've ever had running through your veins, but it will.'

Is it really over, David? You should be elated. But you're not because you know deep down that-

Reed shook away the thought and concentrated on the road. But no matter how hard he tried his thoughts returned to the scene of . . .

Murder? Go on, David. Think it . . . say it aloud!

*

A dark cloud had passed over the warehouse when they had slowly returned to the body, the bright holes in the ceiling winking out of existence one by one like dying stars. But Gladstone stared upwards, seeing something Reed hoped he would not for some time to come. He could keep the secret of the dead to himself! The golden sleeper in his ear lobe shone despite the gloom. For a second he even followed the shark's gaze; then shook his head irritably.

'I've seen enough. Let's go,' Reed snapped, waving his hands as if in submission, about to head for the exit.

'Not yet, sun beam,' said Aaron, gripping tighter on his elbow, pulling Reed closer to the dead meat. 'Take a long good look-'

The ghost grabbed Reed by the throat and pulled him down to within an inch of Gladstone's bloody face. He tried to pull away but it was futile. He could almost taste the coppery blood and smell the stench of piss and shit that pooled about the shark's ravaged carcass. The bile rose in his throat but he was not going to let Aaron see him vomit.

'Tell me what you see,' Aaron insisted. 'TELL ME WHAT YOU SEE!'

'I see trouble.'

*

119

'So now we can leave all this behind,' said Aaron, nodding as a point of fact. The dark clouds had parted some time ago now and warm, bright sunshine passed over the cabs interior, ushering away the deep shadows carved almost in the ghost's face. 'Ring your wife. Tell her you love her and that everything's going to be just fine . . . hey,' he added, smiling crookedly. 'Lighten up.'

Reed couldn't return his smile, he simply kept track of his heartbeat; how it had started to skip, speed up, slow down for a second before thumping hard against his ribs once more. Tiny pin pricks of light spun like Catherine wheels before his eyes and he took a deep breath, hoping that self control would clear his vision and regulate his pulse. To his amazement it did. Now he just needed a little fresh air.

'Hey, what are you doing?' said Aaron.

'I thought you said the dead moved with the times?' Reed said dryly, pulling into a lay-by. He grabbed his mobile phone and opened the door. A rush of cold air invaded the warmth in the cab. 'Didn't you know it was against the law to drive whilst taking a call?'

'Just don't be too long-' Aaron replied, but Reed had already slammed the door behind him. 'We have work to do . . .'

31

Reed could hardly wait to tell Tabby just how much he loved her, could almost hear Paul's jabberwocky already, he thought, smiling broadly. His hands shook as he tried to scroll through the mobile's address book. He couldn't wait to tell her how Johnny and his crew were off their backs for good—how that was exactly he hadn't thought through just yet; he'd have to come up with some excuse, but it wasn't fucking important right now. They were free of him, and that's all that counts!

'Oh, David?'

Reed spun round, grinning.

Aaron had his head out of the passenger window, a cigarette dangling from the corner of his mouth.

'What?'

'Don't forget to tell her that you might be a couple days late getting home,' the ghost shouted over the sound of passing traffic.

Reed's smile faded.

'What the hell for?' he replied, his heart sinking, already knowing the answer to the question. He closed his eyes, his thumb poised above the CALL button. And for a second the ice flowing through his veins prohibited him from pushing down on the damned thing. 'Where are we going?'

Don't ask stupid questions, David! You know where!

'Come on, sun beam,' said Aaron, shaking his head; a bright but jagged smile across his burned mouth. 'Where do you think? Why, good old Silverfield Avenue, that's where.'

It seemed like an hour before he finally made the call. And no matter how he tried to remain calm, no matter how many times he told himself that all would be well and their troubles were finally over, he couldn't help feel as though it was all very far from over . . .

He wondered, listening to Tabby's voice, if he would ever hear it again.

PART B

I'm debating whether to actually grab the knife from his hand and inflict the wounds myself, or simply grit my teeth and bear it . . .

I just want it over with. A storm rages outside but it compares not to the one which burns within . . .

I yearn for the warmth of the fireside and family banter. How I love listening to their idle chit chat about their day. That's what I think about at times such as these. I grow tired each day . . .

Everyone has strange thoughts while inflicting cruelty and pain. It was the only way to escape . . .

Say what they like . . .

Let them tell their lies . . .

But they can't deny it.

I heard that one such like-minded individual often thought of food, large grapefruit and legs of chicken whilst stamping on heads and limbs . . .

But I like to feel the memory of the warm fire against my face, holding it close like a love letter-

'For heaven's sake, do it, man!' I howl, but he is frozen.

So I take the blade, narrowly severing a finger in my haste to have the deed over with, and plunge the rusted piece of metal hilt-deep in the man's thigh. Only the few will truly appreciate just how good that feels; watching the pain pouring from another's eyes, hearing the pleas, the calls for mercy.

Murder's a little like bleeding a radiator. It let's off a little steam!

Now they know how I felt that day in Rossmere Park, twenty seven years earlier . . .

Three onto one was no match, no matter how big I was compared to them. They weren't content with torturing me at school—oh no; they had to bring it to the park on a warm sunny Sunday afternoon. They couldn't wait for a damned school day. All I wanted was a few hours alone, just me and my fishing rod, the small tape recorder beside me set low, a few chewed up Iron Maiden tapes, a can of lager I swiped from the fridge in dad's garage and a few rolled cigarettes, (also stolen from my dad's stash). He would string me up if he found out but wasn't that a little contradictory considering he was my age when he tried this stuff out too? People take ghosts for granted but I tell you, we know our shit!

Fuck it!

I struck the match and went dizzy in a couple seconds . . .

That's when I felt the first fist strike my neck, missing its target. But the shock pushed me out of my small seat beside the glistening pond; a ringing in my ears. Then the kick to the stomach . . . now that fucking hurt! My dad always said I should make a stand and face my enemies, look them straight in the eye and give just as good, if not better, than what I got. But I suppose dad wasn't habiting the same plain that day he decided to share that tiny pearl of wisdom.

The language, as they say, turned the air blue. I caught glimpses of passersby, the shock on their faces . . . but they simply carried on with their own business as though I didn't even exist. There's a strange sounding French term for the typical English attitude, especially in such situations . . .

But it's not important-

Ending it all means all . . .

The blood flows over your hands, your face; despite how careful you are it doesn't make the slightest bit of difference. Gore gets everywhere!

Once again I am left to finish the job before retiring for the night behind the old clown doll in the wardrobe. It's warm in there, but awfully lonely.

I kind of haunted my school the following days of death . . . still unable to let go. The air seemed to smell sweeter as though traffic fumes had never been invented; unpolluted and refreshing. Craft moved through the clouds above me but I knew—I just knew that I was capable of gliding through the ether too . . .

I now believe in myself . . .

My name is Leonard Coast. I was thirteen when they took my life.

Now I'm taking it back.
But first, I'm told, there's a certain lady who needs me . . .

32

That place.

Silverfield Avenue.

Those very words felt like fists driven over and over into Reed's stomach. He had forgotten about Johnny Gladstone and the others that once kept him awake at night like an incessantly wailing infant, constantly having him peer over his shoulder, wondering if that very moment was his last. They had killed somebody. It didn't matter what kind of person Gladstone had been. Good or bad—he was a human being-

But didn't you have that in mind all along, David? Wasn't that the whole purpose behind bringing the gun along? You're a murderer-

I wasn't the one who killed him, so shut the hell up!

But you were in on it-

I DIDN'T KILL ANYBODY!

Reed waited for a rebuke, but silence replied; blessed silence.

Johnny's dead.

Reed, Tabby and Paul were alive.

And that's all that mattered-

Yeah, but for how long-

'So everything's going to be okay from now on, right?' asked Reed. 'Tabby and Paul are going to be just fine?'

Aaron nodded, sighing heavily, his eyes never leaving the road.

'How are they?' he said. 'Good I hope.'

Just stay focused, David . . . Why the hell should he care anyway?

Reed chewed his lip before reaching beneath his seat. He grabbed the road atlas and tossed it over to Aaron.

'I know I'm going to regret this but, show me where the hell it is,' he said. 'I've forgotten.'

'Easy,' replied Aaron. 'We go back the way we came; all the way back to where you set off you bloody liar. You know exactly where it is!'

'Hartlepool-'

'Middlesbrough, David. Don't tell me you've forgotten because I don't believe you,' Aaron replied quietly, a faint smile creasing his lips.

Reed sat in silence, watching the road disappear behind them in the rearview mirror, his heartbeat punching heavily now despite his newfound freedom. No matter how much he tried to gather his senses he felt scattered. He wondered if this was how a lottery winner felt, the ticket in their hand, the winning numbers staring back at them, yet holding back just in case it was made of glass; not wishing to get too close or hold it too tightly should the whole thing shatter.

'I remember,' Reed said finally, brushing his fingertips across his cheek, rasping through the four days growth. 'I just want to go home and start afresh-'

'And you will,' Aaron replied curtly. 'When it's over-'

'I just want to go home,' said Reed, his hands slippery on the steering wheel. He looked down at them and noticed how much they shook now. A bead of perspiration raced down his back, followed by another beneath his arm pit, and another . . .

'I know,' the ghost replied, looking down at his scarred hands, their nails torn and hard. 'But I need your help, David. I helped you-'

'I understand that . . . You scratch my back, I scratch yours—how could I forget?' Reed felt that all too familiar sinking feeling. He knew how borrowing money felt. At the time it was great, liberating. Especially when the bills were getting up to date and there was a little left over for a little sun and sand abroad. Tabby hated the pile of cash he would bring home, but he couldn't help notice that tiny glimmer of excitement in her eye-

So Tabby was to blame now, eh? You got into debt because she got off on it! That's the best excuse I've ever heard-

It was giving it back that hurt the most. And that's how he felt at this moment.

'That's the way it's always been,' Aaron said softly, almost apologetically, as though he didn't make the rules. 'That's the way . . . You know that. There is no way out and no way back . . .' He allowed his words to trail away. He looked Reed in the eye.

He really needs your help . . . He's desperate . . .

'It's going to take quite some time to get there, you know?' Reed piped up, trying to deter the wraith from embarking on whatever crazy adventure he wished. 'A couple of days, at least-'

'Bullshit! We're not that bloody far away from the borough, Davie-boy. So don't give me that crap . . . Besides, I can wait,' said Aaron coldly. 'That's the way.'

You can change your mind, I know you can . . . but you fucking won't . . . Try this on for size then-

'Well, by law I can only drive for ten hours at a time anyway—look,' Reed said, brushing old newspapers and empty burger cartons from the dash board, taking great pleasure in revealing a small window with a disc. 'See how many hours it's recorded already?'

'Oh, that?' Aaron replied, suddenly driving a fist in to the machine, ripping out the paper disc. Then he lowered the window and threw them to the wind, letting them argue over its scraps like vultures over carrion.

'Don't worry, David. You weren't exactly playing by the book any way,' the ghost glanced in the rearview mirror, watching the pieces of paper flutter away on the shoulder of the wind like doves feathers.

'What?'

'Well, when you set off on that little route of yours, you know, the one on the map, the alternative route . . . You gave up your job and you knew it,' the ghost chuckled.

Reed followed suit. 'You're right, you bastard. This was just another fuck-up-and-kiss-your-job-goodbye escapade. I guess I'll be signing on a couple of days from now.'

'I know.'

'That's right . . . You always bloody know, don't you? And you're always right.'

'Haven't I always been? Say, look, this journey may take a couple days, but I need to know you're with me-'

'Aaron,' said Reed, shaking his head. 'What-'

'Whatever I have up my sleeve, you want no part of?'

Reed nodded.

'You will help me because-'

'You keep saying that, Aaron!' Reed slammed a fist down on the steering wheel. 'Just what do you want from me—Give me one of those fucking ciggies, will you?' He nodded towards the pack of cigarettes on the dash board.

Aaron lit one and passed it to Reed.

'I can't tell you,' said the ghost, lighting a cigarette for his self. 'I can't tell you because you won't help me. I know you—I've always known you-'

'That bad, eh?' said Reed, shaking his head. 'But then . . . when did any of your favours smell of roses, eh?'

'Hey, I've cleared away a few of your messes, I know that,' the ghost chuckled.

Reed nodded. He had to agree, the bugger had gotten rid of a few pebbles in his shoes over the years. One in particular went by the name of Tommy Ritter.

If Johnny Gladstone was a tough nut to crack, Jesus, Tommy was the hardest to leave a scratch upon. Not a day went by when the menace wouldn't torture him-

Until Aaron, the friendly ghost-boy, whispered in his ear . . .

Reed didn't like violence, but this was a favour he didn't mind repaying. Didn't mind at all.

How many times did he need to taste his own blood?

How many times did his mum and dad have to replace his spectacles because he wasn't big enough to stop the bullying?

Then he got a taste for blood. Hell, sometimes he deliberately forgot his dinner money—the one thing that kept Ritter sweet.

"Let me help," the voice whispered. It seemed to flow from the walls—no that's not right—it was actually in his head—Hell, he didn't know where it came from, yet it managed to weave through the giggles and shouts of the small throng of kids encircling him. They pointed at his face, the broken glasses and punctured lips.

Those three words he dreaded the most would repeat themselves over and over in his head-

"Let me help."

"Let me help."

"Let me help."

And Reed had ignored those demands . . . until that one day he couldn't stand the taste of blood. That one moment when he knew that enough was enough!

He could see the face, the boy's face, the one he pressed against his window at night. And Reed wanted the pain and the nightmare to end. If this was the only way then so be it!

He had looked up from the pavement, seeing the tiny puddle of blood where his face had hit the road, counting two teeth. Then he stood up, pushed his broken spectacles up the bridge of his bloody nose and smiled-

"What are you smiling at?' sneered Tommy, shaking his head. 'All I wanted you to do was nick a pad of paper from Sir's desk—that's all!'

'What are you going to do with it?' Reed had replied, shakily. 'Roll it up for roaches?'

The fists rained down upon him and he knew that no matter what he did the same punishment would be dealt with day after day after day after day-

It was the second that Tommy spat at Reed's face that things changed.

He wasn't going to take it any more.

Just say it, David . . . Say my name . . . Just two simple words and the nightmare stops. But you know-

'I know the price—AARON BROOKES, wake up!'

'My pleasure,' the ghost had replied, before breaking every bone in Tommy's body.

And Reed only had to sit and watch, the other children in the school yard screamed like nothing he had heard before-

"I didn't touch him, I didn't touch him," was all he could utter, over and over when he was dragged to the Head Mistress's office.

But the children's laughter haunted him. There were reprisals, a fist to the ribs or a kick in the leg at football practice became a common occurrence over the following couple of weeks. He was getting used to the taste of his own blood once more, but it had to end.

He would get revenge some how.

One night, if memory served Reed correctly, the ghost had kept him awake with his infernal ideas of revenge. They were so vindictive. And from nowhere, brain storms from a mind Reed wanted desperately to fathom. Just where the hell did the child come from? Why was he here? Why him? Why Reed? More importantly, why did the boy die, and why?

Hundreds of questions begged for answers . . .

But Reed sometimes smiled, for Aaron had some pretty interesting ideas. His tongue would often brushed over his swollen, broken lip and ponder one of Aaron's ideas; bloody yet attractive as they were. He'd love nothing more than creeping into the Ritter's household in the dead of night, climb their staircase and pass from each room, leaving a trail of bullets-

Jesus Christ! My friend could even provide the gun!

Reed actually believed the fucker would provide a firearm too. But that wasn't going to happen. He just wouldn't be able to live with himself, or so he had said to the boy. He shook his head after Aaron's suggestions; each one bloodier than the last. And when his sore eyelids started to fall, the ceiling getting darker, his voice barely a whisper, the "wows" and the "You can really do all those things?" quickly turned into "It'll never work," "Are you out of your fucking mind?" and not forgetting "Go away, you're sick!"

But one summer's night, a tiny fingernail of a moon visible amongst a smattering of stars that peered between the gap in his curtains like a thousand inquisitive eyes, Reed sat bolt upright. The heat of the day hadn't let up and somewhere distant he could hear the grumble of thunder. He placed his naked back against the wall beside his bed, almost yelping at its icy touch, and whispered: "You know . . . that's not such a bad idea."

Reed sat waiting for his heart to quit hammering a tattoo against his ribs, tiny blotches of light following its rhythm as the seconds ticked by. If he was going to do anything, then that time had arrived to do it, he thought, quickly getting out of bed. He grabbed some dark clothing from the chest of drawers beneath the window then quietly edged around the noisome floor boards of the room. He knew each and every one of the bastards. Then onto the landing he had to stop and take a breath, waiting for those damned blotches to disappear once more. He hoped the bloody stairs wouldn't sound like some orchestra tuning up. So again he had to take his time and tread carefully. Eventually, at the bottom of the stairs, relief washing over him, Reed slid out of the front door and into the warm night.

33

Morning had come quickly. And Reed felt like a zombie fresh from the grave, occasionally tripping on his shoe laces as he made his way to Manorhouse Comprehensive School. His knees shook, and a gust of warm air did nothing to invigorate him. It simply ruffled his hair and made his blazer feel heavier than ever. He couldn't remember getting a minute's worth of sleep the previous night; neither could he recall the time he stole back into the house. But he knew that by mid afternoon his head would be rolling on his neck and his eye lids would be as heavy as lead weights. He just hoped that his tiredness would be worth it. As he made his way through the school gates, seeing in the light of day exactly what he had been up to as the rest of the town slept like babes, he froze.

Spokes of shadow sailed quickly across the sun kissed sports field, a brisk wind now raking through the dry grass. The temperature seemed to drop ten degrees or more as the breeze crossed the back of his neck, raising the hairs there-

'Beautiful, aren't they?' said Aaron, appearing beside him.

Reed was startled and had to remind himself not to have a full blown conversation when others were around, and now was no exception. Other children passed through the ghost as though he wasn't even there, staring wide eyed for a split second; knowing something strange had happened, only to shrug off the crazy notion then carry on with their business.

Reed wanted to look Aaron in the eyes but he was finding it increasingly difficult drawing his attention from what lay before him. But he could feel his smile. And that could only mean trouble-

But are you so innocent? Is this not what you wanted? Are you not the teeniest bit responsible-

Reed nodded, yawning loudly. He glanced furtively about at the bobbing heads and blazers flowing through the school gates, occasionally feeling a rough elbow strike his ribs. But he ignored it. 'Beautiful,' he mumbled out the corner of his mouth, so as not to raise too much attention to himself. 'But will it work?'

Aaron winked one piercingly green eye.

34

The day had crawled along as usual and Reed couldn't pay attention to his studies. His head seemed to buzz; every breath he drew shook him into wakefulness like a slap across the cheek-

'No medals for guessing what you're looking at,' said Sarah Winters without looking up from her drawing board.

Now, David! Do it now!

'Huh?' Reed replied, yawning loudly.

The room was far from quiet despite there being an Art exam in, what could be loosely termed as, progress. But at least he was grateful for Mr. Burton's absence; a chance to relax a little. The old man had slipped out for more supplies from stores and the dinosaurs that ran that place knew how to drag their heels. It was widely known that one teacher had waited forty five minutes for a pack of copier paper and two felt tipped pens. But it was also known that this particular teacher had had an illicit affair with one of said dinosaurs, ruined its marriage then called everything off.

'Down there,' said Sarah, nodding towards the window. 'Everybody's fascinated by the bloody things.'

Come on! Before you grow a set of balls the day will be done!

'Yeah, I know,' Reed yawned once more, a tear forming at the corner of his eye. He peered out of the window to his right, glancing down the three floors to the yard below. 'I thought he was going to the stores for some pencils?' He said suddenly, watching Mr. Burton walk through the yard. 'You'd think the old bastard would be up here watching us like hawks.'

A paper airplane whistled passed his ear but Reed ignored it. The room rumbled with foul language, laughter and the occasional scribbling of pencils from the swats at the front of the class, eager to refine their work with as much detail as possible.

'God, it's just a fucking vase of flowers, man! Lighten up!' someone grumbled behind Reed. He recognized the voice. He smiled.

Now's the time to get this ball rolling!

'They're magic, you know?'

One sentence was all it took.

There . . . That didn't hurt, did it?

'What are you babbling on about, fatso?' piped up Rob Tyne, punching Reed in the back.

'What did you have to do that for? You prick!' snapped Sarah, rubbing Reed's back.

'Oh, fuck off!' spat Rob, turning his attention to a nearby pupil's work, studying the half-completed drawing before crushing the sheet of paper into a ball.

'Real mature,' said Reed, feeling the pain subside beneath Sarah's delicate fingers. His face felt hot at her attention and she pulled her hand away.

'Better watch out, Robbo!' someone shouted. 'He might break every bone in your body!'

'Yeah, I'd better watch my step!' Rob laughed. 'Anyway, It's only one of those stupid corn or crop circles—or whatever you call them. Bugger all, really.'

'No,' Reed insisted, waving Rob over to the window. 'Come here. Look down there.'

He sighed heavily, reluctantly joining Sarah and a few others at the window. Shielding their eyes from the bright afternoon sunshine, they looked down upon the faculty, as they gathered at the edge of the playing field.

'Some of the lazy bastards have been down there all morning-'

'Most of the afternoon, too,' said Reed, shaking his head.

'Fucking scabs!' Rob shouted, beating a fist against the glass, which raised a few laughs from the back of the classroom.

'Who the hell would cut crosses and circles into the field?' Sarah wanted to know, chewing the end of her pencil. 'It just doesn't make sense-'

'God, everything has to make sense to you, doesn't it? I mean, they're magic,' Reed insisted as a matter of fact, watching the technicians and some of the teachers run over the soil with mowers. 'How long have they been trying to get rid of them, eh?'

'They won't get rid of them,' piped up Ben Hendry, a tall skinny individual with a broken voice and greasy hair. Every school had one. He absently picked at a spot on his chin, inspected the smear on his finger tips then wiped them on his dirty trousers. 'They're mowed in, man.'

'I thought it was paint-' said one pupil.

'Don't be stupid! It's carved in, I tell you!' replied another.

Keep it going, David-

'I've read quite a bit about crosses and circles,' said Reed, biting his bottom lip.

'That's it, sunshine,' Aaron said coolly in his ear. 'You're giving them the bait. Let's see if they bite, eh?'

'You would have, you bookworm!' jeered Rob, pulling on Sarah's bra strap.

'Ouch, you twat!' she yelped. Her face had turned a dangerous shade of crimson, but that didn't stop her retaliating with a couple of pitiful punches to the bully's shoulder. She tried to be aggressive but the whole school knew they fancied each other.

'No, straight up,' snapped Reed, wondering if the others would soon lose interest and the whole thing was going to fall flat. 'They're sacred. I mean . . . If you come across a circle with a cross through it, avoid it, mate! They may be holy and it's des . . . des-'

'Desecration,' Sarah offered, shaking her head.

'Did you have a dictionary for breakfast?' Rob chuckled.

'So who the hell marked the fields like that, then?' Sarah said quietly, ignoring his remark. He wouldn't even be able to *spell* the word dictionary, she thought. 'The devil?'

'It could've been,' Reed replied, looking over his shoulder at the students fooling around at the back of the room. But to his surprise, Rob wasn't one of them.

35

Days turned to weeks, and Barry Cussons' patience was wearing thin. As caretaker of Manorhouse it was his job to get rid of the "Devil circles;" a task that verged upon the impossible and not to mention the ridiculous. He had tried everything: weed killer, salt—God only knows the damage he may have caused to the ground in the long run. But only time would tell, he thought, sometimes staring into the circles as though the answer to their removal lay there. He had tried everything except what he was forbidden: to get a digger from a local plant hiring firm and bulldoze the entire ground so that they may start afresh. He supposed his superiors were simply worried in case the disgruntled caretaker would veer off the soil and decimate half the building.

He smiled at the thought . . .

Maybe they were right?

Sometimes traffic would come to a standstill, especially when the sky was clear and the sun shone brightly; the fields could be seen by the busy main road nearby. There were reports of people leaving their cars by the roadside to come and marvel at the markings, minds teeming with mixed reactions as to their origins. After all, they had already read about them in the TOWN POST. And now they could witness the carvings that put the school "on the map," in the flesh, so to speak.

People demanded answers. When new kids passed through town from miles around, hoping to witness some kind of miracle, they'd ask for the "Devil Kid," also known as David Reed; the boy who seemed to know what the damned things were.

And Rob Tyne hated it.

He'd often see the other kids milling around the worm, watching Reed smile and bask in his newfound popularity, and think: who the fuck do you think you are? Look at the girls wanting your time when they never acknowledged your existence before . . . *these* things appeared! I can make up stories about witchcraft and demon . . . demon—whatever the hell!

Reed, you loser!

The worm was popular now that he'd turned. Rob wasn't any longer. Even Sarah was hanging around him like a bad smell, and this infuriated him all the more.

It was as simple as that-

Yes? And what the hell are you going to do about it? Kick and scream? Demand the losers keep their distance from Reed? Think, Rob . . . Use your brain!

*

'Stay calm, David,' Aaron would often whisper when the bully was within striking distance. 'Just ignore him.'

But the ghost's words did little to allay the anxiety rattling his body like a coating of ice. He would peer over his shoulder, especially when the busy corridors fell silent, sending his pulse racing with impending doom. But the lull in the maelstrom was simply influenced by the presence of a teacher or two. The chaos would reign shortly afterwards.

'Expecting some kind of half-arsed wrath?' Aaron sniggered at times such as these. 'It is the way of it, my friend. The threat is very real . . . get accustomed to it.'

'Get used to it?'

'Stay calm. It's working.'

It's really working, David

'It's just a matter of time, then?'

The ghost nodded.

It's like watching a time bomb, isn't it, David?

TICK TOCK!
TICK TOCK!
TICK TOCK!
Then one morning something happened.

36

'Look sharp, David,' Aaron whispered in his ear. 'He's coming. Just like every morning, keep your eyes forward . . . keep him squirming.'

Much to Reed's reluctance of getting up earlier in the mornings to get to school before strangers in the street had the opportunity to bombard him with questions, he sighed at the thought of this whole trick coming to an end. The illusion, the wisdom, the pretense—all of it!

He was the Devil Kid and he didn't want any body to take that away from him.

Reed thought about this whilst standing on the edge of one of the circles, breathing in the chill morning air. His back faced the tall school building and the gates.

You don't need to turn around, David . . . You know what's coming, don't you? He's clenching his fists this very moment-

'Rob sees you standing here every morning,' said Aaron, startling Reed. 'He thinks you're praying or something—hold on, the bastard's coming over. Don't turn around, for God's sake, he doesn't look pleased.'

But Reed wasn't worried about a beating. It was the blue tongues of flame that suddenly appeared about the edge of the circle before him that raised the hair across the nape of his neck.

'Aaron, just what the hell is going on here?' he whispered, eyes widening in awe at the sight of the smoke rising from his shoes. There arose the faint smell of charred leather. Despite being alight, Reed stood still, frozen. He didn't hear Rob's panting breath, nor did he feel the heavy footfalls beating a tattoo in the soft earth behind him, getting closer.

*

Rob knew the markings and their legend was utter bullshit, but he made damn sure not to tread upon one of their edges. It was such a weakness that boiled his blood. What if the worm was right all along? What if the circles truly were sacred? What if-

'You've even got me believing now, you bastard!' Rob muttered breathlessly, gaining on Reed.

*

'Not long now, David,' Aaron whispered, his breath hot against Reed's cheek. 'We make a great team, you and I'

Reed closed his eyes, unwilling to imagine what the ghost had in mind, for his 'favours' involved so much pain-

'He's getting closer, David. He's speeding up-'

'Aaron, I don't like this one bit. Stop it now,' he hissed, eyes tightly shut.

'But . . . I . . . I thought that this was what you wanted-'

'Just tell me what you plan to do! Please, I just don't want to hurt anybody-'

'GET DOWN!'

Reed didn't think twice. He fell to his knees as a blast of wind rushed mere inches above his head.

All I do is cry. I did something that I shouldn't have.

If I didn't . . . then I might've had a chance. But I think it's out of the question . . .

The scent of the flowers rode on the breeze, transporting me way back into the tiny trunk of memories hidden at the back of my mind. I try to avoid it at best but, in times of weakness, I always find the padlock on the floor, tempting me, knowing my soft spot . . . And so I gently climb into the box. I must learn to keep away from the damned thing and make a stand . . . But it's not so easy.

Inside there are toys, old, broken and new. The dolls are clothed—always . . . I can't abide nakedness, whether the flesh is made from plastic, metal or human blood. I sit with my back to the cool wall, in the corner of the trunk, listening to the storm raging beyond its six dark wooden sides. I close my eyes and hold my breath until stars dance in the black and my heart batters a tattoo against my ribs. In there the others can not find me.

My family home is haunted, something mum and dad have gotten used to over the passed four years since I passed away. Not a night goes by without something either moving or disappearing, be it furniture or a damned toothbrush. The lights flicker and appliances turn themselves on and off, even the ones unplugged . . .

But it's not me . . .

It's the others.

I know they're here when I smell the flowers.

That's when I retreat into my tiny box.

When the storm rages about me, lights and colourful shapes only I can see, I let them get it out of their system. Even though I have the capacity to put a stop to their mischief, I had given in long ago. I usually wait an hour or more before they tire. Then I survey the damage they wrought . . .

Besides, they hated me in life . . . so why should they listen to a word from me in death?

Kate and Adam Trent despised the very air I used to breathe. For reasons unknown they secretly wanted me dead. A secret they kept from everyone besides my self. I was their play thing, their scapegoat, the one who took the blame and the punishment for their every wrong doing. They have always been ghosts for as long as I can remember . . .

Now I'm dead, they continue to torment me.

I never thought it possible that ghosts should haunt one another . . . After all, I'd expected us to form a special bond in the dark and scary blackness which is the reality of the hereafter. But I was wrong. You see, I've learned that whatever burdens the soul in life holds on when we die. It doesn't shrug off the hatred like a heavy overcoat at the threshold and enter the blackness pain free. We take it with us.

I can't bear to touch myself. When I was alive the Trent twins knew just where it hurt, made those places hurt for me. So when I got the urge to pleasure myself they had gotten there before me. I was just thirteen and I knew all about the birds and the bees. I knew it was natural to bleed, to have urges I thought was wrong and dirty, but the twins were much older than I and knew what pleased them.

As I hung myself with my school tie, my vision blurring with each, agonizing second, the room spinning, my bare feet kicking at the air, I saw them watching me from the corner of the room. Adam chuckled and slowly shook his head as if in disappointment.

'Do you honestly think this is the end?' he said, turning toward his sister, Kate. 'Hey, sis, get a load of this!'

'Fucking coward's *dropped* a load, more like,' Kate replied, pointing towards the excrement on the carpet beneath my feet.

But then she started to laugh. The sound, as sharp as gravel, cut the silence of the house like a fish's belly. 'Never mind, eh? Come on, Adam . . . Let's leave her out to dry for a while.'

The tears flowed beside my hole in the ground. There were so many tributes, flowers in abundance from family well-wishers and friends to teachers. Even David, my ex stood as still as a statue, flowers clutched in his shaking hands. His face was drenched with tears but I could tell that he couldn't care less what people thought. I know we were just kids but when you meet that certain, special someone you . . . you just know. But he didn't. He was too busy knowing every other girl . . .

We broke up. So did my heart, something that took time to heal. But David broke another virgin. I suppose we all deal with things in our own little way . . .

Mum and dad never recovered from what their only daughter did that day. I know that they would've tried to help me in anyway they possibly could. But it was futile. Something had to give, and it was me . . .

I've heard the twins talking about the future and about a way back to the real world. I don't know whether to dismiss this as a ruse to get me out from my hiding place and beg to hear more, so they can laugh at my gullibility, or keep quiet and pretend I didn't hear a damned word. I chose the latter, not wishing to give them fuel.

And when the scent of flowers disappeared, their words resounding in my mind, I listened to their receding footsteps, waiting for their return. Hopefully they will reveal more the next time . . .

Surely there must be an element of truth to the twin's crazy talk? I tried to convince myself, sitting in the corner of the trunk, tiredness washing over me.

Maybe . . . just maybe . . .

But all I can do is cry, for I regret my moment of weakness.

My name is Erica Thompson, and I was thirteen when I took my own life . . .

For this reason I know I won't be able to go back.

But I think I have one last fight left in me.
If they tear me apart then at least I've tried.
I'm scared but the boy said he'll hold my hand.
I let myself down . . . But I won't let you down, Christine . . .

37

Nobody saw what happened next. Even Reed watched reluctantly through half-lidded eyes.

Of course nobody else saw, David! Do you think anyone could keep this to their selves?

'And what would they have seen, David?' whispered Aaron later that night, his voices converging from all sides, making Reed's head spin.

Reed shook beneath the blankets, covering his head to block out the ghost's laughter at their triumph.

'They'd see a boy leap-frog over another child?'

'Aaron,' said Reed. 'Rob disappeared! Don't you understand-'

'Exactly. That's the beauty of it!' replied Aaron, his lips close to the blanket, almost touching. 'It happened so quickly, nobody would have believed their eyes-'

'But I saw him fall into the circle. And it didn't feel quick. I thought it would go on forever . . .' Reed allowed the words to trail away, as the feeling of helplessness washed over his weary body.

He remembered the rush of the wind then a soft splashing sound as Rob fell into the cryptic circle. The blue flames were almost knee high now but his shoes had escaped the heat. In fact when he stepped back the toe caps were completely unscathed, as though the fire had been ice cold-

Rob screamed, waving his arms like a drowning swimmer, racked by cramp, reaching out for anyone and anything for purchase . . .

God, that look in his eyes, David! He needed your help! How could you've stood by and let him die!

He remembered why.

'Help me, you cocksucker!' screamed Rob, his eyes wide with shock, spittle flying from his lips as grass roots brushed through his hair like teeth, spreading across his crimson face, forcing their way into his mouth and down his throat.

He had felt tempted to help; even reached out a shaking hand. But it was no good-

'You wanted this, remember?' Aaron had whispered.

Reed nodded, closing his eyes as if in resignation.

'You're right . . . But the sounds-'

He covered his ears with his hands, to block out the boy's screams and garbled pleas, the rustling grass forcing its way through to his very core, tearing him apart-

Then it was over.

Reed cried for hours, it seemed; his eyes were sore with tears, even though five minutes had passed. Once there were two boys, now there was one-

What have you done, David? Just what have you done?

As he opened his eyes once more he noticed the throng of children move like a tide of happy faces and strong language towards the school gates, ushering in the beginning of a new day. The fire had gone, so had the smell of smoke. The grass looked untouched-

Let's get away from here, David! The school will survive one day without you!

Without another thought he turned his back on the circle and made his way quickly through the gates before anyone had a chance to even notice.

'Fuck it!' he mumbled, hearing the traffic pass by. He didn't have the faintest clue as to where he would spend his day, didn't really care. In fact, as long as the rain kept its distance he would even walk in circles-

Very clever, David . . . Think that joke up all by your self?

Suddenly he spun round, almost losing balance. His heart was beating fast.

What is it? What did you hear?

'Screams,' Reed whispered. 'I heard screams.'

Rob's gone, David . . . Get used to it-

'Gone,' Aaron said softly in his ear.

Without another word, Reed headed for the local park, where he hoped the screams would not find him. But he knew that somehow they would find a way . . .

That was a long time ago. But time had its way of changing nothing.

38

'Well, I got rid of the bastard, didn't I?' said Aaron.

'I suppose,' Reed sighed, watching the cats eyes on the road hurtle towards them. The excitement over the past couple of days was taking its toll. And now all he wanted—yearned for, was home; to curl up with Tabby in their warm bed and sleep.

Sleep.

And sleep some more.

'Yes, you got him off of my back,' said Reed, quickly wiping the sleep from his right eye. 'But remember what I had to do in return?'

'How could I forget?' Aaron suddenly howled with laughter. 'In fact, if I remember correctly, you didn't let me forget for weeks-'

'Why the fuck did you make me take a shit in the school gymnasium?'

'Oh, come on! It was hilarious!'

Reed shook his head, but eventually he cracked a smile. But he was too tired to laugh.

'I tell you,' said Aaron, barely able to speak for laughing. 'The only . . . only reason I I made you do that . . . is because . . . because *I've* always wanted to to do that!'

Reed simply shook his head.

'Anyway,' Aaron continued, his mirth subsiding somewhat as he wiped the tears from his cheeks. 'It wasn't in the gym; it was on the storage ledge behind the basket ball net-'

'It bloody *was* in the gym! It could still be there after all these years, for all we know.'

Go on, David! It wouldn't hurt to laugh . . . That's it!

'It was funny though, I have to admit,' said Reed, glancing in the rearview mirror before concentrating on the road. He turned his head to the right, pretending to study a passing sign post—any part of the scenery—to hide his grinning face. 'It was fucking hilarious!'

'That's the spirit, man,' Aaron said. 'Fuck it all! It was funny, that little favour, wasn't it?'

'Spirit . . . Get it?'

Aaron's smile faded as he rolled his eyes. 'Not funny, mate,' he mumbled.

'Sorry, couldn't resist.'

'Anyway, David . . . you got an easy deal that day. I got rid of the bane of your life and you helped me to-'

'I helped you to hide shit in the gym?'

The ghost nodded then shrugged his shoulders.

'Well, when you put it like that, then yeah . . .'

'Look, seriously though,' said Reed, his eyes widening with realization. 'Was it because you were literally crap at sports and it was a symbolic gesture-'

'Alright, alright, alright,' Aaron waved a hand, proffering a single fingered salute. 'Maybe I had been a tad disgruntled for being rejected by the hockey team. So what?'

'*You* went to Manorhouse, too?'

'Yeah, so what?' Aaron replied. 'I used to . . . attend. But not for long,' he added quietly, gazing out of the window, all trace of humour had disappeared from his face now. And despite the heating system in the cab, the air had chilled somewhat.

'Missed a lot of childhood, eh?' Reed said softly.

'Too much. Way too much. But you were always my hands, David,' the ghost replied, a smile returning to his jagged mouth. 'My best friend.'

The sentiment only turned the air colder, a sense of unease and dread that raised the hairs on the back of Reed's neck.

'Well, why me? It's one of the two questions I've always wanted to ask you but never knew quite how . . . Of all the kids that you could've approached, why me?'

Aaron was silent for a beat, probably wondering the same thing himself.

'That night I tapped on your window?' he said finally.

Reed nodded, feeling the tiny fists of his heart awakening, taking shots at his ribs.

'Well, yours' was the first house I came to. I was so bloody weak that I didn't think I would make it up your drive let alone the window-'

'Yeah,' said Reed, nodding at the memory. 'I guess we wouldn't be doing this now . . . if you hadn't have found me that night.'

Aaron shrugged.

Is that something to be proud of, David?

Reed shook his head.

Then the ghost smiled.

'I was so badly shaken,' he said. 'I just didn't have a clue as to where I was going or what I would do when I got there. To be honest I still don't know what the hell I'm doing.'

'I've come to believe that when people say "to be honest" they're really lying-'

'Hey, this isn't some stupid tale to help pass the time, mate!' snapped Aaron, his eyes ablaze with anger. Reed nodded, tightening his grip on the wheel.

Let him vent it all, David! Let him talk . . . Just . . . let him talk!

'When I . . . When I died that night . . . Hell, it all happened so bloody fast that I didn't even know I was dead. That was until I saw the blood on my hands; the skin burnt to a crisp—my fingers, my head, my face—it felt hard and . . . my hair.'

'Look,' said Reed, clearing his throat. 'There's a roadside café up ahead. Why don't I get something to eat, then you can answer the second question I've been meaning to ask. Okay?'

Aaron rolled his eyes and chuckled.

'Gee, I wonder what that will be.'

'You're not as stupid as you look, are you?' said Reed, pulling over to the side of the road. He turned off the engine and opened his door, shivering as the cold afternoon breeze invaded the cab. 'Coming?'

39

I know you don't care, David . . . But this isn't over.

The sign said No Smoking but Reed didn't care. There were a dozen drivers and maybe more spread around the room, and only three were too engrossed in their newspapers and dinners to notice the haze of smoke about them. Reed sipped at his coffee, wincing at its bitterness.

Get it into you . . . It'll keep you awake, prepare you for what this fucker has in store for you!

He nodded and took another sip, glancing at the left over apple pie and ice cream on the plate before him. It repeated on him and he wanted to throw up, his stomach turning. But he hadn't felt this hungry in weeks. Ravenous was not the word he would have used to describe the way he had felt. Everything that bubbled and popped in the pots and pans on the griddles smelled so good, thought Reed. In fact *everything* was good! Even the conflicting scent of cheap aftershaves and faint air freshener-

Come on . . . Get a grip! This isn't over! You can do this, you know you can! It wouldn't be the first time now would it?

'No,' Reed whispered, staring at a picture of Walt Disney World on the yellowing wall opposite him and wished his life could be that simple.

Johnny is dead.

Tabby and Paul are safe.

But the question still remained, still burned in Reed's mind: Just how in the hell was he going to get Aaron off of his back once and for all?

'I can't believe it,' Aaron chuckled. 'Did you see that bloke's face when he asked you if anybody was sitting in this chair?'

'Hilarious,' Reed whispered.

'You don't need to whisper, mate,' said Aaron, pointing a thumb over his shoulder. 'We could sing soprano and it'd be drowned out by these dicks.'

Reed shrugged. Maybe he was right, he thought, over hearing the running commentary from a football game that must have escaped him. In fact he had lost track of so much over the past few days—his wife and child, sports, even soap operas—he missed it all and yearned to return home as soon as possible.

Now you're talking, David! That's your goal . . . Just do what this piece of shit wants and then it's homeward all the way!

'Well?'

'Well, what?' said Aaron, raising a patch of burned flesh, where his eye brow should have been.

'Aren't you just a little curious as to the question I'm about to ask you?'

'Oh, I know what you're going to ask me. But I'm afraid that you won't get an answer, David,' Aaron replied, a smile on his lips.

Reed finished his coffee in two swallows, stood up then threw a five pound note on the table. 'Fine,' he said.

'David, what are you doing?'

'Whatever it is you need doing, you can do your fucking self!' he said before making his way across the small room, counting off the seconds in his head as he headed for the door.

One . . .

Two . . .

Three-

'Okay, David,' said Aaron. 'You win. Now will you sit the hell back down?'

Reed smiled, returning to the table, ignoring the strange looks that came his way from all angles. He sat down and took another cigarette from the pack.

'Sorry, mate. I can't offer fresh air a cigarette, now can I?' said Reed, smiling. 'Talking to one's self is quite common nowadays; especially amongst the lonesome long distance lorry driver breed.

Some would say it's a necessity ... Keeps the grey matter twitching. I just don't think I could quite explain a floating cigarette, do you?-'

'Okay, okay! I get the picture, David. Bloody choke on it,' snapped Aaron, glancing around the room. 'The sooner I satisfy your curiosity the better. Just remember what it did to the cat, alright?'

Reed smiled.

'Satisfaction brought it back, my friend. I know the proverb.'

40

'Now you see?' Aaron hollered. 'Now you see why I was so reluctant to answer your bloody question, eh?' Blustery wind pushed against Reed's chest, as though trying to get him back to the warmth of the café, to sit him the hell down and chill out. 'I mean it, David! Don't just walk away like you always have!'

Reed paused momentarily, remembering all the ghost had done for him over the past forty eight hours, and he couldn't tear himself away from the fact that Aaron had saved his family, everyone who gave a damn to him. They were safe and sound.

Tabby . . .

Paul . . .

Alive.

Reed grabbed his mobile from his pocket and jabbed the menu button, searching for Tabby's number. He found it and pressed dial.

'David, come on!'

Reed ignored him, listening for the dialing tone, but as the seconds grew the machine picked up-

'For God's sake!' he hissed, putting his phone back in his pocket.

Do you really believe you could have achieved that if the bastard never turned up, David? Well . . . do you?

Reed shook his head. Maybe not, he thought, heading for the lorry; hoping to whatever sat above the clouds that it could be as easy as this.

If this is what you want . . . Just climb aboard, ignite the engine and disappear-

'David, please!'

Grab your keys and get out of here!

He put his hands in his pockets, his fingers brushed the warm metal of the fob as needles of cold rain pricked his cheek, and he wished for a few shots of whiskey to iron out the creases and alleviate the revulsion now twisting his insides.

Maybe you do and maybe you don't?

'What?' Reed mumbled.

Maybe you want to know . . . Maybe you want a little action to spicen up this life of-

'I've got what I want,' he said.

'David, please don't go.'

Reed stood for a while, wanting to climb the steps to his cab and get as far away from Aaron as possible. Instead he turned around and walked slowly back to the pitiful creature that once ruled his nightmares.

The sun had fallen hours ago, and now a bloodless moon hid behind haggard clouds.

Don't say those words, David . . . You don't need to know-

'You didn't tell me you were murdered,' said Reed, their noses almost touching. He could smell a mixture of cigarettes and dead meat on the ghost's breath, an abhorrent melding pot that pulled at his stomach in a vice-like grip.

And now you honestly believe he will tell you the truth?

Aaron's face was silhouetted in the hot light from the café window behind him. His eyes were sparkling wounds in the darkness of his skull.

'You wanted to know,' replied the ghost, almost apologetically.

'And Silverfield Avenue?' said Reed, trying to keep his voice as low as possible so as not to arouse attention from the cabin. His eyes watered with the cold blasts of wind. 'What's all that about, eh?'

'That's where it all happened,' said Aaron, cracking a smile.

'Where *what* happened?' Reed said with exasperation, clenching his fists, driving his nails into his palms, to cut and draw blood, but it would be futile. The bastard was going nowhere.

Fucking nowhere!

Reed noticed some diners at the steamy window of the café behind Aaron's head. They shielded their eyes against the glass, watching the exhibition of madness unfold; the white mad man shouting at the wind-

They think you're shouting at yourself, David. That's what people do when they shout at the wind . . . It's like spitting: the fucker'll hit you straight in the face-

'Screw them,' he said, giving them the single-fingered salute.

'That's where they . . . *did me in*, okay?'

"Did me in" . . . Did he really say that-

'They?'

'Please, just get back in the lorry so we can talk,' replied Aaron, his smile had disappeared as he glanced over his shoulder at the faces pressed against the window.

'I thought they couldn't see us, mate?' Reed said. But as the ghost stepped forward, he stepped back, the smile falling from his lips too.

'Get in the lorry and I'll tell you everything . . . Everything about that night-'

'I'll believe that when I hear-'

'I swear, David,' snapped Aaron, a fire now burning in his eyes. 'Everything.'

'I can't do whatever it is you want me to—Jesus Christ, this changes everything!'

Reed felt the sudden push of a finger against his chest. He stepped back, glimpsing the puzzled expressions on the diner's faces as they peered from the glass. He wanted to shake his head and smile at his spectators, but-

'I saved you!' the ghost hit him in the chest, punctuating each syllable with the icy tip of his finger. 'You and your fucking family!'

They locked stares for what seemed like an eternity. The rain drops were getting heavier and Reed felt them slap against his cheek.

'Now please, get in the cab,' said Aaron, his eyes gleaming like diamond chips in the darkness. 'I have a lot to tell you.'

41

The vehicle cut like a shark's fin through the night, traveling north.

Faster, thought Reed, unhappily. All he wanted was some way out . . . and soon. Bring on the miles. Bring them on!

He caught a glimpse of the road sign as it swept by like a ghost. He was approaching the bridge at Barton-upon-Humber. It wouldn't be long until he reached Newcastle, he hoped, gripping the wheel as though *it* had control and not vice versa. And he wondered if he *ever* had control.

'I'll tell you what happened that night,' said Aaron finally, plucking a cigarette from Reed's new pack. He struck a match, illuminating his deeply engraved forehead, his fingers shaking. 'It's not easy for me, David. I've not been able to discuss this with anyone since I can remember. But I'll tell you everything. Like I said, it's not so easy. The pain will never truly have mercy upon me. So listen up. I won't repeat a single word. Understand?'

Reed nodded once more, his hands gripping the wheel.

They're shaking, David . . . Stop it. Stop it now!

'I've never been good at telling stories,' said Aaron. 'Heaven knows how you have mastered the art of lies all these years, I'll never know . . . For years I've listened to you and your family. When you and Tabby argued sometimes I wanted to bash your heads together. Instead some nights I'd bang my own head against the walls-'

'That was you? You bastard, I thought it was our faulty water boiler winding down,' said Reed smiling somewhat nervously.

'You people think it's just what goes bump in the night. But do you know how it feels when nobody can see or hear you? Believe me it's not long before you start punching the walls-'

'I'm married,' Reed replied. 'Of course I know how it feels to be invisible-'

The ghost took a deep breath, taking a drag from his cigarette.

'Besides,' said Reed. 'Who else could possibly listen?'

I never classed myself as a hero; super or otherwise. But I knew that someday I had to show just what the hell I was made of. I didn't want a bloody crown or a medal of any sort-

What the hell am I thinking? The time to role up my sleeves and clench my fists hasn't arrived yet and I'm already playing with myself!

I should've told her—should've warned her that there were others out there; that she was not safe!

But first let me tell you how I found her . . .

The damned place must be somewhere around here, I think aloud, waving my arms before me like a blind man cut off from the strings of the real world. I wondered if the old axiom about wishing a little too hard should be carved in stone and built in the walls of every household around the world . . .

I wanted peace and quiet. And boy did I get it!

I remember trudging along the Yorkshire fells with my friends, Kate and Mark. We had argued for hours it seemed. We were lost and blaming each other. I knew that someone would be searching for us, after all, Todd, Sarah and Claire had broken from the pack and decided to follow the noises they claimed to have heard in the forest. I still think they had imagined the laughter of children, for the three of us had searched the woods to no end, for eternity it seemed, and still we hadn't come upon a group of children . . .

Surely they would be returning with help . . .

But something else came instead.

The shadow broke from the darkness, ice chips for eyes. It wanted us to follow it. It could help us, it said . . .

"I can guide you home. Where you can be warm and dry . . . like your three friends."

So we followed, hell, we didn't have much of a choice. We were all wet and shivering with the cold, even though Kate and David kept warm holding one another . . . But I couldn't be bitter for long. We needed to get off the fell before the cold caught up with us. I kept alongside them even though I wanted to break every bone in David's body so I could be the one to hold Kate . . .

That's when we fell down, or were rather led over the edge of the fissure. Well, as one, we reached the bottom, covered in blood and wet earth. My leg was pointing in an unnatural direction but David soon dealt with the crooked appendage, working what he called his "sportsman's magic" on me, pulling the bone back where it belonged. It hurt, but not as badly as I'd expected. In fact I remember hearing a crackling noise, and that was pretty much it.

Now we were following our own noises, never admitting that we were wrong in our assumptions, too bloody stubborn to agree to disagree. We were just kids for crying out loud! I shuffled westward and left them both to it. I knew I'd find help from somewhere . . .

That's when I heard a voice scratch through the silence. It was a conversation between what sounded like a group of grumpy old men and women. I stood, frozen, holding my breath so as not to give away my presence.

"You know it's this way," said one man, his voice breaking up. "I've heard it's this way."

"Well, I'm staying right here," a shrill female voice replied.

I couldn't even see the twinkling of an eye although I knew that they were within close proximity—hell, I could almost smell their rancid body odour. It straddled the shoulders of the breeze like a burdensome monkey. I was about to call out, to get David and Kate's attention, but they were long gone. And I didn't wish to disturb the strangers . . .

"There's talk of a small building around here-"

"It's not around here, stupid! It's everywhere. You just need to find the light in its window-"

"Is she real or just something made up?"

"Never mind that . . . Is what she claims is true not just some bloody fancy? Time and what we have left . . . I suppose we'd better make the most of it . . . That's if she's telling the fucking truth! That's what we should be wary of-"

"Well, I'm looking . . . I know the place exists and believe her story—Jesus, do I have another choice, I ask you! Besides, she didn't lead Aaron astray, did she? He got out and so will we. Might have to twist her arm just a little though."

They chuckled, pushing through the darkness, their feet splashing through puddles of oozing mud.

I followed, creeping along as quietly as a church mouse, hoping not to draw attention to my self. And it worked . . . But then we kind of lost each other as the darkness enveloped us. Looking skyward I thought I'd gone blind. Not a star scraped the heavens. It was as though the universe didn't even exist.

I had no choice but to believe in stranger's words. I called out for David and Kate, knowing now that I was alone. And as no surprise there came no reply.

I had to search for this tiny dot of light, the light from the elusive building the voice ranted about earlier. The woman's name escapes me, I don't really think that was as important as her tale, but there was nothing else I could believe in.

Damn it! I had to believe in something—someone!

I hollered as loudly as possible. My throat was dry and tears coursed down my grubby face but I persevered, trying to fool myself into believing that all would be resolved with time. After all, I thought, the night can not last for much longer . . .

I tried to convince myself that I was asleep and this was some cruel dream. Maybe I had been Jack the fucking Ripper in a past life and now I was paying for my bloody sins-

'Stop this,' I hissed under my breath. 'Stop thinking this way!'

But the time had eventually arrived to start believing the truth of my predicament. I think I knew all along. The dead aren't numb. They feel the dislocation from the real world, except they feel it every second of every hour like the breakage of freshly healed bones; over and over and over-

I'm dead.

Kate and David are too. In fact I think we died before we hit the bottom of the rock fissure. I know that now for this was more than some ordinary dream. The forest soon became a cold expanse of concrete, my voice echoed in this chamber-like void—these things don't just happen!

Then I saw the light!

It shone like a light house in a storm, pulling me toward its sanctuary. It was the place the old voices spoke of, I was sure of it . . . The steps, the door, the sound of the bell tinkling as I pushed it open . . .

There was a blonde lady sat at a table turning over playing cards, hiding their faces, concentration etched upon her face. But as she looked up and gave me a beautiful smile, her brow smoothed and her bright eyes filled with a warmth and brightness that no living person could truly appreciate; only the dead.

"Come on, little man," she said, motioning towards the chair beside her; gently patting the seat with her left hand. "You must be hungry."

Sheepishly I remained still, looking about the dimly lit room, the smell of fried food and strong coffee permeating the air.

"I just want to go home," I said, standing still. "Is there really a way?"

She smiled and I was lost.

That's when I had completely forgotten about the others . . . the dark ones.

God, I should've told her!

I hope I'm not too late!

42

'I *had* a father,' said Aaron, roadside lights stroking his face like a lover's caress, accentuating the depth of his burns to the left side of his head. 'God only knows—looking back—he was more of a rumour; someone spoken of rather than an actual entity. You see, Mum liked the money, and I guess Dad just couldn't win.' His jaw tightened, emphasizing the last words through pure determination; grit. 'Every week she had something new to wear. I can vaguely remember the boxes getting delivered. How she'd parade in front of the mirror, full of smiles and giggles. Even when the letters poked through the letter box she'd catch them before they had a chance to hit the mat. Dad never knew she ripped them up. He'd work on the oil rigs for months at a time, trying to keep a roof over our heads.

'I remember mum's voice: how she feigned the loneliness and adoration she had for my dad—only when they spoke on the telephone, long distance. But the bitch was far from lonely, believe me. Jesus, did dad *really* expect her to live like a bloody nun? Gutless fucker-'

'Hey! Gutless?' replied Reed. 'They were married. She *should* be faithful, that's what it's all about. It's only right. *Right?*'

Aaron chuckled, slowly shaking his head.

'Well, on *this* planet—hey, you've heard the cliché "the female of the species is more deadlier than the male" and all that? They certainly are. Mum knew how to enjoy herself, believe me. And I knew when to keep out of the way. Don't take offence, but I don't believe in marriage. Not now. They didn't act like a married couple at all. To be honest I can't recall mum *ever* wearing a ring. Dad did though. It was a chunky one that seemed to squeeze his finger to bursting point. He had hands like cow's tits, he did. I don't think he could have removed it if he had tried. Eventually he'd wear it like an embarrassing tattoo. You know? At the time it seemed like a good idea, but now . . .'

'How come you knew how to keep out of the way? What do you mean?' asked Reed, taking a long drag from his cigarette.

'Are you joking? Honestly, David, what do you think I mean?'

Reed shrugged.

'Anyway,' replied the ghost, shaking his head. 'Did dad expect her to live like a nun? I certainly did. I mean, she was my mother. But she didn't think I knew about her; what she was playing at, and she didn't fucking care-'

'Doesn't sound like much of a mum to me.'

'She wasn't,' replied Aaron, looking at Reed, who was staring blankly back.

'Step mum,' he said.

Reed smiled in a fashion.

'I understand.'

'So,' the ghost continued. 'Really there was no love there except maybe a duty that she thought she was obliged to carry out when dad was away—I don't know.' He touched his chest. 'There was nothing there. When dad came home and we went out for meals—always expensive restaurants, I might add, we never ate at home—the bloody lazy bitch never cooked—it was all just a pretense. She just grinned and bore it. To be honest I think she just wanted dad to herself-'

'Aaron, I can't see what this has to do with that night-'

'Please, let me finish, David,' replied Aaron, raising his voice. 'It's important.'

Reed fell silent, watching the road.

'Like I said, she didn't care, as long as dad was sending money home every weekend. Catalogues delivered on time . . . what more could she ask for? But it didn't end there. She certainly didn't need to turn to me for company, I can tell you-'

'She was having an affair?'

'To put it mildly, yes. Jesus Christ, it's why he left my mother—my real mother, in the first place. She was screwing around . . . apparently.

Well, that's what he told me . . . Anyway I learned how to keep out of the way.

'Some nights she'd even give me a few quid to go to the arcades. The bitch thought I was stupid . . . But I knew what was going on. She hated me-'

'Didn't you ever tell your dad about it? You know, how you hated her? Didn't you tell him about your suspicions?'

'What suspicions?' Aaron snapped. He rubbed the bridge of his nose, a migraine building behind his right eye. 'Sorry . . . I . . . erm, I knew she was sleeping around, believe me. Because . . . because, that night I . . . I came home from the arcade—well, you know how much money you can lose in such a small space of time in one of those rip-off joints!'

'Yeah, tell me about it! I remember them well,' said Reed.

'I came home early that night, catching her in, let's say, a not so pretty compromising position . . .'

'How did you know that something wrong was going on? I mean, you could've made a mistake-'

'For God's sake, David, don't insult me!' Aaron snapped, eyes wide, glaring in the darkness. 'I know that *I* was in the wrong for catching her and her boyfriend at it! Jesus, they were naked and doing it in dad's bed. I'm not bloody stupid-'

'Okay, calm down. I believe you,' said Reed, his hands gripping the wheel, anticipating a sudden reaction from the ghost; envisioning the steering wheel being commandeered by two burnt hands, a head-on collision-

You're the one who should be calming down, David . . . Breathe.

'Don't make me feel stupid . . .'

'So, erm . . . what did they do? Bribe you? I bet she showered you with bribes to keep it away from your dad—anything just to keep you quiet.'

'She wanted her lifestyle to stay the hell the same,' Aaron grunted, wiping a tear from his right eye, something Reed didn't notice whilst trying to concentrate on the road. 'She wanted everything to stay exactly the way it was. I pleaded with her. I promised not to tell a soul, especially dad . . .' He let the words trail away to silence.

Reed glanced over at the face in the darkness, hanging on his every word.

'I don't think she believed or trusted me. In fact she hated me, hated me so damned much.'

'How did you know that she didn't trust you? I mean-'

'Because she killed me,' Aaron said softly.

43

Reed shook his head slowly, and whistled in amazement at the ghost's last statement.

Surely things like that only happened in the horror movies and books Tabby liked to get her teeth into . . . So you're saying that you don't believe Aaron? After everything that's happened over the past twenty four hours, you find this little nugget difficult to digest?

'Jesus Christ-'

'And you can leave that bastard out of this!' Aaron scolded. 'Where was he . . . Mr. Silent-but-present-invisible-dinner-guest, bullshit? Look, that bitch had help. I mean, I had powerful legs and could kick a football—she'd watched dad and me playing in the park together on Sunday afternoons-'

'I don't want to hear this. Really, I don't-'

'She might have looked stupid but she wasn't . . . So she needed her boyfriend to hold my legs still as she-'

'You don't have to tell me *everything*, Aaron. I get the picture,' said Reed, feeling his flesh crawl across his arms and legs, hairs rising like iron filings to a magnet. 'I vaguely remember the story in the TOWN POST and on the TV, so spare me the details, will you?'

But Aaron was having none of it. A long finger of ash threatened to fall from the tip of his cigarette as his hands moved, yet the ash didn't break.

Let him absolve the vile memories, David . . . Soon it will be all over and you will have Tabby and Paul in your arms.

A faint smile spread across his face, comforted by the knowledge that everything was going to be alright-

Remember what he did to Gladstone? Quartered by carnival horses? This isn't a game-

'I know.'

'I know what?'

'I know you were in a house fire. That's what the papers said. I can't remember anything else,' said Reed irritably. 'You got trapped in a burning house and everyone else survived. An accident is what everyone called it; a tragic accident-'

'It was no *accident*!'

'She . . . she strangled me with her dressing gown belt . . . or something like that,' Aaron stuttered, the ash finally falling from the tip of his cigarette. He chuckled, trying to catch it in the palm of his free hand but failed. He rubbed it into his trouser leg, leaving a dark smudge in the dirty fabric. 'It . . . I guess it was the first thing that came to hand. I can't tell for sure . . . It's . . . All I could see was a blurry, swirling ceiling and a stranger's face looking down at me, laughing nervously; probably thinking that this was all just some fucking game that got a little out of hand. So I kicked.'

Reed nodded, his heart quickening, pins and needles rushing through his hands as he gripped the wheel. His throat had grown dry in seconds and he could feel a cold sweat break out beneath his arms and lower back.

'I kicked that bastard right in the balls,' Aaron sniffed loudly, something akin to pride now blazing in his tired eyes. He shrugged and shook his head resignedly. 'I guess that's when he lost his temper. He was a coward—all the work-shy bastards and smack-heads in that area were. Anyway he didn't want me mum to hurt me . . . you know? I think I could really see that in his eyes.'

'Maybe he thought it was going far too far-'

'He just got swept away in the moment, David,' Aaron replied softly. 'And when I kicked him, fucking Christ, he simply cracked! When he tired of using his fists, then came an old tennis racket-'

'What a cunt!' Reed gasped. 'That's terrible!'

'I just prayed that I'd pass out after the broken wine bottle clawed my neck and body . . . but I didn't. I passed out much much later. Boy, did they have a party with me . . . What kind of mother would allow that to happen to their own flesh and blood?'

'I . . . I just don't know,' Reed said, hearing a dry click in his throat. 'It happens every day—probably going on as we speak.'

'Then-'

'I can't believe they killed you, Aaron . . . That's . . . I can't even describe . . .' Reed let his words fade away as he watched the tear trace a jagged, glistening path down the ghost's face.

You would gladly do time if anyone laid so much as a finger on Paul—I know, David . . . I know!

'I wonder if it was so easy—I mean, dad's working away on the rigs . . .' Aaron's shoulders shook a little as though goose flesh suddenly covered him from head to foot. 'All mum had to do was hide me . . . I'd be found dead eventually—shortly after her reporting my disappearance to the police. It would've been as easy as that. They had plenty of time to get their act together . . . But no. I mean, I don't know what procedure your police of today follow, but back then the authorities didn't lift a finger for twenty four hours before answering a missing person-'

'It's changed a hell of a lot, Aaron,' said Reed-

You were about to say 'my friend' weren't you?

'Twelve hours-'

Reed shook his head. No.

'You've been hanging around for years, you should know all about the tragedies in the News. Anyway, when a kid goes missing these days, it's treated a lot more serious than it used to. I think they wait a couple of hours now.'

'Kids disappeared all the time. So what made *me* any different?' Aaron almost sighed, shrugging. 'Dad would return and his precious son would be gone. It happened everyday in the papers back then too, David,' he wiped the tear away from his cheek. 'I was . . . was just another statistic. Mum would break down in tears, dad would love her blindly—just like he always had, like he always would. Then I awoke at Silverfield Avenue; well, at the edge of the road, to be precise.'

'Did you live there?' asked Reed, frowning. 'Come to think of it, I just can't place you. I mean, I lived round the corner of Silverfield.'

Aaron shook his head.

'I lived about five or six blocks up the road from there. They must've thrown me from their car because I certainly can't remember getting there . . . I just crept from the dirty blanket they wrapped my burned body in, my clothes fused to my skin . . . I remember the ice cold needles of rain dashing against my body, the wet mud splashing over my shoeless feet, bits of glass cutting into my toes . . . walking like a sorry extra in a zombie movie-'

'They threw you into the fallen leaves-'

'God, there were so many bloody trees,' Aaron continued as though Reed had not uttered a word, in fact as though the man didn't even exist. 'At first I didn't know where I was. As I pushed aside a branch another would swing towards me, slapping at my face and clawing the exposed flesh through my charred clothes, pulling at my ankles to hinder my progress. Then I saw a house.'

'My house,' whispered Reed, dots suddenly appearing before his eyes as his pulse started to race, a sinking feeling deep in his stomach.

'It was the first place that still had its lights on at that hour—I say it must've been late, I couldn't recall one car passing me . . . Anyway,' Aaron shrugged apologetically, rolling his eyes.

Does he think this is some kind of joke, David? Yours'-was-the-first-house-so-who-gives-a-shit-anyway kind of look in his bloody eyes!

'So . . . I just followed my feet. Hey, I didn't know where I was really. I think I'd passed the wooded area on Silverfield corner when I rode the bus to school, that's how I knew how many miles I was from home, but I was walking, moving on instinct; following my feet. I guess a part of me really didn't care-'

'What about your dad? What-'

'He went completely crazy,' replied Aaron, twirling his left index finger at his forehead, as though he was toying with a lock of hair. 'He came home from work . . . and then well, I really don't know very much after that. I can't explain it. But I've been living with you guys ever since that night—why, you ask? Well, don't. All I know is that we cling onto whatever's closest and keep hold . . . like a drowning man. That's all we want, you see? God, some of us don't go to that fabled land.'

'Heaven?'

174

'Yeah yeah yeah, that place,' Aaron replied irritably, as though he regretted broaching the subject in the first place. 'And there is—well, I guess there is no hell—but here in the in-between-'

'Limbo-'

'Will you please just let me get a word in edge ways?' the ghost sniggered, but there was no warmth in his laughter. 'It's cold here, so cold. But . . . being some kind of recording . . . and don't ask me about growing up too. Didn't you know that your hair and fingernails grow for a time after you die? God, I don't know!'

Keep your tongue still, David! He's so desperate to describe his confused mind, he's babbling. Just let him talk-

Aaron brought a fist down on the dash board, shaking the console in its fixings-

'Hey, take it easy, Aaron,' Reed snapped. 'I know you're pissed off, but go easy with the rig, for fuck's sake!'

They drove in silence for twenty minutes or more, pretending the last half hour hadn't happened. And as they delved further into the darkness, the headlights raked through the road like desperate fingers, dragging the lorry relentlessly onwards.

'Silverfield Avenue,' Reed said finally, breaking the oppressive atmosphere that had befallen them. 'So what's waiting for us back there, then?'

'There is something I need you to do for me,' Aaron replied.

'But-'

'No buts, David! You said you would help me if I helped you, so you just do what I want and then we're even, okay?'

Reed watched the road ahead, his heart hammering in his chest, threatening to explode.

'Please.'

Reed took a deep breath, a cold sweat trickling down his back. His fingers tightened their grip on the steering wheel. Then he nodded.

'What do you want me to do?'

There must be some way out of this, David! Just think about it . . .

'It's not going to be easy-'

'JUST TELL ME WHAT THE FUCK YOU WANT, AARON!' Reed shouted, almost clipping the wing of a passing milk truck.

'Yeah, you go and screw yourself, too, mate!' he hollered, winding the window down so he could shout a little louder. 'That's it, beep your horn . . . I can do that too, you know?'

'Have we quite finished-'

'This is going to kill me, Aaron,' Reed gasped, glancing over at him. 'Now let's do it—get it over with and make it history because I want to go home to my family.'

'First we go back to the end,' said Aaron, taking a deep breath.

'But you didn't live there!' Reed snapped in exasperation. He ran a hand through his hair and noticed how much sweat had saturated his collar.

'You're right, that's where they dumped me,' Aaron nodded. 'But like I said: we have to begin at the end and make our way back to the beginning. Eventually-'

'Why-'

'We will get back to the start.'

Reed picked a cigarette from the loose pack beside the seat, and with one hand on the steering wheel, he lit up, feeling the nicotine rush almost immediately as he inhaled.

'I just want to go home, Aaron,' said Reed quietly. 'That's all I want.'

'And you will, my friend,' replied the ghost, his blue eyes glistening in the darkness. 'You will, just as soon as we go back-'

'And what do you want *me* to do?'

'Stop them before it's too late.'

44

Just calm down, David . . . What did you really expect?

Reed couldn't drive. He'd lost control. If Aaron hadn't grabbed the wheel to slowly steer the lorry to the side of the road they would just be a ball of yellow and orange chewed up metal now, their flesh bridging the gaps in the panels, welding-

Reed shrugged off the thought like a thick, uncomfortable coat, and sat quietly, barely able to hold the cigarette to his lips.

'You're doing so well, David,' said Aaron. The window was down and a chill breeze peppered with rain dashed across his face. A ribbon of sun light cracked the horizon. 'That feels good,' He sighed, glancing at the road sign up ahead.

They were close to Topcliffe, beside the A19. To their right rolled Hambleton Hills, beyond hid the North York Moors. In half an hour or so, traffic permitting, they would be in Middlesbrough.

You heard him, David . . . You are doing soooo well-

Reed watched the rabbit's foot sway slightly on the key fob in the ignition, wishing its fabled power would come to life; like it was supposed to.

No such luck . . . Think, David . . . Think.

'You know what?' said Reed, quietly, listening to the blood throb in his head; his body shaking. 'I bet you planned all of this. You know about all the shit I was going through and you didn't so much as lift a finger. No, you waited until I was bloody desperate—waited for an opening.'

Aaron grabbed the key from the ignition.

'Put that back!' Reed snapped.

'We're going nowhere,' said the ghost, wiping sweat from his forehead with his right hand. 'At least not for a little while. Understand me? I don't want you to fuck this up-'

'Go to hell-'

'I need you so I'm not going to lose you, am I? You're shocked, David. Take a breather. Chill out-'

'Keys. Now,' said Reed, sharply, holding out a hand, his eyes staring at the quiet road beyond the screen. 'Do you think I'm going to hit the first brick wall that we come to? Give me some bloody credit. Believe me, Mister Ghostie, you're not fucking worth it.'

'That's the spirit,' said Aaron, dangling the keys before Reed like a piece of meat to a starving bear. 'Good . . . maybe keeping our hearts cold might just protect us; being apart could keep it all together-'

'Have you finished talking in riddles?' said Reed, placing the keys in the ignition, his hand pausing there a moment; trying to steady his shaking fingers.

'I won't care about you, you won't care about me-'

'Just one little detail: Just how do I prevent a past event from happening? I mean, this is a *tiny* little detail-'

'Sarcasm. The lowest form of wit.'

'What do you want me to do, Aaron? This here's a great machine, but one thing it can't do, and believe me I've tried, and that's travel back in time!'

His words hung in the air like a sickly smell, refusing to move.

Tabby . . . I know you wish she were here, to deliver you from madness. But you're on your own-

'I need you because I've already tried!' shouted Aaron. 'I've tried. Bloody hell, if it was possible for me to do this on my own, do you think I'd be here right now? Do you think I'd be wasting my time sitting here? Don't you understand yet, David?' he said, tapping his forehead, his face ashen and within striking distance from Reed. And he was getting closer.

Don't, David . . . Just hold it together!

'I'm powerless unless you believe in me,' continued Aaron. 'Christ, you wouldn't be able to see me right now, wouldn't hear me, if you didn't. And what we did to Johnny back there . . . All of that wouldn't have been possible either if you didn't trust in me. He saw me too. I am. Understand?'

Reed nodded then suddenly shook his head, the image of Johnny's ravaged torso appearing in his mind, refusing to go away-

'No!' he said, 'this isn't happening! It's not happening . . .'

There was so much blood, David! His earring glimmered in the darkness-

'Understand me and believe me when I tell you that I've tried to go back to that night all those years ago. So many times, centuries and centuries ago now it seems,' said Aaron. 'But it's impossible. That's why I waited for you, David. Now I've helped you, you can save me. Just like old times.'

'But how do you know that it's impossible? How? I mean, you're still alive—well, you don't seem hurt-'

Reed fell silent as though the words had caught in his throat. Aaron wriggled in his seat, trying to remove his over coat. As the garment fell away, the stench of sweat permeated the air. Then he grabbed the torn hem of his sweater.

'What the hell are you doing?'

Without a word the ghost pulled the article over his head, the sound of static crackling in the silence that ensued. Reed even spotted the tiny blue sparks of electricity as he pulled it clear of his body. And beneath the thick material of his woolen pullover the ghost's flesh crept as though millions of worms coiled and sprung beneath the skin.

'Don't, Aaron,' said Reed, averting his eyes. 'I don't-'

'Look, for God's sake!'

Reed took a deep breath before finally facing what could only be described as an anaemic canvas of scars, slick with sweat, glimmering almost phosphorescently in the darkness. What he had first taken for the disruptive nature of maggots and worms was, in fact, the pallor of the dead skin. How it looks like moon light on a dead fish, he thought, shaking his head, trying to survey the deeply set grooves in the body beside him, secretly wondering how this must appear to a passerby-

'Now do you see me?' said Aaron, turning in his seat, his back now visible in the gloom.

Look at him, David . . . Showing you his scars as though they were something to be admired or proud of! What does he think he is? An ancient sword, folded a thousand times, his blood-run down his middle, a weapon that had claimed a thousand souls-

'What did they do to you?' Reed gasped, trying to follow the curves and swirls of the cuts exhibited across the ghost's back, puncture wounds at intervals. There were tiny burns the size of cigarette ends here and there, turning Reed's stomach. There were a dozen or more stab wounds and he refused to continue counting the rest. Even if he tried he couldn't fathom where one gash started and the other ended.

'Do you see them?'

'Yes,' Reed nodded. He cleared his throat, his voice now barely a whisper. 'Yes, I see them.'

'They burned me, let the house burn to the ground,' said Aaron. 'They knew what they were doing. If they had nowhere to live the council would provide them with somewhere new. But they couldn't leave me there . . . Any way, I thought you'd be interested in the gashes more than anything else. That's what mummy thought of me. You wouldn't believe what they poured into these cuts . . . but never mind. I suppose I've gotten away lightly. Others have not been as fortunate as I-'

'Others?'

'I've had friends, David. But they are no more,' said the ghost. 'They have gone back; those that have not been alone. Others just turned to ash . . .'

'But how do you know that it will all work out?'

'Now you're panicking, aren't you?'

'Hey, we're not kids any more and this isn't a bloody joke-'

'Stop, please,' replied Aaron, turning to face Reed now, holding his hands up in front of him to still his anger. 'I know we're not. But I've just told you that a couple of friends of mine have gone back . . . It *can* happen, it *has* happened. So it can work. It's the only way back because it's the way I left. Remember that girl I told you about, working in a café until she can be reunited with her loved ones? She's real. I've had a coffee there. It tastes like shit, but it's a real place. Fuck, I'm just not ready to spend eternity there. Life here could last just twenty years, at least that's what she tells me . . . So I intend to enjoy it.'

'I turned you away so many times. But you came back.'

'I want to live my life again. The life I should've had . . . not this.'

'Will I burn?' Reed wanted to know.

'It's fire,' said Aaron, unable to suppress the smile on his face. Everything was slowly going just the way he'd planned. 'What do you think? You piss about, take your time, then that's what'll happen. Whatever happens, I'm going back. I'm lonely, David. All I want to do is live again; to have lived and indeed go on living.' The ghost closed his eyes as though to quell the stinging tears there. 'Look, I know that I sound like a bloody drama queen here . . .' he opened his eyes. 'But . . . I've missed so much life, so much life, you wouldn't, couldn't possibly understand. God, how long I've waited for this opportunity-'

'What!'

'Listen to me,' said Aaron. 'There are countless . . . ghosts—God, how I hate that word! But, I guess that if it fits . . . Ghosts like me, roaming about, all alone. But I have a chance, and boy, doesn't that piss some of my kind off! That's why some of us are complete pains in the arse. You're familiar with poltergeists-'

'Slow down, mate,' said Reed, shaking his head. 'Just calm down.'

'Your life has started over, David! I gave you that opportunity, didn't I?'

David nodded somewhat reluctantly.

'What I can't fathom is that some of you envy _us_,' said the ghost, eyes wide, his voice almost shrill with exasperation. '*Envy* us! You contemplate suicide—Jesus, you don't even know what you're throwing away-'

'Not all of us, mate! Just slow the hell down,' said Reed, just able to get a word in. 'Remember when we were kids, when you told us that we could be partners; best friends?'

Finally, blessed silence!

Aaron nodded, his chest rising and falling as though trying to claw back the spent air from his lungs.

'Did you mean-'

'Think about it, David,' interrupted Aaron, speaking softly now. 'If I wasn't dead . . . just think of us growing up together; drinking around the town, making a right mess of the dirty women—all the shit we could've gotten up to-'

'You mean, change history?' said Reed. '*No fucking way!*'

'Save me, and we could change everything!' said Aaron, chuckling. 'Yes, we could be like brothers: you scratch my back, I'll scratch yours-'

'What part of *NO* don't you understand?'

'But I've never even been with a woman, David!' Aaron snapped, running his hands over his dome-like head in frustration as though maggots crawled beneath his scalp. 'I still feel like a child, don't you understand? You can be the catalyst, my one way ticket back. You're my key to that illusive door and I just can't lose you-'

'Christ!' Reed shouted, slamming both fists down onto the steering wheel.

'You keep doing that and you're going to break it-'

'Ring someone who gives a fuck, Aaron!' Reed exhaled loudly, facing the road ahead. 'I do not want this. Are you hearing me-'

'I hear you-'

'But are you *listening*-'

Aaron nodded. But Reed knew instinctively that no matter what he did or said, what was about to befall him was already planned out; to the finest detail.

'You're insane,' said Reed, closing his eyes, a migraine stirring there. 'All that shit you made me do for you all those years ago. Crazy. And that's when—don't look at me that way-'

'What way-'

'As though you don't know what I'm talking about.'

The ghost shook his head, lighting another cigarette.

'But it wasn't just that time with the school yard-'

'Those crosses were a great idea.'

'You know what I'm talking about.'

Aaron smiled as though the vile memory that came to Reed, one he shook off immediately, had somehow rolled through sugar before reaching him. 'Yes, I remember.'

'Memories to you. Take them, relive them as much as you want to but you made me-'

'I made you strong,' replied Aaron.

Reed detected the note of arrogance in the other's voice, his cavalier attitude angering him.

'You made me *hurt* people,' he said, eyes ablaze. 'People who did you no harm-'

'Name one.'

'I told you, the memories are yours. I don't want them! All I remember—the only lesson you taught me back then—was not to trust you. You're malicious, Aaron. I mean, God, do you want to take it out on every kid alive because you-'

'Say it.'

'Okay, I will,' Reed told him. 'You can't hurt everyone because you were murdered all those years ago. It's the past. You're dead. I can't imagine what your final hour was like—Jesus, you must have . . . have gone through so much-'

'Pain, fear, terror,' interrupted Aaron, his voice as dry as chalk. 'You're right, you couldn't possibly imagine, David.'

'All the anger . . . And you were dead. Just imagine what trouble you would've landed us in if we had been friends; living and breathing . . .' Reed stared ahead as though visions of what could have been, was painted on the horizon.

'Maybe I wouldn't be so hateful if I had lived,' said Aaron. He closed his eyes, crows' feet deepening at their corners. 'God, this is giving me such a headache. Forever to move in circles, over and over, when all I could've been was not going to be again. I'm not insane, David,' he whispered now, finally opening his eyes. They seemed to glow, brighter than they had ever been.

'What do you want, Aaron-'

'I don't want to be dead anymore. That's all the dead want: to live and breathe once more. Believe me, when your day arrives, you will wish for the same thing.'

'How would you know-'

'Are you being serious?' Aaron laughed heartily. 'I'm not going to dignify that question with an answer. There's nothing you can say to me, no pearl of wisdom that can teach me about this life. I do share one common sentiment with the hot-blooded, that's what us kind call the ones on this side, and that life is so much better than over there. You're my one chance at getting what I want. I won't give in.'

Reed sneered, shaking his head.

'Are you saying I don't have a choice?'

'Think what you please, David,' the ghost replied flippantly, 'I don't care anymore.'

'You still haven't answered my question, ghost?' said Reed acidly, spitting the last word as though it had crumbled into salt in his mouth.

Aaron stared through the glass to his right. The traffic spilled up the road, gently rocking the cab as they made their way in the darkness. Their headlights resembled marbles of fire.

'Will I burn?'

My God, you're the man insane, David. Not he. You're really going to go through with this, aren't you?

'All I know is that *I* will-'

'But will *I*?' Reed wanted to know, turning the key in the ignition, hearing the engine roar, feeling the monster awaken in the darkness. 'Yes or no?'

'Yes, you'll burn,' said Aaron. 'But it won't kill you. I promise.'

'You promise, do you? Well that's really comforting to know, isn't it?'

'Save your sarcasm, David. It's tiresome. I've seen what's going to happen. Trust me, you'll be just fine. When this is over it'll be like I was never here.'

'Promise? Trust? This goes way beyond all that crap,' said Reed, pulling the vehicle away from the curb, joining the trail of traffic as it made its way into the morning's early hours. 'Do you even know the meaning of those words?'

'Don't you say those things to Tabby?' Aaron replied. 'I promise you this and trust me on that? Well, don't you? I saved you and your family-'

'Yes, yes, I know all of that, but if I go back and you can't, then how can you trust me?'

Aaron shook his head. 'I . . . I don't under-'

'If I do this, go back with you, to help turn all of this around,' said Reed, trying to concentrate on the road ahead, smiling wanly. 'How do you know that you can trust *me*?'

The ghost was silent for a while.

'You know that you can't follow me in the fire? You'll burn if I leave you there, won't you? I could turn my back on you, turn away from the house; make sure none of you escape this time round-'

'I can trust you, David,' Aaron said with a knowing smile.

Reed's smile disappeared completely, his face ashen and almost featureless; as though those four simple words had drained every drop of blood from his veins.

'You sound pretty confident,' Reed replied, quite timidly.

'*You* don't,' said Aaron with a rumble of laughter. 'Besides, I have no choice, do I? As much as it will twist me all up inside, I will just have to stand aside and wait.'

'Wait for what? There you go again with the riddles-'

'Once you go back, if we succeed, we may not see each other again.'

'What the hell makes you think *otherwise*?' Reed gasped, his eyes wild with disbelief.

'You will return and I will be gone. But I'm hoping I'll still be here, you know? Friends 'til the end. Imagine what we can do together-'

'We've been through this, Aaron,' Reed reminded him.

'To feel the warmth of the sun on my face,' the ghost continued dreamily as though the other man hadn't even spoken a single word, as if he didn't exist at all. 'To . . . to talk and laugh with others . . . I can be a good guy. I really can be. Don't you believe in change, of living your life over again-'

'What's done can't be undone,' said Reed, shaking his head. 'It's just not possible.'

'After what we've been through these past couple of days, you still don't believe, do you? How many times must I tell you that everything will go just the way I planned?'

That's what worries me, David!

45

Reed watched the blurred sign up head slowly come into focus, his headlights brushing away the moonless darkness. And his heart sank. Durham Tees Valley airport was at the next intersection. He held his breath a few seconds before cutting into the A67, seeing the lights twinkling on the horizon like a thousand burning candles. A small car weaved between the lorry and another long goods vehicle, screaming its horn like some rabid firefly.

Reed proffered the one fingered salute. He was fluent in the sign language of the road.

'Next time I'll wipe you out, you little shit,' he mumbled, wiping sleep from his eyes with a weary hand.

'Keep your cool, David,' said Aaron, opening the window, invigorated by the icy breeze as it smothered his face like a cold pillow. 'I need you ship-shape-'

'I said I'd do it, didn't I?'

Aaron nodded, yawning loudly.

'I'm grateful to you, David. Don't be mistaken for a moment-'

'I don't have a choice, and you know it. So don't go all squishy on me!' Reed said, as a matter of fact. 'Let's get this over with.'

'I bet you can't wait to get back round the family fire . . .'

'Just let me drive . . . Okay? I'm done with talking,' said Reed calmly, his hands firmly on the wheel. If he'd told anyone about the blood and carnage he had seen on this journey they would certainly stagger in disbelief at his composure. How he can control a potentially lethal machine was almost beyond himself . . .

Well, who else is going to do it for you, David? They're waiting at home . . .

Tabby and Paul . . .

Reed felt the warmth of a smile on his face.

You can do this . . . You can do this . . .

'Yes, I can,' he said.

'Huh?' said Aaron, pulling his face away from the airs stream beyond the window. 'What was that?'

Reed shook his head.

'So, when we get through this, there's a chance we may never meet,' said Aaron with a smile. 'Is that what you want? When this is all over-'

'Aaron,' replied Reed, exhaling loudly, 'you know that I just want my fucking life back—that's all! No disrespect to you but-'

'But?'

'We'll see, okay?' said Reed, trying to keep his cool.

Did you hear what he's just said? If you never meet, if he never even existed in your life, imagine what your life would be like now? No pranks . . . No favours . . . No bloodshed!

Reed gripped the wheel, his palms sweaty. A smile broadened on his lips and he couldn't disguise it nor suppress the sudden pleasure building up inside. He glanced at the ghost, his eyes flickering as the cold wind swept across his pale face.

Look at him . . . He thinks he's got the better half of the deal! What an idiot, David! You're the one that's coming up smelling of roses this time. You'll see . . . it's going to work! It must work!

For the first time in days Reed felt warm inside, happy in fact there seemed to be a way out of this dark chapter in his life. And he couldn't wait to turn the page and see what happens next.

He switched on the radio and found a rock station. As the drums filtered through the speakers and a wild guitar screeched like a banshee, he couldn't help but tap his fingers on the wheel.

46

Reed watched the thunderheads hurtling from the horizon like a plague of locusts, the sun, as bright as a blood shot eye following closely behind.

Not a word was exchanged between them as they approached Middlesbrough.

Reed found it hard to sit still, shuffling in his seat, trying to get the blood flowing through his legs and numb arse; wondering why, after so many years driving long hauls in these contraptions, it still affected him the way it did.

Getting older, David . . .

He glanced over at Aaron, words on his lips. So many questions seemed to float around in his head. If he could just take his hands from the wheel, only for a short while, maybe he could grab one of them-

'Just drive, David,' said Aaron quietly, shifting in his seat so he faced the window. Reed could see the ghost's face reflected in the glass. Those green eyes . . . they were staring at *him*. 'I'll tell you everything you want to know when we get there. But right now-'

'"Want" to know?' replied Reed, shaking his head. 'What about what I *need* to know?'

Reed chewed his lip a moment, gripping the wheel in frustration as he noticed the other had closed his eyes, his breath steaming the glass.

'How can you be tired, anyway?' Reed wanted to know.

Aaron stirred but kept silent.

'You know something? You destroy every preconception that I've ever had about . . . you know, ghosts-'

'That's nice,' Aaron mumbled, yawning loudly. 'I aim to please.'

'Well, let's face it . . . you're dead, but you've grown . . .'

Quit while you're ahead, David . . . This is getting you nowhere fast.

Reed nodded imperceptibly, glancing once more at the dark lump beside him. The passing traffic's light stroked his pale face, illuminating his ashen flesh in the glass-

He's watching you, David . . . Just keep your eyes on the road-

'Just want to go home,' he muttered. But he thought about kicking the door open with one foot and Aaron from the cab with the other. His heart pounded hard in his chest, sending dark shapes across his field of vision. Suddenly he felt the hairs rise like hackles on the back of his neck as out of the corner of his eye Aaron turned about in his seat.

'I thought I had made myself clear,' said the ghost, shadows passing over his scarred face. 'You know about the finger nails and hair.'

'I know, you told me already,' said Reed wearily, swallowing hard. 'But how can that be *possible*?'

Aaron shrugged. 'I suppose those parts of your body are like . . . well, like fungus; they just keep growing for a while.'

'Not in your case though?' Reed glanced up at the ghost's bald head, smiling nervously.

Aaron sighed loudly, curling back up in his seat. 'My mistake . . . For a moment there I caught the scent of an actual intelligent conversation. I guess it was only shit-'

'Hey, sorry for being such a prick, but the past few days haven't exactly been middle-of-the-road . . . if you'll pardon the pun.'

'Give me strength . . .' Aaron breathed, turning round to face Reed once more, his eyes sparkling in the cabs gloomy interior. 'Well, seeing as though I'm not going to get one wink of sleep . . . let me illuminate you. Screw whatever preconceptions you may have about us. Even in death we continue to grow—only if you come back, I hasten to add. You only rot when you go in the box.

'We're just like you, except the only choice we have in our existence is to be seen . . . or forever remain in our little prisons.'

'Like a genie in a lamp?'

Aaron curled his top lip and shook his head. 'Not really, but you're getting close, my friend. We wait for that one chance. Until that happens, we . . . well, we wait. Sheer will power is what it all boils down to. Only the thought, that inkling of a chance however slim stops us from rotting. We have to cling onto hope too, you know. Sometimes it floats, and . . . well, you get the idea. If there is no possibility, not even the remotest opportunity of coming back for real, then even the ghost shall give up the ghost.'

'Like your friend in the café you spoke of-'

'What?'

'You said you knew a girl that's waiting to be reunited with her family . . . She works in a restaurant-'

Aaron shook his head firmly.

'You mean the café? Yeah, Christine is waiting, David. She serves coffee and tea and some things that resemble sandwiches. They taste like shit, but they fill the stomach. The building's just on the border of sleep and the other side—I fucking hate that phrase, but that's the going cliché these days. I love the little place. It may be a tad run down and in need of a lick of paint here and there, but it's cozy. The light bulbs could be upgraded, if you ask me. I mean, it's a little dull in there, hurts the eyes . . . to hell with it, who cares? It's so warm and there's always a smile waiting for you when you get there.

'She's beautiful, Christine I mean; blonde hair, legs that go right up to her neck; I think she's about thirty seven or eight. And eyes . . . whoa, David, you've seen nothing like them. I feel a little sorry for her sometimes. When I'd sit and drink my lemonade, I know it's a bit girlie but the cold liquid helped to soothe the burning sensation that occasionally tormented my stomach and throat . . . anyway, she'd be looking out of the window on what I only know as darkness. Maybe she saw a great deal more, who knows? I asked her once what she was waiting for. That's when she told me her story. Over here I've come to understand that, like life, death is how you make it. That really sounds bizarre, doesn't it? But it's different through my eyes.'

Reed nodded, smiling wanly.

'That's certainly a new one for me.'

'The café,' Aaron continued, staring off into space as though he could see it just beyond the window; a vision so clear that he could just reach out for a glass of cold lemonade. 'It probably has the brightest windows in the surrounding darkness where I . . . live now, so to speak. Well, I use my time commuting, if you like, between here and there. It's a little respite from the hum-drum of this world. Let's be honest, David, watching you gambling behind Tabby's back and getting all messed up by loan sharks sure has its way of depressing one. Anyone who's anyone knows the little shop; those over there at least. It never seems to close. It's not the best coffee but sometimes she gives out bottles of lemonade and sweets when she's in a good mood, which isn't that often, I can tell you.

'I remember waking up all bloody and burnt, stinking of petrol and singed hair. My face was hanging off. I could hold it up and put it in place. But it would fall apart like a mask covered in tomato sauce, the jaw bones were bare for a time, but after a little work the flesh pulled back into place. It's tough, you know, holding your face together. Stumbling around in the dark was like the first time I'd had a beer. If zig-zagging was the way you'd call it, then that's how I walked about. Shit, what happened to me? I remember you turning me away in the night then I appeared over there. When I awoke I was lying on your bedroom floor. You'd turned me away, not only from your life but from your mind too; just closed it off. You didn't need or want me any more-'

'Don't take this the wrong way, Aaron,' Reed said slowly, carefully. 'But why can't I do that now? I'm not saying I want you out of my life, I'm just saying-'

'So, I'd roam the darkness over there, finding my self going round and round in circles,' Aaron continued as though Reed hadn't breathed a single word. 'The years seemed to fly by and I got used to holding my face together, in fact sometimes I'd just let it fall, walk around carefree in this world. Fuck it, no one could see me. But some could. And they didn't give a shit what your face looked like. As long as there was some kind of hole at the other end it was ripe for the taking. One or two shitty encounters with some old creeps led me to her place. They're everywhere, David, skulking about in the shadows, waiting for any piece of unsuspecting meat to stumble across their path. Burns and cuts aren't enough to keep the sex pests away, you know? When they . . . finished with me I stumbled towards a bright light. The coffee house just appeared as of nowhere. It sounds crazy but these bright windows just beamed like a lighthouse on some stormy sea. So I headed toward it, falling over a couple of times on the way, but eventually I climbed the little steps leading up to its front door and sanctuary beyond. And when I fell over the threshold I passed out.

'For how long, I have no idea, but when I came to, Christine was there with a First Aid box, dabbing at my face with cotton wool balls dripping with warm, clean water from a bowl. I noticed just how pink the water was already. After some attempts to sew up my face we decided that there was too much to contend with, and in the end we both knew that it didn't matter, the scars would heal eventually. And besides, we're dead: why bother looking nice?

'Anyway, I noticed the local clientele dotted about the room, sipping at what I could only guess at. No steam arose from their drinks but strange, pale lips blew at the brew anyway as though it was piping hot. They were a little strange and introverted as they were still trying to get a handle on what the fuck was going on. We'd never make eye contact, hell, some didn't have eyes. Then, after returning a couple of times, especially when I couldn't take you and Tabby bitching over money, I noticed the place was starting to fill up. The ice, so to speak, had melted away and I plucked up the courage to talk to them. If it weren't for Christine I probably would be still looking over my shoulder for creeps. So she introduced me to some people too, just to help me along. That's where I met the girl who had been mauled by her parent's dogs. God, some of stories they told me, the abuse they suffered—it turned my stomach!'

Reed shook his head slowly, trying to digest the ghost's bizarre story, but it was going over his head. He wanted to ask so many questions but he knew that they would go for miles and end up back to where they had started: absolutely nowhere-

When all's said and done, David, it'll soon be over. If you listen really closely you can almost hear Tabby's heartbeat—that's how close to home you are!

Reed smiled. He wanted to laugh aloud, but suppressed the joy he felt.

Just a little more time, and you'll be home . . . Just hold it together, David!

'Christine's waiting for her two kids and husband to waltz through the door. That's going to hurt me a little as I've grown to love her, but it's out of my hands, isn't it? Anyway, from what she told me, Darren, her hubby, is a little cross to say the least with her. I hope his anger doesn't last twenty years. That would be such a waste wouldn't it? You see, she kind of tricked him into getting her own way-'

'Own way?' said Reed, his smile fading. 'What do you mean?'

'To cut a long story short, all hell's about to break loose and a lot of dead folk are heading back home to take back what is rightfully theirs. You know what, fucking hats off to them, I say! I don't think they have a clue as to what's going on in the real world right now, and they're in for a shock; especially the oldies that haven't breathed a lungful of air for thirty years or maybe more. There's no justice in the world so you have to deal out your own, am I right? Twenty years is nothing. And when that's all you have left that old saying of living life to the full applies more than ever! You know it, I know it. The thing is, so does everyone else.'

'What about the guys that . . . you, know-'

Aaron shrugged, frustrated by Reed's interruption.

'What about them?'

'Well, aren't you worried they might overhear too? I mean, what if they want their lives back and decide to take whatever means necessary?-'

'They won't-'

'How do you know-'

'They're the least of our problems! If they get through . . .'

'Then good on them? Am I right, Aaron? Do they deserve another shot-'

'I'm not kidding here, David. There's going to be so much carnage you wouldn't believe. And you're the only one, apart from her family, who know about this—sorry to burden you with the secret, but no fucker would believe you anyway if you told them. Christine shouldn't have interfered with what's to be; she meddled with it and lost. She gambled, something you might be familiar with-'

'Just hold it there, for Christ's sake!' Reed snapped, steadying the wheel as the thunderheads above had clashed and split the sky in two. The sudden spark of light shook him fiercely and as the rain hit the screen he knew he would have to take control of his senses. Twenty years left here in this world was short enough, he thought. It didn't need narrowing down any further! 'This is all going over my bloody head. You're talking about what happened in Hamsterly forest last year, aren't you? I read it in the papers. Hell, it even made the news for a few days. That bloke, David or Darren—yes, Darren Barker and his kids almost died there. Half the bloody forest looked like it had been set alight. You're saying this Christine is waiting for Darren and her kids? Just what the hell did she do?' said Reed, trying to steady the lorry about a sharp turn in the road, which was now slick with rain. He shook his head and cursed under his breath, knowing for certain that at any other time he would have had no trouble taking the acute angle. Fatigue was taking a firm hold and it was trying to pull him under, he thought, lowering the window further to feel the bracing wind against the hot sweat on the back of his neck. After a few moments he felt a little invigorated and indeed human once more. Or it could be the absurd conversation they were having that could be knocking his mind off kilter!

Don't push it, David. This guy is sticking to you like glue.

'Christine let, God, I don't know what to say, David,' Aaron stammered, searching for the words. 'She knew exactly what she was doing by letting it live. It should've stayed dead and buried, but no, she couldn't wait to see her family once more. To hell with dribs and drabs, seeing her husband first then having to wait an eternity for her children too. She wanted it all, and it will come in under two decades-'

'*It*? What the hell is that?'

'Nothing that matters anymore, David,' Aaron replied quietly, gazing out the window. Trees along the side of the road swayed to the marshalling winds as if in thrall to the sound of the storm. And drops of rain the size of marbles dashed across the windscreen. The wipers now moved hypnotically but failed to clear the screen of rain for more than a couple of seconds. 'When it comes the world will be wiped of all mankind to make way for a new breed, just the way it had been intended at the very beginning. It can't be stopped, we just have to make the most of whatever time we have left. That's why I'm here . . .'

Separated by silence that lasted all of twenty seconds, Reed started to laugh, shearing the oppressive atmosphere as efficiently as the lightning way up in the grey.

'You have no idea of the gravity of what I've just divulged to you,' Aaron muttered under his breath.

'What?'

Aaron shook his head. He folded his arms and stared out at the falling rain.

'And I thought you shouldn't have a care in the world,' said Reed, glancing over at Aaron occasionally as though he sought, and would indeed find, his answer there in the ghost's eyes. 'I mean, no bills to pay, no money worries; no knackered relationships to endure, no broken heart—hell, no heart at all—in need of mending when someone betrays you . . .' Reed whistled loudly, shaking his head. 'I just don't understand it. I mean . . . life sure can be a prison too, you know? But that's not what it's all about.'

Aaron sat silently for a moment before chuckling. Reed thought the sound resembled a hand raking through the gravel at the bottom of a goldfish bowl, but nonetheless a good, warm sound. He was laughing, and that's all that mattered. For the first time in what seemed like a week, Reed felt the tension in the atmosphere loosen its grip from his throat.

'Sometimes . . . now I could be wrong,' said Aaron. 'But sometimes, when you open your mouth, stuff *other* than excrement falls out.'

'Thank you . . . I think.'

'No no,' the ghost shook his head. 'You shock me, you know? After everything I've just told you . . . the secret of mankind's fall, and you start talking about bills and irrelevant shit such as relationships . . . You're right: I shouldn't have a care in the world. But don't you realize? I've reached a new chapter in my soul's existence.' Aaron's smile had fallen away now. 'I'm not ready for this now-'

'Not ready for what?'

'I believe that the soul lives forever—Christ, I'm proof of that! I know this sounds insane but, I'm not ready for death! I've not been promised a thing. I've missed out on so much . . . Now my flesh is aging like yours'. Pretty soon I will die without ever having lived-'

'Life's wonderful-'

Have you not heard a word these last couple of minutes, David? The world will end in twenty years! You will be fifty seven, Tabby, fifty five; Paul, twenty one . . . Now I've caught your attention, haven't I?

Reed gripped the wheel, the hairs stiffening across the nape of his neck.

'Please, David, let me finish. I know the living have to contend with a lot of shit. Believe me, I know, remember? I've lived alongside you and Tabby for years on end. You think Hell is unpaid bills, mortgage arrears, not forgetting the satanic ritual of dragging yourselves out of bed to earn a crust? Bloody hell, that's only the down side of it, mate. There's no reason to give up and pray for death . . .'

Reed drove in silence, picking a cigarette from the box beside him. Despite the tightness in his chest and the laboured sound of his breathing, he lit up and drew deeply on the smoke. He just needed the kick to wake him up, that was all. He wanted to laugh out loud, but thought it inappropriate at this point in time. It seemed ironic, maddening in fact, listening to a dead person's teachings on life. But he guessed experience sure as hell counted for something. He could only imagine the torment of being life's little spectator, with only the ability to judge, watch and stand aside; tight-lipped . . . powerless. But when he thought about it, he realized just how much it resembled life itself.

'Even if you and Tabby lived like priests,' Aaron continued. 'Treading carefully and thinking a hundred times before carving any plans into concrete, you'd probably still wind up in debt—everybody does.'

'I guess so . . .'

'Do I know more about life than you do?' the ghost added, raising a barely visible eye brow. 'If that kind of trouble, you know, that downside really makes people want to die . . . it . . . it destroys the soul.' He searched the air for those damned elusive words, shaking his head in frustration.

'I suppose I understand-'

'No, you really don't have a frigging clue about what I'm trying to say, alright?' Aaron snapped. A pearl of sweat formed above his right eye and slowly rolled down the curve of his scarred cheek. 'Instead of moaning why don't they just end it all-'

'Why don't you just calm the hell down?'

Stop pushing your luck, David-

'I'm not pissed off!' Aaron insisted. 'I'm just passionate for something I never had. How can I truly miss what I've never had? I see people end it all for nothing!' he added, bringing a fist down onto the dash board, the plastic shook with the impact.

'Hey hey hey! I thought I said calm the hell down, man!' Reed scolded. 'Let's face it, shall we? If we all gave up the grave yards would burst at the seams.'

Why are you taunting him, David? This isn't a bloody game!

Reed breathed slowly, stars appearing before his eyes.

If you keep this up, there's no telling who he'll take his anger out on . . .

He nodded imperceptibly.

By pretending Aaron's talking out of his arse, you think this will all go away . . . What if it's real? What if he's telling you the God damned truth? But you'll never learn, will you? Go ahead . . .

'Let's just drop the whole thing, Aaron,' he said steadily, taking a deep breath. 'Enough, I understand what you're trying to say. I hear it loud and clear. Life's precious, I hear you. But you can't control another person, can you?'

The ghost squinted in the gloom, his green eyes mere slits now as a ray of golden sunlight cut across his face. His once tenebrous pallor seemed less anaemic, thought Reed, which only heightened his apprehension-

He's flesh and bone, David! God, when are you going to realize?

'It's possible,' replied Aaron. 'You just have to know where to push, that's all.'

'Are you serious?

'Do you envy me, David?'

'Don't bother answering my last question, mate,' replied Reed, his smile returning with a vengeance. 'I already know the answer!'

'You wish you were like me-'

'Oh, yes,' said Reed mockingly, 'I'm busted, you got me. Boy, how it would be great to be you right now.'

Tension seemed to build in the atmosphere. Reed could feel the oppressive silence place its hands about his neck; squeezing slowly.

'You envy me . . . us . . . because you presume we have not a care in the world. You said so yourself not ten minutes ago. We come and go as we please, and we've gone through the painful exit, that point of no return, as it were. You want out, the lot of you. But believe me, we want back in. You lot bitch and moan but lack the balls to end it all by your own hand. If the dead took the place of the living, then you'd be in trouble, my friend. We don't want to be there. I don't think Tabby and Paul would like it over there-'

'That's it, Aaron!' Reed snapped. 'Don't you dare bring them into it, understand me? I said: do you understand-'

'Yes, yes, yes,' the ghost hissed under his breath before clearing his throat. 'I'm sorry, David. The problem is: *I* envy *you*.'

'And how's that a problem?' David wanted to know. 'Envy, I can sympathize with; but a problem?'

'The problem is that I'm not the only one-'

'Start making sense, for fuck's sake!'

'We're coming back . . . We're *all* coming back.'

Today I watched my dad cry for the second time. The first time was when they found my mutilated corpse.

If it's one thing we're good at and that's watching.

What else can we do?

A lot . . . It took me such a long time to figure that out.

Back to my dad: I wasn't aware that the bloke had tear ducts! I had many a time been on the receiving end of one of his shovel-like hands, I can tell you! That was back in the day when you could raise a hand to your own kids without fear of a little visit from some unsympathetic, and childless I hasten to add, shit-stuffed suit pretending to be a social worker! After a bit of a knock he'd tell mum that it never did *him* any harm and that would be the end of it. And I suppose he had been right. I think the word is stalwart; a strange word if ever there was one, but that's how I would have described him. Being so hard working was probably the end of him and mum. After a short time at the Steelworks he joined the Police force, worked his way up. In fact the higher he crawled up that bloody ladder the further he moved out of sight.

'Don't turn this into summat bigger than what it is, hun,' I remember dad grumble, a cigarette dangling from the corner of his mouth, wisps of blue smoke closing his right eye as he twiddled with his tie in front of the living room mirror. 'Just be grateful it's plods like me who give a tuppence.'

Mum didn't like dad smoking, it's was what caught up with her dad and it would take her second husband too; but not dad. I don't think he even had the cancer gene, that one. It was the middle of a particularly stormy night, dad had been called out,

199

and she just wanted to climb back into bed. Her curlers were pulled to one side and there was a smidgen of cream on her hollow cheek. I suspect that the rest would be on her pillow.

'You know how I feel, Harold', she replied wearily, carrying the empty coffee cups over to the small kitchenette in the corner of the room. She wanted to get back to dreaming about owning their own little pile of bricks and mortar. 'You just do what y' have to and get back in one piece,' she added, walking passed me in the tiny excuse of a living room.

She didn't see me.

Nobody can see me.

'I'll be back as soon as I can, hun,' he pecked mum on the cheek and stood for a second, about to say something more. I know what he was about to say; it was the usual. But this time dad refrained, grabbed his coat from the nail on the back of the door, and left the room. I stood beside mum, listening to his heavy footfalls gallop down the bare wooden stairs. Mum sighed heavily and locked the door, the key scraping loudly in the silence of the hour. She mumbled dad's last words.

A tear trickled down her cheek as she slowly made her way to the window.

'Maybe tonight, my love. Maybe tonight we'll find him,' she said, pulling the curtain aside to gaze down at the street lights. Dad's tall figure cut through the pool of light, and for a moment mum held her breath as though he were about to turn and look up at her, nod, salute, even just a wave to let her know that all was well . . .

It was the longest night of her life.

Watching my dad cry made me realize just how fragile we really are. Seeing him break a second time confirmed that realization. He wasn't made of concrete and metal, like I always imagined him to be. I guess all nine year olds thought the same of their fathers. But when you were running with the devil the devil kept up. Sometimes he'd let you get ahead, let you think you had the advantage, heck, even let you think you had a chance. But he wasn't called the Father of lies for nothing . . .

That damned phone call.

'Don't answer it,' mum said groggily. 'It's the middle of the night.'

But dad had already jumped out of bed, the receiver in his hands. He growled a few words then hung up the telephone. Within ten minutes the coffee was bubbling and the lights were shining. And now mum's head was on the pillow, the covers still warm, even warmer on dad's side, I thought, lying down on the bed beside her. She grabbed his pillow and inhaled the stain of his aftershave. Her hands passed right through me, but I didn't mind. I had gotten used to it.

Then I felt sick to the stomach, why? I will never quite understand. But I knew that I couldn't spend the night here when my dad was outside in the rain looking for the one person who had haunted his dreams for over ten years. I needed to be there, in the darkness, by his side, trying to touch his hand, his broad shoulders, be there when he broke down . . .

Tonight my father found the man who murdered me.

Everyone knew just what kind of man Robby Kirkland was. Everyone had their suspicions, yet the right to cast aspersions was about as productive as playground whispers. All monsters were protected, human and otherwise. As though he was some kind of endangered species his home had been re enforced with toughened glass windows and high, burglar greased perimeter walls. He was free to bloody come and go, move around amongst his prey and feed when the time was right and a child let down his/her guard. And nobody could do a thing to stop him, such had the world changed.

But this particular night, Kirkland had been careless.

Dad had been alerted by a neighbour to Kirkland's abode, complaining of disturbing noises coming from the house.

'Sounds like a child crying,' the caller had explained. 'I've never liked that pile of muck anyway . . . but I just hope it's not what I fear the most.'

A number of VHS tapes had been seized from Kirkland's bedroom.

It included the movie he made of him raping and killing me. He was enjoying the final scene when my dad burst into his house . . .

I couldn't look when Dad fell to his knees crying in front of the TV screen. For a decade he'd tortured himself wanting to know how I'd spent my last hour, hoping and praying it had been painless and quick . . . And now he knew.

That was the second time he cried.

Kirkland's free to roam the streets once more.
A new home, new identity . . .
But I know who he is.
I know where he lives.

It took ten long years for the light to come shining through the darkness, a pale, beautiful face peeping out at me through the café's steamy window.

But I now know what I have to do.

She gave me hope and I won't let her down.

My name is Alfie Lister and I was nine years old when I had my life taken from me.
The boy is just like me, and he's taking his life back too.
But not yet . . .
Right now I'm needed elsewhere.

47

Despite their tiredness and fresh bruises, the clouds continued to sail slowly across the sky, dragging a thick veil across a waxing moon. The ground was doused with darkness a moment before the moon appeared once more, as though invigorated and ready to paint everything silver. The wind had picked up, thought Reed, turning up his collar whilst trying to ring Tabby. But the damned thing couldn't get a signal.

Now they had arrived in Middlesbrough, Reed, his back aching from the unforgiving road had stopped to stretch his legs in a large car park. Barring the occasional shop worker weaving intermittently between the scattered cars, puffing on a cigarette here and struggling with a tie there, the shopping centre was desolate. He had almost forgotten how it felt to be alone. And now, standing in the cold breeze he was grateful of the peace and quiet. It made him remember one of the reasons he enjoyed his job: the solitude. When he needed to get away from the hustle and bustle of family life, when Tabby's voice grated on him and the arguments became fever pitch, all he needed was the open road, a carton of cigarettes and a route.

But now was not one of those times.

What he would give to be in her arms-

'Can't we hurry things up apace?' shouted Aaron from the cab close by. 'It's just after seven o'clock and we're almost there-'

'Never mind: hurry up!' snapped Reed, glancing over his shoulder. 'I'll get back when—Tabby?'

'Dav—asss,-' came the voice from the mobile, squealing like a strangled cat.

'FUCK!' Reed shouted, wanting to smash the phone onto the road, grind it into pieces beneath his boot. 'Still no signal . . .'

'Try again after,' Aaron replied.

Don't even bother asking what he means, David . . . Just don't

Reed dropped his phone back in his pocket and made his way slowly back to the lorry.

He's in the cab and you're outside, David . . . Now's your chance to run! Get as much distance between the both of you-

Reed shrugged off the thought like an uncomfortable overcoat.

You're right . . . he'll find you no matter where you go-

'You can call home later, David,' said Aaron, watching the other man climb into his seat. 'But right now I want you to listen to something.'

He turned on the radio and twisted the tuning dial, filling the small confines of the vehicle with ear-splitting white noise and static before a voice sounded. It was warped, tinny and sexless at first then, as Aaron persisted turning the dial a fraction at a time, the smoky female voice rung out as clear as a bell.

'. . . Clothing was wrapped about the drowned man as Cleveland police carried him to safety on to the beach. Witnesses claimed to have seen the man, believed to be in his early thirties and of strong constitution, swimming alone nearby. The sea was calm, said one bystander to the tragedy. The man could've suffered a cramp and lost control. Another Seaton resident claims that there had been another person there with him . . . a small child of around eleven years of age and of slight build which made sense when the clothing was carefully removed from the swimmer's body later at Hartlepool Hospital . . . additional life guards have been employed to safe guard the beach, which is usually unmanned at this time of-'

Aaron turned the dial once more, shattering the still with further screams of static; all the while he shook his head, chuckling. 'Fran Shepard, you sly bastard. I guess I won't be seeing you for a while.'

Reed turned to face the ghost, staring quizzically at his scarred countenance and green eyes which had redeemed some of their former brightness. He winced as Aaron slowly turned the dial, searching for more voices on the airwaves, but the static seemed to get louder.

'For heaven's sake, Aaron-'

'There we go,' said the ghost triumphantly as he found another station through the stormy airwaves.

'. . . Blood was found surrounding the broken window, but when the police services reached the scene, only the disemboweled remains of what appear to be two male pit bull terriers lay nearby. There was no little girl being savaged, as previously thought by nearby residents who immediately alerted Cleveland Ambulance services. Paramedic, Caroline Hodgson, described the scene as utter carnage, the animal was completely torn apart by broken glass as though the poor thing had been viciously assaulted . . .'

'Nice one, Sarah,' said Aaron. 'No one will set their dogs on you now, sweetheart.'

'What's going on, Aaron?' said Reed. 'Who the hell's Fran and Sarah?'

'She's the girl I was telling you about, remember? The girl who was mauled . . . never mind,' the ghost replied, turning the dial on the radio.

'Don't . . . I've heard enough-'

'. . . couldn't imagine what those parents must be feeling right now, said a close friend of the Watson family. They had heard the sound of the screams at around four thirty in the morning as they arose for work. There were bright flashes, like fire works, they said. Then the scream rung out, cut short in a second. They broke down the door and found the twin girls huddled together under the stairs . . .'

'I'm going to miss those two,' said Aaron, a tear in his eyes. He switched off the radio, the air buzzing with silence. 'Good on them, I say.'

'Are they . . .' Reed let his words trail away.

The ghost didn't need to nod, didn't have to say a word.

'They've come to take their lives back?' Reed wanted to know. 'They were all hurt . . . like you . . .'

Aaron nodded then swallowed hard.

'Christine told me something that maybe she should've kept to her chest. Bloody woman! The motherly instinct—I don't know! It could stop a train if one came hurtling towards it. It was her only way of a reunion with her babies-'

'So, why shouldn't she have told you? I mean-'

'We want to live—we deserve to live,' he replied finally. 'Is that too much to ask? Twenty years, Christ! What would you do, David? I'm going to live my life over again. There's not a great deal of it left-'

'Then what? I mean-'

'Then we're all ghosts,' he replied as calmly as discussing the weather. 'The window will close . . .'

'Did you tell someone about this?'

Aaron shook his head. 'I think someone over heard us talking in the café that day. And . . . before you know it word got around. I told you, people from miles around came to the café, wanting to know more about what's to happen in the future. And Christine, being the girl she is, she told them what's to befall the living. It was just a pity a guy like me took her seriously. I got away when a few other, shall we say, unsavoury friends were left wandering the darkness . . . Look, we've all got our little plans which we intend to see through to the end.'

No matter who gets hurt in the process, am I right, Aaron?

Reed shrugged off the thought like a damp coat, grateful to be rid of it.

'So how come you knew the name of the victims?' said Reed.

'How many little girls do you know that's been set upon by two pit bulls—If you're trying to catch me out here, mate, it's not going to work. Word got around. And believe me, 'cause I'm proof, that when the dead see an opportunity, a chink in the curtain, a gap in the armour—you fucking name it—we take advantage of it.'

He's lying, David . . . It's his way of getting you right where he wants you-

'How come I've not read up on any of this?' asked Reed, smiling nervously. 'Surely I would've read about it somewhere.'

'Do you believe everything you read?' Aaron replied flatly.

Silence.

The ghost closed his eyes and inhaled deeply, his nostrils flaring as he turned towards the open window. 'You can't beat the smell of good old fresh air, even if it is from Middlesbrough.'

'What happened to the ones they, you know . . . haunted? I mean I'm assuming they're like you, right?-'

'That's not important right now,' said Aaron, fixing him with those piercingly green eyes once more. 'Understand?'

Reed stared ahead, feeling the skin crawl across his scalp. He nodded.

'Good,' replied the ghost smiling crookedly. 'Very good.'

Don't worry, David. Just humour him . . . When this is all over it'll be just like he never existed at all . . . You'll have your shot at redemption.

'Is it true?'

'That man kind is over in twenty years?'

Reed nodded, swallowing hard. The colour had drained away from his face, he could feel it.

'Let's put it one way,' Aaron said. 'The Bible spoke of a flood wiping the face of the earth of all its mistakes. The big guy wasn't talking about water.'

Reed shook his head, chuckling, welcoming the respite from the fear he felt inside. 'My dad used to slam the door in the face of people like you, Aaron. Come on! Flood?'

Aaron smiled, before biting down into his bottom lip. There came the tiniest popping sound as the punctured lip issued a dark red liquid.

48

I'LL BE HOME SOON. I LOVE U BOTH X ;)

Reed looked at the text message, his thumb hovering above the SEND button. There were so many things he wanted to tell Tabby. What he'd done—or rather what Aaron had committed the previous day. Granted Johnny couldn't plague their lives any more, for that he'll thank his stars, but he wondered if he should tell her just how he/they had dealt with him-

Stop those thoughts, David! Tabby doesn't need to know what happened to that sorry piece of shit! He's gone, everything else is just details; history-

He wanted to tell her he would be late home, that there was something he must do to repay a debt to his old 'imaginary' friend from his childhood that just so happened to hitch a ride-

Yes . . . that'll work, David. Are you insane? Well, after what you've been through nobody would fault you losing maybe one or two dozen marbles . . . Go right ahead.

He pressed SEND.

He squeezed the handset as though the action would somehow teleport his fears to her, not only the promise that all was going to work out fine, but also to alert the police—anyone that could help, but despair washed over him. The image of Gladstone, the blood, the carnage . . . those dead, staring eyes—God, what Aaron is capable of-

Just hold on . . . Hartlepool is not far away . . . You can do this.

'Are you ready?' asked Aaron, closing his eyes for a time before glancing in Reed's direction once more. The stars that once twinkled in his emerald eyes had died, and now his skin looked opaque, darkening the scars which crawled along his cheeks and forehead like dying scorpions.

Reed struggled to compose himself. His hands were shaking but his heartbeats seemed to slow apace as he breathed calmly. In through the nose out through the mouth-

He nodded.

'I'll do whatever it is you want me to,' he said, steadily, 'as long as I'm a free man when this is all over.'

'Are you sure you don't want to be friends?'

'Are you deaf as well as dead? You heard me, for fuck's sake!'

'Okay,' Aaron replied, a smile creasing his lips. 'Have it your way. It'll be like we had never met.'

Reed felt the goose bumps cross his flesh; the news readers shocked voice, how they had described the disemboweled dog, reverberating in his head; God, how the image turned his stomach! It shook him even more than witnessing Gladstone's demise, if that was at all possible? But it prompted the question that sent his mind reeling with despair.

'Just how many of them . . . are there? Of your kind, I mean-'

'I'd say around forty seven,' replied Aaron, casually, curling his bottom lip. 'Give or take one or two. But that was some time ago now. Hell, now there could be a lot more of them out there. Why? You only have me to contend with,' he chuckled. 'They'll get dragged out of the shit.'

An awkward silence prized them apart like two cage fighters, but only for a couple of seconds before they were back at each others throats.

'Did they all have to say the names?'

Aaron frowned as though pondering the most difficult question ever posed. Then he smiled broadly, nodding. Either he had found the answer or the lie.

'That's just something we do, David. It's just a formality-'

'A formality? A formality to what?'

'It's just . . . It's . . . Do you remember that old movie, Dracula?'

'Yeah, but what the hell does that have to do with anything?' Reed wanted to know, his frustration growing.

'Well, remember how the blood sucker needed his victim's permission before crossing his home's threshold? You know . . . he can't get in the house unless invited? Well, it's a little like that, my friend. But it's not an invitation to walk around your house; I've been doing that for fucking years. It's . . . It's basically an act of admission. You see?'

Reed shook his head.

Aaron sighed then tried again to explain himself.

'When you say my name it makes everything real. You're admitting that I'm real.'

It's his way of controlling you, David.

'If I remember the story,' said Reed, 'giving Dracula permission rendered you powerless too. Is that what I've done, Aaron? Is helping you going to be the end of me?'

'Everyone's life is in their own hands-'

'Spare me the sermon. You want your life back,' replied Reed, smiling crookedly, unable to wake from the nightmare, or so it seemed. 'We're not so different, you and I.'

'It's universal,' said the ghost. 'It's called hope. I'm just telling you what I've observed, living beside you; sharing your ups and downs. We pray the sun will shine that little brighter tomorrow too—I have a fire inside, David. I'm going to get my life back . . .'

'Fire-'

'Maybe that's why we burn up so god damned easily,' Aaron interrupted. 'You know, when we come back?'

'Is there no other-'

'No,' Aaron insisted. 'There is no other way. The only way to turn back time-'

'Is that what we're about to do . . . turn back time?'

'I can't do this on my own. The only way to turn back time is to retrace your steps. But please don't let me down. You and Tabby have been like a family to me all these years.'

'Okay, I get your fucking point, Aaron,' Reed chided. 'You're sounding desperate and its churning my stomach—I understand, alright?'

Aaron nodded. 'There is one way I can repay you, my friend-'

'I . . . I just don't want anything from you,' replied Reed, trying to force a smile that would never come. 'Let's just put this all behind us so we can both get on with our lives.'

'No, I think you'll like this, David,' the ghost persisted. 'Just think I can make it so you will have never met me–'

'That sounds good to me, Aaron. You got Gladstone out of the way, and for that I'm grateful. And that's it. I go back, do what it is you need me to, then we part. That was the deal. No more favours—an end to the past—No, listen to me! Do you understand? We're *not* friends, never have been and we won't *ever* be in the future! That's the fucking deal! I've learned from my mistakes. I've messed about with my life but not any more. You've preached the preciousness of life. Well, respect my life. It's mine . . . I tried to put an end to you all those years ago, remember? Jesus, I lost count of the times I got up during the night, in all bloody weather, to steer you away from my house and send you on your way. But you were too, I don't know, stubborn to understand I didn't want or need you?'

The ghost turned his back on Reed like a spoilt child, and faced the window.

'Hey, don't ignore me.'

Jump out of the cab now, David! Now, while you still have the chance!

'So . . . we have a deal?' said Reed.

Aaron nodded, gazing out of the window.

'Have you really learned from your mistakes, David? Didn't you at least get a little turned on by the way your enemies cried when I held them down for you–'

'Do we have a deal?'

'Of course,' Aaron replied with an exaggerated sigh. 'I just hope you know what you're doing; for Tabby and Paul's sake as well as your own.'

'I don't need you,' replied Reed, quietly. 'We part, I go my way you go yours.'

Aaron nodded imperceptibly.

'Have it your way.'

Reed smiled broadly, raising his middle finger at the ghost's back.

'Don't worry, I will. Silverfield Avenue, here we come,' he replied somewhat jovially.

Reed turned the key in the ignition, and the engine awoke, coughing and spluttering like an old man for awhile before slowly pulling the lorry away from the side of the road.

'The end of the world in twenty years,' Reed chuckled. 'What a crock of shit!'

Now it was Aaron's turn to smile.

He watched the first specks of sleet hit the glass and traced it with a weary finger as it wriggled quickly down the pane.

49

The vehicle's suspension protested, squealing loudly as he pressed down on the brakes. Bludgeoned by fists of icy wind, the lorry swayed slightly. Sleet had turned to snow within an hour, the roads quickly becoming an ice rink. One moment the lorry had eased smoothly between the small toy-like cars along the road, their lights crystal clear as they passed, and the next Reed could barely move as large snow flakes crossed the windscreen, turning his whole world white. But now the lorry was parked by the side of the road he could relax for a while.

'Where the fuck did all this come from?' Reed commented, straining to see through the white curtains that had been drawn across his field of vision. He placed a hand over the dash board, but still felt a chill encase his entire body despite the hot air blowing out from the heater.

'It'll blow over,' replied Aaron, wriggling to get comfortable in his seat even though he hadn't moved for over an hour. 'It's a test, that's all.'

Reed winced at the sound of the ghost's crackling joints—how he hated that sound-of how it reminded him of his uncle Jack. The old bugger would snap his knuckles, twist his neck and waist. Just to make Reed's skin crawl. And it worked. And now he had arthritis; no surprise.

Don't let the weather dampen your spirits, David! Remember, it'll be over soon . . . Just think: Christmas is just around the corner, and this time you won't have to worry about a knock at the door-

Reed shook the thought away, eager now to crack a smile and pretend all was well and the snow was nothing.

'You're right,' he insisted, smiling broadly now. 'It's a test-' he felt something vibrate in his pocket and his eyes widened. 'Fuck!'

'Well, aren't you going to answer her, David? She'll be wondering what's happened to you,' Aaron mumbled, wiping his face with his dirty sleeves, blinking myopically at the view beyond the window. But through the thin veil of snow there was nothing remarkable except for the long row of houses, their front yards covered in a thick, untouched blanket of snow. He noticed the skeletal figure of a child's climbing frame; the swing at its centre was still, weighed down and frozen. He leaned forward to place his hands over the heater on the dash board, his knuckles crackling as he rubbed at the fingers to generate warmth there. That's when he noticed the large cluster of trees at the end of the road; they too stood skeletal, laden with a fine dusting of snow. But he thought nothing of it and sat back, getting comfortable once more. He closed his eyes.

'Tabby?' Reed shouted into the receiver. 'You're breaking up, sweetheart—I can't hear you . . . Yes . . . Yes, I know I should've been home hours ago—I-I know . . . Oh, and what did *he* have to say, then? Great, just fucking brilliant! Look . . . Tabby, I . . . will you let me explain? Jesus Christ! My battery's dying on me, besides—will you just bloody listen for a minute, please? Thank you . . . Look, there was a change of plan and I confess I couldn't finish the job, and yes, the last of the orders were—but Tabby, you have to understand—please, just listen! You have to understand me when I say that I did it for you and Paul . . . I can get another job when I get home, I don't care if Jay's pissed off. When I get home and tell you everything you won't give a shit either, I swear. I . . . because I can't tell you right now, that's why . . . When, most likely tomorrow . . . Tabby? Tabby?'

Reed stared at his phone and chuckled bitterly.

'Women, eh?' Aaron breathed. 'Can't live with 'em and it's almost impossible to hide their bodies-'

'She cut me off. Can you believe that?'

'Look, she'll understand, okay. Let it go, David.'

Reed lit a cigarette and closed his eyes as he drew deeply on the smoke, trying to calm his double base-drum of a heart. 'God, I hope so. I really do,' he replied wearily. 'Or all of this would have been for nothing.'

'Why aren't we moving?' Aaron said, groggily, sitting up straight in his seat.

Reed turned towards the ghost, and as the pale light from the snow across the lower half of the glass illuminated the interior of the cab, he almost shook at his ghastly appearance. Such dark, heavy bags hung below those piercing emerald eyes. The scars running across his face appeared deeper and somewhat fresh, as though Christine had spliced the raw flesh together the previous day; but not with cotton: with rope. A coarse, thick hemp that ravaged the pierced edges of the drawn flesh with the intention of keeping the whole mess together rather than fuse and seal the wounds. Then it occurred to him that maybe Aaron was right: Ghosts *are* closer to the living than he could ever imagine. They sleep, age, and certainly don't resemble Hollywood teenagers.

Is this evolution, David? Is this thing before you what we aspire to be or do we go kicking and screaming-

'We're here?'

'Yes,' Reed nodded, his breath escaping like a wisp of smoke. 'This is your precious Silverfield Avenue.'

50

'It isn't much to look at, is it?' said Reed, frowning. 'In fact I can't remember it *ever* being easy on the eye.'

'We're really here, Jesus!' Aaron gasped, sitting up rigidly, craning his neck out of the window, surveying the snow swept scenery before him. 'I . . . knew those bloody trees were familiar. The cars look a bit better though,' he quipped, viewing the large Land Rover and Porsche further along the side of the road. 'Christ, a hell of lot better.'

Reed didn't crack so much as a smile, but chewed his right thumbnail instead, watching thick snow flakes scatter across the windscreen. The shiny Porsche gracing the curbside was incongruous; not a common word in Reed's vocabulary, but it seemed to spring to his mind as he gazed at the row of terraced houses. One roof lacked a couple of slates, revealing a black triangle in the blanket of snow like a gap between two pearly white teeth. Another was missing a drain pipe entirely, a blackened butterfly shape tattooed in the pebble-dashed exterior wall. And Reed dreaded to think just how cold and damp it must be in the room beyond.

'Mr. Sporty's family will be paying that fucker off for him when he's six feet under, guaranteed.'

'Yeah,' said Aaron, nodding his head. 'Things haven't changed at all. Everyone's still living outside of their means.'

'Can't we just get this whole thing over with?' said Reed, running a hand across his cheek, hearing the rasp of his fingertips as they scraped along his bearded cheek. 'I'm struggling to remember Tabby's face for crying out loud-'

216

'Lighten up, man,' Aaron replied, wearily. 'Christ! There it is! You see it, David? There it is!'

Reed leaned forward in his seat and strained to see what was causing the ghost so much excitement. But then the air caught in his throat like a chicken bone. Pins and needles jabbed at his fingers and toes, tiny dots encircling his field of vision as though he had trapped a nerve somewhere and now he fought to move.

He nodded.

'I can't believe the bugger's still here. Can you?'

Reed slowly shook his head. 'No . . . I can't.'

The damned lamppost still stood as though sentinel at the end of the path.

'It's like a little lighthouse has guided us home,' said Aaron, a smile creasing his lips. But the humour failed to reach his tired eyes, noticed Reed.

'They should've ripped the thing out of the ground and concreted over it,' Reed replied bitterly.

But the ghost didn't comment any further, he was too busy looking at the trees beyond. Their ancient shadows that consumed him those years ago seemed darker than they had ever been. And as he stared at the skeletal limbs of the weathered trees he found-

'Have you ever stood in an art gallery, David?'

Reed nodded. 'Been a while . . . but I guess so. Why?'

'It felt a little weird just then,' Aaron replied slowly, shaking his head. 'It felt like standing before a really detailed painting, staring at as much as possible until the brush strokes start to move and swirl, draw you into its vortex like water down a plug hole-'

Reed sighed exaggeratedly, folding his arms.

Aaron grinned.

'I thought I saw them moving around back there, that's all.'

'Who are "them"?' said Reed. 'Don't tell me: the tree spirits that the hippy chick warbled on about the other day.'

'You mean the girl on her way to the other tree huggers? You mean Charlie? What a blonde, eh?'

Reed glanced over at the ghost.

'Well, don't you worry about that feisty little one, David,' said Aaron distractedly. 'The arseholes who killed her will need a lot more than the tree spirits to make it through the night. In fact, I bet the police are scraping their bits and pieces off of the ground as we speak.'

Reed closed his eyes and pinched the bridge of his nose with his right thumb and fore finger. 'Great. So she had been the one I'd read about in the papers last year . . . She was a ghost all along . . . Now why doesn't that fucking surprise me, Aaron?'

'Hey, that's what life's all about, isn't it? Mystery, revelation-'

'How can I know who's dead and who's not?'

Aaron shrugged.

'Who cares? Pretty soon you won't be able to move for the likes of me—there! Did you see that?' Aaron gasped, pointing towards the darkness of the trees.

Reed didn't speak; could barely breathe now as it seemed his whole world teetered on the brink of crumbling into dust around him. But first it was going to crush his brain, then his veins-

'Well, never mind, eh?' said Aaron.

Don't break, David! Don't let him get under your skin! Keep it together, man! It's his game—stop thinking "what if he's telling the truth?" He's lying to you and he's winning-

Reed shook his head.

'Takes you back, doesn't it,' said Aaron, suddenly turning to face Reed, his eyes a bright emerald, shining. He placed a hand on Reed's knee, gripping tightly. But there was no time to protest; Reed was too busy trying to wrestle off the black veil that now covered his face.

51

Reed heard the rain punch the window, felt it kick the roof.

'What's happening?' Reed whispered, suddenly sitting bolt upright in his bed, but his voice seemed muffled as though his entire face hid beneath a coating of thick ribbon. His throat was dry and there lingered a metallic taste on his tongue no matter how hard he tried to generate saliva. He squinted at the bright television screen at the foot of his bed as it hissed with white hot static.

There came a sharp scratching noise. It came from the window, and as he slowly pulled the duvet aside, he was overcome with a sense of familiarity. So many times had he stepped out of the warmth of his bed and crossed the room, his heartbeat getting faster with each step; even though he knew what was waiting for him beyond the glass. But wasn't that a kind of madness in itself, he wondered; repeating the same action over and over, expecting a different outcome?

With his eyes closed, so as not to break his night vision completely, he switched the television off. Static crackled, and as he opened his eyes once more, he could see tiny sparkles of electricity cross the screen-

The sharp scratching noise shook him like two rough hands and he slowly made his way towards the window. He could have been blindfolded and would have found his way. He even edged around the small, knee high games table beside his book shelf. Anyone unfamiliar with his room would have shinned his or herself and woke the entire house hold.

Reed looked outside.

The torn face stared back at him.

Of all the occasions he had gazed into that dreaded face and stood stock still without so much as flinching, this time he screamed-

Reed shook his head now as if to shrug off the memory once and for all. Beside him sat Aaron, smiling.

'What the fuck just happened?' said Reed, his voice shaking with adrenaline, lips quivering.

'Knowledge, my friend,' said Aaron softly. 'Did you notice how things were different when you went to the window? Didn't you feel this way all those years ago? I mean, come on! A young boy waking up in the midnight hour to usher away a dead body from his bed room window, and *now* you decide to be afraid?'

'Just tell me what I have to do, okay?' said Reed, grabbing a cigarette from the dwindling pack on the dash board, then lit up. He stared fixedly ahead, as still as stone. But inside he quaked with fear. He didn't dare show it. He probably didn't even need to.

'You weren't afraid of me all those years ago, David,' whispered Aaron. 'So why are you now?'

Reed drew deeply on his cigarette before engaging his mind, letting the bastard's words turn over and over before verbalizing the truth.

'Simple. Something you will never understand, Aaron. Something you can never have or appreciate,' replied Reed, a smile creasing his lips. 'I have a wife and son.'

The ghost nodded imperceptibly, a knot of muscles tightened below his pale jaw. He was the first to break eye contact.

'Let's go for a walk.'

From the moment I laid eyes upon her I knew . . . I just knew that she was the one.

Such a befitting opening line for a thousand love stories!

But that is precisely how it started.

Not a day went by when I didn't think of her.

I knew that she was danger personified—hell, she should have come with a health warning! But I didn't heed the warnings. I just placed my hands over my ears to drown out the sound of alarms ringing, even though they grew louder by the day, by the hour.

Conscience.

Fuck you!

I just thought it would be easier listening to my heart. After all, it's written in all the great love songs, is it not?

I didn't care what it would do to my marriage. That was safe. The certificate was safely tucked in a drawer, stuffed between old coffee table magazines and bill receipts. That's what it amounted to . . . Am I right? a fucking piece of nicely printed paper? Anyway . . . It was going absolutely nowhere. But wasn't this sacrilege? Wasn't I breaking a bond made before the Lord's altar? Being a devout Christian, such a thought should've been deterrent enough, but I knew that the feelings that once triggered my heart to the point of bursting would not slow, like it had not more than twenty four hours following my wedding. And even as I watched the waves disappear on the horizon as we sailed away to sunnier climes, the taste of marzipan on our lips and tiny flakes of confetti in our hair, I knew it had been a mistake. We had exchanged souls in a contract; legally bound, packaged and sent on our way into the big bad world to forever regret what we did-

No . . . this was the real thing.

She was everything to me and she knew it; drew on my weaknesses like a parasite and I was powerless to resist. As she grew stronger, healthier, I got weaker; in body and soul. I stopped eating to make my body just the way she wanted it. I doubled my cigarette habit to kill my appetite. Raised my shirt in the mirror to see the six-pack she wanted from me, despite my deathly palour. I burned so many calories away in the gymnasium, the boxing ring, the swimming pool, the weight watcher meetings, I was becoming a shadow. Stephen wanted to know what had gotten into me, telling me how he loved my bumps and curves just the way they were . . . but it only made me want to burn more fat away . . . set myself on fire for the sheer love, the desire to strip away the imperfections that had burdened me for so long.

I was dying but it kept her alive. I hated every part of me, what I had become. Yet, being a slave to another gave me a sense of purpose. It simply gave her the ammunition and prepared her for our meetings.

Oh how she could work her weaponry, be it barbed wire, a hard plastic cock, or sharp stud-covered leather . . . Sometimes it was nakedness, an old coat, just skin beneath and nothing else to get in the way . . .

We could be animals if we so wished. What was stopping us?

I could run naked in the darkest, smallest of hours with the best of them, I thought . . . We had covered many a mile through rain slicked streets, slapping car bonnets to shatter the stillness with their alarms, giggling, ignoring the pain of our bare breasts as they moved to the curve of our bodies.

For the first time in years I felt free.

Nothing seemed to matter except for how she made me feel.

She stood at my threshold, before my heart, raised her left eye brow knowingly, seductively, and that was her key . . . I gave her permission to cross the line-

Hold on one minute! Wasn't this an unwritten contract? Granted it lacked the bells and whistles, waistcoats, formalities and fakery, but I was letting my guard slip like I had-

ENOUGH!

Drunk on her perfume and weakened into submission by her promises of intimacy the likes of which I would never find scribbled in the contract of any marriage certificate, I actually believed . . . actually trusted in the instincts my Christian bastard God had given me. I soon realized that even the heart liked to play games; with the mind, the soul, dreams and nightmares . . .

I watched her every move. The curve of her body . . . the serpentine sleekness of her hips, the way her eyes changed colour to match her moods; nothing supernatural, just exquisitely subtle changes. When her smile broadened and her lips were close enough for me to kiss, the deep blue of her eyes would darken to a royal blue, virtually black; Black and mysterious. It was almost as though she had become an entirely different person.

In point of fact, she had.

The church had taught me to beware even the sweetest intensions, see behind the words of love, creep passed the guardian of the heart, to read between the lies of men, but those teachings were left behind at the threshold of the house we had built about ourselves.

By day I walked in a dream/spoke to ghosts/lived/existed/ moved/inhaled/exhaled/ate/drank/fucked when beckoned/opened my holes for the fucking/begged for mercy and bled-

That's when she wanted to play . . .

But when my knees faltered she would pull away just in time. When the blood pearls appeared and the tear broke from the corner of my eye, she'd take the knife away, or the dildo from my torn arsehole. After all there were so many games left to play and she was far from done with her toy.

I told Stephen I loved him before turning out the light, quickly sliding between the silk sheets. Those three words meant absolutely nothing now-

Why did someone have to invade another's life, turn it upside down and inside out? Why? Life had been so simple and safe—yes, okay, it was safe . . . there was nothing the matter with that! I came home from work, tidied the house, washed the dishes from the previous night; checked the mail, ironed Stephen's shirts, put the casserole in the oven . . .

I froze.

I needed her.

I really needed her like nothing before.

That's when she wanted me, when I was at my most vulnerable. And she seemed to know the right time. Not when I was happy and full of the joy that Stephen brought to my life, for I won't lie: there were happy times. It was in the small hours that I received the text messages. She'd tell me what to do to myself, what she was doing to herself as we spoke. What others were doing to her at that very moment; the weapons they wore, pushed inside of her; bound by silence. It was as though she could see me in the darkness, describing how I felt, how she wanted me to feel . . .

Down the stairs I'd walk, barefoot, naked . . . just the way she wanted me; as instructed. My phone was in my hand, against my cheek, its coldness to my ear; hands shaking with anticipation. My mind wondering how her voice could command a human body to bend to her will. And she would whisper, her voice coming in hoarse gasps . . . I knew what she was doing to herself and she knew what it was doing to me.

My feet slapped noisily on the cold linoleum in the kitchen, my flesh hard with goose bumps, my eyes attuned to the whereabouts of every single appliance, as though I could see in the black. I wrestled with her voice, her demands in my head . . . I needed time to think, I'd reply. She had to give me time . . .

No, she'd whisper. If she gave me that then nothing would happen.

There was a time for everything.

Now was not the time to feel or think.

I did as instructed.

I took the sharpest knife in the drawer and made my way back upstairs.

I wondered what she saw in me. I wasn't something to look at. In fact I couldn't quite fathom what Stephen sensed in me either. Here I was, a twenty eight year old mathematician teaching secondary school kids their times tables, dying my roots every couple of weeks from grey to brown; folded weight-watcher pamphlets tucked away in my purse, the promise of change always on my mind; the elusive new year resolution. I just can't understand the blindness of love, provided that was what it was. But life was short and she often told me her take on equations; something I prided myself in knowing quite a bit about. We'd chat over the internet or even meet in cafeterias, always hidden in the farthest booth away from prying eyes. She gave me strict instructions as to the topic of conversation. Each day it would change. But this one particular day it had been equations. To the layman nothing made sense, we spoke in numbers and her shoes had fallen away, her feet slowly stroking my inner thighs. I reached down and held her foot with both hands, caressing her toes, pulling my panties to one side so the digits could know me more intimately. The numbers were harder to understand, the mathematics more complex as her toes fucked deeper into my pussy.

She didn't care that I was melting in my seat.

She didn't care that a bunch of kids sat eating burgers in the booth opposite, probably eavesdropping our every word.

She didn't care about drawing blood with her sharp toenails.

She cared about come, nothing more and nothing less. Whether it was inside her cunt, over her face, arsehole or breasts, it didn't matter.

'That's where life begins for some and ends for others,' she'd once said, her toes working their magic, 'a frivolous disregard for human life; every drop a million children. Sex is murder for pleasure . . . don't you agree?'

'You spoke of equations?' I said, heart beating quicker as her toes delved deeper and faster.

She nodded, curling her top lip, eyes sharp slits, her foot pushing harder against my pussy.

And Stephen had to be cut away from that equation, she told me.

That's when I came.

I made my way through the room, doused by blackness. Not even the moon light lancing through a chink in the curtain illuminated my sweat-slicked body. It glanced across the knife edge though. I dropped the phone and held the knife in both hands, holding it above my head-

What on earth was I doing?

She had me enthralled. I needed her. I would do anything for her-

That's when the lights came on and the figure burst from the wardrobe.

Stephen sat up straight in bed, smiling as she took the knife from my hand.

I begged them, pleaded to know what was going on.

But I should've known.

She wasn't in love with me. It was Stephen that she desired!

My husband of eight years kept smiling, even when the woman I thought I loved turned the blade on me.

My name is Rebecca Runer, you know how old I was when my life was taken from me. I'm not in the habit of repeating myself.

I followed, listened and trusted my heart . . .

Such a fool I had been.

She took my life . . .

Now I'm taking it back.

There's only one woman I can trust now. And I have a feeling that I'm not alone.

She was there for me. And I'll be there for her . . .

52

'I told you this was the only way!' shouted Aaron, grabbing Reed's forearm in a vice-like grip. 'Don't walk away from me, David. I'm warning you-'

Reed flinched, expecting the onslaught of a hundred bloody memories to come flooding back to him, converge upon him like stock cars, without a care of the consequences, but he only felt his skin tighten beneath the ghost's cold fingers.

'You promised me.'

Reed shook his head defiantly. 'I can't remember promising you a fucking thing. This is just one bloody revelation after another, isn't it?'

A car passed slowly by, tyres cutting through the sludge in the gutter, its driver frowning at the crazy man arguing with himself. Reed gave him the one fingered salute.

'You must do it, David,' said Aaron, pleadingly, his grip relaxing on his forearm. He quickly surveyed the street to make sure no one was watching now, then actually whispered: 'You know that . . . I'll . . . I'll die if you don't.'

Reed shook his head in disbelief, but before he could utter a word, the ghost tried to push a small object into the palm of his hand. But it fell to the ground.

Aaron bent down to pick up the box of matches, the sound of his crackling joints cut through Reed's nerves as though he was tied up in front of a large school chalk board and the ghost was playfully dragging his fingernails down its surface.

'Here,' he said finally, placing the box in Reed's hand. 'Just take the damn things.'

'I . . . I don't like this, Aaron. I swear to God that I don't,' replied Reed quietly, turning the box over in his hands, hearing the tiny rattle of its contents. 'I mean, what if I hurt somebody? What if they-'

'What if, what if, what if? You can't go on forever thinking that way!' Aaron snapped, closing his eyes a moment as though his anger would boil and bubble over and out from between his eyelids. 'We'll just have to be extra careful then, won't we? Besides, if, and it's a big bloody if, it happens . . . then tough. What's one life? I mean, whatever happens here—look, are we going to dwell on the what ifs? For fuck's sake, where are your balls, man!'

'Balls?' Reed spat. 'I'd understand if this was funny, but it's not!' he lowered his voice. 'You're asking me to . . . Is this it?'

Aaron nodded, kneeling down in the snow.

The trees on the corner of Silverfield Avenue were skeletal and leaned to one side as though weighed down by the very oppressive silence on this wintry morning. No birds twittered or stretched their wings high up above. A delicate dusting of sleet fell across the ground before them like blessed offerings to some twisted deity. The blood beating in their ears was the only sound shattering the stillness.

'This is where they threw me from the car,' said Aaron. With shaking hands he brushed aside the crisp white snow to reveal the thick mud beneath. Before the next beat he had pierced the earth with his tired fingers, pushing them as far into the soil as they would allow.

'Are you alright?' whispered Reed, placing a hand on the ghost's shoulder before quickly pulling it away as though it had brushed hot coals. But in fact he had been shocked by the coldness of the other man. He bit his bottom lip, regretting what he was about to say-

It's the only way, David. You know that it's the way back to your own life. Tabby . . . Paul . . .

'How far away are we from your house?'

'Like I said,' replied Aaron flatly, shaking the soil from his fingertips, wiping his hands of the earth and its memories for good it seemed. 'It's a couple of mile up the road.'

'So we still have a bit of a trek ahead?' Reed uttered wearily.

Aaron snorted, watching his breath encircle his face like a poisonous gas in the icy air. 'No. We don't have to go very far at all to get this little show on the road. They killed me in a fire then scattered me here,' he added bitterly, looking down at the ground once more.

'I don't know what you mean-'

'All we need is right here.'

53

'You mean . . . now?' Reed stammered. He looked down at the box of matches before surveying the quiet avenue about them. 'Here? I mean, I thought we had to return to the place where, you know . . .'

Aaron shook his head.

'No, David . . . Like I said: this is where they dumped me. It's where it all truly ended for me. But I died in flames. Light one and save me from it. It's as simple as that.'

Reed pocketed the matches and stepped slowly, tentatively across the snow covered ground before him as though doing so would prevent leaving evidence that he had ever been here. Despite the cold, he felt the unmistakable tickling sensation of hot sweat as it wriggled down his back, raising the hairs across his scalp, pasting his shirt to his skin.

'I really can't do this, Aaron,' Reed admitted. He wanted to fall to his knees in supplication, beg for some reprieve, a way out of this insanity. Tears welled in his eyes and he could already feel the cracks beneath his skin travel across his entire frame. It would be a short while, imminent in fact, before his nerves left him entirely. 'What if . . .'

You're a bloody wreck, David! He's beating you. Don't you see? You're his puppet . . . always have been. He's pulling the strings right now and you're letting him. Come on! Grow a spine! When this is all over it will be as though he had never existed at all-

'What if?' the ghost whispered, baring his teeth in a maniacal sneer which bordered upon feral, the emerald of his eyes gleamed brighter than ever as though etched with delicate strokes of silver and gold. 'I'm not in the habit of repeating myself, David. But that's all I seem to do with you, don't I?' He suddenly rose to his feet and, in less than a second, closed the gap between them.

Reed remained steadfast, aware of the jack-hammering of his heart, as the ghost's eyes fixed upon his own, their noses mere inches apart. The hardness of the face's contours appeared sharper and terrifying in their clarity. Reed resisted the urge to reach out and touch the ghost's scarred cheek; just to confirm the reality of his predicament. He caught the vapour of the other's breath, almost tasted something akin to death itself, if there was such a taste. His tongue seemed to retract, pull itself away from the front row of teeth, almost like a cowering animal in mortal fear, pulling itself down its own throat . . . But he forced it back to the front.

'Then the cycle will never end, will it?' Reed said, almost shaking his head with disbelief. 'Can't you see what you're doing? Are all of you so fucking oblivious-'

'I don't know what you're inferring.'

'Fuck right off! You know exactly what I'm saying, Aaron!'

'Look, are we going to dwell on the what-ifs? This is how you 'living' ones go on day in day out, wasting the precious hours-'

'Then why be one of us?'

The wraith bit his bottom lip, speechless. Yet he maintained eye contact.

'That's new, David,' he said softly, nodding imperceptibly. Colour, like blood, spread through the pale surface of his flesh, but only for a split second. 'I think I can speak for the others too when I say that I don't want to waste what little time there is left . . . don't you?'

'You're asking me to set fire to a house,' said Reed, not caring who might be watching. 'And you expect me not to give a shit? You want to know something? You really don't care, do you? You just get what you want regardless of who you hurt in the process.' Reed turned away and stumbled on a slippery patch of muddy snow. He found the nearest tree and leant against its cold, rough bark. He felt earthed, grounded, his feet on solid ground and so many other clichés. But it reminded him of his chat with Charlie; of how he had slapped the steering wheel to demonstrate just what he believed in-

Aaron moved quickly, grabbing Reed's collar with both screwed up fists.

'The longer you talk, piss n' moan,' the ghost spat, his voice shattering the quietness of the sleepy street. 'Well . . . the longer I have to wait-'

What did I tell you, David?

'Remember, I have the patience of a saint-'

I told you he would haunt you like never before.

'I've waited this long for you to start believing in me,' said Aaron, finally, releasing the other man's collar. Reed almost staggered off balance, his back hitting the tree once more. 'You know I can wait a little bit longer. Care to try me? There's still a lot to be had of twenty years . . . so much I can use.'

Reed needed no convincing of the ghost's malicious intent should he not get his own way. It shone in his eyes. And if they truly were the windows of the soul, then he no longer dared gaze into their depths should he see-

'Choose one and let's get it over with.'

'And that's where it'll begin.'

'What will begin?'

'The dreams,' replied Reed.

'The guilt, you mean?' Aaron sneered. 'Did my fucking mother and her bit of rough tear their hair out with guilt when they threw my body from the car?'

Silence separated them like reason between burnt lovers.

Aaron smiled crookedly.

'I don't care if another home is in its place. Hell, I couldn't care less if it is a fucking primary school let alone a bungalow occupied by a little old couple settling into sixty years of marriage—I don't bloody care! It means absolutely nothing to me. Understand?'

The small cluster of trees swallowed shadows whole; drew them in like a star-hungry black hole. Reed wished he could disappear also, just rush head-long into the sanctuary of the darkness and never-

And leave Tabby and Paul to put up with this unforgiving bastard for the rest of their lives, David? If what he said was true and time was short for mankind, would you have their last remaining years ruined at the hands of this piece of shit?

Reed glanced over at the row of houses, exquisitely renovated from the dilapidated shit-holes he remembered from an age long dead. The sun blinked occasionally from between bruised clouds, flashing across the double glazed window panes. Hungry solar-powered panels gazed skyward from snow covered roof tops. A skateboard lay on its side at the side of the road, choking the gutter, creating a small dam of dark leaves and muddy rain water. He remembered the winter when this road split in two. Some called it a small earthquake but the sewers had broke due to flooding. The tarmac looked almost freshly laid, he thought, returning his attention to the windows of the surrounding houses. Not a curtain twitched or blind moved. Searching for signs of life was eating his time.

'What if somebody sees me?' he asked finally.

Aaron smiled.

He knows you're going to do it, David . . . And now he's resting in the knowledge that his life will be returned to him, but what about your life? What happens when he has what he wants from you!

'Fuck you. Go away,' Reed whispered.

Reed shook the voice from his head. He didn't want to listen to reason any longer. He couldn't care less if he never heard that irritating sound again. But of course it would be back. And so would Aaron if he didn't put an end to this-

Reed jumped at the unmistakable sound of a door handle being turned, the creak of a hinge cutting through the quiet street like glass through a wrist. Instinctively, he turned around, averting his eyes from the stranger now leaving the house behind him. The lorry wasn't too far away. All he needed to do was head for the bugger, climb aboard and start her up-

He heard the slamming of a car door, quickly followed by a finely tuned engine being awoken. Now it purred softly, pulling slowly away from the curbside like a shark following the scent of blood.

'Stay calm, man,' said Aaron, grinning. 'What's the bloody matter with you?'

'We're being watched, for fuck's sake,' Reed hissed between gritted teeth. 'What do you—shit, here it is. God, I knew this was a bad idea . . .'

The car passed him by, slowing at the end of the road. Then it stopped as though waiting for traffic to pass by.

'Why can't he just piss off?' Reed whispered. 'Why's he waiting at the corner?'

Aaron grinned once more.

Reed felt needles of sweat prick at the nape of his neck, a heat that not even the icy breeze could cool. The discomfort crept down his collar, sticking his shirt to his flesh. The scent of burnished steel filled the air as though a storm was on its way, could taste stale cigarettes on his tongue . . .

This is it, he thought. The bloody driver's spotted me. Christ Almighty, I must look suspicious . . . Hell, he's probably been watching me argue with fresh air from his window for the past half hour and now he's going to turn back . . . He's going to turn back, wind down his window and ask me all sorts of awkward questions . . . Great, I've picked the classic curtain twitching, finger in everyone else's pie, friendly neighbourhood-

Then the car turned the corner, the sound of its engine fading on the shoulders of the chill breeze.

'*Now* can your heart slow down a little, David?' said Aaron. 'You're nothing but a bloke passing through-'

'A lot of things have changed since you pegged it, my friend,' Reed replied, raising his voice just above a whisper. 'You can't just wander anywhere you please. We're probably being watched right this minute-'

'Point taken,' conceded Aaron. 'But we do know one thing for sure.'

'Oh, and what's that?'

'That one's house is empty. All we have to do is wait a little while then-'

'Screw this,' said Reed, turning around. As he almost lost his balance on a patch of slush, the matchbox rattled like a death watch beetle in his pocket.

'Where the hell are you going, David?'

'If you think I'm walking about in the cold when there's nothing wrong with the lorry, then you're sorely mistaken, Aaron. Let's just get this over with. Some of us have homes to go to.'

'Very funny,' replied the ghost. 'We're walking.'

'Are you insane?' gasped David, frozen in his tracks.

Aaron shook his head.

'The exercise will do you good. Come on, it's not that far. Maybe we'll come back, maybe we'll find a better, quieter place.'

Before he could utter another word, Reed watched the ghost make his way down the avenue. The pale sun glanced across his bald pate, his shoulders pushed up tight as if to ward off the chill wind.

'Great,' Reed said flatly, quickening his pace to catch up. 'Maybe I can see what's become of my old house. Maybe it's a betting shop. Now there's an omen if ever there was one.'

54

Although Reed had turned his collar up against the brisk wind, feeling tiny needles of sleet scratch his cheek and forehead, he held his head up, trying to look as inconspicuous as possible. What did he have to hide after all?

He glanced over his shoulder at the lorry parked at the corner of the street and thought that maybe leaving it behind had been prudent. That way, when the shit hit the fan—and boy, Reed could already smell the rancid stuff—the last thing he needed was linking it to-

Linking it to what, David? Arson, murder-

'I thought I told you where to go,' Reed murmured, his teeth chattering with the cold.

His head filled with silence.

That didn't hurt, he thought, a slight smile on his lips. That didn't hurt at all-

Suddenly his heart quickened, stars danced before his eyes. His mobile phone was vibrating in his pocket.

'Must be the missus,' said Aaron wearily, shaking his head. 'Women?-'

'I know I know,' replied Reed, trying to get at the phone before it had a chance to switch to the answer machine. 'Can't live with them; impossible to hide their body parts. Very funny . . .'

His smile faded, words trailing away; forgotten. The screen was flashing, but not to indicate a received message or indeed a missed call. He wanted the throw the damned thing as far away as possible; smash it into a hundred pieces if he could. Instead he stuffed the phone back into his pocket and kept his hands there for warmth.

Aaron chuckled, and the sound washed over Reed like acid.

'What kind of an idiot embarks on a long haul delivery trip to the other end of the country and back . . . and forgets to pack a phone charger-'

'Point. Fucking. Taken. Okay?' Reed snapped, taking the phone back out of his pocket to switch it off to preserve some vestige of the battery's energy. And should he need to, provided he acted swiftly, he might catch a few minutes' worth of call time. He nodded quickly, a spark of hope igniting in his heart. And he moved on through the slippery snow.

An icy breeze pushed litter across their path, shattering the early morning serenity, yet Reed unbuttoned his coat, his back now slick with perspiration. Spokes of hot sunshine pin-wheeled through the heavy banks of grey clouds, unveiling the most beautiful rainbow Reed had ever seen.

The ghost inhaled the cold air and smiled.

'Today's going to be a good day,' he said, slowing his pace. He pointed toward an old knee-high wall. Gaps appeared in the structure, blackened and broken, like rotten teeth poking up through cancerous gums.

'What is it?' said Reed, frowning at the small jagged rocks up ahead.

Aaron shook his head.

'It's nothing really. I can . . . I feel us getting closer, that's all.'

'I know what you mean,' Reed replied. 'I think we've already passed my old house. The streets seem smaller, I give you that-'

'They aren't,' said Aaron, patting Reed on the stomach. 'You've gotten fatter, my friend.'

'Fuck you,' Reed mumbled, unable to resist smiling. He remembered his old school was nearby. The very thought of that damned playing field and the crosses he had daubed-

He shook the memory away.

Aaron laughed. 'Good, David. You don't need to go there any more. And before you ask me: No, I don't know what the hell happened to the boy. Well, that's what you were thinking, right? That little arse hole that made your life hell . . .'

'I often wondered where you'd sent the poor bugger-'

'He just . . . disappeared. Simple.'

Pendleton Drive comprised of a small cluster of detached houses that, even back in Reed's childhood, exuded an atmosphere of discomfort when he walked by; as though the homes themselves were embarrassed being in such close proximity to their run down semi detached neighbours from the street adjacent. And not surprisingly, that feeling remained, even though the piles of bricks and glass were nothing remarkable; at least not by today's standards. Yes, they had small, finely groomed emerald green lawns, and their rooftops were flawless. In fact, Reed remembered how his dad once cursed the Pendletons. During a major storm which lasted but fifteen minutes, Reed's bedroom ceiling caved in, as did his mum and dad's. The rain shot against the roof's loose tiles like bullets in a carnival rifle range, the guttering over flowed, destroying what little flowers mum had planted only weeks earlier. Or did dad plant them? he thought, mentally pin wheeling his arms through the wall of spider webs. The weather report described those delightful fifteen minutes as the tail of a hurricane which had passed the United States of America, making its merry way to the North east of England . . .

Dad had almost cried whilst chatting with his insurer. Reed had never seen a grown man cry and so he went outside to play, or more to the point, investigate the storm damage.

The white plastic garden furniture had toppled over. Reed knew it wasn't heavy so commenced straightening out the mess; cursing as cold rain water spilled over his hands, soaking his jumper through to his wrists. He noticed the sorry-looking plants, their stems bent and broken; their pots over flowing with muddy water-

Then his world stood still.

Nothing else seemed to move or matter when dad attacked his mum.

Maybe it was the drink . . . but most likely it was something to do with the home insurance. They didn't pay out against the storm. Three Pendletons had new roofs within three weeks. Apparently not one of the bastards actually worked and were entitled to free refurbishment . . . But the Reeds had to scrimp and save for forever it seemed.

Reed shook away the memory. Not the image of the storm and the mess it made, but the sound of his mum's screams, the unmistakable clap of a hand striking flesh. The silence that followed always hurt more than the foul language because he never quite knew what to expect in those pregnant pauses. Kids conjured up the wildest things, and Reed was no exception. So he'd anticipate a gun shot, the whisper of a samurai sword as it left its scabbard, damn it—even the humming of a light-saber-

'Are you alright, David?' Aaron said, his breath but a fine mist about his face.

Reed nodded, swallowing the bitterness of the flash back, grimacing as it reached his stomach; turning over there. 'The council still seems to favour some streets over others,' he piped up.

Aaron shrugged his shoulders, moving along quietly. His footsteps were tentative, kicking aside the occasional crushed tin can that crossed his path. His eyes focused on the ground, always at his feet.

'I think I'll ask you the same thing,' said Reed, placing a hand on the ghost's shoulder.

Aaron pulled away.

'I'm just like you,' he replied. 'I'm nodding my head.' But then his voice softened, adding almost apologetically that he was okay, except for his stomach, which was spinning like a top.

Then he stopped still.

'Well, did you feel it?'

Reed laughed at the ghost's outburst. 'This is fucking insane. Feel what, for God's sake?'

'This is where you'd take me during the night,' continued Aaron.

'You mean when I wanted you to go home, because of the rain and the fact that you had outstayed your welcome? Yes, I suppose you're right, Aaron,' replied Reed, his words dripping with contempt. 'Feel? You know what? I didn't feel a bloody thing.'

He glanced over his shoulder at the pavement Aaron spoke of. He noticed the different shade of concrete where an old grate used to be. Maybe a lamppost had been there too, but to hell with it! He smiled.

'What the hell do you have to smile about?' said Aaron wearily.

Their feet slid through a patch of sleet, almost throwing Reed off balance.

'Well,' Reed replied. 'At the end of the day you could be feeding me as many lies as you want and I would be powerless to stop you. I think you're wrong about that bit of concrete, Aaron. I mean I thought we had already passed it. Hey, I could be wrong! I'm just suggesting that maybe you've got your facts wrong here and there.'

Silence hung in the air, suddenly carried along on the shoulders of a brisk wind.

Aaron nodded, looking over at Reed. The ghost's eyes had paled as though he was struggling to keep his very soul awake.

'Can I ask you something?' said Reed, his voice now barely a whisper before clearing his throat to be heard above the wind.

Aaron shrugged his shoulders as way of agreement.

'Where the hell did you draw your strength from? I mean, how did you do . . . *that* to Johnny? Christ! That coaster must have weighed at least-'

'If I had such strength then why do I need your help?' said Aaron flatly. 'That's what you really want to know isn't it?'

Reed didn't need to reply. The ghost already knew the answer.

'Contrary to what you believe, I'm not flesh,' said Aaron, holding out his hand. 'Here, feel . . . You chicken-shit! Never mind. Take my word for it that I may feel like skin and bone, but I'm more than that. My mind is more powerful than you could *ever* imagine, David-'

'But just not powerful enough to do this on your own?' Reed replied.

'I know what you're doing,' said Aaron, the crack of a smile on his thin, pale lips. 'And you can see it makes me happy. I just can't be arsed right now but if you really want to know then you'll find out everything that niggles at your curiosity when you're dead. Do you think you can wait that long?'

'Why are you playing games-'

'I can play all the games I want, my friend. But that won't change a bloody thing.'

'So you can't be hurt, like real flesh can?'

Aaron's smile broadened as he gazed skyward as though the answers were written there. 'There's nothing to equal the texture, David; the soft touch of a woman's brea-'

'That's not what I asked you,' interrupted Reed. 'Can you be hurt? I mean, you've certainly aged, haven't you?'

'Do you have something in mind?' said Aaron, grinning. 'Are you planning to catch this weary old goat off-guard? You can try if you want to, you know? It'll be interesting. No there's a lot of life still left in this body before . . .'

'Before what?'

'Before we become simply a noise or a voice,' replied the ghost, a dry click in his throat. 'Or one of those little bumps in the night. Some of us just end up one bad smell. You know when a song sometimes takes you back to a certain point in your life? Well, that's close to what we become. That's why-'

'That's why Elvis is still alive,' said Reed.

'Kind of . . .'

'But what you did to Johnny . . .' Reed let his words trail off as the image of the eviscerated shark opened up across his mind like a bloody canvass. He threw the thought away.

'Ask any of us why we can do all those things,' snapped Aaron. 'Ask away. But you're wasting your time because we don't know. Like I told you: over there all you have, all you need, is what's between your ears,' he said, tapping his temple with a boney finger. 'Believe me there's a lot up here we don't use.'

'If that's all you need then why do you want your life back?'

'What the hell *is* this?'

'Look, all I want-'

'No,' said Aaron, grabbing Reed's forearm. 'I asked you what this is: Interview with the ghost? Maybe I should call you Anne Rice from now on.' Before another word was said he quickened his pace, leaving Reed behind.

The grip on his arm loosened but his flesh still crawled where the ghost's fingers had been. And the voice inside still obeyed Reed's orders; keeping its distance. Right that moment he didn't need any other distraction or train of thought spinning through his head; this living walking talking nightmare before him was quite sufficient for two life times. Then he noticed how the ghost's narrow shoulders shook slightly as he made his way forward through the icy wind. So he quickly caught up.

'Not long now, David,' said Aaron, his voice as dry as tinder. He was gazing down at his feet, watching the right one follow the left.

'Are you crying?' said Reed, leaning forward in order to establish eye contact, but Aaron just shook his head and carried on unsteadily along the path. 'Christ, I swear you're crying.'

'We're almost there, that's why my eyes are watering,' replied Aaron, his smile now narrow and crooked.

Reed frowned. 'Quit talking in riddles-'

'I can almost taste the smoke.'

55

'Breathe, Anne,' said Aaron, standing at the corner of the street. It was an attempt at humour which didn't quite work. He glanced at Reed who stood beside him, as still as a mannequin, his jaw slack. 'You can relax now, we're here.'

The grey clouds had disappeared now and, although the scent of burnished steel hung on the air, a bright sun traced its warm fingers along the back of Reed's neck.

The inclement weather was far from over, he thought. In fact, judging by the goose bumps crawling across his arms and legs, the storm was approaching. It was simply a matter of when.

Reed could almost hear the sound of the sea, but in fact it was the blood pounding in his ears.

'Here we are,' he said, trying to sound up-beat and carefree, clapping his hands together to generate some warmth there; but his tone was just as fake as Aaron's joviality. He waited for the ghost to change his mind, waited for the sudden snap of reality—anything . . .

Aaron stepped off the curb and made his way across the wet road.

Reed followed but froze, noticing how curtains twitched, bedroom lights flickered into life and somewhere a dog barked.

'Aaron,' he hissed, keeping an eye on the front doors of the houses surrounding them, just in case one should open—'Hey, Aaron! Bloody wait. We're being watched,' he said, trying to walk as casual as could be. He reached the other side of the road and mounted the curb.

'Why should it bother *me*, Miss Rice?' Aaron replied, taking a cigarette from his pocket. 'It's not me they're watching . . . is it?' He placed the cigarette in the corner of his mouth. 'Got a match? Don't tell me: your face, my arse-'

Reed grabbed the cigarette from the ghost's mouth and flicked it away.

'It's so fucking simple, isn't it?'

'There's no other way, David,' said Aaron. 'If you're seen, you're seen. But it'll be over before anyone realizes what the hell we're up to.'

Reed watched the tiny dots appear before his eyes, beating to the rhythm of his heart. His right hand squeezed a small object, and it took him a few moments to realize just what it was. Slowly, as though he had just discovered the use of his hand he opened it, palm upward.

'That didn't hurt, did it?' said Aaron, grabbing the box. In moments he had lit another cigarette, returning the box back to Reed's hand before he had time to close it. Aaron took a long drag before offering Reed the rest, to which Reed declined with the shake of his head. 'Suit yourself. Come on, time's a wasting.'

Can I come back, David?

Reed smiled.

There was a pause before the voice continued. But after a few moments it seemed like it had never been away.

I know what you're feeling right now is hard, David. Don't tell me to shut up or go away! The severed head of an executed unfortunate can still look upon it's executioner for a number of seconds before finally drifting off into oblivion . . .

And you wondered why I wanted you to go away? thought Reed, shaking his head.

There are so many questions rushing around your mind right now, rising to the surface—yet your tongue is inoperable . . . there is nothing left . . . there is so much left undone . . . and you imagine the answers will elude you. You believe in many things, David. But you can't persuade yourself to accept what's real any more . . . Look in your hand—Go on, look!

'See that old house over there?'

'Eh? What?' Reed mumbled, shaken from his reverie. He looked at the box in his hand as he had been instructed.

'That one,' said Aaron, pointing to the house before them. 'Can't believe how good the place's looking,' he continued in awe.

Gone were the single glazed windows that felt loose when pressed, especially during the winter. Now it boasted double glazing. The old pebble-dashed fascia, with its trellis of creeping ivy, some of which spread dampness through the spare bedroom, had been replaced with a smooth coating of cement. Now that the rain water was channeled through a fixed drain pipe at the side of the edifice, the clean lick of cream paint was unmarked. 'Looks good as new, doesn't it?'

They walked down the garden path. Closely cropped dark green grass glided passed them in the darkness. No bicycles and any other toys to speak of littered the yard, noticed Reed with something akin to relief. Even though the evidence of a child living here was far from conclusive, the tidiness that only a childless home could boast looked hopeful. The last thing he wanted was the death of an innocent child on his conscience . . . anybody's death for that matter!

Think about what you're doing, David. Please, don't do this!

'There are no lights on that I can see,' Reed said flatly, glancing over his shoulder occasionally at the surrounding houses. 'No car parked outside either-'

Do you hear how cold you sound, David? Think about what you are about to commit-

'I just wish I could say there were good memories-'

'Fuck this, Aaron!' Reed spat, approaching the front door. He took a scrap of paper from his pocket without bothering to see what he was about to destroy. Hell, it could've been a ten pound note and it wouldn't have made the slightest bit of difference to him. Then he grabbed a match from its box and struck it across the abrasive strip.

Aaron drew deeply on his cigarette before dropping it to his feet, where he crushed it beneath his right boot.

Before the tip could touch the edge of the slip of paper the match extinguished immediately.

Reed shook his head, grabbed another match then tried again. His fingers were now numb with the cold breeze.

It extinguished.

'For God's sake!' he muttered, trying again.

'Take your time, David,' Aaron breathed. 'Take your own sweet time.'

Suddenly the flame took hold of the paper. And slowly, slowly, it grew.

Aaron grinned.

'Good lad,' he said, grabbing Reed's wrist; guiding it towards the front door's letter box. 'Easy, easy does it . . . there you go, my boy.' He lifted the brass lid and delicately helped the flame squeeze through the dark.

Reed let go of the paper.

The fire had begun.

He squeezed his eyes shut.

'What now?' he whispered, searching the ghost's emerald eyes, for what, he didn't know.

'What do you think?' replied Aaron, grinning.

'Think?' said Reed, shaking his head. 'I don't do that any more. It gets me nowhere.'

PART C

After a while you learn to forget that the sun ever existed at all.

It was something to put down to experience; something beautiful from a bygone age.

You wonder if the here and now was your real 'life' and planet Earth had been some wild and vivid dream.

That's what you feel at the beginning, when you're all alone.

But when pale, confused faces, some familiar, others strange, suddenly peel away from the blackness and cross your path you realize that you were wide awake all along. And despite what I'm going through right now, I do not believe that two people can have the same dream.

I used to sit at the window and watch for the moon to break though the darkness, hoping to catch a glimpse of its shiny face behind a thin grey veil I once called clouds. But there was nothing up there where heaven was supposed to be. If that place is real then I'm in purgatory; my life had been hell, and the promised kingdom . . . well, it's taking it's time in coming.

They say that death isn't the end. They were telling the truth. It isn't the end but one interminable pause. It's like standing at the curb of a busy road: just when a gap appears in the rushing traffic and you prepare to take one step forward, another vehicle comes hurtling along, pushing you back.

So you wait for the next available gap . . .

And you wait.

Now when I peer through the dark glass I see my face staring back at me. Sometimes I don't even bother wiping the condensation away with my hand, the way I used to. How I'd pat the nape of my neck with the icy water from the pane, feeling the goose pimples rise along my entire body. But now . . .

'Penny for them,' said Christine, placing her chin on my shoulder. 'What you looking at out there, eh?'

I was just a teenage boy, and before I found my way here my hormones were crazier than shit-house rats. In death nothing changed. I closed my eyes for a moment to savour her sweet perfume. If I had my eyes open then one of my other senses could steal the show—uhuh—nose only.

I shrugged, mumbled something stupid and then opened my eyes once more. I saw her face beside mine and suddenly the heat rose about my cheeks, the glass misted over with the touch of my breath. My heart was beating like a bunch of jungle drums and I think she knew it too.

Christine cleared her throat and sat down in the wooden chair beside me. The wood creaked, despite her slim figure. I suppose the only thing that grows old is the furniture-

'Can I get you something?' she said, absently brushing a rogue lock of blond hair behind her left ear. 'As you can see, we're not that busy tonight.'

I surveyed the room. She was right. In fact we were alone. Together . . .

I shook my head. 'No, I'm fine. Thank you.'

She smiled broadly, that smile I knew I had fallen in love with. Its warmth always reached her radiant eyes; always brightened her beautiful face. I turned to look at her mouth and imagined myself tasting the wax of her pale red lipstick, the tip of my tongue exploring the warmth of her mouth, connecting, feeling the slight sharpness of her teeth as they scraped against mine. Such clumsiness was simply a part of the fantasy's charm. I can't help glancing toward her blouse and I avert my attention to the empty tea cup on the table before me.

'It's okay,' she replied, clearing her throat once more. I felt her hand on my thigh and secretly prayed it would wander further, but it remained still. She knew how strongly I felt about her and I even think she didn't adjust her clothing in case it hurt my feelings.

I knew deep down that I could look all I wanted, but out of respect I stared at my tea cup.

'We all get lonely,' she said. 'It's okay. I have a teenage son-'

'Anthony,' I said. 'I remember you told me he's just turned thirteen.'

She nodded, her smile waning somewhat as she stared ahead.

I wondered if she saw him sitting in the chair opposite us. But then surely I would be able to see him too.

'You must miss him.'

'Yes. Yes, I do. But he's fourteen now. You're not much older,' she whispered, her hand gently squeezing my thigh before letting go. Now she was staring right through me, to my very soul it seemed.

'I'm almost sixteen,' I said, an edge of desperation in my voice. I tried to maintain eye contact, but she quickly looked away once more. 'By law-'

'Daniel, we've gone over this before,' she said, closing her eyes for a second as she bit her bottom lip. Her smile had faded, but she tried to maintain the joviality she had felt moments ago, as though nothing had been said. 'It wouldn't be right-'

Just then we both jumped as the sound of the door bell shattered the silence surrounding us. The door flew open, ushering in an ice cold breeze, upon which carried the scent of tobacco and alcohol.

'We're closed, gentlemen,' Christine piped up, almost knocking the tea cup over as she stood up. 'I thought-'

'You thought you'd locked the door but you didn't,' said the tallest of the three men. His voice was a little slurred, as though he was full of drink. But I knew that outside, in the darkness, pubs didn't exist.

At least they looked like men. The tall one had a long beard that almost reached his navel. His jacket was open. A black leather jacket, it was. And beneath shone the whitest tee shirt I have ever seen. His eyes were blue, but they seemed vacant.

His companions couldn't have been more different. They were of similar height and build: short but stocky. One had a scar running straight across his . . . no, it was female-forehead. Her hair was pulled back into a bun. Her eyes were wide but empty as though she could see for miles. But I'm not as stupid as your average fifteen-going-on-sixteen. They were as high as kites. The other one looked male, although I could've been mistaken. He actually looked intelligent. His dark brown eyes were nothing more than slits behind thick-lensed spectacles which were balanced precariously on the bridge of his long, bird-like nose. If he was sane, maybe, just maybe he would've been capable of an intelligent conversation. For some reason they wore leather. But I failed to hear the grumble of motorcycles outside. Nor did I see the arc of bright headlamps cut through the umbra as they approached the café.

'I'd like-'

'I said: we're closed,' said Christine, approaching the trio. 'You'll just have to buy something you like elsewhere-'

She didn't even see the fist fly towards her jaw, but I felt it. She fell to the floor and lay still-

Beard shook his head, his hand raised. 'Don't, son. Don't even think about it. Sit back down. There's a good boy,' he said. His voice sounded as deep as an ocean.

Christine was just a pile of twisted arms and legs on the floor, blood pooling beside her face. I prayed she was alright.

'Who do we have to fuck to get a coffee around here?' sniggered four-eyes, looking down at the still figure at his feet. His hands reached for his belt buckle as he looked down. 'Oh, yeah-'

'Leave her,' growled Beard, fixing the other man with his ice blue stare. Immediately the grin fell from four-eye's face. 'If that maggot leaves your pants then, God so help me, you'll be picking it out of a puddle of blood. Understand me?'

Four-eyes nodded, glancing over at scar-face. But she didn't respond because . . .

She was staring straight at me!

'So,' she said finally without breaking eye contact, 'do we wait until she wakes up or will you be a little forthcoming?'

'I don't know w-what y-you want,' I stammered, unable to remember the last time I was nervous enough to speak this way-

I heard a sharp clicking noise and noticed the sudden appearance of the blade in her hand.

'Put the flick-knife away,' said beard, his eyes never leaving mine, 'before he pisses his self.'

Four-eyes sniggered.

Scar-face folded the blade and put it in her jacket pocket.

My heart was hammering wildly, threatening to burst from my chest, but I didn't take my eyes from them.

Beard looked down at Christine and shook his head. 'Don't know my own strength sometimes,' he said, much to his idiotic friend's amusement. But as he looked towards me once more his smile melted away.

'Do you think he knows?' said Four-eyes.

'They did look pretty close, didn't they?' replied Scar-face. She stepped forward, but suddenly a hand grabbed her arm and pulled her back.

Beard shook his head.

'But there's not much time left-'

'There's time!' beard snapped, pushing Scar-face back towards the door. 'Plenty of time.' Then he returned his attention to me. I felt dwarfed even though he was nowhere near me. Then he kicked Christine in the ribs, to which she cried out.

I felt the tears well in my eyes but I was frozen by fear; fear and anger. My fists clenched into tiny balls of hate but what the hell was I compared to these three gorillas?

'Tell her we'll be in touch,' said Beard, heading for the door, the others following him like lap-dogs.

The bell above the door rang out as they set foot outside and became one with the darkness. I heard the squeaking of leather boots as they descended the steps, their laughter now receding as nothingness swallowed them whole.

Cracks appeared in the ice holding me to the spot, and I crossed the room to be by Christine's side. She was still, congealed blood spread about her mouth and-

I almost jumped out of my skin as her eyes flickered open.

'I I thought y-you were dead!' I almost screamed. 'Th-thank God! Can you sit up?'

She shook her head, slowly shuffling onto her back.

'Let me lie here for a little bit, flower,' she replied breathlessly, squeezing her eyes shut a few seconds before staring up at the ceiling.

'What did they want, Christine?' I demanded to know.

'Not now, sweetheart,' she replied softly, trying to crack a smile. But it became a grimace as pain lanced through her side where beard had kicked her. 'Not now.'

56

Their feet slammed the pavement as they fled the street, a fire already burning in Reed's lungs. His face beamed a dangerous shade of red as beads of sweat formed on his brow, threatening to roll down into his eyes; but he kept moving. With the bloody racket he was making he wasn't sure which pointed the finger of guilt at him the most: loitering the quiet street or running as if for dear life away from it-

Reed slowed down, realizing he was alone. Stopping to catch his breath, bending forwards with hands clutching his knee caps, he turned about. A white hot skewer of pain stabbed his side. He couldn't remember the last time he had moved quick enough to get a stitch!

Aaron walked casually along, without a care in the world it seemed, before stopping for a couple of seconds to light a cigarette.

'What?' he asked, raising a barely visible eye-brow. He glanced at his fingers. 'Oh shit, I was going to offer you one but there aren't many left-'

'Don't give me that rubbish, Aaron-'

'Look, the lorry's just around the corner from here,' the ghost replied, pointing over Reed's shoulder. 'Just relax.'

'That's easy for you to say, isn't it? They can't see or hear you,' Reed snapped. 'It's *my* head on the chopping block-'

'Nobody's head's going on the chopping block,' Aaron chuckled quietly, stepping off the curb. He didn't bother looking both ways as he crossed the road. He waved a hand, beckoning Reed to hurry up. 'I know, I know. If I were alive you'd kill me.'

Reed smiled.

That was one way of putting it, he thought.

*

Reed's hands shook whilst trying to insert the key into the ignition. A cold sweat broke beneath his arms, sticking his shirt to his back like a second skin.

'Breathe, David,' said Aaron, shifting in his seat to get comfortable. 'It's a bit chilly in here, isn't it?' he commented, quickly rubbing his thin hands together to generate a little warmth through the digits. 'Knock the heating on, then-'

'Just hold on, will you!' Reed snapped, finally driving the key home. He thought about how much noise this big bugger was going to make and just how the neighbours were bound to react . . .

'Fuck it,' he mumbled, turning the key.

The engine coughed, spluttered then died.

'Nice work,' replied Aaron, quietly. 'Way to go-'

Suddenly the engine roared, awakening the dashboard instruments.

'You were saying?' Reed said, the tyres cutting through the thin layer of sleet as they pulled away from the gutter. 'Yeah, that's what I thought.'

'You really did it, David,' said Aaron, nodding his head. 'I didn't-'

'Didn't have much of a fucking choice, did I!'

Aaron wiped the condensation from the screen and practically pressed his face to the glass, watching the houses pass them by.

'Stop the lorry, David,' he said suddenly, tapping the dashboard with his right hand. 'Hey, I said stop!'

'No way,' Reed replied, pressing his foot down on the accelerator. 'I won't rest until we're at least half a dozen streets away. Besides, I just can't sit there and watch; I'll go nuts. The police will-'

'Screw the police, David. Believe me you *don't* want to leave it too long.'

'Why?' Reed said, weaving through a drizzle of lazy traffic, almost clipping a Ford's wing. The irate driver sounded his horn then waved his middle towards him. *'Same to you, mate!'*

'Forget that idiot, David!' Aaron said, grinding his teeth with frustration, wanting to beat the dashboard with all his might. 'Look, I guarantee that within the next few minutes the first cloud of smoke will rise from behind that house over there.' He pointed toward the edge of the road. 'And when that happens . . . you do *not* want to be sat here.'

'Shh, just shut the hell up,' said Reed pointing to a small shape in his rear view mirror, then he pressed down on his brakes, bringing the vehicle to a bone jarring stop.

Aaron cursed but did as instructed, winding the window down to stick his head out and see what the fuss was about.

'Big deal.'

'What the hell do you mean: big deal?' said Reed. 'Can't you tell me what's wrong with this picture? Honestly-'

Aaron raised a hand to silence Reed.

'Fuck you.'

They watched the two little boys kicking a football against a brick wall, absently tapping the toy down the road.

'We're too late, David,' said Aaron, slowly turning round. There was a grin upon his scarred face that broadened at the sight of sheer panic in the other man's eyes. 'What did you expect-'

'No! Don't go that way!' Reed shouted, bringing his fist down onto the steering wheel. 'Aaron, do something for God's sake!'

They watched helplessly as one of the boys pointed at what appeared to be a curl of grey smoke rising above the edge of a roof top. And as the moment rolled into the next the children had followed their curiosity and broke into a gentle run.

'Now, David.'

'Now, what?'

'Listen carefully. We don't have much time.'

57

'Great!' Reed shouted, walking briskly towards the burning house. 'You know something? I didn't expect anything less of you and this *fucking* situation!' Lights appeared in the windows they passed by, probably awoken by his loud voice, thought Reed. But he no longer cared.

'Look at the idiot screaming at his own shadow!' Aaron shouted at the silhouettes at the curtains, quickening his pace to keep up with the other man. His feet barely left a mark in the worn rug of snow. 'Just keep calm. The lorry is fine where it is, just out of the way so no one will suspect-'

'I can't believe all of the . . . the things I did for you when we were kids,' Reed replied, his face blushing with a mixture of conflicting emotions: anger, fear, frustration—God, he felt everything! 'I hurt people for you; innocent people . . . and the animals I tortured for you. I mean, Christ, what the hell was all that about? Don't tell me the whole world was against you! And now this?' he gasped, pointing at the house across the street. 'Now I'm an arsonist!'

'Nobody is hurt,' said Aaron calmly. 'The place is empty-'

'How do we really know that . . .' Reed allowed his words to trail away as he noticed one of the children he had seen not moments ago staring at him from across the road. Other little street urchins had gathered also. And much to his surprise they were standing a substantial distance from the building.

He stopped suddenly as thick smoke belched from a shattered window pane on the ground floor. Inside an explosion sent shockwaves through the path. Reed looked down at the crack in the concrete, frozen by the sight of the gash that measured at least three inches wide

'There's nobody inside, mister,' piped up one small boy, his tiny, grubby hands gripping onto a football as though for dear life. 'They're—No, don't, mister-'

'Get out of the way, for Christ's sake!' Reed spat, making his way towards the house.

'Up yours then, mate!' the boy shouted back, now tapping the pavement with his ball. 'Fuckin' burn!'

Reed pushed two pig-tailed girls out of his way, glancing over his shoulder at them, noticing how similar they were: same hair, same style of dress-

Probably the same crazy thoughts dashing through their minds too, David.

Reed shook the voice from his mind.

You are insane for going through with this, David!

'Shut up!' he snapped back at the voice, watching the little girls giggling and pointing their fingers, laughing at the freak who raked his hair with two shaking hands.

'You know what you must do,' said Aaron, weaving through the throng of children, his body disappearing then reappearing as though he were not even there.

'Where do I look?' Reed said anxiously, about to take a step towards the house but the heat of the fire was palpable, his flesh crawled as though a poison raced through his veins. And he stepped back a pace.

'What did you say?' said one of the twin girls, her chin covered in chocolate.

'What? No, never mind,' Reed replied, waving the child's question away with a shaking hand. 'Aaron? Which bloody door? Where do I look for you-'

'Bloody hell!' shouted the boy with the ball, laughing with his friends. 'He's really going in there! Here, Jimmy, give us your mobile-'

'You gonna phone the firemen?' replied a tall, thin figure of a boy. His glasses were perched on the tip of his nose, and he jerked his head back suddenly to reposition them. But in seconds they had made their way back to the edge of his beak.

'Don't be so round shouldered, you fuckin' flamingo!' retorted ball boy, hitting the buttons before bringing the handset to his ear, a grin spreading across his face. 'Gonna get the rest of the lads round. This'll be a laugh!'

'Aaron, speak to me!' Reed shouted, taking a tentative step, feeling the heat of the fire on his face as he approached the buckled front door, the glass cracked in its frame; tasting the smoke in his mouth even though there was none to speak of here . . . yet. Fire belched from the edges of the broken window, sending tiny splinters spiraling skyward.

'I've told you!' Aaron shouted. 'I don't know which door will lead you to me.'

Just keep your head, David! Don't let this destroy you-

'Too late.'

The ghost ignored Reed's words, pointing at the door. 'You have to step into the fire and find your own way. I can't help you now, you know that-'

'You're mad! There must be some other way—Some better way! I could die in there!' Reed screamed, pointing at the thick black smoke which now haloed the entire roof.

'Every moment you waste, the less time you have!'

As though they were encased in concrete, Reed's legs remained rooted to the spot, only feet away from death itself. As a little boy he used to think fire was beautiful; its heat, its colours and the way it marked one of his most favourite nights of the year: Guy Fawkes Night. Candy by the bucket-load, jacket potatoes split and spitting on sharp sticks, cooking slowly but surely amongst the flames. And the whole family encircling the flaming tower, chatting and sipping beer as the burning effigy fell apart. But now he hated the damned thing!

Reed clenched his fists and turned to face the ghost.

Through gritted teeth he said, 'And when it's all over you want me to return the same way, right? RIGHT?' he bellowed, stepping around the ghost and away from the house. 'You're out of your mind. I've had it with you-'

Aaron pushed Reed back with all his might, much to the gawping children's amusement. They shook their heads, giggling as the strange man fought his way *away* from the burning house, pulling at his clothing as though his skin was crawling with angry bees.

'You must, David! You must do what I need you to do,' shouted Aaron, but the gathering didn't hear a word from the wraith. Even if he *were* audible they were transfixed by the strange man levitating a couple of inches above the broken path, his collar raised as if pulled by sharp little hooks towards the house. 'You have to return the same way you went in-'

'You're crazy!' Reed screamed, unable to touch the floor, kicking his feet wildly, the heat intensifying with each passing second. 'By then this place will be ash—do you understand? I'll die-'

'Then you'll have to pull your finger out, won't you?'

Reed felt ice cold hands pressing on his back, pushing him onwards through the wall of black smoke that had now engulfed the front door. He choked and wanted to vomit, deafened by the noise of crackling glass, eyes watering, stomach turning with the stench of burning furniture-

He stepped or rather fell across the threshold, the door slamming shut behind him.

*

This is the end, thought Reed, trudging through the smoke, barely able to see in front of his face. But he knew that he would have to try if he wanted to see-

Tabby . . .

Paul.

Those two magical words were all he needed to galvanize him into action.

That's it, David! Move!

He started with what appeared to be a kitchen, waving dark smoke from his streaming eyes on his way, wading through the permeated air. He cursed as he stumbled over something hard. A toy car? An action figure? He didn't know and quite frankly didn't give a damn. Pain shot up his right thigh as he collided with the edge of what appeared to be the wooden edge of a table top. The air rang out with the clatter and crash of porcelain bowls and half full coffee mugs as they fell to the hard linoleum floor.

Suddenly, through the thick, poisonous cloud he discovered a door; his left wrist caught the round knob. He tucked his hand into his sleeve to act as a glove just in case the thing was hot. He wanted to compose himself, wanted so desperately to take a deep breath, but there was no clean air left to take. So he turned the door handle.

It was warm.

It was jammed.

'Fuck!'

The smoke and heat seemed to intensify with each passing second, thought Reed, alarmed at the limited vision But he had to keep moving-

That's it, David . . . Keep moving!

The urge to scream until blood filled his throat was overwhelming, but he knew that saving his breath was paramount. So he cut through the lounge and crossed the narrow hall.

That was easy. You're really doing it!

There was nothing obstructing his path and smoke hadn't drifted this far through the building yet, but it was quickly taking possession of every pocket of air in the damned place!

Reed noticed the small cupboards under the stairs, almost tripping over what appeared to be a box full of tools-

'Straight in and straight back out: That's all you have to do,' Aaron whispered in Reed's ear.

Reed's heart beat faster; felt its tiny fists batter the inside of his chest. He was at the foot of the stairs now, and he gazed up at a pale light shining at the top of the landing. A single lamp, haloed with smoke seemed to shift positions. One second it was to the left then to the right-

You must hurry! You're starting to lose your senses-

'And that's it? Then it's all over between us, right?' Reed shouted.

'I told you that I can't really promise that.'

'No! I come back and we're finished!' Reed shouted but his throat was growing increasingly sore as the smoke thickened before him, its arms squeezing him tightly, enveloping him-

'If that's what you *really* want,' the ghost whispered.

'THAT'S WHAT I WANT!'

'You really wish to have nothing to do with me when you come back? You probably wished we'd never met, don't you?'

'You . . . know I-I don't have to answer . . . that,' Reed stammered, his head swimming. Tabby and Paul's faces should have flashed across his mind, instead Aaron's green eyes and scarred face jumped out from the darkness.

Reed passed through the vision as if it didn't exist, emerging through the other side with something resembling a smile across his face. He didn't know if it was through stubbornness or stupidity, but it actually felt satisfying.

Do this for Tabby and Paul . . . Do this for them . . .

With his sleeve now shielding his mouth against the smoke, his eyes stinging with tears, Reed made his way up the stairs.

The fucking door must be here somewhere!

Stay calm, David—Don't lose your mind-

'Don't tell me to stay calm!' He wanted to shout but what he did instead almost made him wonder if maybe his mind and sanity had already parted ways some time ago.

Three days ago Reed didn't believe in anything apart from what he could see in front of his nose, and especially what was in his wallet (or more to the point: what his wallet lacked). But now, if a neighbour of his mentioned seeing strange lights in the sky at night, or if they told him stories about the little girl that lived two doors down, of how her head rotated three hundred and sixty degrees like Linda Blair from the Exorcist, he'd believe in a heartbeat. Even if they told him they'd magically painted "Gullible" on the ceiling, he'd break his neck to take a look.

He couldn't help thinking that maybe magic didn't disappear when childhood ends-

He entered a bedroom, pulling wardrobe doors from their hinges-

Nothing.

Age doesn't kill everything, he thought, quickly leaving the room, wondering why these crazy ideas crossed his mind when he should be looking for the way out! He didn't understand his behaviour-

You're not going crazy, so stop thinking that way!

'WHERE THE HELL IS THE DOOR?' Reed hollered, running now across the landing, doubt breeding fear breeding anger, creating a terror inside he could only equate to drowning. It filled his lungs, his mouth, burned his eyes and made him lose control of his bodily functions. Piss ran down his legs-

Then he saw a tiny flickering light. And as the darkness surrounding it calmed the raging sea inside, he still fought to keep afloat. That light . . . it . . .

It was a door.

It was a door and his last chance, he decided, desperately trying to reach that gloriously bright light. Then he suddenly stopped, his heart now beating like a war drum. Thoughts, thoughts—*cursed thoughts*—they always got in the way!

But what if there is fire waiting on the other side?

He watched his shaking hand, blurred by the tears in his eyes, reach out toward the dark handle. Slowly, his fingers numb with fear, they encircled the warm metal-

He froze once more.

What about the phenomena known as . . . He searched his mind for the word, knowing he'd remember-

Back-draft, David! That's the word you're looking for! This is insane! Stop thinking and move your arse, for God's sake, man!

He squeezed his eyes closed, a galaxy of stars swirling on the canvas of his fevered mind. Then he turned the handle and opened the door.

Christine shook her head, unable to conceal the thin smile as yet another dead artist warbled from the small speaker at the farthest corner of the room. They couldn't come more dead than Elvis, she thought, plunging three dishes and a cup into a sink full of hot soapy water. It was company at least, she admitted, sighing as Jailhouse rock switched to static. But when the white noise lingered she didn't bother changing the station, even though the dials were right beside her. She couldn't even if she'd tried, much to her frustration, for there was only the dead silence between songs. No deejay, no news flashes, no weather—nothing. No truly living thing could reach this place, hell! Not even the air waves! In the two years she had been here she couldn't remember ever having heard the voice of a living human being travel through the damned speakers. Nothing live, that is. Recordings from a bygone time, yes. Interviews conducted twenty even thirty years previous certainly, as though the operators of the white noise struggled to find something, anything to fill the void. And as for the weather? There was only darkness beyond the window. But that was okay, she would often tell herself; that was the way it would have to be until the time came.

She concentrated on the simple task of washing the dishes, as banal and mundane as the task may be, it kept her grounded. She looked over her shoulder at the dark window, condensation dripping over the edge of the sill, the droplets gently tapping on the floor, and a shiver ran through her entire core. It was at times such as these that she thanked her lucky stars. After all she could have been one of the others: condemned to walking through the impenetrable darkness with her arms outstretched like a blind person or like Frankenstein's monster, she mused, shaking the thought from her mind, a grin blossoming across her face. But the smile soon vanished, for the wanderers out there often fell victim to the cruelest acts of debauchery. In fact she had lost count of the poor souls that had found her lights in the darkness beyond. How they had relayed their pitiful stories . . . This place, its bricks, glass and lights was more than the halfway house of the dead. It was a beacon, a lighthouse for the lost souls out there. They'd turn up, eyes squinting with the brightness of the overhead lights, step in from the icy ocean of nothingness and embrace the warmth and hospitality that she had worked tirelessly to protect. She had made it her own; the décor had been her idea, after all her employer had passed away since she had taken over residence, and so it was now her own establishment. The best thing was that she didn't have to pay taxes. In fact, she didn't even need a penny the place was taking. And she smiled at the thought, wondering when she had inherited such responsibility; if she ever did at all. The thought had occurred to her that maybe this was her atonement. Age followed age and she had reincarnated from one body to the next, almost as casually as stepping from a bus only to jump onto the next one that so happened to be there. Many lives had passed, children lost, husbands murdered and buried; all because of her oath; the one promise to protect a pile of bones that meant nothing to her, yet everything to mankind. The child had been born of violence in the forest of Hart in Hartlepool back in 1587 and she had helped in it's destruction . . . but that, as they say, is history.

She knew that this had been her salvation, where her soul had sought refuge after being . . . Christine often struggled to think the word, let alone say it, but she had been murdered. And it was all because she had fallen in love with the very man she was born to kill.

This was the place their lives together had started all those years ago, when two bodies fused into one. It's where her real life began. Darren Barker was a lonely, penniless student and Christine's job was to lead him to the site of the child's burial, watch him find the creature's remains then kill him where he stood. It was her destiny.

But in the end she couldn't kill the one person that gave her two beautiful children. No, the only way for them to be together as a family once more is to make sure the creature survives, even if it left twenty years for all of mankind to enjoy before it returned to destroy everything God created.

All ghosts know that when the tide of death comes to sweep you off your island you try to cling to the only thing or memory that helps to keep your head above the rancid water. This place is her buoy. Always will be.

Darren Barker, her husband, had fought to protect the one thing that spelled the end of the human race and all that was good on earth, and it's name was Sally. Christine had almost torn her sides laughing at the choice of names for the creature also, even though the bloody thing was male! But her daughter, Taylor, had insisted on the name as though the horrible, triple-jawed creature with the gruesome mercury eyes belonged on her shelf with the rest of her dolls and play things, not deep in the earth, where it was meant to be; wrapped in the blessed cerements and the very wire that had severed its entire body, and kept him apart from his father.

They should never have assembled the bones, she thought, remembering that night two years ago at Hamsterly forest. Darren had been so brave. Not just in the face of adversity, when George Valentin, the burnt husk of a man and his cohorts, Shaun and Peter tried to kill him with his own fears, but by protecting Anthony and Taylor and that damned strange creature that should never have been. How the fucking tables had turned when the old man's prisoners, the very parts of his own body that had disbanded in revolt, fell from the very bones that controlled them.

Nineteen, long, dreaded years before the reunion with her loved ones. She hoped they could be reunited sooner, in their dreams. That was of course if they would speak with her. After all she had deceived them. If her husband were there to wrap his arms around her and tell her that she had had no choice then it would be fine and good, but she knew that that wouldn't happen for some time, in fact it might never happen at all.

She couldn't shrug off the memories of her past lives. Her time spent with the brotherhood of Hart Village and the church of St. Mary.

It had indeed been a year since she'd confessed to poor Darren of the game of which he had become a major player. Of course the news had been destructive, but only for a short while. Time was a great healer after all, even though time itself had but nineteen years left. He still loved her. She could feel it, even though his visits had dwindled over the past year. In fact she couldn't remember the last time he had dropped in for a coffee. Well, he was always the stubborn one in their relationship.

Right now she hoped that her only son, Anthony, now aged fourteen, was having the time of his life. She knew he was bitter. Christ, who wouldn't be carrying the burden of knowing that time was short and it was partly because of him and his family? Maybe that was part of the reason why he declined visiting? Maybe she would never know.

And what about her princess, Taylor?

Nine years old going on twenty one!

Fuck, Christine couldn't remember the last time she saw her gorgeous little girl let alone held her in her arms. How she longed to smell the scent of her blond hair, feel the softness of her skin. And that hurt more than being a party to the creation of the end of the world; a contradiction in terms if ever there was one. Darren refused to let Taylor wander here in her dreams, he had told her so; for that was the only means by which the living could see Christine. The dead didn't have to try . . . but the living had to use a little more imagination: try that little harder, actually want to be here. How she longed to hold her, tell her everything was going to be alright in the end and that they would be a family again some day. But it would just have to wait. The little angel still played with dolls, for crying out loud! Let her enjoy her childhood, thought Christine.

Children walked in here every day, asking what was to come or what the Christ happened for them to be here at the café, but all she could do was talk and comfort them. It was heart breaking. For all it could do. Jesus, when they would cry, scream the place down, Christine didn't know what to do-

Suddenly Christine heard the bell and froze.

She hadn't locked the door.

She heard the footsteps across the floor, approaching.

She saw the large bread knife on the drainer, and suddenly grabbed it before turning round-

'Hey! Easy, tiger,' said the stranger, holding her hands to the sky. She was smiling, eyes twinkling.

'Kerry?'

'I wanted to surprise you with my new look,' Kerry replied, her smile now fading away as she saw the bruises to her friend's face. 'But screw that! What the hell happened to you?'

'I love the blond look by the way,' Christine stuttered. 'We could be sisters. And you've lost a little weight. I wish I could—hey, what're you doing?'

Kerry grabbed her by the soapy hand, taking the knife from harm's way and placed it on the drainer. Then she led her to the nearest table, took the chair from the table top and sat Christine down.

'What the fuck are you doing?' Christine chuckled, wincing suddenly as pain rushed through her sides. She ran a weary hand through her unkempt hair. 'I've got pots to wash-'

'You're going to start telling me what's going on while I put the kettle on,' Kerry called over her shoulder whilst filling the kettle. She grabbed two mugs from the drainer, scooped coffee and sugar from the tiny jars on a shelf beside the stove and grabbed a bottle of fresh milk from the tiny refrigerator by her knees.

'Look, Kerry, I'm tired-'

'And I'm not going anywhere until you tell me where you got that black eye.'

'How much time can you spare?' Christine chuckled, delicately pressing a finger tip at the swollen flesh before suddenly leaving the affected area as pain lanced through her skull like a drill bit.

'Hmmm, I'd say around nineteen years.'

58

Reed staggered from the door and fell to his knees, clutching his throat as if vomit constricted his airways. He looked up at a boiling sun how it seared his neck and face. He couldn't remember breathing air so fresh. It tasted clean and icy, as though he had stepped from some great time machine, the dials flashing:

0:00
0:00
0:00

Over and over again the dials flashed. It was the beginning, when everything was new, uncorrupted and sacred.

Expecting to witness a towering inferno, he spun around on his knees, covering his face with weary hands, awaiting the blast of belching black smoke, the stench of melting plastic, crackling timber and the spitting glass shards from the buildings devastated window frames-

But all was calm. Nearby bushes hummed with hidden life, he could hear the insects and birds battling in the shadows of the undergrowth as if for supremacy. And somewhere, far away it seemed, a hound made its presence known. The soil beneath him felt soft and mushy, but he didn't mind. It was real and so far from the dreaded world that he once knew.

Reed quickly stood up, examined his weary, shaking body and brought his sleeve to his nose. He almost gagged at the stench of smoke. Not the scent of cigarettes, he always carried that dark stinking cloud with him, or so he had been told, but actual smoke. It wasn't his imagination at all; he could even feel the heat on the soles of his feet where he'd stepped through the burning house.

But . . . it wasn't burning now, he thought, his skin crawling as though ants scurried beneath it. In fact it didn't even resemble the same house. The one before him looked much smaller and-

I know the windows are whole, David! And there is no smoke here but-

'I don't care!' he snapped, a smile spreading across his tired face. 'I made it through in one piece.' His eyes widened, searching his mind for a few scrambled moments. He'd gone back . . . even though the house wasn't the same—Hell, that didn't matter! It all made sense; he's stepped back in time: of course it's not going to be the same house-

Beyond that door . . .

Home.

Reed closed his eyes for a moment and exhaled slowly, stars swirling across the universe of his mind, as he composed himself. This was no time to get carried away, he thought; there was a job to do.

He surveyed his surroundings, noticing the calm atmosphere; how it spread goose bumps across his entire body. Even the air tasted sweet as though some sugary spore rode the shoulders of the gentle breeze that now stroked his cheek. The town had refused to succumb to the dragon's breath of the motor engine-

Calm down, David! Just breathe slowly-

Just where are the cars? He thought, turning his head in both directions, not caring how bewildered and spaced out he must appear. He couldn't even hear the *beep* of a horn!

The hound barked again.

Reed glanced over his shoulder, at the door waiting there. His heart tripped for a moment, a lump catching in his throat. And he wondered if a fire still raged on the other side-

The sobering thought stilled the air in his lungs, his pulse battering in his ears as though some one or thing was holding his head under water and was reluctant to let go of the scruff of his neck. If he was to return that very moment, he thought, just how bad would it be on the other side? How much of its shell would still be standing-

Reed had to shake the thought from his mind. He didn't even want to imagine what was going on back there; a time that didn't—hell! Didn't even exist yet! And right now there was no time to waste; for every moment he devoured here, the hotter and deadlier the seconds grew back . . . there-

Stop these thoughts, David! We don't have much time remaining! You must-

'I know!' Reed said, nodding. 'I need to find Aaron.'

He took one last look at the house and its calm, sweet smelling garden, making a few mental notes:

Number 43

Check!

Single-glazed windows—sash

Check!

Three upstairs, Care Bears stickers at the corner of the middle one. Two windows downstairs

Check!

Broken bicycle propped up against wall, pebble-dashed facade; front wheel missing-

Got it!

Reed allowed the details to run through his mind a couple of times, letting their hooks gain purchase, so as not to let anything filter through and escape him. He watched a blue glacier of a cloud sail across the glass of an upstairs window, the garden gate hanging loose on its hinge-

Enough with the nitty-gritty, David! Move!

He made his way to the end of the broken path and slowly closed the gate behind him. It creaked as splinters fell from its rusty hinges. He tried to close it properly but it seemed reluctant; almost as reluctant as he felt, heading down the quiet street towards the corner of Silverfield Avenue. Number forty three, his only way home, was disappearing behind him.

Three windows upstairs, two down, one with teddies-no, care bear stickers, bike, no front wheel, broken gate, three windows upstairs, two down, one with teddies-no, care bear stickers, bike, no front wheel, broken gate-

'Fuck off, for God's sake!' he cursed under his breath, unable to suppress the laughter that boiled in him like lava. He was finally losing his mind, if he hadn't already! He wanted to stand still, hold the insides and force out the pent-up frustration—let it all go—but he couldn't!

He smiled at memories that hadn't been conceived, a past that might never go by. He saw Paul bouncing his beloved children on his knee; Reed's grandchildren; eavesdropped the old boy's sketchy adventures . . . of time travel, ghosts, burning houses and carousel horses coming to life: The life of their grandfather.

Maybe they'd believe their father, thought Reed, feeling tears of . . . tears of what? Sorrow? Joy? He couldn't fathom his true emotions for they swam together like creatures from forbidden universes, uniting and pulling them selves apart-

Please hold on, David . . . Just hold on

He nodded then took a deep breath, swallowing hard, the sound of a dry click loud in his head.

Better?

Reed agreed.

Good . . . Now let's keep it together. Let's find Aaron and get the hell back to Tabby and Paul

Reed realized what kind of tears were falling down his cheeks. A smile spread across his smoke-stained face.

Let's go home . . .

The boy couldn't be far away, Reed thought, reaching the corner of the street, a hot sun burning the nape of his neck. As much as he hated to admit it but for the first time in almost twenty years, he couldn't wait to see the little bastard.

Kerry offered Christine another cup of tea, but she declined, picking a packet of cigarettes and a disposable lighter from a small handbag which hung from a rusty hook on the wall beside the kitchen sink. She noticed the other woman's smile; the way she shook her head. And as she lit the tip of the cigarette, she felt the warmth of a smile spread through her weary face.

'I know, I know,' said Christine, blowing a stream of blue smoke into the air. 'Why the hell do I still have a handbag? Your guess is as good as mine.'

Kerry shrugged her thin shoulders and took a sip from her cup of steaming tea. The small, wooden chair creaked beneath her weight. Age it seemed was catching up with the place, she thought, but she stared intently at her friend.

'I couldn't care less what you carry round, sweets,' she said. 'I'm just bewildered that you've kept all this to yourself—No, it's my turn to speak now, Chris!'

Christine sighed resignedly, drawing deeply on her almost spent cigarette before throwing it in the sink with the tepid water.

'Three arseholes waltz in here, show you the back of their hands and you just get on with the washing up? And I still managed to walk in here! No locks on the doors-'

'OKAY, KERRY! I GET THE FUCKING MESSAGE, LOUD AND CLEAR!'

Silence filled the space between them and even the darkness beyond the café would have seemed more vibrant than the very moments trickling away within these crumbling walls.

274

'How long have we known each other?' Kerry wanted to know, her voice now as soft as her cheek. She absently flicked a rogue lock of blond hair behind her left ear and fixed her friend with eyes of green, so incredibly clear and bright, that Christine looked and indeed felt decades older. 'What have we been through, Chris?'

'I'm not going to get Darren and the kids involved with this,' Christine snapped, shaking her head, before self-consciously running her weary hands through her mop of unkempt hair, fastening the top button of her grease-stained blouse. 'They've been through enough because of me . . . and they don't deserve this.'

'They're your bloody family, for crying out loud!' replied Kerry, eyes wide. 'Do you think they'd want to see you in trouble-'

'I'm not going to mess up what time they have left,' Christine said vehemently. 'I haven't seen them since-'

'I know, I know,' Kerry almost whispered, gazing down into her tea cup.

'Darren thinks we've been selfish wanting the world to end so we can all be a family together-'

'You can't exactly blame him, now can you?' replied Kerry incredulously, shaking her head. 'You disappear, presumed dead, haunt his dreams, then confess to murdering every man whose ever fallen in love with you—and all for the sake of a couple of stones-'

'YOU TOOK THE OATH, JUST LIKE I DID!'

'I know I did,' Kerry snapped back, but she kept the edge of calmness to her voice, refusing to succumb to the madness that was slowly taking control of her friend. 'And, as you know, I've spilled my fair share of blood-'

'Not to mention falling in love with my husband-'

'When you begged George to kill you, because you couldn't go through with it yourself, It was my job to take over . . . But you're right, I did fall for him. Who wouldn't? And what about those two munchkins of his? What a pair of cuties! I bet Anthony's breaking all the hearts at his school. And as for Taylor, well, it won't be long before she's doing the same! I knew just what dilemma you faced a couple of years ago. There had to be an end to the bloodshed . . . And it had to start with someone worth fighting for. Even if we think the fight is already lost-'

Christine wiped her eyes with her sleeve, but was unable to suppress the sobs that now shook her completely.

'Hey, sweets,' said Kerry bridging the distance between them in a heartbeat. 'It's okay . . . We'll get through this, you'll see . . . It's okay,' she let her soft words trail away as her friend cried into her shoulder.

'I just don't want it to be like this until the end,' Christine said groggily, shaking still. She broke free of her friend's embrace and gazed into her kind eyes. 'I just can't keep the secret for the next nineteen years.'

Kerry nodded slowly before letting Christine rest her head on her shoulder once more.

'I know, sweets,' she whispered. 'I know.'

'I can't let another Aaron Brookes get through-'

'You've just got to stop falling for the bad 'uns,' replied Kerry, chuckling softly. 'They tell you their fucking sob story and, being the little softie you are, you help them on their way. But-'

'It stops now, Kerry,' said Christine pulling away from her friend's loving arms. She wiped her tear stained face on her sleeve then straightened up as though fortified by her resolve. 'Only the good go back. Those three arseholes are going to return . . . and we're on our own. But I don't want Darren or the kids involved in this, okay? Swear to me, Kerry! Swear to me that you'll help me and keep my family out of this-'

'Of course, sweets! I swear, I swear! That's the girl I know and love,' said Kerry, smiling broadly. 'So what do we do?'

Suddenly the crash of broken glass destroyed the silence of the room as a brick hurtled through the window, narrowly missing Christine's face.

59

Number forty three, bike outside, Care Bears—got it!

Reed smiled but listening to the mantra in his head no longer amused him. He smiled because anxiety and fear always made him appear to be a million miles away, content and so far from harm's way that a bullet could strike him between the eyes without him feeling a thing for hours.

Come on, David . . . You can do this; stop torturing yourself. It's all in your mind-

He nodded, gaining some frail form of control of his senses. But it was composure nonetheless, so he fought to keep the words between his ears before his mind threatened to tear his skull to pieces. It was working, he thought, now smiling for real-

Suddenly a car Reed hadn't seen in an automobile magazine let alone on the road, passed slowly, appearing as if from out of nowhere; it's driver staring wearily at him.

'You're just like mice in a cage,' he whispered, nodding in reply as the vehicle slowly reached the corner of the street then disappeared from his life forever. He fought to rid his senses of the thick stench of leaded petrol, the grey cloud blowing over him from the cars exhaust pipe, but it was futile. He held his breath a few seconds to let it pass. 'You don't have a bloody clue about me.'

He felt almost invisible on the sun kissed path, the heat of the concrete soaking through the soles of his shoes. He couldn't be sure just what season this was. Hell, it certainly wasn't winter . . . it was back in his time, he thought, but not here. Maybe it was summer-

'I couldn't care less,' he mumbled.

The trees to his left stood tall and somewhat foreboding, like dark sentinels, guarding something, but what exactly he couldn't fathom. He envisioned an eager limb lurking and flexing its muscles in every shadow cast, his body unsettled in their close proximity, waiting for one gnarled branch to reach out-

You're getting carried away again, David-

'Don't make me banish you again . . . because I can,' Reed mumbled, inhaling the fresh air once more, now that the car was long gone.

Silence replied.

Reed nodded, smiling brighter than ever. But the smile soon faded as he remembered Aaron's demise, of how his poor little burned carcass had been thrown from a car; left to smolder and rot amongst the wet leaves and earth-

For God's sake, why me!

Couldn't the damned trees have clamped onto Aaron's soul? Why did this have to happen?

The answer's easy and you know it. He's already told you, David! He wants his life back-

'They all do,' Reed whispered.

What on earth must you do for him, David?

'Repay a favour-'

Just like in the olden days?

'Just like in the olden days,' Reed mouthed the words but not a sound fell from his dry, cracked lips.

I know . . . I heard his story, David. You don't need those images going through your mind right now . . . Stay focused.

All he wants is his childhood back, thought Reed. Another chance to relive his years without spending his days in fear; used like a worthless play thing to throw to one side when the mood struck. Is that too much to ask?

I know you're thinking it's a small price to pay-

If it weren't for Aaron, thought Reed, then I wouldn't be able to watch Paul grow-

It's not that simple, don't you see-

He's offering me a second chance, to be with my family; to make everything count again . . . another try-

How can you be so sure? You know what he's capable-

I know what he did to Johnny Gladstone-

But, David-

He got the fucker off of my back and out of Tabby's life! He's literally saved my life, don't you see that? He's about to change my future, in fact he already has. And if this works, maybe my entire past will change . . .

You mean that if you save him then-

'Then he wouldn't have . . . existed at all,' Reed spoke softly allowing his words to trail away.

The hot sun rays beamed across Reed's face and he couldn't remember ever feeling so confident.

David . . . for the first time in days you're actually beginning to make sense.

He quickened his pace.

Christine headed for the window but yelped as Kerry grabbed her shoulder tightly, almost pulling her off her feet.

'Are you bloody mad, woman?' snapped Kerry, dragging her friend behind the cash counter, to take shelter should another object come hurtling through the shattered window. But Christine still managed to curse despite the taste of smoke in the palm of Kerry's hand, pulling it away so she could breathe at least.

'Am I mad?' gasped Christine incredulously. 'Whoever threw that bloody thing's still out there-'

Kerry slapped a hand over her mouth once more to shut Christine up, waving her other hand before her pale, wide-eyed face. She understood and nodded, prizing the smoke scented fingers away from her face.

Christine's eyes were wide and bright, their eye contact remaining, even when they heard the sound of voices coming from beyond the broken window. And when she recognized the speaker her shoulders slumped as though a pin had pierced her guard and now she was quickly deflating. It was Beard and his cohorts, for that there was no doubt, she thought. Jesus, she should've known from the start.

'Maybe I should just tell them what to do?' Christine whispered.

'Are you fucking crazy?' Kerry hissed, shaking her head. 'No way! You know that they don't deserve to go back-'

'But who are we to say who can and who-'

'We're not going to put up with this for the better part of twenty years, Chris!'

'I know . . . do you think that the arseholes out there have it in for me because-'

'Because you let one of them through, you mean?' said Kerry.

'Don't say his name,' replied Christine, closing her eyes. 'You know I made a fucking mistake by falling for-'

'Aaron Brookes knew how to play you,' said Kerry. 'You fell for his sob story and he stomped all over you. You told him how . . . Don't you see that this is where you're going wrong? You're as soft as shit!'

'Okay, I felt sorry for him! Just like I felt sorry for a whole bunch of others . . . why's he different, eh?' Christine hollered, much to Kerry's surprise. After all she actually stilled her tongue at her friend's outburst. 'You can roll your fucking eyes at me, but I don't care. I'm lonely, Kerry—there, I said it. I don't think I can take another nineteen minutes, never mind nineteen years!'

'Why's he different?' Kerry chuckled, shaking her head. 'Are you taking the piss? He's scum, Christine, that's the difference. He belongs out there with his little pathetic gang that trawl the darkness for fresh, fearful meat-'

'I'm going to tell them what they need to know,' said Christine about to get to her feet. But Kerry pulled her back down behind the counter.

'Wait,' she said, a fingertip at her lip. 'You hear that?'

Christine held her breath for a couple of seconds to concentrate.

'I don't hear a thing-'

'Exactly,' whispered Kerry, slowly standing up, before peering over at the window, noticing how the dull light over head caught the sharp edges of the glass shards scattered about the floor.

The small red brick lay amongst the pieces.

'They've gone,' said Kerry, carefully bending down to pick the object up off the floor. The brick was just . . . just an ordinary house brick.

'I hope so-'

'But not for long-'

'So what do I do-'

'We,' said Kerry, crossing the room to deposit the brick into the waste paper basket. She clapped the dust from the palms of her hands and smiled. 'What do we do?'

Christine smiled but it didn't last. As her bottom lip quivered, the first tear raced down her pale cheek, followed by another. As they embraced, Christine's tears falling freely, Kerry felt herself sobbing softly, but quickly shrugged off the feeling.

This was no time for weakness, she thought.

*

I watched the shapes scatter, the sound of their heavy footfalls filling the silence as they passed me by, consumed by the hungry nothingness. Their sickening scent filled my nostrils and almost threatened to turn my stomach. I held my breath, hearing the blood thump in my ears, hoping they would fail to realize my presence. Noise moved so quickly here, and could be one's worst enemy if not kept in check. Stars sparkled in the darkness, and I counted the moments before breathing once more. After ten seconds the footfalls and maniacal laughter faded into utter silence. And I exhaled . . .

The shape crossed the broken window but something pulled it away, leaving the bright light behind the grubby net curtains-

I heard voices whilst approached the bottom step leading to the café's front door and saw the pieces of shattered glass at my feet, stopping me in my tracks.

I wanted to tell her the good news, wanted so much to ease her pain and fear; to tell her that everything would be alright, that she didn't need to worry any more-

My smile faded, hearing the sound of sorrow, the cries of fear, weariness and desperation invade the silence surrounding me.

I knew that I would have to try harder.

This wasn't going to be easy and there was no time to rest.

I turned my back on the café and disappeared into the darkness once more.

60

Reed glanced at his wristwatch.

11:30 AM

It can't be, he thought. No, it must be a mistake, surely. But the damned thing is digital so there can not be a problem with the batteries. Jesus! Where was the time going? It must be different here-

It's almost noon-

'I know,' Reed replied, quickening his pace. 'Where the hell would children hangout at this time-'

Think about it, David—Don't! What are you doing-

'Hey, excuse me,' he shouted over to a woman passing on the opposite side of the road. She was struggling with some bags of shopping. 'Wait there. I'll help you,' he said, quickly crossing the street.

The woman smiled crookedly, revealing a row of brown, equally crooked teeth. Warily she squinted, appraising the stranger before her. And immediately he wondered just how disheveled he must appear; standing there, panting, twitching uncomfortably in his grubby clothes, heat from a fire way-back-when still pressing against his skin. He could almost taste the smoke permeating the air between them.

Reed reached for the old lady's shopping bags, but instinctively, she pulled away sharply as though recoiling from a figure cut straight from some dark bible-

'Hey, I'm sorry,' said Reed, holding up his hands to show that he'd meant no harm. 'I just thought they looked a little heavy and that you could use a hand.'

'That's okay, flower,' she replied softly, flicking a lock of silver hair from her weathered face with a quick nod of her head. 'But I can manage. Always have and I'm not about to start-'

'Look, you wouldn't happen to know the right time, would you?' he asked, biting his bottom lip, wondering if it was such a good idea to be talking to another person here-

Stop it, David!

'Yes, it's about . . . ,' she replied, screwing up her face as though she had placed a shard of lemon on her tongue. The wheels were turning and maybe she would never know. But then—'It's about half past five.'

That can't be right, David . . . That can't be right—You must think fast!

'Shit,' he said. 'I'm supposed to pick up my little brother from school and I'm bloody late-'

'Yes,' she chuckled loudly, nodding her head, 'you could say that.' And without another word she stepped onto the road and shuffled her way to the edge of the street. But suddenly she turned to face him and smiled softly; a look of sympathy in her warm brown eyes.

She must have children of her own, maybe great grand children-

'Look,' she said, raising her voice to be heard even though not a sound stirred between them, 'If you've missed him—what's his name?'

Think fast-

'Aaron,' he replied, his heart battering the inside of his chest. 'His name is Aaron Brookes.'

'Well, I don't know any boy of that name, but if you've missed him there's this big shop full of those . . . erm, what do you call 'ems? One armed bandits—that's it! Rob you blind they will if you're not careful. One of my friends at line dancing used to-'

'Can you tell me where I can find the shop?' Reed snapped impatiently, softening the blow with a winning smile. 'Please. I'm . . . I'm worried about him.'

'Well don't be,' she replied. 'I'd bet every moth and cobweb in my handbag that he'll be there, safe and sound on them space games-'

'Space Invaders? There's an arcade around here?'

'Yes, the place is a bloody eye sore. Kids standing about outside, smoking-'

'Shit, of course! The arcade,' he said shaking his head. How the hell could he have forgotten the arcade? All those fantastic hours spent there when he should've been sitting in a sweltering classroom! His mind raced with the memories, his heart pounding hard in his chest—he suddenly grabbed his left arm as though he could feel a heart attack approaching.

What's wrong, David?

He shook his head. 'I'm fine, really.'

The old lady stepped back apace. 'Do you need an ambulance-'

Maybe that's not such a bad idea-

'I SAID I'M FINE!' he yelled, surveying his surroundings as though he had just awoken in this crazy world. 'This shopping parade, where is it?'

'You'll have to speak up, flower-'

'I SAID-,' he replied, suddenly lowering his voice, noticing the fear on the lady's, pale gentle face. 'I'm so sorry . . . I'm-'

David, what the fuck is wrong with you?

'I feel-'

'The arcade is just a couple of blocks away,' she said, pointing to the corner of the street, then she scuttled away while she had the chance to flee from this crazy individual.

'I feel like I'm . . . ,' Reed panted, pulling at his collar, beads of sweat formed on his forehead and wriggled down his face. 'I feel like I'm on fire.'

Come on, move! We don't have much time! Remember, when this is over-

'I know,' Reed said, wiping his face on his sleeve. 'It'll be as though he never existed at all.' He tried to smile but his whole body shook.

*

Reed shielded his eyes with both hands, squinting as he peered through the dark glass window of the arcade, feeling the vibrations as music beat like a human heart inside; shadows danced, shifted and merged, it seemed, to the thumping tunes. It was just as he remembered it. Jesus, even fat Jenny was there dishing out change in her little upright coffin of a booth, telling anyone who cared, or was indeed able to hear above the din, that she wasn't going to do this boring job forever.

The same words, day in day out, Reed thought. Words that changed nothing.

He stepped inside the shop, his shoes felt tacky against the grubby, cigarette burnt carpet, its faint dark blue swirls, patterns now blackened with the filth of careless human traffic, reluctantly allowing him to venture further into the converging shadows of the room. It was like a cheap and nasty night club, he thought. He felt drawn to a couple of coin-op games beside a COKE machine, lights flashing across their screens-

This is not the time-

'House of blood,' Reed gasped. 'I don't believe it-'

'Hey, watch where you're going!' a small boy with bright ginger hair snapped, wiping the spilled drink from his thin pale forearm where Reed had walked into him.

'Christ, I'm sorry, son,' Reed replied-

See what I mean?

Reed nodded, his shirt now sticking to his back like a second skin.

Can you feel the flames?

Surveying the small crowd of children without looking suspicious was not an easy task, Reed thought. Even though some of them were waist height, their features twisted out of true, beguiling their age and in some cases their sex, he wondered just how he was going to pull this off without drawing too much attention to himself. There were so many wide eyes, lips mouthing obscenities, and tiny fists bashing the control panels in frustration before grabbing more pieces of silver from their pockets; stuffing them into the slots as though their very lives depended on it.

He heard a squeal of delight to his right and the rattle of change as the machine's small collection trays filled with coins. The same din erupted on his left. Reed wanted to laugh, after all, he couldn't remember one of these damned rust buckets actually coughing up a penny-

Then he spotted Aaron.

Reed quickly turned away, looking down at his reflection in the glittery, flashing surface of a ROCKY pinball table. An old Culture Club track poured from the speakers above his head, but he could still hear the blood pulsating in his head. He pushed a coin in the slot so as not to look conspicuous. But nothing happened. No lights, no funky bleeping music. Then he chuckled, not surprised at all when the contraption didn't register. This was the past, he reasoned; the new coins hadn't been pressed yet.

Reed quickly glanced over his shoulder at the boy.

Yes, it was him alright, thought Reed. He couldn't mistake those piercing eyes. Even though they made eye contact for a split second, Reed knew that there dwelt the tortured soul of a child-

He doubled up in pain.

David, you must hurry-

But all he needed to do was wait a little longer.

Easy.

Easy to think and even easier to say, Reed thought. But all of that changed when the only way home was burning away each second that passed by. He slammed in another ten pence piece despite knowing fine well what would happen. But he had to look convincing, nudging the controls, dramatically raking his hands through his hair in mock defeat; feigning despair. He exhaled, shaking his head as he moved on to the next game, all the while taking another step closer toward the boy.

Reed glanced at Aaron, watching the boy jam silver into the machine, its body suddenly bursting with noise and bright colours. Christ, he thought, catching a glimpse at the boy's balled left fist, wondering where the hell he had laid his grubby digits on so much money. How much pocket money did his mum give him-

Maybe she just wanted the poor bugger out of the way!

Reed nodded, watching another coin fill the slot-

And another.

He closed his eyes for a moment, hearing the clutter of metal in the collection trays, the chatter of children and the beat of their little fists against the control sticks, and he could feel the heat rush over his body. Sweat was pouring down his back now. He was afraid to keep still incase, like an insect under a magnifying glass, he should suddenly burst into flames. No, he had to keep moving.

He opened his eyes and his heart skipped a beat.

Aaron had disappeared.

Reed surveyed the room, air almost constricted in his chest, a culmination of panic and fear squeezing the very energy from his body. The grubby faces swam in the darkness, how they split and contorted with spokes of bright light from the screens before them; held in thrall as though hypnotized-

'God, this can't be happening,' he muttered, now gasping for air.

Calm down, David!

'So . . . fucking . . . close-'

The room was spinning as the pop music grew louder, so loud that the machines fought to be heard. Maybe it was the blood pounding in his ears which forced out all other noise, he thought, spinning round, desperately trying to find Aaron.

You will find him! Just breathe, for God's sake!

He didn't want to listen, all he wanted to do was scream; press 'pause' on this horror movie—simply stop everything for one blessed moment. No, not for a moment, he wanted out of this scene completely.

There's the little bastard!

David, it's not Aaron-

Despite the dark and the convoluted voices, Reed spotted him . . . it was the little toe-rag, alright, he would bet his life on it!

'Come with me, you little . . .' he said, parting two youths who were huddled together before a flashing screen, spinning them round to face him.

'What the fuck are you doing, you wanker?' said one boy, straightening his ruffled collar, frowning angrily at Reed. He pushed his spectacles, which had the thickest lenses Reed had ever seen, up the bridge of his greasy little nose.

'Yeah, go stick it up your arse, you perv'!' his companion shouted over the music. He looked just as greasy except his acne covered his chin and his nose.

'I'm . . . I'm sorry, lads,' said Reed, holding up his hands in way of apology. And as he backed away from them, quickly leaving the shop, Reed never felt so deflated in his life. He didn't have time for this!

'I don't know what you want me to say,' Christine said softly. She wiped the tears from her cheek and looked down into the tea cup, seeing her face reflected back in the still tepid liquid. She could smell the tea and it turned her stomach. Tiredness and age—hell, even ghosts aged. It was a hard lesson to learn, if ever there was one. Crows feet at the corner of her eyes, dark lines and puffiness to boot . . . A sorry sight, she thought, shaking her head. 'I told you I was lonely . . .'

Kerry nodded, taking a sip from her mug, wincing at the bitter taste. 'Urgh, it's cold!'

As she rose from her seat and crossed the room to pour the liquid into the sink, Christine noticed how she quickly glanced over her shoulder at the shattered window and the pieces on the floor. And she smiled a little.

So the big bad Kerry wasn't as fearless as she made believe? Christine thought, clearing her throat.

'I know,' replied Kerry.

'I mean-'

'No, Chris,' snapped Kerry, slamming her cup down onto the counter, shattering the silence of the room. 'Please, don't even go there! You're lonely. And so am I. Don't you think I'd give my right tit to get a little tail? Well?'

'I miss Darren-'

'So do I—Don't look at me that way, Chris . . . you know I love him too,' replied Kerry, taking a pack of cigarettes from her pocket, lit one then offered Christine one. To which she accepted.

'So we're in love with the same man,' said Christine, drawing deeply on her cigarette, feeling her muscles relax with the rush of nicotine. 'I've known all along.'

'It was my job, and you know it,' Kerry replied. 'And I couldn't do it either. I can see what you loved about him. He wasn't the funniest of blokes but there certainly was a certain something-'

'Love.'

'What?'

'Love,' repeated Christine, tapping her cigarette in the ashtray on the table before her. 'You say the word in the wrong tense. I love him still. Our time isn't over just yet.'

'I wonder how many times we've used that fucking word in the past ten minutes.'

'What word?' said Christine, raising her eyebrows, a grin spreading across her pale, weary face.

Kerry chuckled, shaking her head in a halo of blue smoke.

'I must admit, Aaron does have a certain charm,' said kerry, taking another drag.

'I told you,' replied Christine as calmly as possible, despite the anger that slowly smoldered inside 'He's nothing. I was lonely and he was there, I thought you'd understand that.'

'I understand alright. I just don't like the way you open yourself up to any Tom, Dick or Harry-'

'You're walking a very fucking fine line with me now, Kerry,' said Christine, squeezing the handle of her cup to the point of shattering the damned thing. 'It was a mistake . . . that's all. Besides, getting all pissed off with each other doesn't resolve a bloody thing. Agree?'

Kerry was silent.

'Does it?' Christine demanded an answer.

'Yes, for fuck's sake! Okay?'

'I just . . . I just told him what to use,' said Christine quietly as though she could see the words before her and whispered them should they blow away. 'He needed to delve as far down into his soul as possible . . . to latch onto the first thing that his soul's instinct attracted him to, and I'm not talking about something trivial here, I mean he had to go with his gut-'

'I know-'

'I'm talking about the first thing—not the second. There are no second thoughts,' said Christine, glancing over at her friend. 'One mistake and it's all over. I was stupid to tell him what to look for: how to manipulate the soul who could help him . . . I can't believe I fucked it all up-'

'He's just one prick that got through, Chris. George taught us what to do should we need to come back and you let that information slip. We're only human. We did no wrong. Where he learned the lessons I hope we never know,' Kerry cooed, crossing the room to wrap her arms around her shoulders, feeling them shiver at her touch. They felt so cold and thin. 'His . . .'

'Do you think his friends want the same thing?' said Christine, fresh tears running down her cheek. 'He got a second chance at life, now his so called buddies want to go too?'

'What else would they want?' Kerry replied softly, unable to hide the fear in her voice. She hugged her friend, feeling her shoulders shake. 'We could just let them know how to cross over-'

'No way!' said Christine, breaking their embrace, turning around to make eye contact. 'No fucking way, Kerry! I don't care what happens over the next nineteen years! They can throw as many stones at that bastard window as they want to but what time remains are for those who deserve it!'

'Calm down-'

'No, I won't calm down! I took the life from my world. Darren won't speak to me, won't let me see the kids—and you know why? He said that if nineteen years are all he has with the children, as living people, then he wants nothing to do with . . . with the dead-'

'Meaning-'

'Meaning: me.'

Kerry nodded, licked her lips and sniffed.

Silence hung motionless on the air.

'This isn't trivial, you know?' said Kerry finally. 'You've started something that you must keep up for the next nineteen years. That's a long time. Why don't you just let any fucker go back?'

'I can't believe you're saying that, Kerry,' said Christine, slowly shaking her head. 'You know what the stones said about the worthy walking the earth in light of the fragility of the time remaining; it's borrowed . . . they don't deserve what's left-'

'God, you make them sound like carrion birds pecking at carcasses—Chris, who are you to judge who stays and who makes a go of what's left over the other side, eh?'

There was silence between them for a moment.

'As long as I look after this place,' Christine replied, composing herself. 'As long as there is air in my lungs, I will decide who goes back and who remains.'

Kerry knew that it was unwise to utter argue.

'Come whatever may?'

'Come whatever may.'

*

I felt the pain lancing my soul, knew the feeling of desolation as I wandered through the darkness, searching for bright eyes in the umbra. There were armies in the night. I just needed to find them, to keep looking when the sleepers turned their backs, and the believers saw the error of their ways. But most of all keep the badness as far away from the café as possible. The nights weren't over but they were abundant. Or that's what I once thought. Except the only question was: when the time came, did I have it in my soul to keep searching? There was an end to everything-

'I can't let her down,' I said, searching the local haunts. 'I love her and there's no way I'm going to let her down.'

Up ahead I noticed a bright light.

61

The sunlight hurt his eyes but Reed was grateful for the fresh air. Despite the brightness there was an edge to the breeze and he detected the aroma of cooking meat and fried onions. Someone was having a barbeque. But it was a damned better scent than stale cigarettes and body odour from the arcade, he thought, raking his hands through his unkempt hair. When was this? It certainly wasn't winter like back home! Summer? Spring? Fuck it!

He yearned for a good hot bath and a shave-

It won't be long, David! That and more is waiting for you-

'I understand. I get it,' Reed mumbled, his head spinning with the culmination of bright light, traffic crawling nearby, the squeal of excited children as they poured out of the arcade-

'I've got to get away!'

Just be careful-

Just where the hell was Aaron? He thought, watching a couple of infants cross the street. But he shook his head. No, they were too small-

The cars brakes screeched to a halt on his right, the driver screaming like a banshee: 'Move it, you little shit! Go on, be home with you!'

The child waited for the car to pass before sticking two fingers up in the air, laughing as he crossed the road.

It's him!

Reed nodded.

'It's him, alright,' replied Reed. 'It has to be.'

Reed ran across the road, his right hand merely inches from the boy, fingertips encircling his collar, quickly spinning the boy round.

'Get off me or I'll tell me mam!' shrieked the little girl, spitting in his face.

Reed froze a moment, shocked as he watched the girl run further up the street. Spittle ran down his cheek. He quickly wiped it away with his sleeve, looking about self-consciously as though he was a pervert about to be caught with his hand in the cookie jar.

That was a girl?

This wasn't going as smoothly as he'd hoped. He wanted to cry, just give in and collapse into a pile of fear and meat on the pavement; to stay in one place to let the fire consume him.

'It's over . . .'

This isn't over, David!

'STOP CALLING ME DAVID!' he shouted at the top of his voice. Pedestrians spun on their heels to see the source of the comical outburst, shaking their heads before moving on with their lives and dismissing him as just another mad man in the afternoon heat.

What do you prefer-

'Reed,' he whispered, swallowing hard. 'Only Tabby calls me David.'

He felt something inside nod its head. It was the strangest feeling he had ever encountered. It was like being watched by a thousand eyes rolled into one. And he was glad that the connection had been made, established and acknowledged.

No, Da—No, Reed . . . You're not mad. I'm not your guardian angel either . . . just a voice I wish you'd take a little seriously now and again-

'Okay—*aaaaarrrghh!*'

Reed fell to the ground and curled up, his knees in his chest, his flesh crawling as though he had been doused with iced water.

Come on, Reed, get up! You must keep moving otherwise-

'I'll burn, I know!' Reed replied, veins prominent in his throat, eyes bulging with pain as the burning sensation engulfed him. 'Just leave me here-'

So you can do what you've been thinking about for so long? So you can commit suicide? You FUCKING COWARD!

Reed looked up at the azure sky, quickly beginning to believe he'd never shake free from this whole nightmare. All he wanted to do was go home. He managed to release his hands from his sides and wiped away the stinging tears from his eyes. A car went by . . . and another. But he remained still beside the road, watching the world, and a time that was dead and gone go by; deep, fresh air now coursing through his lungs as though they had been skewered. Dots peppered across his field of vision, but only momentarily as his anxiety slowly passed-

That's it . . . slow the hell down, Reed.

'Time's slipping . . . away,' he muttered, seeing the first licks of gray smoke appear on his knee caps. 'Time can have me . . . I give up-'

Just what I thought you'd do, Reed, David—whatever you want to call yourself! But it all amounts to one thing: SHIT!

'Please . . . God-'

What is it now, Mr. Reed? Have you spotted something good and sharp? Something you can draw across your yellow wrists-

'Wait . . .' he whispered, his vision coming into focus. 'Yes, It must be . . . It's that little bastard . . .' he said breathlessly.

The boy walked quickly up the street-

Your heart's going crackers, Reed! Just calm down—what are you doing?

Reed staggered to his feet once more, his head spinning.

'Just need to keep pace with the little bastard,' he mumbled, swallowing hard. 'Got to keep moving . . . I'm burning-'

Only if you stop, Reed. Keep moving and you'll be fine-

'The little fucker's over there . . .' Reed said, taking deep breaths as he got to his feet. 'Got to . . . keep moving.' He patted the gray wisps of smoke away from his clothing.

Hours seemed to pass but he knew that only minutes had passed between them.

'He's . . . so slow,' Reed muttered.

Who can blame the poor bugger?

Reed frowned.

Think about it! An arsehole for a mother and a creep for a step father! Would you be in a hurry to get home?

Reed's heart sank, remembering Aaron's story. He hoped that the boy had been given enough money to pass over the time the arsehole spent with his mum-

To come and go, you mean?

'I'll ignore that last remark,' Reed said, staggering along the path like an extra from the movie Night of the living dead. And he knew it wasn't so. This was a recording. He had to keep reminding himself-

The boy now paused at his garden gate, staring fixedly at the bedroom windows. He knew it too: the abuse, the beatings . . . just the same day, everyday.

Nothing was ever going to change.

A part of Reed wanted the boy to hurry up and go inside. He walked passed him and made for the corner of the street, disappearing among the trees. He breathed softly, cloaked in dark shadows. But then . . . the horror that was about to unfold was oblivious to Aaron, but not to Reed. It was the end of the boy—Or maybe he did know? Thought Reed-

'Come on, Aaron. Just get inside,' Reed whispered through clenched teeth. 'I promise I'll be right behind you.'

That's the plan . . . Real quick-

'Save the boy then go home.'

That's right-

'Save the boy then go home.'

Sigh-

'Save the-'

Get a hold of yourself, Reed! For the love of God!

Reed shook his head. It was all he could think about. The plan was simple; he just needed to put his fears aside. Screw that hippy hitchhiker he'd picked up way back when. Let there be ghosts and hungry spirits in this place, he thought warily, peeking over his shoulder at the dark shadows surrounding him. The real world was far scarier-

'Number forty three . . . bicycle with one wheel . . . sticker in the window . . . this is it—just get inside for Christ's sake!' he hissed, digging his nails into the hard bark of the tree shielding him from sight. 'Come on—there, good boy . . .'

The screech of the rusty hinge cut through the silence of the hot afternoon. And as the gate slowly opened, Reed's breath caught in his throat. Only did it escape from between clenched jaws the moment the boy set his first tentative step up the cracked garden path.

There. Now can you relax?

Reed felt the relief wash over him as though his fevered mind had suddenly been unplugged from the supercharger that threatened to explode behind him at any given moment-

So move before the house is razed to the ground!

'This is really happening,' he mumbled. 'I can't believe this is-'

Then he froze. The look on the boy's face was one of pure dread.

I can smell the fear too, Reed . . . even from this distance. That's why we have to move . . . NOW!

Reed made his way towards number forty three, watching Aaron slowly open the front door, step inside then close the door behind him. And as he did so he couldn't erase the image of a little lamb from his mind, a gentle little lamb on its way to the slaughterhouse.

The lights cut through the darkness like demon's eyes but I kept moving, driven by the promise of extra hearts and souls; some goodness that could help keep the bloody jaws and nails at bay. I knew that despite my fatigue and the prospect of encountering the monsters that roamed this empty quarter, I had to persevere. I heard Christine's cries and pushed them to the back of my mind. She needed me more than ever; needed me to stand up and be a man.

'I am a man, Christine,' I whispered, quickening my pace toward the flickering lights. 'See how I move? Only God knows what's up ahead . . .'

'Hello?' a voice hollered.

I stopped but my heart hammered hard against my ribs as though it tried its damnedest to break out. Holding my breath unleashed tiny sprites in front of my eyes and blood pulsed loudly in my ears.

'We know you're there!' the voice shouted; a female voice I noticed. 'Just . . . please stay where you are. The fire is shining in your eyes . . . Don't move.'

I could be callous like the horrors hiding round every corner of black nothingness; the rapists and the murderers, I could close my eyes so the female wandered forever . . . but I wasn't one of them. I thought a man like myself could reach the limit of horror and turn his back upon it, unable to face it any more. But I had to destroy what destroyed me: fear itself.

'I'll be right here,' I said softly. Shouting was merely a waste of energy and drew unwanted attention to ones' self. 'I promise.'

I detected another voice, it seemed gruff and laboured. And as they spoke softly, closing the distance between them, I heard panic and something akin to confusion in their tone; their Geordie accents were familiar-

'No way . . .'

It couldn't be . . . could it?

I broke my promise, moving one foot before the other, sweat wriggling down my back, pasting my shirt to my skin.

The lights grew brighter, nearer-

I picked up the pace, praying that this was just a nightmare. But . . .

The cigarette lighters were swallowed by the inky darkness but suddenly burst into life once more, unveiling two faces I hoped not to see for another nineteen years.

'Jackie?' I said, tears welling in my eyes. 'Is that you, sis? Is it really you-'

'God, we never thought we'd ever see you again,' Jackie cried, letting her lighter fall to the floor as she wrapped her arms about my thin shoulders, tears pouring down her face.

I looked over at the other burning light, my mum's kind eyes twinkling in its warm orange glow. 'My boy,' she said, her bottom lip quivering, her emotions about to spill over their brim it seemed.

'Why are you here?' I cried, hugging my sister. 'You must tell me what's happened-'

Then my eyes widened and I grabbed her shoulders, prizing her away from me to find the answers written in her face, for I wouldn't get any truth tonight-

'Just take us somewhere warm and safe,' said Jackie.

'I'm going to fucking kill him!' I snarled. 'I swear-'

'You can't do a thing now . . . Anyway, Dad's in prison-'

'What did he do, Jackie?' I pleaded. 'The bastard's gone too far!'

'Please,' she cried, shaking. 'Please, just take us somewhere warm . . .'

I held her in my arms and hugged her for all I was worth.

'I know a place.'

62

Reed waited in the shadows, unsure exactly of the right time to strike. Once again time had shifted. He couldn't tell if it was five thirty or even ten thirty. The digital face of his watch had blackened as though the LCD had turned to liquid and washed across the screen. He pulled it from his wrist and threw the piece of crap in the gutter to rot amongst litter and leaves. His heart was pounding hard, white shapes drifting in the gloom before his eyes. Twice he had shook with panic when shooting pains lanced through his left arm, but as the moments rolled by he could feel his body relaxing. The heat was starting to fade, even though his clothes were soaked with sweat. Whatever he was doing in Aaron's old house, he was using his brain for once-

'That's it,' Reed mumbled, wiping his forehead with his sleeve. 'Keep away from the flames and smoke . . . You can do it.'

Let's pray that the heavens have opened up on the otherside-

'Yes, that . . . that makes sense,' Reed replied. His eyes were wide and hopeful. 'Let's hope it's fucking biblical!'

Ghostly thunderheads moved across the sky, their bruised underbellies rumbling loudly as they cast a dark veil across the street. And as the first needles of icy rain touched the concrete the air had already permeated with the familiar scent of burnished steel.

The sun had fled, and the rain wriggled down his collar and the back of his neck. But as he crossed the street to Aaron's house he noticed the light bulb glowing dully, as though it was covered in dust and webs, almost close to bursting, through the grubby cream net curtains in the upstairs window.

He then looked about.

No curtains twitched, nobody opened their front doors to see the suspicious looking character loitering on the door step of number forty three.

Screw them anyway, thought Reed, reaching for the door handle-

It's locked, Reed-

'No shit,' he whispered, turning the handle once more. But it was no use.

Must remain calm, he thought, taking a deep breath.

Just close your eyes and count to three

'One . . .'

That's right, Reed-

'Two . . .'

Everything will be different-

'Three.'

He opened his eyes but his heart still beat a tattoo inside his chest. He glanced to his left, at three dustbins fit to bursting, cluttering the entrance to what appeared to be a narrow alley way. Then he smiled wanly, thinking that things weren't so bad after all. He surveyed the street once more before quickly pulling the dustbins aside. In seconds he had cut through the darkness of the alley way, the stench of blocked drains and torn rubbish bags threatening to turn his stomach inside out. The path stopped at an intersection, separating two backyards.

Slowly, wincing as the latch screeched upon its rusty hinge, Reed opened the gate on his right and slipped through like another bad smell.

63

Aaron made his way as quietly as possible along the corridor, avoiding the two floor boards by the skirting board to his far right. They squealed like strangled cats if you weren't careful; and that was a big mistake. He had learned that children should be seen and not heard. He'd learned the hard way.

Maybe "mum" was alone, he thought, slowly unzipping his coat and placing it on the hook under the stairs. Her name was Diane but she had insisted, somewhat reluctantly after dad had introduced her to him, that he called her that dreaded three lettered curse. Maybe she had been cooking something sweet for tea, just like she used to when dad was home from work; rice pudding was his favourite. Just the thought of it made his mouth water, and a smile creased his lips. She'd use just the right amount of milk and sugar: not too much, not too little. Even Diane's cottage pie had been divine. Care: that was the key. Alas, the key had been well and truly misplaced. Those days were over. He couldn't smell the sugary aroma or meaty essence of home cooking. That was simply a dead memory; one he was too young to pine for. Now they'd share a tin of hot dogs or a plate of watered down Spaghetti Bolognese, the rest of the tin thrown in the fridge to be used another day. There simply was no effort any more.

His dad, or the "Mountainous Mick Brookes" as his old friends from his days at British Steel used to call him, spent more time working on the oil rigs. In fact he needed to; sacrificing his home life just to keep up with the bills. It wasn't a home, it hadn't been since Aaron's *real* mum walked out, or rather "out stayed her welcome" as his dad had once described that day. Out walked one woman only to be replaced by another, much more hurtful creature. Aaron was too young to feel it at the time but he had known the moment Diane had been introduced to him that there was something akin to hate in her eyes. She didn't want the young calf, just the old bull.

Mountainous Mick, thought Aaron, shaking his head at the absurdity of such a nick name. Maybe it was one of those stupid names that meant the complete opposite to a person's personality? A little like calling a man with straight hair "Curly".

Aaron's stomach growled but he'd learned to accept hunger pains. After an hour or so it would pass. He had to tolerate a number of things and skipping the occasional meal was just one of them. At least the kids at school couldn't call him names about his weight, he thought. The sight of the dirty workman's jacket hanging on the hook beside his own overcoat was another sight which disheartened him.

He wasn't stupid, even though his bitch of a step mother would have him think otherwise. He knew when his hands filled with loose change, when Diane smiled in front of the mirror, touching up her make up and red hair, that it was his time to make his self scarce for an hour or so while she . . . attended to some other business upstairs.

What had once been a monthly occurrence quickly became a weekly event. How long was it, thought Aaron, before he would have to play this game daily?

Who cared?

She most certainly didn't!

After all, it wasn't Diane's money he was spending at the arcades every week. It was his dad's. That's why Aaron tried to spend as little of it at possible in order to save it up so that he could go and stay on the oil rig. But if Diane had her way, he thought, he'd be out of the house and the way morning noon and night-

Aaron's stomach growled once more, his gut somersaulting. But this time he couldn't endure the pain. To hell with it all, he decided, pacing up and down the dimly lit hallway, suddenly heading for the kitchen.

There had to be something worth eating. He painstakingly, slowly opened the fridge door to peer inside. No luck. A half-full tin of baked beans, a stick of celery and a smelly bottle of milk adorned the shelves. He jumped suddenly to the sound of heavy rain drops lashing the dusty window pane across the room, a cool breeze from the fridge drying the sweat on his forehead. Sighing, he let the light die as the door closed. He looked up. Above him loomed high, oak-paneled cupboards. He couldn't reach their handles, but the void inside insisted he tried—then he winced as the pain in his stomach clawed at his ribs. The last time he had felt such pain was after completing his two mile swimming certificate at school the previous year. His head, or rather the room, started to spin. And he knew that if he didn't have something soon he'd topple over. Surveying the room as though he were about to commit some heinous crime, searching for anything that would fit the job he noticed a bar stool in the corner behind the door. And in that moment he felt a pang of hope. The seat was covered with old newspapers and coats but it would do, he thought, tip toeing across the kitchen. He removed the papers and placed the coats up on the pegs behind the door—not under the stairs beside that bastard's overalls, he thought. Home work isn't *that* hard, mum! He carried the stool over to the work units by the sink. Maybe later he'd wash the filthy pots and pans that piled up onto the draining board. Somebody had to-

He froze, air caught in his chest, at the sound of movement coming from directly above his head. He didn't need the brains of Aristotle to fathom just what was going on upstairs.

Bed springs creaked erratically, the sound of Diane's moans, how they made him nauseous. But like always, they didn't last long.

After a few moments Aaron climbed onto the stool, wobbling a little at first. He held his breath for a few seconds, standing like a statue, waiting until he felt it was quiet enough, and indeed safe enough, to move. Then he slowly opened the cupboard. He wanted to swear at the top of his lungs, to call Diane all the whores under the sun. He suddenly remembered what she had insisted yesterday about there being no food in the house for a couple of days until dad sent some money through the post. But now his eyes narrowed in the darkness.

The highest shelf, the one she knew Aaron would never reach, was straining under the weight of chocolate bars and packets of crisps. Poking between the glossy bags were the familiar brands of fizzy drinks he had seen the other kids at school drink in their lunch hour. Real COKE, not the copied brands, but the good stuff; red covers with the white swoosh along its side. There was a bottle of gin, although he couldn't understand why the bitch would place this out of reach! What the hell was he going to do? Turn into a drunk like her? He shook his head, noticing the two large plastic tubs of jelly sweets. There wasn't a bit of fat on Diane's bones, he thought bitterly, so why the hell did she hoard this stuff? But then her "boyfriends" often got the munchies after . . . There was so much delicious junk glaring back at him that he couldn't keep himself from salivating. He reached up as far as he could to grab a packet of crisps, the salty taste of prawn cocktail already tingling on his tongue.

The shelf was so bloody high up! But he had to get some. His sheer sanity depended upon it! The stool wobbled beneath his feet, but after a second or two he steadied, cold sweat wriggling down his back, heart hammering in his chest.

Christ, there had to be an easier way of getting something to eat around here, he thought, stretching his arm, finger tips almost reaching the bag, the thumping and creaking bedsprings above him slamming louder and heavier against the wall, so much so that the lampshade vibrated. At any other time it would have been comical, he thought. Many times he had crept upstairs and pressed his ear to her bedroom door. Sometimes he'd masturbated to the noises she made in the pillow, the words that came from her mouth: so demanding! Sometimes he only lasted seconds-

Fuck! Why did he need to be so precarious? It wasn't as though he would be heard over the noise they were making, he thought, his tongue sticking out the corner of his mouth, eyes now slits with concentration. Sweat dripped down his back like the rain now trickling down the window pane-

Suddenly the stool came out from beneath his feet bringing an avalanche of confectionary and tin cans crashing down onto the hard kitchen floor. And as he lay on his back, pain firing through every fibre of his being, he knew that tonight things were going to go from bad to worse.

The lampshade stopped vibrating, even the springs fell silent. And Aaron listened to the blood pulsating in his temples. He had to keep the pain inside, to suppress the screams that rampaged in his ribs and lower back.

"Children should be seen and not heard," he whispered, black blotches throbbing before his eyes. "Children should be seen and not heard."

He repeated the words over and over like a mantra; counting the moments before the springs started squealing again.

It took ten seconds. Each moment passed agonizingly slowly, thought Aaron, fire hot pain scratching its nails across his sides. Ten little seconds to get back on the fucking horse!

He shook his head, wanting to cry out, but as he slowly got up and pushed chocolate bars and packets of crisps into his pockets, he knew that tonight if anything he wouldn't go hungry.

'Are you sure, Daniel?'

Jackie and mum said, holding each other at the foot of the stairs, while I made my way to the front door. I turned round.

'Trust me. I'm sure,' I replied softly, trying to smile, but the warmth didn't reach my eyes; I could feel it. They were empty as though my soul and all the gold buried inside of it had been pilfered and driven out; stolen. And she knew the thief only too well—but that bastard didn't matter any more.

In that moment, Jackie saw just how much her little brother had aged—or matured to be exact in the years he had . . . well, passed away. I could read her mind like a book. A fact she would have to try to get her teeth around. Age here didn't make sense—hell, it shouldn't exist! And for the first time in God knew how long she felt vulnerable. Fuck! She was supposed to be the strong one! Compared to her thirty one years, Daniel was and always would be the baby of the family. But now . . .

Jackie nodded, shaking uncontrollably, despite her mum's arms about her. But the question was: who was holding onto whom for dear life?

I turned towards the door once more.

*

'Couldn't you've brought something a bit stronger?' chuckled Christine, sprinkling the tiny bits of cannabis resin along the

308

stripe of tobacco cradled in the three cigarette papers on the table before them.

'What, needles?' replied Kerry, unscrewing the cap of the bottle of vodka.

'Don't talk out of your arse, woman,' said Christine, shaking her head, pointing at the bottle she held, 'I mean whiskey. I could never stand that clear stuff. It's like nail varnish remover!'

Kerry poured the liquid into two glasses she had filled moments earlier with ice and pushed one towards the other woman, her eye brow slightly raised with a sardonic grin to match. 'Just drink up, "woman." Besides, when did you learn how to do that?'

Christine raised her left hand, brandishing her middle finger before grabbing the glass of spirit, bracing herself for the first sip. She shook exaggeratedly as the fiery liquid went down to her empty stomach. 'I went to Uni, you know?' she replied as though those three little letters were all the ones she needed to justify her guilty secret. And she nodded, frowning.

'And?' said Kerry. 'What the hell does that have to do with the price of eggs? And what to study? How to wash pots in a café beyond the veil?' she emphasized the last three words in a posh Victorian voice.

'Well, you ate noodles and smoked dope,' said Christine, rolling the joint. 'You stole the former and sold your backside for the latter-'

'FUCK OFF!' Kerry laughed, taking the offered cigarette carefully between thumb and forefinger so the thing didn't fall apart like a small bag of candy. She flipped open the lid of her silver Zippo lighter and turned the wheel, watching the sparks ignite the petrol as though it was truly a sight to behold; a formality to magic.

'Never mind how I learned,' said Christine, taking another sip of the vodka. 'Where the hell did you get the stuff?'

Kerry inhaled the sweet smoke, rolling it around in her mouth for a couple of seconds like a fine vintage wine before spitting it into the air. The blue cloud drifted without the intention of moving a muscle. She drew deeply on the joint once more before passing it to Christine, who took it deftly between thumb and forefinger, like any other cigarette.

'Well?' she said, watching the tip burn a brilliant red as she sucked on the roach.

'While you're eating noodles I'm out there selling my backside-'

'FUCK OFF!' Christine chuckled, waving the smoke away from her head like a pesky insect.

'Is that all my university-educated friend can come up with?'

'You know that when the darkness-'

'Hey!' whispered Kerry, holding her hand up before her. 'Did you hear that?'

'Are you—now you're just taking the piss out of me!' replied Christine, grinning. She took another drag from the joint and giggled some more. But her friend was being deadly serious. She put the cigarette in the ash tray then sat up straight, her eyes wide and vigilant.

'What is it?' she mouthed silently, as still as stone.

Kerry pointed towards the door.

Immediately Christine appeared to deflate somewhat, expecting at any moment a reign of terror to come flying through the door, tear her and Kerry to pieces-

Kerry quickly got up out of her seat and made her way towards the door, slowly placing her left hand against the frame, her right hand on the handle. She put her ear to the door and then turned towards Christine.

'There's someone out there,' she mouthed silently, pointing a finger toward the window on her left.

Christine shrugged her shoulders, after all, what could they do? She held up her cigarette then rolled her eyes.

'It's not the blow, you daft cunt,' mouthed Kerry, shaking her head.

Then they screamed as the door handle turned.

*

Kerry jumped away from the door as it slowly opened, revealing a small figure cut from the very fabric of the darkness and cold.

It stood stock still.

Christine squinted, almost falling from her chair.

'Daniel? Is that you, honey-'

'Honey?' said Kerry.

Christine threw her a glance that Medusa would've been envious of.

Kerry rolled her eyes.

'You must be freezing, sweetheart,' Christine cooed, grinding her joint in the ashtray before crossing the room. She grabbed the boy from the black.

Then she noticed the others. The girl and the old woman, how their eyes shone in the nothingness-

'We need somewhere to stay,' whispered Daniel, peeking over his shoulder at the two pitiful creatures cowering together at the bottom of the stairs. 'Please . . .'

'Come inside.'

64

Aaron had lost count of the number of jellied sweets he had consumed. Hell, he couldn't even remember the amount of chocolate bars he had stuffed down his throat either. Four, maybe five-

He didn't care! He was going to get a beating anyway, so why not make the most of it?

His stomach turned but not because of the junk food. Diane's little stash had been found and there was no where to hide. He'd be punished alright, for that there was no doubt, he thought, standing up suddenly at the sound of the bedroom door opening. He wondered if it had been worth it: filling his stomach only to have a fist thrust into it-

The scent of cheap after shave and over priced perfume drifted its way down the stairs as though the noise he'd created had stirred a dozen wraiths from their slumber and now they made their way through the dark to see what all the fuss was about. Not only could he smell cigarettes, but the familiar citrus odour that often came with Diane's tobacco. He wasn't stupid. He knew what was in those long roll-ups she sometimes built when she thought he wasn't around. But he'd often notice the little card board roaches crushed in the ashtrays littered about the house. Sometimes Aaron wondered if maybe that had been her plan all along: to remind him that this was life and these small things helped the big things go down a whole lot easier. And a habit that grew with time soon took over her every hour of every day. But it was also something Aaron cared little about, for as predictable as rainfall in the school summer holidays,

Diane would clean up her act when the prodigal Mick Brookes, his father, returned from the North Sea oil rigs.

Weathered, his neck sun-burnt and creased, dirt ingrained in every wrinkle in his broad face, the mountain would scoop his woman up as though she was made of balsa wood. His face knew hardship, his eyes dull and tired, and not forgetting blind to what his beloved was up to . . .

But then . . . What if Aaron had it all wrong? It was a thought that, together with the bruises and taste of blood on his tongue, kept him awake at night.

What if he knew about . . . what she did to me? What if he knew about her boyfriends and her dope? Maybe he didn't want to interfere lest the bitch pick up sticks and leave him-

When Mick was home the floor was clean enough to eat off of. Every surface was as bright as a mirror and the air looked misty with the scent of fresheners: pine, rose, vanilla—a different scent in every room, to hide . . . just to hide what was underneath. Fake, just like the paper covering the dampness on the walls. It was there, you just couldn't see it. And all it took was a few licks of paint.

Despite their time together, thought Aaron, staring at the shadows as they clawed their way across his bedroom ceiling, dad and Diane barely knew each other. He couldn't remember the last time they had shared a kiss. Dad was too caught up with keeping a roof over their heads. Love was just the garnish. He hoped he didn't turn out like him. Not about the loveless relationship, no! Fuck that, he meant the blindness. He couldn't see or just damned *refused* to see what was going on.

Aaron held his breath a moment, looking up to the ceiling. The sex was over, he could tell. The bed springs were silent although he detected a low rumbling sound, like a deep voice through the palm of a hand. He wanted to kick himself for missing out on the fun of watching Diane getting nailed. Well, she wasn't his mum . . . That was his justification to anyone who might enquire. He didn't feel awkward or uncomfortable; he enjoyed it. Sometimes when her little squeals turned to screams, he'd take the picture to his tiny chest of memories in his head, save them for later when he can jerk it out of his system.

Aaron smiled at the thought, popping another sweet into his mouth-

He started to choke! Stars flashed before his streaming eyes; felt his face burning up. He fell to his knees, clutching his throat to squeeze the sweet beneath the flesh, forcing the fucker down. It hurt so badly that he failed to hear the thumping foot falls on the stairs, nor the sound of breaking glass in the back door.

The kitchen door opened and the hand reached towards him.

'Here,' Christine said softly, gently placing a thick red blanket over the girl's shoulders. 'The kettle's on and there's a pan of soup boiling its arse out on the hob over there,' she added, hooking a thumb over her right shoulder. 'If there's-'

'My name's Jackie,' the girl whispered, her bottom lip quivering uncontrollably now as tears glistened at the corners of her eyes. There they remained as though frozen by the coldness that now raised goose bumps over her whole body. 'C Call m me Jackie . . .'

Christine took her in her arms and gently rocked from side to side. She could smell the apple and strawberry scented shampoo and it reminded her of Taylor-

She threw the thought aside and prized herself away from the girl.

No, this wasn't her little girl, and Christine refused to torture herself this way!

She stood up and crossed the room, grabbing the cigarettes and the bottle of vodka on her way to the front window by the door.

I swallowed hard, wiped my clammy palms on my jeans then quickly made my way to the cooker, just in time to turn off the gas before, what appeared to be oxtail soup, bubbled over the rim of the pan. Taking a couple of bowls from a shelf by my knees and carefully filling them with the hot steaming liquid, I placed them on a tray and carried it over to the table. I glanced over at Christine for a second. She was looking at me, a cigarette poised a matter of inches away from her lips. She smiled then took a drag, returning her attention to the condensation-soaked window beside her.

'Please, mum,' I said, placing a bowl before her. 'You must eat-'

'Why did he have to kill us all?' she replied wearily, barely able to keep her head from lolling to one side. 'First you-'

'Mum, no!' Jackie snapped. She was equally ruined by exertion but she could still hold her own. 'Stop it . . . What's done is done. Don't you-'

'What did he do to you, sis?' I wanted to know, sitting down beside her. Suddenly I heard the toilet flushing loudly behind me and I caught a glimpse of Kerry straightening her clothing as she left the small room. She stopped suddenly, noticing how the room temperature had plummeted from a few minutes ago, before joining Christine at the window. She cleared her throat self-consciously and poured herself another glass of vodka. She glanced at Christine but the other woman stared at the glass.

'Please-'

'WHAT DID HE DO?' I shouted, bringing my clenched fist down onto the table top.

Kerry was about to rise from her chair when Christine grabbed her arm, shaking her head.

'Just leave it, Kerry,' she whispered.

Kerry nodded before reluctantly sitting back down again.

Hot soup tipped over the edge of the bowls and spread like spilled blood across the surface. 'I want—I need to know, Jackie . . . He killed me, that which we know. But, please . . . you're my flesh and blood-'

'You might want to grab a glass of vodka, little bro,' replied Jackie, her voice sounded stronger now, more composed. Then her weary smile broadened at the sight of the long cigarette sitting burning in the ashtray. 'And you may need one of those after I tell you-'

'Just tell me,' I said firmly but quietly.

'He's in prison, that's all you need to know-'

'At least now I know where he is,' I replied, smiling bitterly. 'He's safe for now . . .'

316

'What are you talking about, bro?' fresh tears wriggled down Jackie's cheek. She leant forward in her chair trying to bridge the distance between us, but I sat back firmly, raising my hands before she could make contact with me. I don't think I could handle the intimacy right now.

'Tell me what I want to know . . . then I'll shed some light.'

Jackie closed her eyes.

*

Christine blocked my path, knowing that if she had been anybody else she would be sharing the overturned tables and scattered chairs about the café. In fact, judging by the hate she saw burning in my eyes, she would now be more than a wraith. That's precisely why she had pushed Kerry aside when she had tried to subdue me. Now I stood before Christine, her arms outstretched across the door, her back against the cold glass.

'Please, sweetheart,' she said softly, reaching a hand out to stroke my cheek. As the contact was made I opened my mouth to speak.

'Just get out of my way . . . please,' my voice crackled, bottom lip quivering.

'Not until you tidy up the mess you've made, mister,' she replied, a trace of humour in her voice, but the warmth failed to reach her eyes. 'Come on, sweets . . . let's sit down for a bit and think things through.' She peered over my shoulder at Jackie and her mum as they sat huddled together in the corner of the room, shaking, despite the thick blanket covering them both. 'Your family need you now; more than ever before-'

'Dad used to beat me when he was drunk,' I snapped, my eyes never leaving hers. 'One night he came into my room and-'

'You've told me, darling,' said Christine.

'So you understand why I hate him so much!' I said. 'When they found me in the river, the bastard got away with it. When I stood there watching his reactions when they asked him to . . .

to identify me . . . I thought that maybe, just maybe that he had . . .'

'Had what, sweetheart?'

'I thought fear might have . . . changed him,' I whispered said finally. 'That he had seen the worst thing that a father ever could: his own flesh and blood lying dead on a slab . . . But getting rid of me wasn't enough. He had to . . . hurt them too.'

I heard the sobbing from behind me but refused to turn around. Instead I wiped the tears from my eyes and sniffed loudly, resuming some kind of composure.

I took a step towards her.

'We need you here, my darling,' said Christine, smiling broadly now, the warmth reaching her eyes. She quickly wiped away the tears before blocking my way once more. 'We need you strong-'

'I'm not walking away from you . . . I'm sick of being scared, Chris . . . Tired of being walked over,' I said, my voice barely a whisper, taking another step closer to Christine, our noses almost touching. 'I'm the man of the house now. I couldn't do a thing before . . . but now there's something I have to finish.'

'How long will you be?' Jackie said.

I spun round to see my big sister had regained some of the colour in her cheeks. She had her arms round mum's shoulders, just two tiny heads peeping out from a thick blanket in the dimly lit room. Kerry joined them on the floor and embraced them both.

But I turned to face Christine once more.

'I won't be long,' I whispered. 'Take care of them, will you?'

Christine nodded as she slowly stepped aside.

'Be careful,' she said finally before opening the door. But before she could say another word, I had brushed passed her, clearing the steps in one leap and quickly disappeared into the darkness.

65

Reed stifled a scream as the glass cut into his wrist. Blood started to pulsate from the wound, tapping quietly onto the back doorstep like spilt ink. He cursed under his breath, pushing the jagged slivers aside so that he could find the latch on the other side of the door. As he entered the house the pain that rushed through his arm started to subside. All he could feel now was coldness as he squeezed the appendage, pulling his sleeve over the gash to regain some warmth there; but the blood saturated the material in a matter of seconds.

'Fuck it,' he mumbled, quickly making his way through what appeared to be a utility room to the kitchen, almost tripping over the pile of confectionary lying in the middle of the floor.

God, it's exactly like the house back home, he thought.

Of course it is, Reed . . . What was that?

There came a noise from upstairs. It sounded like a heavy foot fall. His breath caught in his throat as he stared at the ceiling.

Reed, you must get this over with-

'I am, just stay out of this-'

The house is burning down around us!

Reed heard the words but they didn't seem to make a bit of sense. After all, he could smell smoke although he couldn't see it. Then he felt the burning sensation envelope him once more. He was going to burn to ash if he didn't move!

Reed headed for the stairs, hearing the sound of voices far up there in the darkness. Then he froze at the sharp sounds of skin hitting skin-

God, no! It's started and I'm too fucking late!

He continued up the stairs unaware of the trail of blood he left in his wake like lit petrol, following his every move. He was becoming light headed, weakening with each passing second. He tried to shrug off the lethargy but it was futile. He saw faces of angels in his mind.

Tabby.

Paul.

It was all that invaded his mind right now as he stood on the dark landing. All the broken promises; the gambling; the shitty attitude towards his responsibilities; the loan sharks—it all came flooding back.

This is it, Reed . . . Let's do this and go home.

He swallowed hard, blood pounding in his ears, white blobs flashing before his eyes. He heard the droplets of blood hitting the carpet.

Kerry dried her hands with a tea towel and left the clean bowls to dry on the draining board before leaving the kitchen, grabbing her pack of cigarettes from her purse on the way as she sought out the others.

She didn't see the grinning face pressed against the window by the front door.

'Do you have any more screws?' asked Jackie breathlessly, standing on her tip toes to reach the top of the window frame. 'I'm almost done here.'

She turned around and smiled wearily at her mum who was still wrapped in the blanket, staring into space. But she didn't return the gesture. Almost an hour had passed since Daniel had left them and now Jackie was beginning to worry that he had gotten his self into trouble out there. But then she smiled at the thought before showing it the proverbial two fingers. 'Out there' was total darkness, she thought. What trouble could he possibly find? But she didn't want to go there. There was business to attend to here.

Christine grabbed a few screws from the old coffee tin and handed them to the young girl. Their eyes met for a moment and they both laughed. The light bulb at the centre of the ceiling flickered then beamed brighter than ever for a few seconds before settling down.

'He never mentioned you or your mum,' said Christine. 'Oh, no offense, honey—I know he had a lot on his mind when he strolled on in here-'

Jackie giggled. It was a sweet sound that Christine hadn't heard for almost three life times, and it seemed to turn the ambient temperature up a few degrees.

'Honestly, it's okay. Really,' she said, grabbing a screw from the coffee tin. 'Daniel's never been a one for conversations. But If it's football or girl bands then watch out!' she said, returning to the task at hand.

Christine shook her head.

'Boys will be boys, eh? I don't know,' she chuckled, tapping gently at the other window frame with the hammer. 'You know what? I bet I end up putting this window through-'

'Do you really think they'll try to get in here?' said Jackie in a hushed voice as though just uttering the words will make it come true.

Christine sighed, a chill shooting through her as though a goose had waddled across her grave. And she gazed out of the window. Darkness stared back.

'Why can't you just let them go back-'

'Listen, love,' snapped Christine, closing her eyes for a moment, 'let's not go over that again. I told you already: I made the mistake of letting one of them through—and don't mention his name, okay? I made the mistake of giving the bastard the means to relive his life when all he wants to do is manipulate and take take take! Understand me when I tell you that nobody, I mean NOBODY who doesn't give a fuck gets through!'

Jackie cleared her throat and turned to the window, absently placing the screw at the frame before proceeding to drive it through the wood.

'Look, I'm sorry, sweetheart,' said Christine, putting the hammer down on a large box of canned drinks. 'I made a big mistake a long long time ago and now I want to do something good, you know? I hurt a lot of people-'

'And why the fuck should arseholes enjoy the privilege of a second chance?'

They both spun on their heels, almost toppling off balance at the sound of the voice.

'Kerry, you bitch!' said Christine, placing a hand on her chest. 'You scared the life out of me!'

322

'No sign of Daniel?' asked Jackie.

Kerry shook her head, blowing a long stream of smoke into the air. Her heels tapped noisily on the bare stone floor as she slowly made her way through the narrow store room.

Jackie seemed to physically deflate.

'Hey,' said Christine softly, 'he'll be just fine-'

'But what's he up to, eh?' Jackie replied, forgetting the task and crossed her arms. 'Rushing off into the the fucking God knows where without so much as kiss my arse! We need him here-'

'Just calm down, flower,' said the little old lady wrapped in the blankets.

Kerry almost screamed at the sound of the croaky voice, the only four words the old lady had uttered since arriving here over two hours ago.

Jackie rushed to her mum's side and gently rubbed her frail shoulders, kissing her cheek. 'I love you, mum,' she whispered, embracing her tightly.

'He's not daft, that lad,' her mum said. 'He definitely doesn't take after his dad, I tell you.'

'That's right, mum,' said Jackie, tears wriggling down her cheek. 'Nothing like him. They broke the mould when they made that one.'

Suddenly they all screamed at the sound of a knock at the front door, a scream that soon turned to laughter.

'That bloody bloke, I tell you!' laughed Christine, throwing the hammer onto a crate of canned soup as she left the room. 'Doesn't he know opening the door lets the cold in something chronic?'

Kerry shook her head before following her friend into the shop, a freshly lit cigarette dangling from the corner of her mouth. 'What a tit!' she mumbled. 'Just wait 'til I get my hands on him!'

But as they made their way towards the front door they froze.

Daniel wasn't at the door.

That wasn't his face pressed against the glass.

It was someone else.

66

'You little bastard!' cried Diane, picking the sweet from the carpet and holding it before Aaron's face. 'You can't leave anything alone, can you? I bought them for myself. But you have to go snooping, don't you, eh? When I want a bit of time on my own, to do what I want to do, you spy on me. I don't have a fucking life because of you!'

'Take it easy on the lad, pet,' mumbled her latest squeeze, dragging his feet over the edge of the bed. He pulled a dirty work shirt over his massive beer gut and grabbed his jeans from a pile of dirty clothes on the floor. 'The lad's only young. He's doing no harm-'

'Don't you be going soft, Eddie,' she replied, shaking a fist at the boy, her red hair falling across her face, but she flicked it aside in one move, revealing a countenance so twisted with anger that Aaron gave out a cry. 'This little bugger's the bane of my life!'

Aaron let the tears flow, grateful for the blurred vision. Anything was better than watching her furious eyes scour him-

'Aren't you, eh?' she snarled, the scent of those strong cigarettes on her breath. 'I just can't wait until your dad comes home so I can tell him how much of a little shit you've been. We might even put you up for Foster care,' she hissed, winking at Eddie. But he just rolled his eyes and shook his head.

'Come on, pet,' he said. 'Don't you think that's a bit strong, eh?'

'You wimp!' hollered Diane, her voice cutting through the silence of the small room. 'That's what you are: a wimp.' She pointed a bony finger at Aaron. 'He's my step son and I can't change that, but you're just a fat-'

Eddie moved fast, striking her cheek with the back of his right hand. Aaron jumped, startled at the sound of the skin, the loud crack echoing about the room. Diane almost crossed the room, her pink nightgown coming undone at her waist.

Aaron caught a glimpse of her breast and stomach, the green and black bruises there, and he knew that his dad would never do that to her. He turned towards Eddie, his eyes wide with rage and his fists like tiny balls of steel.

'Don't you ever hurt my mum again!' Aaron screamed, punching the bastard squarely between the legs.

An old Bible story played in Aaron's mind, one he had read in the school library. It was the tale of David and Goliath. That was how the beer-bellied lout looked at that moment, thought Aaron, smiling broadly as Eddie rolled about on the floor clutching his groin and squealing like a dying pig.

But the boy's smile faded.

'Are you bloody stupid?' Diane screamed. 'Don't you ever hit him again, do you hear me?'

The boy watched the giant slowly uncurl from his feotal position on the floor, froze in dismay as he rose; his clenched fists as large as oil derricks. The room seemed to grow older in the man's shadow.

Diane cowered from her lover as he quickly crossed the room, expecting the full brunt of those mighty fists of his. She had felt them many times before and bore the scars to prove it. She squeezed her eyes shut, feeling the vibrations in the floor as Eddie's footfalls passed her by.

Aaron cried as the fists came down, his tiny face quickly blackening. And he couldn't cry any longer. All he wanted, all he prayed for, was death. Maybe if he struck out again the bastard would end it all quickly, he thought.

Between swollen, blood-filled eyelids, Aaron watched Diane remove the belt from her dressing gown.

'Here,' she whispered, handing it to the giant. 'Use this.'

*

325

Aaron's face and neck throbbed, and no matter how much he fought, the belt tightened. He heard the twisted laughter ringing somewhere in the gloom, tasted blood on his tongue as he bit down on it.

He didn't even flinch when the dark figure burst into the room, shouting words—such nonsensical words. He recognized fragments: "too late" "here sooner" and "my last chance" but he could've been mistaken as one side of his face was pressed against the carpet-

Then he almost jumped at the sound of screams. It was Diane, he thought, and the . . . the ghost of a man—had to be a ghost, it's edges were smoky—throwing her across the room. But the scream ended as her face struck the wall, leaving a bloody smear on the dull nicotine stained paper, before she fell in a heap in the corner.

Eddie grabbed at the ghost's hands as they tightened about his throat, trying to prize them free, but it was too late. The crunch of bone seemed to cut the room in two and, like earlier, the giant crumbled.

Suddenly every muscle in Aaron's body screamed with white-hot pain, stomach churning with the sweets he had gorged his self on earlier-

The room wouldn't stop spinning!

One minute he stared into the darkness as though some cruel god had scribbled black ink across his eyes with a razor sharp quill; fingers like talons picking him up from the floor, shooting white hot spears of light across his mind, through his arms and down one side of his limp body. His heart beat faster and he thought this was how the thing can turn, like an abused dog, and bite back. His heart was attacking him!

The smell of smoke and blood filled his senses now as he spun round in the air, his arms dangling by his side, blood pounding in his skull. He was sleep walking, he thought, leaving the room, the temperature of what seemed to be the landing falling dramatically as he glided passed room after room after room . . . after . . . his feet scraping across walls, knocking pictures onto the floor; their smiling faces shattering like Aaron's world.

He wanted to cry with the pain searing his sides, the ghost's fingernails clawed his flesh, but it was the heat-

The damned thing was smoking! It was going to burst into flames!

-and now he descended the stairs, the air in his lungs filled with pieces of broken glass it seemed, struggling to be free.

The world, his world, his past, his entire being and all the pain inside disappeared . . . as though it had never been.

*

Reed felt the pain burn through his wrists and fingers, trying desperately to keep hold of the boy as he descended the dark staircase; except, he noticed to his dismay that there was a light about them, an aura that made his head swim, lighting their way-

YOU'RE ON FIRE, REED! MOVE, MOVE, MOVE!

The fire had caught up with me, he thought. This is it, Reed: you're going to die!

NO, YOU'RE NOT!

In that moment Reed felt one final surge of energy rush through every fibre of his being. Smoke stung his eyes, tears streamed down his face-

'Tabby . . . Paul,' he mumbled. The two words that pulled him, got behind him and pushed, dragged him, slapped his face and struck his cheek like anvils.

That's right . . . they're waiting for you, Reed! Keep moving!

I'm really going home, he thought.

Home . . .

That's right . . . home.

He cleared the last few steps with one final leap, running towards the front door, the boy now an unbearable weight in his arms. Fire spread across his legs and torso, licking around his face, singing his hair, burning his eyes-

Then he cursed, the door was locked to high heaven! He fumbled with the chain, trying to balance the boy on his hip, pain skewering every nerve ending in his body like tiny flaming acupuncture needles-

Come on, come on! COME ON! YOU CAN DO IT!

As the chain snapped and the latch came loose, Reed thought of two names. And the new life he would make for them:

The ones, the only ones he loves.

Tabby . . . Paul . . .

Now the tears evaporated on his cheek as fire engulfed him.

He opened the door to a new life.

A life without Aaron. As though he had never existed at all.

A life without pain and tears.

A life without causing pain to others.

He eagerly stepped outside.

Christine was the first to scream as she backed away from the door.

The face looked crushed and painted with what appeared to be scabrous, black blood, glaring back through the condensation. Eyes as cold and sharp as ice chips, scoured the dimly lit room, and the blood shot orbs moved erratically, as though recording what they saw-

'Get the fuck away!' shouted Kerry.

Christine's heart skipped at the sudden outburst. But she stood transfixed, unable to take her eyes from the ghastly countenance staring back at her.

The face grinned, a hand suddenly slapping the pane, slowly dragging its torn flesh down the glass, nails scratching-

Then another face appeared beside it. This time it nodded at Christine, knowingly, chuckling, a scar across its throat, hair pulled back.

'God, no,' Christine muttered, backing away from the door, the faces suddenly disappearing as though made from sand, borne on an icy breeze.

'What?' said Kerry.

'It's them . . . The ones I told you about,' she replied, shaking as though her whole body had been dowsed with iced water. 'They want to know how . . . they want to know how to get back! This is it . . . This is it . . . this IS IT! I shouldn't have let that bastard through . . . It's all my fault-'

Kerry grabbed Christine's shoulders and squeezed them tightly.

'Get a fucking grip, woman!' she snapped, spinning her around to face her. 'We're going to be okay! Understand me? We're going to fight this! We're not going to let them know. Aaron's gone . . . Okay? He got through, but who cares about that piece of shit? Get a hold of yourself for God's sake!'

Christine nodded, thin cords prominent in her throat as her whole body shook; her eyes were as wide as saucers.

'What's going on?' asked Jackie, entering the shop.

They both spun round, shaking.

'This is it,' said Christine.

Jackie froze, her hands covering her mouth to stifle the screams.

'This is the end!'

'Don't fucking listen to her, Jackie. Understand?' snapped Kerry. 'She's gone with the flippin' fairies! Just keep an eye on your mum and everything will be okay!'

Jackie nodded, her shaking hands wiping the tears from her cheek. 'Don't you worry about her,' she stammered. 'She's just fine!'

She crossed the room and pulled the curtain aside, staring out of the window. It was as black as pitch out. No stars twinkled in the heavens and no moon shone through the umbra. Except . . . there was something. It, whatever it was, shone like a distant star. It moved like a dense shadow across their field of vision like a puppet in the dark-

It laughed!

'What the fuck was that?' screamed Christine, jumping away from the glass. 'There are more of the bastards out there!'

They neared towards the glass and peered outside. Through the darkness, faces, as white as snow with eyes glowing like hot coals, suddenly appeared. And like sentinels they stood, watching, chests heaving, vapour billowing about their faces as though a fire burned deep inside what was left of their souls.

'Why aren't they moving?' said Kerry, turning to Christine.

'Why do you think?' she said, turning from the window. 'They want us-'

'Well . . . what's going to happen then?'

330

Then another face appeared, grinning maniacally, teeth white and jagged.

And another face broke through the black . . .

Then another-

'Where the hell are they coming from?' said Kerry, her heart beating a tattoo in her chest, threatening to burst forth at any moment.

'We just stay right here and-'

'Shut the hell up, Kerry!' said Christine acidly. 'So what do we wait for, eh? We wait for daylight, for morning to come? Then we're going to be waiting a fucking long time.'

'JACKIE!'

They spun round at the scream.

The store room.

'Mum?' said Jackie, heading for the back of the shop. 'Mum, are you alright? I'M COMING, MUM! JUST HOLD ON!'

Christine turned to Kerry, skin as white as snow, realization draining the blood from her face.

'We didn't secure the back door,' she said, following Jackie. 'We forgot the fucking back door!'

As they reached the store room they found Jackie trying to console the old lady, wrapping her arms about her thin frame to generate some warmth there. But her mum wriggled and wrestled her daughter's arms away from her, pointing a shaking finger towards the back door.

'What did you see?' Jackie wanted to know, desperately trying to keep her mum away from the door but she was too slow.

'Someone . . . a face . . . I saw it—them . . . they're here to . . . here to save us! We must get out of here!' the old lady gasped. In three heartbeats she had reached the door handle-

'NO!' Christine hollered. 'Don't open the door! Don't let them in!'

The door swung open, hinges creaking loudly like old joints.

The next ten seconds stopped their hearts, the air caught in their throats.

It was Christine that broke the stillness, stepping slowly over the threshold. An icy breeze lifted rogue locks of hair from across her forehead, goose pimples wriggling down her back.

She was smiling.

'Daniel?' she whispered, her breath curling like smoke about her face in the cold. 'Is that you, sweetie?'

I nodded.

'Did you think I wouldn't come back?' I said softly as she jumped into my open arms.

Her goose flesh disappeared against my body, its heat enveloping her, destroying the fear she held deep inside. It was wrong . . . she knew that, but the heart ruled.

'I love you, Daniel,' she whispered, warring with her emotions. 'I love you so much!'

I closed my eyes, feeling the electricity between us course through me.

Reluctantly, I pulled away from Christine and stared at her tear-stained face.

'Darren and the kids?' I said, a dry click in his throat. 'You won't remember me when the time comes-'

'But-'

'I'm not alone,' I said quickly, turning around. 'It's okay . . . Come on.'

'Oh, my God!' Kerry gasped, watching the figures appear behind me. Then she chuckled. 'Well well well, look at what the cat dragged in!'

'Hello, Kerry,' said Richard, hand waving sheepishly like a little white glove. 'Nice to see you again.'

'Penny!' Christine laughed, breaking away from me to embrace the young girl. 'How long's it been? You know what, that doesn't matter. You're here now.'

'Hi, Chris,' Penny giggled, squeezing her tightly. 'Daniel said you were in trouble-'

'No, sweetheart,' she replied, shaking her head. 'No, I don't want you—don't want any of you getting hurt-'

'But Christine, are you insane?' shouted Kerry.

'They're just children for God's sake!'

'Let us help,' I said. 'We're all in this together, remember? We don't have much time-'

'He's right, you know?' said Kerry, looking over her shoulder at the back door. 'They aren't vampires, they won't wait for an invite-

CRASHHH!

We all jumped at the explosive sound of broken glass coming from the café.

'Come on, everyone inside, quickly!'

And so we followed Kerry into the store room and beyond, to what end, none of us knew.

67

Reed jammed the number on the key pad. He didn't have to look at them; he knew them by heart.

And so he waited, listening to the slow beeps.

'I'm not putting the phone down,' he muttered almost musically, a yawn almost paralyzing his jaw. 'Come on, for heaven's sake, pick up!'

And he waited-

'David Reed, why the hell are you phoning me at this bloody hour?' said the sleepy voice.

'Tabby? Thank God it's you,' he said before clearing his throat. 'Erm . . . good morning.'

Yes, Reed. She's alive. They didn't get to her. You can calm down now . . . breathe . . .

He composed his self, feeling his heartbeat slow even though a cold sweat had broken beneath his armpits.

'Look, I know it's the middle of the night, but I wanted you to know I'm okay and that . . . and that I love you so much!'

'I love you too, honey,' she replied warmly. 'Are you sure you're okay?'

I'm just glad you're still alive, he thought. *God, if only you knew—and I hope you never find out-*

No body is going to find out what you're up to, Reed. Soon this will be all over and you'll be by their sides once more! Nobody will find out what you're going to do.

Reed took a deep breath, swallowing back the tears.

'I'm alright, really,' he said, sniffing. 'I've nearly delivered all the beer now and have only a couple of breweries left on the sheet and then I'm heading back up North . . . Hey, put Paul on the line. I want to speak to my little future England footballer.'

'David, it's one o'clock in the morning and the baby's asleep—all he'll say is goo-goo anyway-'

'The words of a future king, I tell you, Tabby. The giggling gibberish of a future monarch,' he replied, laughing. But a tear ran down his cheek.

'Look, darling, I'm really tired,' said Tabby, before yawning loudly. 'Can you ring me a bit later? I've got a lecture at the university in . . . ten hours and I'm wrecked.

'Of course, baby . . . Sorry, I just wanted to make sure-'

'Well, we're just fine, so stop worrying. Just like an hour ago when you rang. And two hours ago—and three hours ago, and-'

'Okay, okay, okay,' Reed chuckled. 'I get the picture. Just love you, that's all.'

'We know that, love. See you when you get back, okay? And please be on time, you don't want to anger-'

'I know, I know, I won't. Okay? . . . See you later,' replied Reed, rubbing the bridge of his nose with his thumb and forefinger, a migraine building there.

'Good night, pet,' said Tabby.

'Night. Sleep tight-'

The line went dead.

He lit another cigarette, his smile quickly disappearing. Beyond the window, to his right, where a cold wind swept the rain-slicked road, he thought of his journey ahead; of Johnny Gladstone, of his family back home in Hartlepool . . . and the revolver stashed in his glove compartment.

'Johnny's just going to have to accept I can't pay a bean back,' Reed mumbled, turning the key in the ignition. And as the engine purred into life he wondered If he would ever change.

68

'Mr. Brookes?'

The man come mountain rose from his seat as though a bolt of electricity passed through him and the seat seemed to sigh in relief, gently reshaping itself after the onslaught of such a monster.

'Yes . . . Erm, call me Mick, please,' he stammered, reaching out a hand to the tall female stood beside him. She accepted the gesture, her hand like a tiny child's in his massive mitt, which surprised her with its gentleness.

People usually exuded warmth, an aura of naturally hot body heat, especially, she thought, under these circumstances, but the mountain radiated an icy chill. She shivered.

His eyes were wide as if in fright, deep lines carved in his red forehead. And his ruddy complexion added many years to his thirty four years. The bright fluorescent lights shone across his bald pate, a small scar at the corner of his right eye looked like a badly executed tattoo.

'I'm Doctor Regis,' she said, smelling the mountain's body odour as he towered over her.

Mick nodded, feeling his bottom lip quiver.

'I tried to get here as quick as I fucking could—sorry, I didn't mean to swear. I just . . .' he allowed his words to trail away.

'That's perfectly understandable,' replied Regis, smiling. Then the smile melted away as she cleared her throat.

'So, when can I see him?'

'Aaron's sleeping right now-'

'Why won't anybody tell me what's going on?' he snapped.

'Keep your voice down, mister-'

'My name's Mick-'

'Just remember that this is a hospital; people are resting . . .'

'I want to see my son,' he said quietly and calmly.

'I'm afraid I can't allow that at this present moment in time-'

'What?' Mick said, pushing passed her, covering the length of the hall in four large strides. 'You can't stop me-'

He peered in the dimly lit room and saw the tiny figure sleeping peacefully on the bed. As he stepped forward, he didn't see the other figure move through the shadows.

The policeman blocked his path.

Their eyes met.

'I'm afraid I have to ask you to step away from the door,' said the uniformed officer, his voice hushed so as not to wake the sleeping child. Although he stood some six or seven inches shorter than Mick his eyes glowed intensely.

He backed away into the cold clinical brightness of the hall.

'Please . . . he's my son,' Mick said, stifling the tears. 'I got here as soon as I could-'

'Well, right now we need to get him rested so we can ask him a few questions.'

'What the hell are you going on about? Questions? What bloody questions—I was told he had burns-'

'That's right, sir,' replied the policeman. 'He has burns about his waist which are being treated. The problem is . . .'

'Then the house has burned down-'

'That's just the problem, sir . . . You see there wasn't a fire at all. But there was something else-'

'I wish you would start making fucking sense!' Mick shouted, rousing the attention of two nurses close by. They peered round the corner, whispered a few words then disappeared once more.

'Two bodies were found at the scene. One female and-'

'Diane? She's hurt?'

'She's dead, sir,' replied the policeman. 'But that's all I can divulge at present. We don't know the other body's identification-'

'That fucking slag!'

'Just calm down, sir,' said the policeman. 'I need to ask you something.'

'What? What the hell do you want to know?'

'A nurse who accompanied your son in last night informed me that the boy was delirious, that he kept mumbling about-'

'Mumbling about what, for fuck's sake?'

'He mentioned something about a ghost that picked him up and carried him to safety-'

'Kids are kids, mate,' replied Mick, shaking his head exasperatedly. 'Ghost? That's bloody nonsense. So he was picked up by a ghost, he must've been dreaming the whole thing-'

'Well, that's just it, sir,' said the policeman. 'The burns in his body-'

'What about them?'

'The house wasn't on fire-'

'I know that!'

'Well, the burns are in the shape of hands.'

ABOUT THE AUTHOR

Andrew was born in 1974. Currently lives in Hartlepool on the North east coast of England, with his wife Claire.

Ephemera is his third novel, book one of a trilogy; a story which follows on from Every heartbeat counts.

Lightning Source UK Ltd.
Milton Keynes UK
UKOW050824290313

208391UK00006B/120/P